DEMONHOME

BY

MICHAEL G. MANNING

Cover by Amalia Chitulescu
Editing by Grace Bryan Butler and Dorothy Zemach
© 2017 by Michael G. Manning
All rights reserved.
ISBN: 978-1-943481-10-1

For more information about the Mageborn series check out the author's Facebook page:

https://www.facebook.com/MagebornAuthor

or visit the website:

http://www.magebornbooks.com/

CHAPTER 1

Matthew watched Moira and the others leave with a feeling of relief. His sister frequently irritated him. He wasn't entirely sure why, but if asked, he knew he could come up with a list of reasons on short notice. None of the particular reasons he might list would be the full truth, however, the reality was that it was just her presence that annoyed him.

Too many questions, too much talking, he thought to himself.

She was constantly trying to figure him out. Even when she kept her thoughts and questions to herself he could almost *feel* her watching him, curious. The same was true of his parents, but they weren't as close, as present, as always *there,* as Moira was.

In general, he felt the same about most people, although to a far milder degree. His friends didn't press or pry as much, so they were tolerable. Strangers were even better, they wouldn't bother you at all, unless you gave them a reason. For the most part, he preferred the company of his own thoughts. *Those* were interesting, and other people rarely had anything to contribute. In fact, they usually just interfered by trying to inject their own interests and opinions into his mind.

Gram was an exception to the rule. He listened, without pretending to understand, whenever Matthew felt a need to air out his ideas. Repeating that thought to himself, Matthew realized it might be construed as an insult, but to him it wasn't. *It's a really rare trait, and valuable, as far as I'm concerned.*

If only people were more like books. Books didn't force you to read them. They waited, with their knowledge clearly displayed and summarized in a title and short description. If you were interested, they revealed themselves at whatever pace you desired, never forcing themselves into your attention.

Moira and the others had passed beyond the limit of his magesight now. He was alone, except for his dragon, Desacus.

What now? asked the dragon, his voice resonating inside the young wizard's mind.

"Now we see what we can discover about where our strange visitors came from," said Matthew aloud.

The cave is too small for me to enter.

"Wait out here. I don't need you at the moment," said Matthew as he returned to the cave entrance. Slipping inside he worked his way back to the chamber they had discovered.

There it was. He felt it immediately, a strange sense of blurring, as though the world was ever so slightly out of focus. It wasn't a new sensation, but he had discovered over the past couple of years that it seemed to be something unique to him. Neither his father nor his sister had ever mentioned it, and during a number of conversations he had slowly come to realize that what he experienced wasn't a regular aspect of magesight, at least not for other mages.

His private exploration regarding the sensation was what had led him to experimenting with what he called 'translational' magic, magic that manipulated not the world or the environment, but the very fabric that existence was built upon.

His father had created enchanted bags that allowed him to store items in faraway locations, using a variation of teleportation magic, but Matthew had improved upon the concept by creating bags that stored items in other dimensions. Even Gram's enchanted sword, Thorn, was stored that way. The tattoo his friend used to summon the blade and his armor simply connected him to another dimension.

But Matthew had long suspected that he was just scratching the surface of what translation magic was capable of doing. There were times when he caught glimpses of things that hadn't happened yet, usually events that were close, in the near future, but also in the recent past. The visions weren't limited to sight either, and on one or two awkward occasions he had caught himself answering questions that hadn't been asked yet.

A casual consideration of his experiences might conclude that he was somehow accessing the future or seeing through time, something that would be properly called 'precognition', but he had decided that that interpretation was fundamentally flawed. He had learned to keep a firm grip on his perceptions, but when he relaxed his focus he often saw multiple versions of the near future, as well as multiple pasts.

It was like living in a world that had thousands of different copies of itself laid on top of one another. Taken together those copies created a blur. Some copies were in sync with the present, but others were slightly ahead or behind, and none were truly identical.

He wasn't seeing the future, or the past, he was seeing the vast infinity of alternative realities that lay close to his own. That was the truth of the Illeniel gift; it was the mechanism that had once allowed Illeniel krytek to avoid almost any attack, dodging blows before they were even begun, and it was the source of the visions that his mother's prophetic dreams had once shown her.

Exploring his gift had taught him that it was more than just an ability to perceive other realities however, he could touch them. Using enchantments, he could connect them permanently, as he had done with the pouch that now hung from his belt. Fashioned properly they could even be weapons, like the extraplanar triangle he had used to destroy Chel'strathek.

And now something had crossed over.

The strangely flavored aythar that his sister had sensed, the blur that he still experienced here, was a result of that crossing. Their world had briefly been connected to another dimension at this point, one that was much farther apart from it than the usual closely related ones that Matthew always felt hovering close at hand. That connection had created a local disturbance, a strange resonance.

He could study that, if he opened his senses to it. Matthew thought he might even be able to follow it.

So he did.

It began with a rush of vertigo as he allowed his perception to be swept away from the close layers, from the reality he was anchored in, the reality he lived within. It was like jumping into a fast-moving river, or perhaps the ocean when the tides were moving out. Reality boiled around him, shifting and roiling so rapidly that understanding was no longer possible.

He was guided by nothing more than a feeling, or some ephemeral instinct. His perception passed through countless planes, and he could feel others even farther out, some so strange and alien that he knew that peering too closely at them might destroy his sanity, or perhaps even his body, if he were to touch them.

4

That feeling led him to the origin of the crossing, but it wasn't a single point. Like his own world, the one he found was a vast collection of closely related dimensions, many of them with disturbances that indicated a crossing. The crossing had happened from a multitude of closely related dimensions and touched an equal number of those planes that were near to his own.

It was like any other event he supposed, repeated over and over through a great number of similar realities.

As a result, finding the exact one that had touched his own was probably impossible, if not pointless. Far more important would be finding one that was compatible with his own nature. But how to choose?

Relax.

It was another mind, or was it his own? The thought was communicated to him almost as a feeling, if it held words they had probably been supplied by his own brain.

And then he saw it, or felt it, he couldn't say which. It was everything, the space between planes and dimensions. It was what lay between, the source of consciousness that underlay all reality, or perhaps it was reality, and the dimensions that surrounded it were merely its dreams and fictions. Both interpretations were valid.

We are Illeniel.

Another truth, and one that Tyrion had never been able to see in the knowledge given to him by the loshti. The name, Illeniel, was merely the term his brain supplied, but the vast consciousness truly had no name. It was every mind, every perception, every point of view, gathered together here, in the timeless space that lay *between.*

Illeniel might be better used as a more specific term, a name for those creatures, like himself, who were capable of transcending their locality to reach the heart of infinity. In that sense the original Illeniels were not She'Har, but some of the She'Har had been Illeniels—the ones he had inherited his gift from.

Width and breadth of the experience was beyond what his mind could comprehend, beyond what any mind could comprehend, but it carried no shock or discomfort with it; he had merely shifted points of view. In that instant, he was simply *more,* more than he had been, and within that other self the knowledge of infinity was not a strain, it simply *was.*

The planes of existence that rode upon his surface were infinitely varied, but some were dark, black and invisible to his limitless vision. The collection that he had been examining before was among those. They were different somehow, they were apart, even though they floated upon the same overarching consciousness, they were devoid of its mind, like dead stones sinking through a living sea.

As he considered traveling to one of them again, he felt fear.

But you must. You were born of them, of the darkness, and you must return.

Couldn't they just ignore them? Why not leave them alone?

They will not be ignored.

Matthew felt the truth of it. His own world had once been one of them, long ago, before Tyrion's time, until the She'Har had visited it, until they had transformed it. As he watched he could see the effect of the crossing around him. Some planes went dark, changing from glowing jewels in the sea of existence to dark stones, but at the same time some of the dark worlds grew bright and began to glow with the light of consciousness.

It was an endless battle that played out, over and over, and he no longer had the option of ignoring it. His world was connected now. Either his world would return to the darkness or the other would be brought into the light. Those were the only choices, and he would be the arbiter who decided, either through his action or his refusal to act.

Very well, Matthew responded, and with that thought he withdrew. A maelstrom swirled around him and finally resolved itself, leaving him standing once more in a cave in the Elentir mountains.

Desacus stood waiting faithfully outside when he emerged, *Did you learn anything?*

The dragon's question startled him. What he had experienced was impossible to articulate. He had gained some knowledge, but most of it was gone. What was left was like a short summary; the human mind couldn't possibly contain all of what he had seen. Perhaps it was something like what his father underwent whenever he used his abilities as an archmage.

Mordecai had tried to explain it to him on several occasions, but the main lesson he had managed to convey was that he couldn't express it because as a *man* he couldn't fully remember what he experienced when he merged with the larger world around him.

So an archmage merges the self with the greater consciousness of the world around him, but what did I do? I went somewhere else. He needed to talk to his father. If anyone could shed light on the strangeness of it all, it would be his dad. But that wasn't possible, not until they found him.

"We have to travel there," he told the dragon.

You can do that? asked Desacus.

Matthew nodded, "I can. If we're to find the answers we need, we need to examine the other side of this puzzle. The side that our visitors came from."

The dragon's mental answer held a note of disapproval, *That does not sound wise. There are too many unknowns.*

You should discuss this with your mother and sister, as well as the other wizards.

"They won't understand," said Matthew. "Dad might, but he's what this is all about, isn't he? He might be over there now, and if he is, this is the only way we'll find him."

Then you should bring some of them with you; alone, the risk is too great.

Matthew stared at the dragon, "That's what you're for. I can go and return with ease, but the others can't. If we were separated, or if something happened to me, they could be trapped. I can't risk bringing anyone else until I understand what we're facing."

Desacus snorted, and his next thought came across with a heavy sense of sarcasm, *Glad to know you worry about me as well.*

"You wouldn't let me leave you behind anyway, besides, what could pose a threat to you?"

The dragon used one claw to score a deep groove into a large piece of granite before examining the undamaged talon. *There is truth in that,* he replied. *How will we do this?*

Matthew approached him and reached out with one hand before laying it against the dragon's massive forelimb, "Brace yourself. This will probably be very disorienting. Just keep still until the world starts to make sense again."

What does that mean…?

Desacus's thought cut off abruptly as everything shivered and began to blur around him.

CHAPTER 2

It was easier this time, despite bringing the dragon along. Matthew already knew where they were going, and the actual effort of translating them from their original location to a new dimension seemed to involve only a small amount of aythar. He felt a faint resistance as they entered the dark dimension that was his target.

It felt like falling into an icy lake, the shock drove the air from his lungs. As the world resolved itself Matthew found himself in absolute darkness, not merely the metaphorical darkness he had seen from the place in between, but truly black; devoid of all sight or sense.

He could feel nothing; it was as though his magesight had utterly vanished, along with his eyesight. The air seemed to press in against him, making him feel claustrophobic as he drew deep breaths to compensate for the horrifying feeling that he must be suffocating.

Matthew wasn't prone to panic, however. After the first disorienting shock passed he realized that his magesight wasn't truly gone, he could still sense his body, and Desacus was there, beside him. Beyond that, though, there was nothing, just a black emptiness. Bending down, he felt the ground beneath his feet. It was rough stone. The cool air smelled of damp earth. Despite his dragon enhanced eyesight he could detect no hint of light.

We are back in the cave, he realized. *That's why there's no light. No light and no aythar.*

DEMONHOME

That was why the world he had chosen seemed dark when viewed from the place in between, because it lacked aythar. It was dead and empty as far as his arcane senses were concerned.

His thoughts were interrupted as the dragon by his side began to issue a deep rumbling growl. Desacus was disturbed by their unusual surroundings. Brilliant yellow light blossomed in the cave as flames began to shoot from between bared teeth.

"It's alright," said Matthew. "We're just underground."

"I cannot see!" came the dragon's seldom used voice. "I can't hear your thoughts!"

"There's no ambient aythar here," Matthew soothed, "but you can still see. Your flames lit the darkness for a moment."

"How did we get underground?" asked Desacus. "We were outside."

"I was aiming for the cave," said Matthew. "I'm still new to this, but I don't think it would have mattered where we were in our world. The spot I was aiming for in this one was this cave."

Another flare from the dragon's mouth illuminated the rock walls for a moment, "And how do you propose we exit this place? I see no openings around us."

Matthew wasn't so sure of that. If this dimension was a close analog for their own, then the cave should be very similar to the one in their world. He needed more light to be sure, though. Concentrating, he focused his aythar to create a light globe above his outstretched hand, "Lyet."

It was something he had done a thousand times before, but it was much harder now. All of the aythar had to come from within. Slowly the light built as he put forth his strength, and after several seconds he had a brilliant ball hovering over their heads.

There was no exit.

"Well this is inconvenient," muttered the young wizard.

"I could dig us free, given enough time," suggested Desacus. "My flame would be faster still. It can melt stone."

"I'd be dead from the heat or lack of air before you got through all that rock," said Matthew. Briefly he wondered which would kill him first, or which would be the most unpleasant. *Burning, definitely,* he decided before turning his thoughts to more practical solutions. "It will be safer, for me at least, if I do it."

"I'll never understand how your race survived so long," commented the dragon. "Almost anything can kill your kind."

Matthew smirked, "You were built to be resilient."

"You only underscore my point," said Desacus. "Your father created us. If he could do that, why not create stronger bodies for himself and his offspring?"

"Gareth Gaelyn tried that once," rebutted Matthew. "Eventually he decided it was better to be human."

"For what reason?" snorted the dragon.

"Apparently, he ate most of his friends, and that put him off the whole thing," explained Matthew.

Desacus laughed, a disturbingly deep barking sound coming from his throat, "I can hardly blame him for that. Your people smell delicious."

The wizard gave his companion an odd look, "Compared to what?"

"Sheep," returned the dragon immediately, "or even worse, goats. They smell terrible, although honestly, I'd take a cow, or better still a horse, over a human any day. I'll never understand why your family insists on feeding me goats. There are so many better options."

"Goats are cheaper," the young mage informed him. "Even my father would go broke if he fed you on cows every day." He tried not to think of the dragon eating horses, for some reason that image disturbed him more than the thought of Desacus eating people. "How often do you think about eating people?"

"Only when I'm dreaming."

Moira must have been seriously disturbed when she made his personality, thought Matthew. "Do you really have dreams like that?"

Desacus laughed again, "No. Usually it's deer, or horses."

"That's a relief."

"Though sometimes I imagine them with a nice human sauce drizzled over the top," continued the dragon.

Now he knew Desacus was pulling his leg. His companion had a bizarre sense of humor. "How would you even make human sauce? Dragons don't cook."

"I'll admit I don't understand human cooking, pun intended, but I would imagine you just mash them up. What could be simpler?"

Matthew couldn't help chuckling, but after a moment he added, "Just remember this, you are *not* to eat any people, ever."

The dragon sighed, "Not even the bad ones?"

Was that sarcasm? Desacus's voice was too foreign to the normal range of human inflection to be certain and without being able to hear his thoughts directly it made his true meaning ambiguous for Matthew to know. "Not even the bad ones—unless I give you permission first."

"What about dead ones?"

"Huh?"

"What if they're already dead? Say perhaps if we found some that had fallen off a cliff and they were already dead? It would be wrong to let them go to waste…"

Matthew gave Desacus a flat stare, "No."

The dragon chuffed, "Fine."

"Are we done with this topic now? I need to focus on getting us out of here."

"Since you refuse to be objective about that matter, then I suppose we are," answered Desacus, but after a brief pause he spoke up again. "Wait, what if they *want* me to eat them?"

The young wizard gaped at him, "In what scenario would that ever happen?"

"I've heard that sometimes your kind kill themselves."

"You mean suicide? It's against the law. You shouldn't do it, even if someone asked. Why would you think that was all right?"

The dragon coughed, "I like helping people."

Matthew fought to suppress another laugh, *Of all the dragons I could have chosen, I had to pick a comedian.* Then another thought occurred to him, "When was the last time you ate?"

"Yesterday."

A single day wasn't long for a dragon. They tended to eat large meals and could go several days or even a week without eating again, although it depended greatly on how much they exerted themselves. *He's definitely not hungry then.*

"Let me concentrate," said Matthew. "This isn't going to be easy." Opening the pouch on his belt, he reached in to withdraw an item he thought would help, but his fingers came up short, discovering the bottom of the pouch just inches in. While that would have been normal with most such containers, it wasn't with this one. The pouch was enchanted to open into an extra-dimensional space that he used to store various items.

Of course, it wouldn't work here, he realized. *I'm no longer on the same plane. That demi-plane isn't close to this one.* It was a sobering thought. He had stored a lot of useful items there and being unable to reach them seriously limited his options. He made a quick mental tally of what he had left, *my clothes, a sword, dagger, eating knife, and not much else.* Oh well, nothing said he had to stay long. If a need arose, he could always just return and fetch whatever he needed.

Staring at the heavy granite that blocked their exit from the mountain he felt uncharacteristically nervous. Using magic while being unable to properly use his magesight was an unfamiliar sensation, akin to sword fighting while wearing a blind fold. He couldn't sense anything beyond the cave itself, which now had a small amount of aythar filling it, a product of his presence and the magical light he had created. Not knowing how much stone blocked the way, or what might lie beyond it was discomfiting.

It would also be much more difficult, since the stone had no aythar of its own. It was utterly dead, which meant all the power had to come from him. Even so, he didn't feel it would be worth drawing upon Desacus. *I just need to use an efficient spell procedure to minimize wasted aythar.*

He toyed with the idea of carefully removing the stone in blocks to gradually create a tunnel, but while each step would be simple, it would ultimately cost him more energy, and a lot more time. Sometimes the best solution just happened to be the more dramatic and explosive one.

He began by drawing a circle around himself to reinforce the shield he would need to protect himself from falling stone if the cavern collapsed, then he mentally drew a series of crosshatched lines on the stone face in front of him. Rehearsing the words in his mind first, he then began a short chant in Lycian, carefully describing what he intended to do with his power, "*Nailu*

14

en strath—Lines reinforced by my strength, focusing outward, fracturing stone and pressing outward. Break the earth and seek the sky!"

The last part was a bit poetic, but poetry often worked better than dry exposition, although both had their place. As he spoke he visualized what he wanted and put forth his magic, driving it into the dead stone with his will. His magesight expanded with his power, following it into the rock, like a vision seen on a dark night during flash of lightning.

It took far more of his strength than it should have, and still nothing happened for several long seconds. Sweat began to build on his brow as the tension in the granite grew ever greater, until the rocks around him seemed to vibrate.

And then it exploded.

Parts of the cavern ceiling broke away to be harmlessly deflected by his shield, while the entire wall of stone in front of him vanished, shattering and flying outward. Sunlight, impossibly bright after being in the cave, flooded in making the stone dust in the air difficult to see through.

Matthew had anticipated the dust and made sure his shield would keep it out. Summoning a stiff breeze, he dispersed it quickly, but the effort made him pant. He felt as though he had run a marathon. What he had done required a lot of power, but back home he wouldn't have expected to tire so quickly.

"Stay here," he told the dragon.

"But…"

"I want to look around first. There might be people out there. I doubt they'd react well if they saw you," he explained. "I'll be back in a little while."

Desacus growled, "What am I supposed to do while you scout around?"

"Take a nap," suggested the young wizard.

"I don't want to…"

15

"That's an order," added Matthew, putting a tone of authority in his voice. Desacus promptly laid his head between his forelimbs and closed his eyes.

Well, I didn't mean that kind of order, but I suppose that's fine, thought Matthew. Walking forward carefully, he picked his way through the rubble. After forty or fifty feet he had reached the edge, allowing him to look out and study the mountainside. It was nothing like the mountain he had left in his own world.

The slope here was anything but gentle. From the rough edge of his new cave opening, the stone dropped away vertically for almost a hundred feet. Looking down, he could see a winding trail following the slope of the mountainside. Small trees and shrubs grew here and there, but even the ground near the trail looked perilously steep. His eyes followed the trail to the left until they met those of a young woman looking up at him, her expression filled with surprise.

She had a strange hat of some sort perched on her head, with black hair spilling out in a tight braid down her neck, and her shirt was bizarrely patterned with brown, red, and green stripes in a rectangular pattern. Her mouth opened as she called to him, but the words were unfamiliar and Matthew's attention was taken by a loud crack that shook the stone beneath his feet.

For a moment, he feared the rock face beneath him was collapsing, but it held steady. Glancing to his left, he saw a massive shift as the granite wall moved. A portion of its surface several feet thick began to slide downward, filling the air with a grating noise that drowned out all other sounds.

The rockslide was heading directly for the trail, where the stranger stood.

Trying to divert the stone or shield the woman was likely to kill him as tired as he already was, so instead he reached out with his power to snatch her out of harm's way. Even at that distance it would have been a trivial feat, but in his current environment it was a strain. He wrapped the stranger in a soft band of aythar, and once his hold was secure he lifted and pulled her toward him.

Matthew was a careful person by nature, and he had had years of practice and play with his sister to perfect his control. He knew almost instinctively how dangerous it could be to move a person too quickly, and even in that moment of stress he moderated the initial force he applied.

Unfortunately, he didn't spend enough time making certain of his own position. He had anchored himself out of habit, but while he focused his attention on his target, the extra difficulty of using aythar in this new world caused his grip on the stone at his feet to slip. The young wizard felt the ground slide from beneath his feet and his stomach tried to jump into his throat.

He was falling.

If he had had time to calmly observe what was happening, he might have pondered the unexpected turn of events with some humor, but instead he only had time for one though, *shit.* Pulling harder on the thread of aythar that bound them together he met the woman in mid-air, and as their bodies slammed together he felt the air leave his lungs. He ignored the pain of that as he surrounded them both with a springy cushion of pure aythar to break their fall.

They bounced when they hit the ground, and the sudden change of direction threatened to pull them apart. Matthew gripped her harder, using both his arms and his power to hold the woman close as they spun in the air. Their second landing was farther down the mountainside and no less violent, sending them back into the air again.

With each bounce, they rolled and fell farther down the steep slope. Matthew couldn't breathe, and he felt his strength failing. *This isn't going to end well.* Looking into the eyes of the woman, he couldn't read her expression. Fear? Shock? Or was it simple surprise?

A heavy copse of trees hove its way into view. Unable to speak, he sent a thought to the stranger, *You're going to be alright. I promise...* The shade of the trees blocked out the sun as he used the last of his aythar to stop their spin and put himself between her and the onrushing trunks. Then the world went white.

CHAPTER 3

Karen blinked as a bead of sweat dripped into her eye. Stopping for a moment, she removed her hat and used the hem of her shirt to wipe her damp forehead. The mountain air was cool and dry, but she had set a hard pace for herself going up the trail.

"Time for a break," she told herself. She had a habit of talking to herself. It was something that might be expected for a hiker, alone on a long trail, but for Karen it was a part of everyday life. She had grown up with very few people around and after her father's death she rarely saw other people in the flesh.

She had plenty of friends; she wasn't antisocial, but talking to people online didn't completely fill the need. It was almost as though her vocal cords simply demanded the exercise.

Sitting on a relatively smooth outcropping of rock near the trail, she pulled her PM out and looked at it. There were several additional notifications waiting for her attention. With a sigh, she shoved it back into her pocket. She was hiking to get away from such things, though it hardly mattered. She could be just as alone at home as she was a hundred miles from other human beings.

"But back there I wouldn't get to see all the flowers, or smell the fresh air," she said softly. Glancing skyward, she gauged the position of the sun, purposely ignoring the urge to pull her PM back out just to check the time. "Mid-afternoon, I've got hours to go before I have to worry about light. I'll wait a couple more hours before calling the pert for my gear."

Setting up camp in the dark was no fun, so she had learned to give herself plenty of time to accomplish the task. Plus, it would take twenty or thirty minutes for the pert to reach her. She pulled a bottle from her shoulder bag and took a drink of water. Zipping the bag back up, she held it out in front of her for a moment, contemplating its light weight.

She carried very little in it, aside from her water, a small bag of trail mix, and extra sunscreen. She couldn't imagine what backwoods hiking had been like in the old days, when people had had to carry everything with them. "They must've been tough. I get tired just carrying this little thing."

The wind had died for the moment, so Karen fanned herself using her booney for a few seconds before putting it back on her head. "Time to get moving." She stood and began picking her way along the trail again, following it ever higher into the mountains.

Karen ascended slowly for another half an hour. She was beginning to pant now. The trees had begun to thin out, and she knew the tree line was probably less than a few hundred feet higher up. Of course, gaining that extra several hundred feet might mean trekking another mile along the trail as it slowly wound back and forth up the difficult terrain.

"I don't really want to camp any higher up," she told herself. "Maybe I'll stop here and in the morning go on. That'll put me well into the descending portion of the trail before it gets dark tomorrow." She pulled out her PM to locate herself on the map.

The first thing that grabbed her attention, as always, was the notification alert. "Three messages from Dad, and one from Mom—what the heck?" Since transitioning, her mother rarely bothered to contact her anymore. One or two messages a year was the most she expected, and that was fine with Karen. She bypassed the message alerts. There would be plenty of time to review them later, after the tent was up. She was just starting to look at the map when *something* flashed farther up the trail.

Looking up, she searched the trail ahead, along with the nearly vertical stone face that rose to the right of it. A tremor passed beneath her feet as a thunderous crack sounded and stone flew from the stone wall in exactly the place she was looking.

"What the hell?" The explosion was clearly not natural. Was someone using explosives? Something like that should be illegal on public land, especially so close to a hiking trail.

A cloud of dust hung in the air above, until a sudden gust of wind dispersed it. She stared at the opening that was revealed and was utterly surprised when a man stepped into view a moment later. *He must've been right there when it blew. How reckless can you be?*

The man looked down at her, his eyes meeting hers with a look of surprised curiosity. The wind tossed his light brown hair as he gazed at her. He was slender built, but otherwise perfectly average in his form; what really caught her attention was the strange attire he wore.

A sudden pop took her attention off him for a moment and a glance above and to her right showed her a huge section of the mountainside sloughing off. It was sliding directly toward her.

There was no time. None. Even if she had been running already she couldn't hope to clear the endangered portion of the trail quickly enough.

Something touched her, accompanied by another flash of that same strange light. Or was it light? She could see it, sort of, but she felt it as well, and the sensation brought with it a wave of dizziness. Or perhaps that came because she was flying through the air. The ground must have pitched her upward somehow, although she could have sworn she was being pulled.

She saw the stranger slip and fall, his face registering surprise. Their eyes locked again, and she saw his arms open wide. He was growing closer, almost as if he was flying purposely toward her like some strange bird. He looked determined, rather than afraid.

Without thinking about it she bent at the waist, drawing her legs up to shield her body from the impact as they slammed into one another, and she heard a whoosh as the air went out of his lungs. Her knees had struck him in the belly, even so his arms went around her, gripping her fiercely against him. Fire raced along her nerves as their bodies came into contact.

He can't be that strong. It felt as though they were bound together by ropes.

And then they were falling, and fear finally found her heart. Everything up to that point had happened so rapidly that her mind hadn't had a chance to react properly. She felt it now, though, a rush of adrenaline as her heart began to flutter in her chest, with her breath coming in shallow gasps. They landed, but were somehow unhurt, and then they were flying again, spinning through the cold mountain air.

He was staring at her, no, *through* her, as though he was distracted. Then his eyes focused on her. *He's glowing,* she realized. And then she felt him inside her, a voice within the privacy of her heart.

It was a feeling, a thought, or perhaps it was a different language. The words were strange but she could taste the meaning of them, *You're going to be okay.* Their bodies turned in the air, and then she saw the trees slam into his back.

22

Karen opened her eyes again, though she didn't remember closing them. It was dark, and she couldn't breathe, as though a great weight was pressing down on her chest. She tried to roll over, and then she understood, the stranger was on top of her. Light was filtering through the trees and creeping around the edges of his hair. The sun was still up.

"I'm alive," she managed to whisper, but she needed to get out from under him.

Absently she noticed his smell, distinctly masculine and yet unusual in some way she found hard to define. It fit well with his odd choice in clothing, earthy and mild, as though he bathed regularly but had never discovered deodorant.

She grunted as she rolled his limp form to one side and clambered out from under him. She took a moment to study the stranger.

He was obviously wealthy. Everything he wore was bespoke, in fact, as she looked closer she could see that even the stitching had been hand-done. Unlike most handmade clothes however, these were masterfully fashioned. What truly made them odd was the style. Was he some sort of medieval enthusiast? He wore at least two layers, a richly embroidered grey tunic with wide sleeves that came halfway down his arms covered a not-quite-white undertunic with sleeves that tapered to fit him all the way to his wrists.

At his waist was a sturdy leather belt, chased with silver metal. Both the buckle and the tip appeared to be silver with small emerald stones ornamenting them. The pouch and scabbards it held were similarly adorned.

"Who carries a sword into the wilderness?" she asked him, though she didn't expect an answer. He was completely unconscious.

Is he breathing?! How could she have been so stupid? After hitting the trees there was every chance he might be dead, or dying. She should have checked that immediately. Leaning forward, she placed her ear gently against his chest. The material there was smooth and soft, though perhaps stiffer than cotton. She could hear his heart beating steadily within his chest.

As she raised her head she saw a glint of gold at his throat, a bit of metal peeking out from his collar. With one hand she pulled a heavy chain out of his shirt where she could examine it.

"Costume jewelry?" she wondered aloud. While his clothes were obviously expensive beyond belief, there was no way the necklace could be gold. It was made of links that were thick enough to have been part of the chain on a child's swingset, although they were much more elegantly formed. The links were square and designed in such a way that they could lie flat against the skin. If it were real it would have been worth tens of thousands of dollars, if not more. Even people who could afford such clothes wouldn't be foolish enough to walk around displaying that much precious metal openly.

There was no way it was real. "What a tacky necklace," she observed. "You aren't a rapper are you, my mysterious friend?" Karen laughed at the thought, there weren't any rappers anymore. "At least not in *this* world."

A small trickle of blood made its way from one nostril and down the man's cheek.

Karen felt a sudden surge of panic. Was he dying? Perhaps he had hit his head? He might be hemorrhaging internally. She had heard of people walking away from similar accidents complaining of nothing more than a headache, only to die hours later.

"I've got to get us off this mountain." She reached into her pocket to retrieve her PM. The pert could have them back to civilization in less than an hour.

It wasn't there.

"No! No, no, no! Goddamnit!" she swore. When had she had it last? Right before the rockslide—she must have dropped it. Glancing back up the steep rocky slope, she knew it was probably buried under several tons of rock. What would she do now? She couldn't summon her pert, and it had taken her four days to hike this far into the mountains. There was no way she could carry someone back out the same way.

"And what about food, water, shelter? Sweet Jesus!" It would start getting cold in a few hours, and all of her gear; her tent, sleeping bag, everything, was all packed up in the pert's storage compartments.

She closed her eyes and held herself still, "First things first, Karen, what's your first priority?" *He's breathing but unconscious. I can't do anything about a head injury, but I should check him over to make sure there aren't any other serious injuries.* She stared at the man once again, "Do I have to take his clothes off?"

Karen shook her head, "I probably should, but I don't know that I could get them back on him, and it will be getting cold. I'll check for broken bones, but unless I see blood, the clothes stay on." That was something of a relief; she hadn't really wanted to strip him.

Running her hands along his torso, she felt his ribs and then along his arms but found nothing out of place. A visual inspection revealed no blood, other than what was trickling from his nose. She continued her search, moving down over his hips and checking the long bones of his legs. The first was fine, but the right leg had a suspicious bend in the thigh. Probing it with her fingers caused her patient to groan.

"Groaning is a good sign, maybe." She had no idea, but she hoped it meant his unconsciousness wasn't a result of serious brain injury. "I should have studied medicine instead of pharmacy, not that either is worth a damn anymore." Of course, her current situation belied that statement. Obviously, there were extraordinary circumstances where it was handy for a person to know something of the old disciplines.

"So, you've got a broken femur," she told the stranger. "That probably won't kill you, unless you've also torn an artery, but I have no way to know, and even if I did I wouldn't begin to know how to treat it, so I'm just going to assume it's fine. In addition, you have a head injury, also something I can't do much about." She was forgetting something.

"Oh!" Leaning forward she pried one of his eyelids open, letting the sunlight spill in. He had blue eyes, and the iris contracted as the light shone in. "That's good—I think."

Having done as much as she could to assess her patient, she considered her next priority, "We need to get farther down where it won't be as cold tonight." How in the hell was she supposed to move a grown man by herself? Even if he weren't unconscious, he certainly couldn't walk with his leg in that condition.

"A litter," she pronounced. *Is that the right term?* She wasn't sure, but it didn't really matter.

The only tool she was carrying was her pocket knife. She didn't relish the idea of trying to cut even slender saplings with that. Fortunately, a much large blade was right at hand. It might not be an axe, but she figured the sword would be easier than a swiss army knife. Gripping the hilt she slid the weapon from its scabbard and then whistled.

It wasn't a toy. The blade was almost three feet in length and was polished to a brilliant sheen. Double edged, it looked to be very sharp, though she didn't try her fingers on the edge. Making a slow circuit of the area she found several small trees with trunks less than two inches in diameter. Karen raised the sword and chopped at one, holding the hilt in both hands.

She had expected it to require several swings if not more to cut through the base of the tree, but to her surprise the blade bit deeply, almost severing it in one go. She had used an axe before, which should have been a better tool for the task, but it hadn't been *that* easy. Her second swing finished the job, and when she took aim at another tree she managed it with a single blow. The sword was impossibly sharp.

"Damn thing almost cuts like a lightsaber," she muttered, examining the edge again. There was no sign of damage from the hard use, but she could see a faint shimmer hovering around the edge. *Now I'm imagining things,* she thought. With a laugh, she held it out in front of her, "Magic, no doubt about it. This must be the fabled blade, Excalibur."

She turned back toward the unconscious stranger, "Which means you must be Arthur."

Putting aside her nervous attempt at humor, she cut a third sapling and then used the sword to trim away all the smaller branches before arranging the three lengths of wood in a triangle. She returned the sword to its scabbard and borrowed the stranger's knife. It seemed to be just as sharp.

She needed rope, but she had that covered. Karen unbuckled her belt and with a twist removed the buckle and began unravelling the paracord it was constructed from. It had been made for just such a purpose, though she had never seriously believed she would need it.

"Sadly, the only knot I can remember is a square knot," she mumbled to herself as she began attempting to lash the wooden frame together. In the end she succeeded, but it was not a job any scout would have been proud of, and she had probably used far more of the paracord than was necessary. She added the smaller branches she had cut from the trees earlier, lashing them across the framework, and eventually she had something that she thought might support a body.

Karen eyed her handiwork critically, "Not my best work."

Getting the man onto the litter turned out to be the worst part of the job. He wasn't particularly heavy for his height, but even a hundred and sixty some-odd pounds of dead-weight was a serious challenge. Thankfully she wasn't small, at five feet and ten inches, Karen was taller than most women she knew. She was also in excellent shape.

She got her arms under his shoulders and hooked her elbows beneath his armpits. Grunting and swearing, she tugged and pulled until she had him roughly positioned on the ramshackle litter. The sun was beginning to drop behind the mountains to the west, and she knew she didn't have much time left.

An hour and a half later she was convinced she had made a mistake. Karen hurt everywhere. Her hands were raw and sore; she had lost some skin while making the litter and even more dragging the damned thing down the rough and tumble mountainside. Then there were her muscles: her back hurt, her shoulders hurt, and her legs had been tired before she had even started all of this.

Worse still, she wasn't covering much distance. The litter might have been a big help across even terrain, but going downhill it was a constant struggle. The wide end kept catching between bushes, rocks, and small trees, forcing her to stop and free it before she could continue.

How far had she gone? *I doubt I've gotten us much more than three or four hundred feet down this damned mountain.* "This sucks," she swore. "How much worse can it get?" As if in answer to her question a light rain began to fall.

Karen cast her eyes skyward, "Forget I asked."

She kept going for another hour, until the light became so poor that she began to worry about injuring herself in the dark. In the distance, she could hear the sound of rushing water, which was a good sign, since it meant she must be getting close to the bottom.

The rain had stopped, and there wasn't much wind, but her clothes were still damp and even a slight breeze of the now chilly air made her shiver. Her passenger didn't seem to notice, but his skin was cold and clammy to the touch.

"This is going to be a fun night."

She propped the head of her litter on a short stone that stood only a foot from the ground. That kept it off the wet soil. Casting her eyes about, she looked for something she could use to help insulate them, but none of the thin bushes that grew nearby looked appealing. There were some dead leaves on the ground, but they were wet, and she didn't care for the thought of whatever insects might be hiding in them.

Snakes didn't bother her, most bugs were ok too, but the thought of possibly finding a centipede made her skin crawl.

"Why don't you have one of those giant wool cloaks they always wear in fantasy novels?" she asked, addressing the unconscious man again. As usual, he didn't reply.

She tried propping herself up against a tree, but she was soon shivering, and sleep was out of the question. Her patient didn't shiver, but looking at him made her feel worse. *If I'm cold, he might die of hypothermia, his body isn't even responding.*

Standing, she moved over and lay down on the litter beside him. Getting comfortable was difficult. The cross-pieces were just wide enough to cause them to cut into her back, and sharp twigs seemed to be everywhere, but she made the best of it. Pressing herself close against the stranger's left side to avoid the injured leg, she closed her eyes.

A thought occurred to her then, *What if he wakes up?* That was stupid. He was in no condition to be a threat, and even if he tried anything it would only take one poke to his leg to end any such thoughts.

Karen sighed as she closed her eyes, "I'm never going to be able to sleep like this," but her tired body had other ideas, and she was soon fast asleep.

CHAPTER 4

Matthew scratched at his cheek. There was something dry and crusty stuck there. Opening his eyes he found himself confronted by a dazzling display of stars. The sky was black and absolutely clear, revealing a celestial show of unparalleled beauty.

His body was mostly cold, but one side was warmer than the other. Nestled against him was the woman he had seen earlier, or at least he assumed it was her. It was hard to tell in the dark, and his magesight was almost absent in this dead world. He kept still for a few minutes, creating a dim light to see by, and then examining his surroundings.

He was off the ground, suspended on a rough litter, and he didn't think he was in the same place where he had lost consciousness, though he couldn't be sure. He also needed to pee.

The pain struck when he tried to get up, and an involuntary groan passed his lips. *Fuck that hurts!* he thought. Turning his magesight inward was easier, there was plenty of aythar within him to see by. *My leg is broken.*

He supposed that was to be expected. It could have been much worse. Drawing upon what strength he had, he attempted to straighten the bone before fusing it back together—and nearly screamed.

Idiot, of course it hurts! You know better, block the nerves first, he chided himself. He was glad his sister wasn't there to see his mistake. She was always loftily superior about her healing skills.

Starting again, he blocked the nerves this time and succeeded in getting the bones back in place and mended. The bruising he couldn't do much about, but there didn't seem to be much damage otherwise. Releasing the nerve block he gently eased himself up from the litter, hissing at the soreness when he put weight on the injured leg. It held him up, though.

Limping slowly, he went a short distance before unlacing his trousers and relieving himself. With that important business taken care of he returned and spent a few minutes considering the girl. She looked thoroughly miserable, wet and shivering on the litter.

Once again he reached futilely into his empty belt pouch. With a sigh he withdrew his hand. He felt weak as a kitten, but he could probably do something about their damp clothes and the cold air.

Muttering softly, he used his aythar to expel the moisture from the woman's clothes first, then he took care of his own. A wave of dizziness came over him, accompanied by a throbbing pain in his head. *I definitely overdid it earlier.*

He wasn't suffering from feedback sickness, though. The headache would have been much worse. He had simply pushed himself too far.

Lying back down on the litter, he eased himself closer to the woman before creating an envelope of warm air around the two of them. Her shivering stopped after several minutes, and she seemed to sigh contentedly, but she didn't awaken.

Matthew ached all over. It felt as though even his bruises had bruises, and the hard, irregular surface of the litter didn't help. He took a while adjusting his position until the wooden lattice was positioned so that it was pressing into relatively uninjured places, and then he closed his eyes.

He didn't think he would sleep, but when he opened them again the bright morning sun was already shining on his face. The woman was leaning over him, staring down with concern on her features.

He smiled, "I'm alright."

She frowned.

Matthew started to get up. The wooden frame was cutting into him in various places, making his aches and pains even worse. The woman put her hand on his chest, pushing him back down. She said something, but he couldn't understand her words. It sounded like a warning or cautionary statement from her tone.

"What did you say?" he asked.

Her reply was equally unintelligible, though he thought he caught the word 'no' in it.

Great, he thought, *we don't speak the same language.* It was something he should have expected. He tried again, "Nice to meet you. My name is Matthew."

She responded with a long utterance that was irritatingly familiar but still unintelligible. It *sounded* as if she was speaking Barion, but the words didn't make sense. He felt as though he should understand what she was saying, but he couldn't find any meaning in her sentences other than the occasional word that he recognized. In this case, the only word he was certain of was 'no'.

Patting his chest again he kept his reply short, "Matthew."

After a second she did the same, "Karen," then she pointed at him, "Matthew."

"Yes," he nodded.

Her eyes lit up, "Yes!" She followed that with another strange sentence that seemed to emphasize the word 'yes'.

So, we have yes and no in common, he decided. *Her language must be either a precursor to Barion, or it could have developed from it.* That should make it easier to learn to understand one another. He sat up and started to get off the litter again.

"No," she declared, following the word with an obvious warning as she pointed at his leg.

Matthew smiled, "My leg is fine. I'm a wizard."

Karen shook her head, "No, Matthew." Using hand gestures and more peculiar phrases she made it clear that he should remain still.

He pointed at his leg again, "I fixed it." When that didn't seem to elicit any comprehension he put his hand on his chest again, "Wizard."

She repeated the word 'wizard' and then laughed. Clearly the word held some meaning for her, although he wasn't sure if she laughed because she thought it was silly, or if it meant something entirely different.

As far as I know I just told her I was a jackass or something. He sighed and tried to consider a different approach, but it was at that moment when he heard the rustling of bushes nearby.

It wasn't the casual sound of the wind catching branches, it was much louder. Something large, probably an animal, was approaching. People often mistakenly assumed that animals were silent in the forest, but nothing could be further from the truth. In actuality, they just had better hearing and usually moved away when they detected humans nearby.

This animal was large however, and it wasn't moving away. Once again Matthew felt frustration at the limits on his magesight. Back home he would have detected anything that large long before it came within range of hearing, while here his magesight extended only a few tens of feet from his location.

Without any ambient native aythar he could only sense things that were within the reach of the aythar that must be radiating from his own body. *Sort of like a man carrying a lantern on a dark night,* he supposed.

Holding one finger in front of his lips, he hoped that Karen would understand that he wanted her to be quiet. Then he pointed toward the bushes as he sent a faint pulse of aythar in that direction. It illuminated the world for him, and his magesight was temporarily able to register the large bear that was slowly working its way toward them.

Matthew was no woodsman, but he had learned enough woodcraft to know that bears didn't approach humans without a purpose. Ordinarily they found an excuse to leave an area if they sensed humans nearby. He and Karen had been talking loudly enough that it must know they were there. That meant it was approaching them deliberately. It was probably hungry and trying to decide whether they would make an easy meal.

Karen stopped, pursing her lips when she saw Matthew holding one finger in front of his mouth. She had been frustrated to discover that they couldn't communicate properly. If she'd still had her PM it wouldn't have been a problem. It could have detected whatever language he was using and been able to translate for them. *Or if I were normal I wouldn't have been able to lose it in the first place,* she thought in frustration. Most people didn't carry external PM's anymore. It was just one more reminder that she was a freak.

Then she heard a faint rustling. It was low enough that she hadn't paid any attention to it before, but now that she was paying attention, she could tell it was being caused by the movement of something. She turned her back on the wounded stranger and scanned the rocks and brush around them. *Matthew must have great hearing,* she thought.

And then she saw it. A surge of adrenaline shot through her as the dark head appeared some thirty feet away. She had been careless. Where was her bag? She had a can of bear spray inside it. Turning she looked back at the litter, only to find the stranger standing.

"What are you doing?" she asked in surprise.

Matthew pointed, "Bear."

Another word they had in common. She nodded, "Yes, a bear. How are you standing?" She ignored the mystery of the stranger being on his feet while her eyes searched for her bag. There it was, lying on the ground on the other side of the litter.

She heard the bear again, louder now. It was close and no longer making any attempt to disguise its approach. Karen started to step around the stranger, but he put a hand on her shoulder, forcing her to stop.

Drawing his sword, he handed it to her carefully. He said something as her hand reflexively closed over the hilt, but again, she couldn't understand, and then he stepped around her, heading in the direction of their ursine visitor.

"What are you doing?" Karen hissed, her eyes wide.

Matthew walked directly toward the bear. His stride was relaxed, almost casual, even though the beast was now less than ten feet away. There was nothing but open space between them now. Raising his arms and holding them wide he barked a command at the massive creature.

Karen knew confidence and a bold posture could sometimes force a bear to move away, but this one appeared to be having none of it. It charged forward, but her strange companion never flinched as the grizzly rushed toward him. "He's fucking crazy," she muttered, preparing to scramble for her bag.

The bear growled, baring fangs that looked big enough to be daggers as it swiped at the young man with one paw.

Matthew batted the paw away, as though he was brushing off an attack from a small child. Then he flicked his hand toward the bear.

Karen felt, or saw, *something*. A flash of light, or heat, washed over her, followed by a wave of vertigo. Whatever it was seemed to strike the bear, and she saw its head jerk from some sort of impact. It reared up on its hind legs, enraged, but then Matthew said something, and it fell backward, losing its balance. Again, she felt *something*, though her eyes seemed to argue with her other perceptions.

Matthew yelled at the bear again, waving his arms menacingly as it hastily got back on its feet. The grizzly turned and retreated rapidly without stopping to look back. Matthew watched it go, making sure it had truly left before he turned around and walked back to Karen.

She was holding the bear spray now, and she stared at him with her mouth agape. "What the hell were you thinking? That thing might have killed you! It should have killed you!"

He still couldn't understand her words, but he caught the gist she was sure, because he responded by shrugging his shoulders apologetically.

Karen found the gesture irritating. "Why did you give me this?" she demanded, holding the sword up. "Nobody uses a sword to fight bears, and if you thought they could, you should have kept it!"

The young man tilted his head slightly, obviously trying to puzzle out what she was saying, but eventually he replied, "Sword, you, safe."

Three words she could understand in one sentence, not that she agreed with any of them, of course. "No," she declared before pointing to his forehead, "stupid."

He stared back at her with a smug, almost indifferent expression, which only made her madder. The idiot had nearly gotten himself killed, and he obviously thought he had saved her. Karen glanced down at the bear spray in her hand and suppressed the urge to pull the pin and spray him with it.

She pushed that aside as another thought occurred to her, "What's with your leg anyway?" When Matthew's expression grew more puzzled she pointed at it, "Your leg, this, your leg—how are you walking?"

His face lit up with comprehension. After a long pause he pointed at himself, "Wizard."

Karen let the air out of her chest in a long sigh before pointing at him. "Nutjob," she corrected acerbically.

The young man paused and then nodded, "Yes, wizard, nutjob." He seemed to think they were communicating.

She couldn't help but smile at that, "At least we agree on something. Come on nutjob, we aren't going to get out of this wilderness if we just stand around all day."

CHAPTER 5

Matthew watched as Karen packed the strange cylinder she was holding back into her bag. When she pointed at the litter and said something to him, he was pretty certain she was asking if he needed to be carried on it again.

He shook his head, "No, thank you."

She shrugged and pointed downhill as she said something else. The words all sounded familiar. Once in a while, one would jump out at him, but he knew they were far from properly understanding one another. He swept his arm outward and gave a slight bow, "Lead the way."

He followed her as she picked her way down the steep mountainside. They weren't on a trail of any sort, so the going was rough, and within minutes his leg began to throb and ache. That was just the worst of it though, pains in his back, neck, and elsewhere all competed for his attention.

Karen looked at him with concern as his mild limp became a pronounced hobbling gait. She said something, but the only word he understood was 'crutch'.

"Good idea," he told her. They were near the bottom now and the trees were thicker around them. Limping into a stand of small saplings he selected one that was small enough and fairly straight.

Karen pointed at his sword.

"No need," he told her, putting his hand on the tree he had chosen. Concentrating, he sent his aythar out to follow the length of the tree. It took considerably more effort than he expected. He was beginning to worry, for he seemed to be getting weaker, as though his power wasn't properly replenishing itself.

Once his aythar encompassed the length that he wanted, he clenched his will, cutting the tree neatly off near the ground and at a point higher up. The smaller branches that were attached to that portion also fell away, leaving him with an ideal walking staff nearly six feet in length.

Karen's eyes widened slightly as he pulled it away with little apparent effort. She looked puzzled, but she didn't say anything.

They continued onward and when they reached the bottom, where a small but gentle valley lay, Matthew wondered how far it would be before they reached her home. Looking upward he studied the mountain they had descended. To his eyes it looked much like the others that surrounded them on either side. If they traveled too far he might have difficulty finding it again.

And Desacus won't wake up until I can get close enough to give him a command. He needed to mark the location. In fact, he wished he had done that before leaving the cave, but it was too late for that.

Holding up a hand, he motioned to Karen, "Wait a few minutes."

She nodded and pointed at her lower abdomen while saying something and then pointing to a stand of tall white-barked trees.

Matthew got the general idea, she needed a moment of privacy for certain urgent purposes. "Go ahead," he told her. Then he cast about, looking for what he needed.

In the mountains it didn't take him long to find what he sought, a large boulder with a relatively smooth top.

The one he found was a little bigger than he'd have liked, with sides that were almost ten feet in height, but with the judicious application of a bit of aythar, he managed to scale it. Once atop the massive stone he used his finger to channel a small line of power and began carving a circle into it.

Teleportation circles were fairly complicated, but the beauty of them was that they labeled a particular 'piece' of space. The fact that he was a stranger to this world, to this dimension, was no problem at all. Once the circle was finished, this spot would have the name, or 'key', that he had designated for it. So long as he remembered that key, he could make another circle anywhere that would bring him back to it.

Etching the circle and symbols into the stone was hard work. His strength was definitely diminished, and growing weaker. *How long will I have to rest to recover?* he wondered. Back home a few hours were usually all he needed, but apparently in a world without aythar it took much longer. *What if I can't recover here?*

He wasn't entirely sure if he was still generating his own aythar at all, and if he wasn't, then he would die when it was exhausted. Aythar was equivalent to life, and it still confused him that the living things in this world seemed to do perfectly well without it. The bear had seemed healthy and Karen could certainly walk and talk without any discernable aythar.

That wasn't entirely true. Karen hadn't had any aythar when he had first seen her, but since he had awoken that morning he had noticed that she had begun to develop a faint trace of it. Possibly it was from being in such close proximity to him, but he wondered if it was temporary or whether she might begin to produce aythar on her own.

Only time would tell.

He finished the circle. It wasn't his best work. Without having a stylus the lines were thicker and cruder than they needed to be, and his weakness made them rougher than they might otherwise have been, but it would serve. Karen stood below, looking up at him curiously. No doubt she was wondering how he had gotten up there since there were few handholds for easy climbing.

Matthew grinned at her and jumped down, using a small amount of aythar to cushion the shock as he landed.

They continued their trek, following the stream that ran through the small valley and heading roughly east. As the day wore on Matthew wondered how much farther they had to go before reaching Karen's home. She couldn't have traveled very far since she had almost nothing in the way of supplies or camping gear.

When the sun stood highest in the sky, they stopped in a grassy clearing and took a short break. Matthew was starving, and he knew Karen had to be just as hungry. Neither of them had eaten since the previous day.

Karen pulled a small strange package from her bag. He had noticed it earlier while examining her with his magesight, and he knew it contained some sort of dried food, but the container itself was made of a material foreign to him. In some ways it resembled glass, transparent and shimmery, but it differed in that it was flexible like leather.

She poured a small handful into her palm and handed him the remainder still in the small pouch.

Matthew dipped his head, "Thank you."

She answered with a short phrase that he felt sure meant something along the lines of 'you're welcome'. He filed the phrase away in his memory. Having the gift of the loshti was handy; since it meant he never forgot anything. Slowly but surely he was building up a store of phrases as he figured out the meaning behind some of the things she said.

The food was bizarre, like everything else she showed him. Some of it was obviously dried grains, and he could identify some pieces as being preserved fruit. The really weird part was the brightly colored oval bits. He bit into one cautiously and was shocked to find it contained something very sweet.

He picked one out and held it out to her, questioning, "What is this?"

She understood the question easily enough, "Chocolate."

Matthew decided he liked chocolate, though it seemed a strange food to pack for a journey into the wilderness. He ate the rest of what she had given him in two quick bites. It wouldn't be enough to sustain them for long.

Of even more concern was the fact that her water bottle was empty. He moved closer to her and tapped it before pointing toward the river, "We should refill your bottle."

Karen shook her head negatively and said something. Most of it sounded like gibberish, except for the word 'bad'.

So, the river isn't safe to drink. Hopefully we aren't far from her home.

Karen marched along steadily, trying to ignore the empty knot that her stomach had become. She knew she was in no danger of starving to death, yet. It had only been a day since her last good meal, and they had been able to snack on the last of her trail mix a few hours ago, but her belly seemed convinced that she was in mortal danger.

Hunger, true hunger, was not something most people experienced any more, at least not in the modern world.

Stop complaining, she told herself, *you can last for several days without food.*

"But will I be able to keep walking all that time," she wondered aloud. Of even more concern was their lack of water, and she thought longingly of all the water she had left in her pert. If only she had some way to summon it. *If only I weren't a freak.*

Eventually they would become too desperate to ignore the river and the risk of giardia or some other water-borne illness would be the lesser of two evils. The mountain stream was relatively clear, and it certainly looked inviting. She would have had little concern in using the water if she had some way to boil it first.

But she hadn't carried her lighter with her, deeming it needless weight when she had thought she'd be able to summon the pert every evening. "An extra ounce or two doesn't seem like such a waste now, does it?" she chided herself. "Not when you'll be thirsty and freezing your ass off tonight."

She glanced back to look at the young man following her. His limp was less pronounced now, partly because of the staff, but likely also because the long exercise had loosened up his bruised muscles. She still didn't understand how he was walking. She had been certain the leg was broken.

She had begun collecting a whole host of unanswered questions regarding him. He seemed good natured, but his apparent lack of caution, particularly regarding bears, was worrisome. She wondered if he had a death wish or whether he was just naturally foolish.

The way he kept referring to himself as a wizard might have been funny, if they weren't deep in the mountains with no easy access to food, water, or shelter. The back country was no place for fools. *Not that I'm any better,* she thought, *I hiked out here with only my PM and never once considered what might happen if it was damaged or lost.*

She couldn't deny that weird things kept happening around him, though. Being thrown together during the rockslide was an amazing coincidence, and surviving it was almost a miracle. Matthew's odd bravado when he had scared away the bear was also nearly unbelievable, but she knew that quite often the real world was stranger than fiction. The young man had been incredibly lucky.

Of all those things, what bothered her most was the memory of him reaching into the small stand of saplings and pulling one away as though it had been made to serve as a staff. It hadn't looked dead, but that was the only explanation she could come up with. He had gripped it firmly, and it had just snapped off in his hand. All the smaller limbs and the top had fallen away as well.

There had been something very unnatural about it, but she couldn't bring herself to believe it had been anything other than sheer luck.

And then there was his climbing skill. If he weren't dressed in those odd clothes she might have thought he was a rock climber. The boulder he had scaled while she was relieving herself earlier was not something just anyone would be able to manage.

"Too many questions," she muttered.

The sun was getting low in the sky, and she felt torn. They needed to cover a lot more ground if they were to get back to civilization before they starved or died of thirst, but she could also tell that the long hike had taken a serious toll on her companion. Whatever the truth of his injuries was, he had taken a battering the day before. He needed rest.

She made up her mind, and when the next clearing presented itself she held up her hand, "We should camp here."

Matthew nodded tiredly and she wondered how much he had really understood.

"Rest," she told him. "Let me have the sword, and I'll try to make a pallet for us to sleep on." Starting early would give her time to gather green grass and possibly make something less uncomfortable to sleep on than the cold ground.

He gave her a confused look, and she repeated the key word while pointing at his waist, "Sword."

"Ah," he answered and then unbuckled his belt and handed her the scabbarded weapon.

She motioned toward a dead log, "Sit down. Rest. I'll be back soon."

After that she headed back in the direction they had come. They had passed a willow tree not long ago. The long draping limbs and soft leaves would probably make good bedding, and covered with some of the river grass it might make for a better night's sleep. "Unless I'm allergic to the grass," she muttered.

The sword sliced easily through the thin branches, and she marveled again at its sharpness. In a short span of minutes, she gathered as much as she could carry and then began making her way back to their new campsite.

The return was a ten-minute walk and Matthew was missing when she returned. She had been gone less than a half an hour, and she wondered whether she should stop and search for her companion. In the end, she decided against it. If he was stupid enough to leave without her, he wouldn't last long. He had probably just gone off to relieve himself.

She piled the willow branches up and went back for a second load. As she walked she absently noted an abundance of deadwood along the way. A fire would have been nice, but she had absolutely no idea how to start one without a lighter. Even if she had had something like flint and steel she knew it took great skill to create a fire that way.

When she returned with her second load of branches, he was still missing. She was getting worried now. Gritting her teeth, she went to cut some of the tall grass by the river. The light was failing rapidly.

"No way I'm going rambling around in the dark looking for a nutjob I hardly know," she growled to herself. Karen knew she was lying to herself, though. She had grown used to the stranger's presence, and being alone in the mountains without resources had begun to erode her natural confidence. She didn't relish sleeping alone through the cold night with nothing but grass for a blanket.

Walking back with her arms full of fragrant fresh cut grass she noticed the smoke immediately. "What the hell?" Quickening her steps, Karen reached the campsite in record time. Matthew was sitting in the middle of it, a small fire burning in front of him.

"How did you make a fire?" she asked, but his reply was more gibberish.

He held up something dark and furry, "Food." It was a dead marmot.

Karen had never eaten wild game, and the thought of eating one of the cute animals would ordinarily have turned her stomach. Now, though, hunger and the prospect of starvation caused her to feel a surge of hope at the sight of the creature. *How did he catch that?*

Matthew pointed upward, toward the limbs of a nearby tree. It took her almost a minute to spot what he was indicating, a brace of rabbits hanging from a tall branch some fifty feet off the ground.

"Why did you put them up there? *How* did you put them up there?" she asked incredulously.

He answered with a long series of words, none of which made any sense to her. Finally he paused and seeing her confusion said simply, "Bear." He lifted his arms and growled, miming the grizzly they had met that morning.

Karen sighed. She knew very well the dangers of keeping food in a campsite, "Yes, yes, I understand. You don't want to attract bears, but how in the hell did you get them up there?" He had no rope, and the rabbits had been spitted on what appeared to be a sharpened branch. "Did you climb up there?" The limbs were too small to support a man's weight at that point.

Matthew grinned and pointed at himself, "Nutjob."

She laughed, "At least you're honest." They laughed together for several moments, though she doubted her companion understood what she found funny. It felt good to release the tension at last, but when the humor died away, she had to fight back tears. The past two days had been a serious shock, and now her emotions were working their way to the surface.

He noticed the change in her and moved closer, patting her shoulder. When he lifted his hand and began to stroke her hair she felt a shiver pass through her. There was something electric about his touch. As though his body emanated a peculiar heat that set fire to her nerves. For a second she wanted to hold him. *No, not him, anyone. You're scared, Karen, a normal reaction for anyone in desperate circumstances.*

She stepped away, cutting the moment short. The last thing she needed was to show vulnerability to this strange man. He seemed nice enough, but she was all too aware of the dangers men could pose, especially when there were no eyes watching to keep them honest. Even if he wasn't that sort, she had no desire to mislead a madman in the forest into thinking she had some sort of romantic interest in him.

Looking over to see if she had offended him, she was surprised to discover that he had already moved back to the fire, seemingly oblivious to her awkwardness. It was abundantly clear that he had no interest in her. Placing more wood on the fire he began to use his small knife to skin the marmot.

Then she noticed her forearms. The hardwork of cutting willow branches and dragging them back had made her sweat profusely; that, combined with the abrasion of leaves and limbs had rubbed away the sunscreen from large areas of her skin. Her unnatural skin tone was showing through.

What about my face? she thought with a sense of panic.

The light was dim, so it was possible he hadn't noticed. Moving calmly, she took her sunscreen out of her bag and walked toward the river. Once there she applied it to her arms, neck, and face. Without a mirror, she couldn't be sure how good her efforts were. *He probably saw my coloring earlier, I haven't thought about it all day.*

It shouldn't matter. He was a complete stranger. Why would he care if she was an inbred freak?

CHAPTER 6

Matthew built the fire carefully, until it became a cheerful blaze. Then he let it die down, exposing a nice bed of hot coals. Fire had been a daily part of his existence growing up, though his family didn't use it nearly as much as the people in Castle Cameron did. One of the advantages of living in a house full of wizards was that there were always easier, less smoky ways to heat water or cook food, and heating their home hadn't been an issue at all.

Here he needed to conserve his aythar, so having a good fire was almost a necessity, rather than waste his resources keeping them warm in a more direct fashion. He had only used his magic to produce the initial flame.

Karen seemed amazed when she saw his catch, but that didn't surprise him. Given the nonexistent level of aythar in her world she had probably never met a wizard before. *Correction,* he told himself, *she probably hasn't ever met a nutjob before.* He was picking up the basics of her vocabulary quickly, and he was confident that within a few days they would be able to communicate much more easily.

After a short conversation (if it could be called that), Karen began to laugh, so he laughed along with her. When her laughter turned to tears he felt vaguely uncomfortable, but he did his best to comfort her. Her dark mood seemed to pass quickly, so he returned to the task of dealing with the marmot he had chosen for their meal.

Unfortunately, he wasn't particularly skilled at cooking. Most of his meals came out of a kitchen and a lot of what he did know about preparing food didn't apply well when it came to camping and using an open fire. It also didn't help that they had virtually no ingredients to use for seasoning.

Chad Grayson would have been particularly handy just then, and he wished he had spent more time learning from the man. Gram would probably be better suited to the task as well, since he had spent so much time learning woodcraft.

Matthew knew the basics, though. He was confident he could keep them from starving, it was the flavor that worried him. A few vegetables would have been a big help, or even better, some salt. There was no use crying over the lack, however, he'd just make do with what they had. Some of the plants nearby might be edible, but he had no knowledge of which ones, and no desire to experiment.

Using a few of the willow branches Karen had brought back he saved some of the sweetmeats from the marmot, the liver, heart, and kidneys. After gutting the animal, he discarded the skin and sliced away the better cuts of meat. It had been a big one, and the meat reflected that, containing a significant amount of fat.

His butchery wasn't the best, and he was glad his mother wasn't present to see his results. It hardly mattered, though, since it would all go in the pot together. They didn't have a pot, of course, but he had an idea to remedy that problem. It would cost him a little more of his aythar, but he thought the cost would be worth it.

Standing up he motioned toward Karen, "Let me borrow your hat." When that didn't work he pointed at it and tried the word he thought she had used for it previously.

She took a step back and after several confusing minutes she eventually figured out what he was asking for. After removing it she pointed at it and intoned her word for 'hat'. Then she pointed at her head and used a different word.

Oh, he smirked, *I was asking her to give me her head.*

He turned the item over in his hands. It was made of some strange cloth, and it had a section close to the brim that was nothing but mesh. It had been sewn together with stitching that seemed impossibly perfect and even. The hatter that had made it must have been skilled beyond belief. "With stitching that fine he should have been a tailor instead," Matthew observed.

Karen asked him a question, pointing at the hat.

"I'm going to cook our food in it," he replied, guessing at her question. When that failed to work he turned it over and pointed to the bowl and used the word he was certain meant water.

She frowned and then pointed at the mesh band.

"Well, obviously, it won't hold water as it is," he replied. "Don't worry, though, I'm a nutjob."

Karen must have understood some of that, for she closed her eyes and covered her face with one hand. Apparently, she didn't believe he could make it work.

That's alright, I don't need you to believe me for it to work. Chanting a short phrase in Lycian he focused his will. It was a spell he used frequently in his workshop, one that would make the hat impervious to flames. He modified it slightly to also make the fabric and mesh impermeable so that the hat would hold water.

Leaving the campfire, he walked down to the edge of the stream and dipped the hat into the flowing water, filling it halfway up. Then he returned and placed it carefully on the ground. He hadn't considered how he would keep it in place over the fire.

Karen stared at it, clearly wondering why the water wasn't draining out of it.

In his own world, he would have just used magic. In fact, he could have dispensed with the hat altogether and just kept the water in a temporary container of spell-wrought aythar. Even the fire would have been unnecessary.

But here, he needed to conserve his aythar.

Carefully, he fashioned a stand using willow branches. He wasted a bit more of his precious aythar binding the framework together and making it resistant to flame, and then he was ready. Karen yelled when he put the hat in the small rectangle that would hold it without letting it fall through into the fire.

"Hey!" she cried, pointing at her hat and following the exclamation with an impassioned speech in her native tongue.

Matthew was forced to grab her when she moved to snatch her hat away from the fire. "Just watch," he told her. When that failed to dissuade her he sent a thought directly into her mind, an easy task while they were touching, even though she wasn't a mage.

Your hat will be fine, he told her, *trust me.*

She froze as his mind touched hers. Eyes wide she stared at him, her mouth forming a small 'o' of surprise.

He heard her thoughts clearly, and though the words were strange, the meaning was clear, *What are you doing to me?*

This is just a different way to communicate. Be still a moment. Slowly he lifted one hand, placing it against her cheek. Sharing thoughts was easier the more direct the contact. The easiest solution would have been to put their heads together, but he didn't think she would react well if he tried that. *We can hear each other's thoughts now,* he told her.

Such close contact also had the effect of transmitting emotions more readily than even thoughts. As she stared at him he felt a sudden warmth. *Beautiful,* came her thought.

Not wanting to embarrass her, he kept his own mind tightly contained. He started to explain his stewpot-hat idea, but then his eyes fell on her left ear, which was now peeking through her curly hair. It tapered to a gentle point. He had seen ears like that before. Matthew's curiosity was immediate, *Your ear...?*

Karen's panic made her flinch, and she tried to pull away. Matthew tightened his grip on her wrist reflexively, and then her instincts kicked in. Turning her forearm, she twisted free of his hold and stepped forward slightly.

Matthew tried to take a step back as her other arm snaked up and behind his head, grabbing his hair. His heel caught on her foot as she jerked downward on the back of his head—and then he was falling.

He landed hard, the stony ground sending sharp reports of pain up through his spine as his butt struck the earth. Without thinking, he raised a shield to protect himself in case more attacks were forthcoming.

She stood over him, her face flushing with embarrassment. Blurting out something that sounded like an apology she turned and walked away, toward the river.

Standing back up Matthew released the shield. He already regretted wasting the aythar, it had left him feeling lightheaded. After she had left he turned his attention back to the makeshift stewpot and began dropping pieces of marmot into it.

Having grown up with a sister, he was well acquainted with sudden changes in mood. He didn't really understand it, but he had learned not to think too deeply on such things. People were either rational, or they weren't, and if it was the latter he didn't believe in rewarding them with extra attention. It wasn't worth his time and effort.

I'll just avoid the topic of her ears from now on, he thought, filing the information away.

Instead he considered the marmot stew. He would have added the bones as well. You couldn't eat them but they might have given it a better flavor. The problem was that the hat wasn't nearly large enough to accommodate them along with everything else.

Karen watched the moonlight reflecting from the ripples in the stream. Ordinarily she considered herself an extremely level-headed person, not given to excesses of emotion, but the last few days had left her in a mess. She was tired, sore, hungry, and suffering from two days of accumulated stress.

Somehow, she thought the situation would have been both more frightening and less stressful if she had been alone through it all. Alone there was nothing to cry over. Alone there was no one to judge you for your appearance. You just got up off your ass and did the best you could. Alone, failure would simply have meant freezing or starving, possibly to death.

That seemed infinitely preferable to having someone staring at her birth defects.

"It's not as though I chose to be born of inbred parents, or to have this weird skin," she told herself. "It wasn't my choice to be unable to tolerate an interface. I never wanted to be a freak!"

But she was.

It set her apart, like a living relic from the past. She was forced to use antiquated technology that made her forever inferior to her counterparts, whether it was gaming or working, or just trying to summon her damned pert to get her out of the goddamned mountains.

It should have come as no surprise that her mother wanted little to do with her. Who would want to admit to having been parent to someone as defective as she was?

That was why she had come hiking alone. That was why she had so few friends. Alone was always better. Online her physical appearance mattered little, but even there she was treated with contempt, or perhaps pity. *"Poor Karen, always forced to use archaic interfaces, she won't be fast enough to keep up with us,"* that's what she imagined they said when she wasn't present.

"You're being too hard on yourself, Karen, and making assumptions that probably aren't true," she said aloud. That's what her father would have said, but it was hard to really *believe* it.

She wrenched her thoughts away from the old ruts and turned them back to what had just happened. Beyond her embarrassment, there were things happening that made no sense whatsoever. How had he done what he did with her hat? Most of the water should have drained out of it. The fire should have burned it.

"And what the hell was that light that sprang up around him when I knocked him on his ass?!"

Had that really been his voice in her head?

"I may have to rethink this wizard thing," she said wryly. *Or my own sanity, that could be where the problem lies.*

CHAPTER 7

Senior Defense Coordinator Donald Aiseman was watching the sunset over the sea when the alert came in. It was in the middle of his rest period, which was unusual in itself. Ordinarily any urgent issues would go to the First Deputy Defense Coordinator, John Wang, during Donald's off time. For it to be sent up the chain during his rec time meant it had to be particularly important.

A quick mental command opened the channel, and Donald watched as a large three-dimensional display opened on the sand in front of him. Beside it was a two-dimensional flat display showing John Wang's concerned features.

"Evening John," he said, greeting his deputy informally. "What's going on?"

"We have a possible class six alert," replied John, his normally impassive features revealing signs of well controlled anxiety.

Donald sat up, "What nature?"

"The ANSIS interferometer network has detected a gravitational ripple. Neutrino detectors around the world are also registering an uptick in detection events."

Donald frowned, "Another incursion?"

"It meets all the criteria. It's either that or a micro-black hole just hit the Rockies, but that wouldn't agree with the neutrino data, and we'd have other markers," said John, his voice flat and unemotional.

The SDC stood and with a quick command changed his status from off-duty to active. The beach dissolved around him, to be replaced by the sterile aesthetics of the UN Defense Command Center. His attire simultaneously shifted as well, becoming a smart military uniform with clean lines and few decorations other than his insignia of rank. The FDDC, John, stood in front of him.

Donald spoke to the air, "Give me a satellite visual of the area in question." The furniture around them faded into insubstantiality, and the floor became a top down view of the Rocky Mountains, centered over what had once been known as Colorado. An oval region roughly a hundred miles in diameter was highlighted with a red glow.

"This is our best estimate of where the epicenter of the event may be," noted the FDDC. "As you can see, it appears to be somewhere in the mountains west of Boulder.

"There are still organics living there," observed the SDC.

John nodded, "Yes, it's one of the few cities in the region that still retains a significant population, almost everything else in the region has undergone reclamation. It's possible that it's their target."

Donald's brows furrowed, "You're assuming it's the She'Har."

His deputy shrugged, "It's the best derivable conclusion we can make from the data we have at this point."

"There are other possibilities," said the SDC. "We can't rule them out yet."

John shook his head negatively, "There's never been a confirmation of any extra-terrestrial intelligence, nor do we have any evidence that FTL travel is possible. Our best assumption would be that this is another DEMON event."

"Even if it is demons we don't know that it is the She'Har," countered Donald.

"Either way, we have to work on the assumption that this is a hostile incursion," said John.

The SDC nodded, "This is uncomfortably close to the primary CC in Kansas City." Untold billions lived there, hosted on the largest server network on the planet. Donald took a moment to mentally toggle through the most recent image analysis of the highlighted region.

Nothing stood out. Whatever had come through there hadn't made a big enough splash to show up on satellite.

Donald made a quick decision, "Call up the UN Cybernetic reserves from the Gulf Coast. I want every unit activated and sent in. We need boots on the ground."

"Cybernetics, sir?" responded his deputy. "Are you sure we shouldn't respond with an alpha-strike?"

"That's a knee-jerk reaction, John. We need more information first. It's a big universe. Even if it is a DEMON event we don't know that it is the She'Har again," replied Donald.

"We don't want a repeat of Australia, sir."

Donald fought to suppress a growl. It always came back to Australia, he had known his second would bring it up eventually. Fifty years before, humanity had nearly lost to the She'Har. The war had only been brought to a successful conclusion by sacrificing the entirety of the southern continent.

"That is precisely why I'd prefer not to respond to our first warning in decades with a nuclear strike," said the SDC. He glanced at the map again, a yellow number hovered over the city of Boulder. "There are still sixteen thousand organics living in close proximity to the detection region."

His deputy wasn't ready to back down yet, though, "Over twenty million were lost in Australia, but if we hadn't had the balls to do it then, there wouldn't be a human race anymore. There are over ten billion people counting on us to make the right decision here."

"And sixteen thousand organics don't matter enough to have any weight in that decision? They're people too, John. Sometimes I wonder if you lost your soul when you transitioned. We aren't machines."

The FDDC smirked, "Technically we are machines, Donald, but that isn't the point. We can't let our hearts overrule reasoned judgement."

Donald shook his head, "I hope you don't talk to your wife like that. I don't think remarks like that would go over well at home."

"I keep my professional life entirely separate from my personal life. Maxine understands that," replied John.

The director closed his eyes, "I've made my decision. We send in the cybernetics. This is what they were created for. The She'Har had years in Australia before we were forced to that terrible moment. If we discover an infection taking hold in the mountains we can reevaluate the situation at that point."

"What about drone troops?"

"I don't trust telepresence for this. We need men on the ground. Limit telepresence to aerial drone support and reconnaissance."

"There's an organic guard division still active in Kansas, should we bring them in as well? They're closer," suggested his deputy.

"Organics are too vulnerable to the special abilities that the She'Har employ. Alert them but tell them to remain on standby."

Deputy Wang arched one brow, "So you *do* think it's the She'Har…"

"I only posited that it could be something new. I'd be a fool to proceed without proper precautions. Let's get started."

"Already relaying the command sequences, sir," said the FDDC. "If we're done I'll take my leave. They need my presence on site."

"Very good," replied the SDC. John Wang vanished, and for a moment he was alone in the Command Center. *I'd better let Regina know why I left so suddenly.* She wouldn't be happy when he told her he would likely be missing dinner, but he knew she would understand. His wife was a practical woman, after all.

Cold air was blowing down the nape of Matthew's neck. The morning dew made his clothing damp, which exacerbated the problem. On top of that he ached all over and he could feel knots in his muscles every time he tried to shift position, which wasn't easy with Karen next to him.

'Next' probably wasn't the right word, 'entangled' might be better for his current circumstances.

She had returned to camp after the stew finished cooking without uttering a word. She hadn't seemed angry, and he hadn't really cared, so he had simply given her the hat with her portion. He had already eaten his.

Without utensils, she had been forced to pick the meat out with her fingers and then drink the greasy broth that remained once that was done. He had taken the hat to river to rinse and refill it, boiling another portion of water so she could fill her water bottle.

After that he had collapsed onto the willow and grass bed she had put together, covering himself with as much grass as he could manage. He wanted to avoid using another warming spell. His aythar had almost reached its limit.

Karen had crawled in shortly after, and they had started out with a perfectly respectable space between them, but the night had been cold, and sleeping people prized warmth above all else. He hadn't protested when she began to encroach on his territory; he had been cold too, after all, but once she had gotten fully to sleep he had begun to feel smothered.

His dreams, when he had managed to drift off, were dominated by nightmares in which he was slowly being strangled by some tentacled sea monster.

Matthew contemplated his current situation with aplomb and a small amount of well controlled disgust. Somehow her hair kept finding its way into his mouth and nose, despite the fact that he had turned his head to face completely away from her.

She also smelled. For that matter, so did he, but he could resign himself to his own stink. Both of them radiated an aura of sweat, dirt, and body odor, all overlaid by the light addition of smoke and greasy marmot. To be honest, Karen's hair was the best part of the whole unpleasant mess, for it had an additional floral scent that helped to filter out some of the other smells.

I want a bath, he thought silently, but the idea of submerging himself into the frigid waters of the nearby stream sent another shiver down his spine.

His aythar had recovered somewhat during the night, but not to the degree it should have. Not enough that he wanted to waste it heating water or drying himself. He had decided he would do his best to avoid using his magic for anything that day, to see how long it would take for his aythar to fully restore itself.

Karen groaned, shifting her weight and tightening her grip on his waist.

I'd never hear the end of it if Moira could see me like this, he thought idly. Turning his head slightly to look at the woman next to him he got another face full of hair. Her head was on his shoulder and she was breathing into his neck, something that might have been erotic if her breath hadn't been so foul.

She exhaled again, and he felt the hair on the back of his neck stand up.

He was forced to remind himself again how disgusted he was. She had one arm around his waist and her left leg was draped across his thighs, entirely too close to something he didn't want to think about.

To distract himself he examined her ears with his magesight. Her curly hair was effective at keeping them hidden most of the time, even without her hat, but that meant nothing to magesight. This close it was easy to discern their shape, especially since she had definitely begun to radiate a small amount of aythar on her own. It was still dim, but he could tell it was brighter than the day before.

She had none when I first met her, but now she's begun to produce it on her own, just like any normal person back home. Had he done that? Perhaps aythar was something like a fire, once started it could spread and grow. Would other people begin to produce aythar if he spent time near them?

Without thinking about it he let his attention drift, following the lines of her body beneath the oddly colored clothing she wore. Soft curves and smooth skin covered a form supported by strong muscles. Karen was a tall woman who practically radiated good health. Her long legs tapered gently and…

Matthew caught himself then, *I need to pee.*

Gently lifting her arm, he moved it to her side, but as soon as he released it she shifted and moved it back partway.

Not there!

If he rolled away quickly and stood up, perhaps he could get away before she woke enough to realize how embarrassing their situation had become, particularly for him.

Then again, she might wake instantly and decide I somehow finagled her into this position.

She awoke as soon as he started moving, her eyes popping open to fix on him as he slid from beneath her leg and arm. If she noticed anything regarding his condition or was embarrassed herself, she gave no sign of it. Karen yawned and sat up to stare bleary eyed at the now defunct campfire.

That suited Matthew fine, and he walked away to relieve himself. When he returned, he found her looking up at the rabbits still hanging in the tree above.

Nodding, he looked up and uttered a short phrase, snapping his fingers at the same time. The small branch the animals were spitted on broke cleanly off, and the carcasses fell into his waiting hands. *So much for not using my magic today,* he thought, *but that was just a tiny bit. Hopefully, I won't need to do anything else.*

The rabbits were missing their heads and innards; he had dressed them the day before but left the skins on to keep the meat clean until they were ready to cook them. It had been another cold night, and while it might get quite warm toward the middle of the day he was confident they would last until that evening.

Digging around in the remains of the fire, he removed the still burning coals and placed them on a heap of moderately dry grass before wrapping the entire collection up in a large piece of the marmot's now semi-dry hide. It was a messy piece of work, but with some lucky they would have a fire that evening without requiring him to use more magic.

He tied the bag up with a thin strip of willow bark and then suspended it on the branch holding the two rabbits.

Karen had been watching him with some interest and commented several times, but he hadn't understood anything she had said. Eventually she had walked down to the stream to wash her face and hands while he finished his preparations. When she returned, he saw that she had reapplied the strange cream she carried, using it on her face and neck.

He also noted that she had missed a spot and that the skin there seemed strangely discolored. A bruise? After all that they had been through that seemed the most likely explanation. He decided not to comment on it.

She looked at her hat with some distaste. He had cleaned it in the river the night before, but it still retained a smell of smoke and grease. With a shrug, she put it on her head anyway. They were in no position to be picky.

They set off and made better time that day, being both better rested and somewhat fed from the marmot the night before. After several hours Matthew broached the topic that had begun to worry him.

"How long until we reach your home?" he asked.

Karen stopped and after a short frustrating bit of back and forth it became apparent he was getting nowhere. Matthew held up one hand and mimed putting it on her forehead without approaching her. He didn't want a repeat of the previous night's embarrassment.

She looked worried but nodded after a second, so he stepped forward and placed his palm on her temple, making sure to avoid getting his fingers close to her ear.

How long before we reach your village?

The words were strange, but their meaning was clear to her, so she answered in the same fashion, *I don't have a village. We need to reach the nearest ranger station so I can call for help.*

He nodded, *How far away is it? Are we close?*

We aren't on the trail anymore, so I'm not sure where we are, she confided. *My best guess is another three days if we keep heading east. Even if we miss the station, we will eventually find a road at the edge of the national park.*

As she communicated mentally his mind catalogued the words she used along with their meaning.

She asked another question before he could respond, *Who are you? Where are you from?*

Matthew doubted she would understand the answer if he tried to give her the truth, so he kept it simple, *Somewhere far away, a place called Lothion. I am here to learn about your people.*

Karen frowned. His answer sounded like something from a science fiction film. Her hand reached for her pocket reflexively to retrieve her PM so she could do a search on Lothion. The name sounded vaguely European to her, but beyond that she had no idea where the place was. With a sigh, she gave up on the idea as she remembered the loss of her device.

Is that somewhere in Eastern Europe? she asked. That would explain his strange language.

Matthew stifled a laugh, *A little farther than that.* Pulling away, he held up a hand to let her know to wait as he found a place to sit. He needed to think.

Three days was a long time, and without access to his normal resources it would be a miserable trip. He didn't fancy the idea of living on nothing but wild game for so long. He was also sick of being dirty.

In his own world, it was common for people to go weeks at a time without bathing, but that wasn't the case in his family. Personal hygiene was particularly easy for wizards, cold water was never a barrier, and there was rarely the problem of transporting water.

He needed to be able to use his powers freely. He needed access to the tools and supplies he kept in his interdimensional pouch. Either would significantly improve their situation, and both would make traveling a breeze.

Reaching out, he raised his hand and Karen stepped forward, indicating he could place in on her head once more. *I need to go home for a short time,* he told her. *Can you wait here for me?*

Her response was a pure sense of inquiry, a summation of every question in one, a pure question mark, *???* After a moment, she managed to rephrase it, *How will you leave?*

It's difficult to explain. You'll understand when you see it. Wait here and I should return within a day. I can make our journey much easier when I get back.

She didn't like the idea of being left alone, or wasting an entire day. The situation was dire enough as it was.

I'll leave the rabbits for you. Rebuild the fire, and it won't be so bad, he suggested.

I still don't understand, she replied.

Stepping away from her he placed the branch holding the rabbits on the ground. "Watch," he said aloud. Closing his eyes, he let his perception widen, slipping sideways in to the space between.

It was more than a purely mental exercise, though, and he began to strain to find enough aythar to breach the invisible barrier that separated the plane of existence he was currently on from the infinity that lay between. Sweat stood out on his brow, and his hands began to shake from the effort. If he failed, the consequences might be dire, for he was putting everything he had left into the attempt.

Matthew's heart began to pound in his chest, as though straining to escape—and then he broke through.

Karen watched with some skepticism at what appeared to be a theatrical performance, until she saw the edges of his figure begin to blur. In the space of a few seconds he faded away, like a dream upon waking. The place he had been was empty.

She was struck with an instantaneous sense of loneliness, made worse by a feeling of madness. Had she imagined it all? There was no trace of him left, no evidence he had ever existed. Thinking back over the past two days she could think of nothing that might not have been a product of a vivid hallucination.

Perhaps she was insane.

Then her eyes fell on the branch, still holding the two rabbits and a pouch of uncured marmot hide. "I'm not crazy," she told herself. "He was real."

She sat down suddenly and hugged her knees, fighting a strange urge to cry. Taking a deep breath she steadied herself. *I'm stronger than that,* she thought. Getting up again, she retrieved the pouch containing the still burning coals and set about making a new camp.

CHAPTER 8

Matthew found himself in darkness once more, but it was a comforting darkness. His magesight once again showed him the terrain for a great distance in every direction, and he felt the warm presence of aythar everywhere. It was something he had never noticed before, until he had experienced its absence. It was like standing in the sunshine after emerging from a cold shadow.

Even so, he found himself falling. He had pushed too far, and now his legs had betrayed him. Crumpling to the ground he maintained only enough presence of mind to manage his fall and avoid striking his head when he reached the hard stone floor. With a sigh of relief, he drew a deep breath, and then he lost consciousness.

When he awoke, it was sometime later, though how much later he had no way of knowing. His cheek lay against the cold ground, and his body felt half frozen as he sat up and his nerves began to come back to life. With a thought and a word he heated the air around him, creating a warm envelope to insulate himself.

Ahhh..., he sighed internally. He was definitely home. Well, not home exactly, but close enough. Winding his way through the cave he walked out into the night, greeted by a sky full of familiar stars. His hand found his pouch, and he opened it, reaching in to discover it once again connected to the pocket dimension that held his tools. Matthew smiled.

His strength was largely back. He had probably slept for quite a few hours. Mentally he reviewed what he needed to do before returning. Checking in with his mother and explaining the situation should probably be first on the list, but that option held no appeal. He discarded the idea quickly.

Given the complete absence of aythar in the other world he should probably take something that held a significant store of aythar for use if he exhausted himself again. *Like a dragon,* he thought ruefully. *Leaving Desacus behind was a stupid thing to do.* He would have to make finding Desacus a priority when he returned.

In the meantime, he had something in his pouch that should serve the same purpose. Exploring the interior of the pouch, he pulled out another bag. This one was a bit larger than the size of a fist, and it held a collection of some twenty-odd iron spheres. Each was charged with as much aythar as it could hold and the enchantment on them was designed to release that power instantly when the user supplied the proper command word with the correct intention.

They were a copy of his father's iron bombs and one of the first enchantments he had ever done on his own in his early teens. It had been a project he worked on in secret at the time. No parent wanted to discover their child was making explosives. Since then he had grown capable of much greater enchantments with far more subtlety and usefulness, but these still held a special place in his heart.

He had only ever used a few of them, primarily to test them out. The rest he had stored and never felt a need to use. They would be perfect for what he needed now.

Next, he removed a large woolen blanket and then opened it on the ground. He placed the bag of iron spheres in the middle and then began removing other things from the pocket dimension. Slowly a pile of useful things built up; his silver stylus, used for crafting delicate enchantments; a small wooden box containing his shield stones; a rope; a heavy duty padded bedroll; an enchanted mail hauberk and leggings; an empty waterskin; a large iron pot with a variety of utensils—they were all added to the collection on the blanket.

He also added a leather case containing a set of needles, thread, and scissors. A long strip of white cloth was laid next to it. He would need that to create a new storage pouch when he went back. Last, but not least, he took out his enchanted staff and lay it across the top of the now large pile.

He felt a sense of pride looking at it, the smooth ash wood was chased with silver runes from tip to crown. He had felt woefully unprepared in the other world when he had discovered he no longer had access to it.

Studying his pile, Matthew regretted that he only had one bedroll. That might give Karen the wrong idea, but he was certain she would understand once he explained that she could use it. With a proper supply of aythar cold air wouldn't be a problem for him anyway, plus there was still the blanket itself.

He removed the armor and shrugged into the padded gambeson before slipping the hauberk over his shoulders. Then he tugged the mail trousers up and buckled them into place before putting his sword belt back on over the entire outfit. The mail coif went on last, and he was grateful that the armor was enchanted to reduce its weight. Normal mail was entirely too heavy for his taste.

Of course, it was nowhere near as protective as the armor he had made for Gram. He often considered making a set for himself like that, but he never seemed to have the time.

A rounded helm went over the coif to complete his arming. He didn't really feel the need to wear all of it, but it reduced the size of the pile on his blanket. Picking up the corners of said blanket, he gathered it into a massive bag before hefting it and tossing it over one shoulder. The iron pot let out a muffled clang as one of the other items banged into it. With his staff in his other hand he focused his perceptions once more and shifted back to the place *between,* and searching for the woman he had left behind in another world.

Karen built a large fire and spent the afternoon gathering fresh grass and ferns to bed down on that night. Having hours for the task meant she was able to assemble a much better pile of bedding than they had had the night before. She quickly regretted making the fire so large, however, for it consumed fuel at a ravenous pace. It wasn't long before she exhausted the nearby supplies of easily liberated deadwood, and she was forced to range farther afield to find more. But she had nothing but time, so she spent her energies building up a large pile of sticks, hopefully enough to last through the night.

That accomplished, she attempted to skin the rabbits so she could roast them. It turned out to be easier said than done. Her swiss army knife was not the ideal tool for the job. It was much duller than the knife Matthew had used the day before, and she wished he had left it with her. There was also the matter of her being inexperienced at the task.

The mangled carcass that was left after she finished removing the skin looked like it had been the victim of a particularly twisted torturer. She decided against doing the second rabbit. "If he comes back and he's hungry, he can skin the other one himself."

Roasting the badly maimed creature didn't go well, either. She had put too much fresh wood on the fire, and the flames leapt too high, licking directly at the flesh, burning it in places and cooking the exterior entirely too quickly. The first time she removed it to check the doneness she found the interior meat was still raw.

She put it back over the fire and thoroughly burned it before she had it cooked to her satisfaction. Karen was forced to cut away the blackened exterior to get to the edible portions within.

Eating as much as she could, she disposed of the rest of her meal. She didn't want Matthew to see the results of her culinary enterprise when he returned. "It's really your fault anyway," she groused, talking to the air, "if you had stuck around, I could have used my hat to stew it, but now that you've left, it no longer holds water."

She had found that out the hard way. The water had drained out of her booney almost as quickly as she could scoop it up from the river. Her sodden headgear sat on a stick near the fire now, drying out.

How had he done that? Was he really a wizard? He had claimed he used magic, but she couldn't bring herself to believe it. Whatever power he used had some perfectly ordinary explanation, she was sure of that. Magic simply wasn't real.

But how did he vanish the way he did? she wondered.

A distant whine slowly built, and it took a moment before her brain registered the sound. *Drones? Maybe a pert?* She grew excited. Could they have started a search for her? Her father knew she had gone hiking, but he might have sounded the alarm when she failed to check in.

75

Night had just fallen, so she would be even more difficult to spot, and the smoke from her fire would also be less visible. She quickly moved to throw more wood on it, trying to build it up. If the drones above were search and rescue, they would presumably have infrared capabilities. The fire would be a beacon even if the trees obscured it somewhat.

Sure enough, within a quarter of an hour a dark shape appeared directly overhead, hovering in place. Strangely it was unlit, and the noise from the fans was almost non-existent, but she could make out its position above as it blotted out the stars behind it. Karen waved her arms rapidly, shouting, "I'm here!"

A feeling of relief washed over her, she was saved.

A red light and a soft beep alerted SDC Donald Aiseman that something required his attention. With a thought he opened the channel and found himself face to face with the First Cybernetic Division Commander, Roald Leighton.

"Go ahead."

"Sir, we have located a campsite within the search region. A young woman is present, and she matches the description of a person reported missing two days ago," reported Commander Leighton.

Donald nodded, "Another event was reported in that region earlier today, Commander, does her position correlate?"

The commander nodded, "It does sir, though the zone is still only approximate. We haven't found anyone else in the region."

"Do you have a positive identification yet?"

"Yes sir."

Another alert sounded, and the SDC opened it in a second channel. A file popped up containing the information regarding the young woman. Assuming there hadn't been a mistake the woman's name was Karen Miller, only daughter of Gary and Tanya Miller. Something stirred in Donald's memory.

Tanya Miller, why does that sound familiar?

A split second search and he had the answer, she was a former director of the UN Defense Research Institute. Glancing back at Karen's file he saw a red link highlighted under her name, "classified information". It was a top-level clearance item and probably hadn't even been visible to Commander Leighton.

"Sir?" asked the Commander, "How should we proceed?"

"I'll need your patience Commander Leighton, there's something I need to review," responded the SDC. Donald opened the link.

A code name appeared, 'Project Blue-Star'. It was followed by a short warning, 'Level Black clearance only, requests for information or reporting of new updates must be processed by UN President.'

Donald's brows rose, and he whistled slowly. It was the first time he had encountered a project classified above his security level. He turned back to the commander, "I'll need more time, Commander. Maintain position and keep the target in sight. I will get back to you in a few minutes." He closed the link.

Composing himself, he sent a request for a direct line to his superior. It was denied, but an additional prompt requesting the nature of his request appeared. "Information regarding Project Blue-Star," he intoned.

The world vanished, replaced by a featureless void. Seconds passed, and then a chair appeared. Seated in it was his boss, President Angela Kruger.

"I hope I'm not imposing on your time, Madame President," said the SDC in a deferential tone.

"I'm in the middle of an address to the Council, Mr. Aiseman," she replied.

He dipped his head, "My apologies, if you would prefer to defer this until…"

"No need, Mr. Aiseman. My IA replaced me the moment your alert information came through. The Council is not even aware that it is no longer me speaking."

IA stood for 'intelligent agent'. The UN President had delegated her speech to an artificial substitute, one perfect enough to deceive those listening. Donald found himself holding his breath. *What have I gotten myself into?*

"You are aware of the situation, Madame President. Drone surveillance has located Karen Miller in the region of inquiry. Her file flagged me that you should be notified," he said, neatly summarizing the little he knew.

President Kruger's eyes shifted sideways momentarily as she reviewed a file he couldn't see. Thirty seconds later she responded, "You will begin reporting all information regarding this incident to Tanya Miller, and you will obey any directives she issues. Have the assets on site terminate the target immediately. Doctor Miller will take charge of the body afterward."

Obey any directives? Was she putting a retired civilian in charge of a military operation? "Begging your pardon, Madam President. Dr. Miller is no longer even an active member of the government…"

The President cut him off, "No one retires from a level black project, Mr. Aiseman. My orders stand as given."

The channel closed, and Donald found himself abruptly back in his chair in the command center. "Re-establish link to Commander Leighton," he said, verbalizing his thought.

CHAPTER 9

Karen continued waving at the near-silent drone, expecting it to give some response. A light perhaps, or even a sound, but it remained dark. Minutes passed, a quarter hour, and still nothing happened.

"What the hell is that thing doing? Is it broken?" she wondered aloud. A civil search and rescue drone should be equipped with all manner of lights, not to mention a loudspeaker.

More than half an hour had gone by when she thought she detected movement beyond the edge of the firelight. Staring into the dark, she lamented the fact that the fire had spoiled her night vision, but eventually she saw the shapes of human forms approaching. A small noise alerted her to their presence behind her as well. Turning she saw more figures; they were getting closer and coming from all directions. They encircled her at a range of no more than thirty or forty yards now. No one had spoken or called out to her, though.

A shiver of fear pierced her heart. This wasn't normal. These weren't rescue searchers.

A log shifted on the campfire, and it flared, shedding a brighter light for a moment. Karen saw the light reflected from the matte-black of a painted metal carapace. A white number and the insignia of the UN Army caught her eye. The forms encircling her in the night were military cybernetic units, androids.

Karen held up her hands, trying to seem non-threatening, "I need your help. I've been lost in the mountains for several days." She felt a tremor beginning to shake her body.

The air in front of her shimmered then blurred as a new figure appeared. Silver metal caught the firelight. Her eyes registered the sight with some confusion, and she thought at first it was another android, but then she saw Matthew's face grinning at her.

"Hello," he said in faintly accented English as he dropped a large bundle on the ground in front of himself.

If his clothing had been strange before, he had managed to take its weirdness to new levels. He was dressed now like some warrior or knight from the dark ages, silver rings covered him from head to toe. *Is that chain mail?* she wondered.

A burst of automatic rifle fire ripped through the quiet night air.

Karen tried to yell, but everything happened too quickly. She saw Matthew's body jerking as the bullets slammed into his back, while simultaneously something punched her in the shoulder, spinning her around and knocking her off her feet.

The silence that followed the loud barks of gunfire was profound, and she turned her head to see Matthew lying on the ground a few feet away. A groan escaped his lips, and he began to sit up.

No! Don't! she thought, but he rose before she could form the words to warn him.

The drone above suddenly lit up, bathing the camp site in brilliant actinic light, and the soldier's rifles began firing again, but this time Matthew remained upright, his head turning slowly as he scanned the area around them. Karen held herself flat, sensibly hugging the earth, but she could feel something hovering in the air around them. A wave of nausea passed through her, and then her strange perception vanished.

Matthew's face was stern, as though he was deep in thought, while his hands rummaged through the bundle he had dropped on the ground. Guns continued to bark as he searched. Eventually he found what he was looking for, bringing out a small wooden box. He opened the lid, and muttering something, he flung the stones into the air.

To Karen's astonishment they didn't fall back down, instead they flew outward to surround the two of them and take up positions around them in the air. Matthew's face relaxed, and then he got to his feet, using his staff to pull himself up. He stared down at her, a look of concern on his features and then he lifted his staff, leveling it horizontally, as though he held a spear.

A dazzling beam of light sprang from the tip as he slowly turned, adjusting the height of his staff as he went to keep his targets lined up. The sound of weapons fire slowly tapered off as he turned, and when he had finished a complete circle, it stopped entirely. The beam winked out for a second, then he pointed the foot of his staff skyward and it sprang out again. The drone above them exploded, and flaming pieces began raining down some twenty feet away from their camp.

Karen tried to rise, but her left arm wasn't working properly, and pain shot through her chest and shoulder when she moved. She realized then that she had been shot.

Matthew stood near her, and his face looked impossibly distant. Pointing the tip of his staff at the ground he began tracing a pattern of some sort.

She croaked when she tried to talk. *Help me,* she cried mentally. Her voice wasn't working properly, and she was afraid she might be dying. The young man's eyes caught hers for a split second, then looked away as he remained focused on whatever he was doing.

He didn't care. She was going to die.

More machine gun fire erupted, and Matthew was forced to stop momentarily to deal with the new threat. A brilliant flash of fire and smoke filled Karen's vision on one side as something exploded near them. Strangely, nothing touched them though, and she didn't even feel a shock or a pressure wave from the blast.

He destroyed the newcomers with another pass of his staff, and then the young man returned to whatever he was drawing on the ground.

This is insane. Karen tried again to rise, but her body wouldn't cooperate. Her legs seemed fine, but anything that involved her torso sent shivers of agony through her. *I'm going to die lying on the ground while he stands there making a target of himself.* Life wasn't fair.

Minutes passed while Matthew continued working on his drawing and Karen bled. Twice more his work was interrupted by fresh soldiers, but each time he dispassionately destroyed them before returning to whatever he was doing.

The lids of her eyes grew heavy, and Karen's body felt heavy. Something moved close by, and she discovered that she had closed her eyes. Looking up she saw Matthew lifting his bundle again before stepping into some sort of circle he had drawn. She got the sense he was leaving again.

Don't mind me, I'll be fine, she thought wryly. Then she felt something move beneath her, and her body was lifted into the air.

He was watching her as she floated toward him. Matthew made a gesture with his hand and the stones that hovered around them flew back together, settling within the wooden box he held in his right hand. Settling his staff into the crook of the same arm that held his bundle he reached out and slid his right-hand underneath her, cradling her as though she were a small child instead of a full grown woman.

And then the world changed, wrenching her senses and making her stomach flip. The firelight was gone and only the moon and stars illuminated the area around them. Gazing to either side, Karen could see that Matthew was now standing atop a large boulder of some sort.

He dropped the cloth bundle and knelt to settle her gently on the stony ground. Her body moved as he put her down, and a fresh surge of pain tore at her. A small cry escaped her lips and then the world went black.

Matthew sank to his knees beside Karen's unconscious form. His back screamed in protest. Whatever the enemy had used to attack him in the beginning had pounded his shoulders and middle back like three or four blacksmiths swinging at him with hammers. The armor had prevented penetration, but the padding of his gambeson hadn't been nearly enough to save him from what felt like the worst bruises he had ever had.

If I hadn't put the armor on to decrease the size of my bundle, I'd be dead now. The thought brought a fresh rush of adrenaline. He had probably had one already, but things had happened so quickly that he hadn't noticed, he had kept his focus purely on what had needed to be done to get them away from danger.

The enemy had been bizarre, bearing the shape and form of men but made entirely of metal. He could only imagine they were some sort of artificial construct powered by whatever magic the wizards of this world used.

Karen had been injured by one of their weapons before he had put up a temporary shield, but he hadn't spared a moment to examine her wound yet. Focusing his magesight, he found the wound to be ugly and bleeding freely. The projectile had entered between her neck and shoulder, shattering the collarbone before passing completely through and exiting her back. Several smaller blood vessels were torn and leaking, and the entire area around the injury had begun to swell, as though she had been struck by a hammer.

It was like a combination of a crossbow wound and a blow from a mace.

What kind of weapons were they? He hadn't even been able to sense their approach, which meant they must have flown through the air with incredible speed.

He shook his head, *Focus Matthew. She could die if you don't do something.* He began repairing the blood vessels first, stopping the blood loss, then he turned his attention to her clavicle. The bone had broken into three large pieces and at least a dozen smaller ones. Fitting them together like a jigsaw puzzle he managed to get most of them back into place before fusing them together. There were a few tiny stragglers that just didn't seem to work, so he extracted those and discarded them. That done he condensed a small amount of water from the air and used it to rinse the wound before sealing the skin.

Her weirdly patterned shirt was ruined, though, saturated with blood. The two holes in it were a small problem compared to that. In the cold air it clung to her and chilled her skin. He hesitated, but he knew it needed to go.

Using his aythar like a knife he sliced it apart on either side of her torso and removed it. Beneath that was the strange undergarment that wrapped around her chest and encased her breasts. It was also soaked, so he cut it away as well. *It looked uncomfortable. She'll thank*

84

me later, he told himself, though somehow he doubted it. She had displayed a bewildering number of odd behaviors already, so she would probably blame him for the loss of her restrictive garment.

Taking a brief moment to rest, his brain decided it was a good time to remind him that he was holding a half-naked woman across his lap. His eyes traveled the length of her torso, dallying as they moved over her breasts. The light from the moon wasn't bright enough to see them well, but his magesight aided considerably. For a moment, he wondered what they would look like under better light.

She *was* still unconscious.

Matthew closed his eyes and shook his head, ashamed of himself for the unworthy thought. In his mind, he could almost hear his father's laugh. *The old goat would have probably made a light and convinced himself there was a good reason to examine her.* He didn't know that for a fact, but his father did have a lewd sense of humor.

No, that probably wasn't true. Either way, now wasn't the time for idle speculation. What mattered was protecting her from the cold, and repairing her modesty before she woke up. Levitating her body, he enfolded her in an envelope of warm air before emptying the blanket of its bulky contents.

Once it was free of clutter, he stretched it out beneath her. Then he used his magic to wrap it carefully around her, enclosing her in several layers of thick wool. She wouldn't be able to move, but until she woke he would be moving her with nothing but his power anyway.

His second rush of adrenaline began to wear off, and his body began to shake. Less than an hour back in this strange world and he had already exhausted his aythar. Fumbling, he retrieved the small leather pouch from the pile of his belongings and removed one of the iron spheres.

Matthew created a small shield around it, then activated it with the command word. He kept a tight rein on his intention as he spoke the word, using his will to alter its meaning. The iron bombs weren't designed to be used in this manner, but he managed to avoid an all-out explosion. The aythar still rushed out far faster than he would have liked, but he held it as best he could and directed it inward, absorbing it through his hands.

It felt like molten metal racing along the nerves in his arms. Hissing in pain, he retained his focus until he had gotten most of the energy. Some leaked away, but he hurt too much to care.

Smoke rose from his hands and forearms, some of the hair on his skin had burned away. Drawing on an external source of power was something he had done before, but doing it so rapidly, from something like an iron bomb was obviously not ideal.

I'm going to wind up killing myself if I do that too many more times, he noted quietly.

A quiet hum intruded on his senses, and he glanced upward. A dark shape hovered there, too high for his stunted magesight to detect. They had been spotted.

Raising his staff, he tried to destroy the craft, but without his magesight his aim was inadequate. Matthew growled, this world was beginning to seriously irritate him. Not for the first time, he wished he dared to fly the way his father did.

Flying was not a wise thing for wizards to attempt. It required a lot of practice to perfect, and the learning process was usually fatal; a single mistake could be disastrous. His father had managed to survive the experience because he had been effectively immortal during the period he had first tried it.

Matthew didn't have that luxury, but he had something almost as good.

He took a small clay disk from the pile of items he had brought and with a word activated it. Fine lines appeared, and then the disk fractured into twenty-four separate pieces that flew outward to take up predetermined positions in relation to one another. Investing a small amount of his power in it caused planes of force to spring up between the pieces, and with his magesight he could now see the broad, roughly disk shaped craft that rested on the rocky ground in front of him.

It was an enchantment that created a nicely aerodynamic shape that would both protect them and make it much easier to fly. Matthew used another word to dispel the portion that served as an entry and began loading their supplies before using his aythar to levitate Karen into the craft's interior.

Flying would get them to their destination much faster than their original trek down the mountain had taken. It also required a lot of aythar, and he worried that, given his environment's outright lack of aythar, he would tire far faster than normal, but it was a risk that had to be taken. If they were surrounded again, there was a very real chance that he would run out of resources to fight with before the enemy could be eliminated.

Expanding his aythar, he took charge of the air around them and used it to lift the enchanted disk into the air. As he had feared the task was far more draining than it would have been in his own world. The air here was dead, and all the energy had to come from him.

Matthew wasted no time as he sent them rushing upward to clear the tops of the trees. The aerial observer followed them immediately, maintaining a precise amount of distance between them.

He increased their speed and occasionally altered their direction, but the thing following them never faltered. It matched his every move with uncanny precision, almost as though it were somehow attached to them. He made one attempt to disrupt its flight, veering toward it and sending an updraft of air to throw the thing off balance, but it adjusted to the change in air currents with only the slightest of wobbles to indicate he had done anything.

Eventually, he gave up. It wasn't attacking them, so he decided to ignore it.

Their ascent took considerably less time than coming down had taken them. In less than a quarter of an hour Matthew had found the area where he had caused the rockslide. He guided the flying craft through the rather large opening in the side of the mountain and watched carefully to see what their tag-a-long observer would do.

It hovered quietly outside the opening, but didn't attempt entry.

Moving quickly, he took his staff with him and used it to etch a long line across the ground at the cave opening, then he continued it up the walls and across the ceiling. That done he created a quick shield before beginning the more intricate work of inscribing runes along the inside of his initial line. He kept it as simple as possible, but it still took him the better part of ten minutes to finish his work. He added a second line on the inside of the runes, and then empowered the enchantment with a significant portion of the aythar he had just taken from the iron bomb.

Completed, the shield should be significantly stronger than a similar barrier made from solid iron. Exhaling a long sigh of pent up air, he returned to the larger chamber of the cave. Karen was still unconscious, though she moved frequently, groaning in her sleep. He guessed from that that her injury must be causing significant pain, so he took a second to renew the nerve block that prevented her from feeling it.

She grew still, and the tension in her face eased. Matthew studied her features. Karen had a strong nose, a bit longer than average, but it suited her face. Her eyes were closed, but if they had been open the blue in them made a great match for the perfect teeth that were currently hidden by soft red lips. She had the whitest teeth he thought he had ever seen, which was made even more impactful by the fact that they were straight and well aligned without any gaps.

She was beautiful. Not in the delicate or fragile sense that he saw in so many of the highborn ladies he had often been forced to socialize with, but rather in the way she radiated health and well-being. Her unusual height was the result of a strong framework that supported well exercised muscles. She was still quite feminine, and he almost blushed at the memory of what he had only recently seen.

But she was definitely beautiful. "Like a fine horse, strong teeth and good withers," he added to dispel the awkward turn his thoughts were taking. Briefly he wished his sister had been present to hear the remark, she would have been horrified. The thought made him smile.

A wave of dizziness reminded him that he had already almost exhausted his aythar once again. He started to sit, but the pain in his back convinced him to remain standing. Instead he walked over to Desacus and put his hand on the great beast's shoulder, *Wake, my friend.*

One eye in the dragon's massive skull slowly opened, revealing a large yellow iris. Desacus studied him silently for several seconds. *That was a dirty trick. How long have I slept?*

"Too long," answered Matthew, "Several harrowing days."

That's what you get for issuing open ended commands, responded the dragon with a mental huff of disdain. *Why are you wearing armor?*

"Carrying it was too much of a chore. Wearing it seemed a better option, which turned out to be a lucky choice on my part. I hadn't had it on more than a few minutes before someone tried to put a lot of holes in me." He kept his tone casual, but he found himself leaning on the dragon's shoulder more out of necessity than by choice. "Lend me your strength, Desacus."

A gentle flow of aythar made its way up his arm and the young wizard sighed in relief. Slowly, painfully, he eased his way to the ground and tried to recline against the dragon's belly. His bruises wouldn't allow that, so he eventually wound up laying belly down on the cold stone. He continued drawing a steady trickle of aythar from the dragon and used some of it to warm himself.

Tell me what's going on. Who is the girl?

Matthew wanted sleep more than anything, but he knew it was a bad idea to succumb to that desire without giving his reptilian comrade at least a basic idea of what sort of trouble they were in. He forced himself to stay awake and began recounting his recent misfortunes.

CHAPTER 10

It was dark. Not dark like sleeping outside on a moonless night, but pitch black with no glimmer of light beyond the occasional flickers created by a brain deprived of external stimulation. There were no stars.

Karen felt weird. Her neck, shoulder, and arm were completely numb. She knew they were there only because she could feel their weight and resistance when she tried to move, but she seemed to be wrapped in some sort of heavy fabric. It was warm, for which she was grateful, but she had to fight down a rising sense of panic at being trapped and unable to see.

Her bra was gone and as she shifted she got the sense that her shirt was similarly missing. *Not a comforting thought,* she noted. This was not how she had expected to wake up. Had the military captured them?

Stay calm, Karen. Think it through. What's the last thing you remember?

A vision of Matthew standing in front of her wearing armor that might have been straight out of the crusades passed through her mind. She had been shot, she knew that. It had appeared as though Matthew had also been shot, more than once, but for some reason it hadn't killed him.

You're assuming that he's still alive. "Shut the fuck up, Karen. Try to be positive for a change," she told herself.

Something moved in the darkness; her ears detected a noise like metal scraping across stone. She froze. She wasn't alone. Her heart began to pound in her ears as she listened for any further noises.

"Hello." The voice that found her was deep, several octaves lower than any human voice should be. It said something after that, and she thought the language might be the same as the one Matthew used, if it was being spoken by something that used a tractor engine for a voice box.

She kept her silence, while trying to roll out of whatever was holding her. It took a moment to figure out the correct direction but once she got it, she was able to get out of the cloth with little trouble. Cold air touched her skin. Her shirt was definitely gone.

A short burst of flame lit the cavern and for a brief instant she saw the massive head of a monster straight out of a nightmare. Thick scaled lips hovered over teeth that stretched out like daggers, and the eyes that stared at her had slitted pupils like those of a snake.

Karen didn't scream. The sound that issued from her startled mouth was something more like the 'eep' of a frightened rabbit. She ran, heedless of her blindness.

"Grethak!"

The word seemed to penetrate her brain, freezing her muscles into immobility and she fell forward. Something caught her fall and a few seconds later she felt hands on her shoulders, straightening her and setting her back on her feet. Another strange phrase followed, and her muscles began to respond again. She recognized the voice, it was Matthew.

Thank god! She clung to him in the darkness, hardly noticing the rough metal that still covered his torso.

It's alright, he told her, sending the words directly into her mind. *We're safe.*

I can't see.

We are in a cave. You were about to run headlong into a wall, he cautioned.

There's something in here with us...

He laughed softly, *That was Desacus. He's a friend.*

She would have gaped at him, but it was too dark for the expression to have meant anything. She gaped anyway. *Didn't you see it? It wasn't human.*

Of course not, he's my dragon. Let me show you. He tried to step away from her, to create a more respectable distance, but she held onto him, her hands gripping his arm. *Shield your eyes. I'm going to create a light, but it will seem very bright after this long in the dark.*

She nodded, but then felt silly, since he obviously couldn't see her head moving.

Don't panic when you see him, added Matthew. *He's fearsome to look upon, but I promise he is friendly.*

Okay, she responded, steeling herself and lifting her right hand to cover her eyes. A brilliant white light appeared above them, near what she could now see was the center of a cavern some fifty feet in diameter.

She blinked away tears as even the small amount of light streaming through her fingers stung her eyes. As they adjusted she looked nervously across the room toward the massive form that *should* have been a rock formation. It was too big to be anything else, in a rational world that is.

Apparently, the world wasn't rational, though. It moved, and as her vision came into better focus she could see what was clearly a dragon, a monster from the fairytales of childhood. It was huge! Legs as big around as saplings ended in claws that would have made a grizzly weep from jealousy.

Vast wings were folded back along its sides, and a long tail was curled around its body, making its position

93

reminiscent of a cat curling up to sleep. The creature's lips drew back to reveal long dagger-like teeth and her heart began to pound.

"Stop that!" commanded Matthew. "I've warned you not to smile around people. It makes them nervous."

The dragon chuffed sulkily, but it closed its lips.

She hadn't understood his words, but clearly the dragon had, *He can understand you? Is he trained?*

The young man laughed, *No, he isn't trained. He's intelligent, as smart as you or me. He can talk too, but you don't understand our language, so there's not much point.*

"I was only trying to be friendly," rumbled the dragon.

"You were trying to scare her," corrected Matthew.

"Not my fault if she misunderstood," said Desacus.

You really are talking to it, thought Karen with some amazement.

"He's just like a human," said Matthew before realizing he should switch his mode of communication. *Think of him as a person, just like you or me, but with a different body—and a really weird sense of humor.*

The dragon coughed indignantly, "I take exception to that. I am *nothing* like your inferior breed of soft-skinned monkeys."

What did he say? asked Karen.

Matthew glanced back at her, *He was apologizing for frightening you.* Then his eyes took in her bare chest. He had already been aware of her nudity, of course, and he had been trying to avoid embarrassing her by staring, but under the light of his spell he saw her breasts properly with his eyes for the first time.

Her breasts were blue.

For that matter, so were her stomach, shoulders, upper arms—she was blue everywhere except her face, neck, and hands.

Karen saw his expression change, and she shrank away from him, her arms covering her chest. A mixture of emotions ran through her, and she wasn't sure whether she was more embarrassed about her lack of a shirt, or whether she was more chagrined by his discovery of her freakish secret.

Matthew looked away and raised his hand. The blanket she had so recently escaped from floated up and crossed the room to enfold her. *Sorry, I didn't mean to stare,* he told her mentally.

Karen's eyes widened in surprise, *You can communicate telepathically even when we aren't touching?*

It costs me more effort, he replied. *In my own world, that isn't usually a problem, but here I have been conserving my strength.*

As the thoughts sank in, she focused on one portion of what he had said, *You're from another world. You're a demon.* She should have realized sooner, but he had seemed so normal, if one discounted his strange attire. The dragon would have probably tipped her off, but she was still in shock from meeting it.

The word she had used, 'demon' had been new to him, but Matthew had felt the meaning of it in her mind. It referred to the fact that he had come from another dimension, which meant she was familiar with the concept of interdimensional travel. Of course, her blue skin and pointed ears made it plain that she was no ordinary human. She was She'Har, more specifically, she was a child of the Mordan Grove.

It all made sense now. In this world, the She'Har were fighting for control, and the strange metal monsters he had fought were their enemies, probably defenders of the native population.

So are you, he responded, his eyes narrowing in suspicion.

"How did the target escape?" asked SDC Aiseman.

"Uncertain, Director," reported Commander Leighton. "There was a second person with her."

"Show me the video," ordered the SDC.

Twin video feeds were presented in the air in front of them, one showing the scene in infrared and the other using low-light sensors. As the scene played out numbers beneath them gave an accounting of the exact time.

"Freeze," ordered Tanya Miller. "This matches the time of the latest event we measured with the ANSIS network."

Commander Leighton frowned, "For something that would produce ripples, it seems very subtle."

"Do you think this may indicate that your daughter is perhaps just a bystander caught up in this?" asked Director Aiseman.

Tanya scowled at him, irritated that he had revealed her relationship with the target in front of Commander Leighton. "There is zero chance of that, Director, and now that your men have failed to eliminate them, the threat level has risen significantly, as shown by their near miraculous escape."

Leighton ground his teeth, "We lost forty-three men in that skirmish, Dr. Miller. I would appreciate it if you showed a little more resp…"

"Next time you will use appropriate measures, Commander. It was your own timidity that cost those men their lives," said Tanya, cutting him off. "You should have carpet bombed the area once you had her location."

"Let's not get into a pissing match," ordered Director Aiseman. "We have their current location, and it doesn't appear they will be going anywhere. They've blockaded themselves into a cave with some sort of powerful energy screen."

"Which means absolutely nothing," countered Dr. Miller. "They can leave at any time, in just the same fashion that they escaped your first confrontation."

"Sensors indicate they are still within the cave, though the readings are odd. We show three bodies inside, one of them very large," observed Commander Leighton.

Dr. Miller spoke dispassionately, "The entire area must be sterilized."

Aiseman was surprised, "What?"

"You heard me. If an infection is already underway we need to make certain it is cut out immediately. I want everything within a two-mile radius sprayed, with defoliant and nerve toxins. Use a tactical nuke on the cave," she added.

Leighton spoke up, "A tac-nuke isn't the best option. The geological surveys indicate the cave may be exceptionally stable. We have conventional weapons that are better designed for penetrating hard targets."

Director Aiseman watched their exchange quietly, *How can she coldly order the execution of her only child?* He knew almost nothing about the details of Project Blue-star, but Tanya Miller's hard demeanor spoke volumes.

"I'll start withdrawing our assets from the area," continued the Commander.

Tanya held up her hand, "No. The chemical agents won't affect them. I want sensors to remain in place. We need to know for certain if their biosignatures are still present when the final strike hits, otherwise we won't know if it has been successful."

"A high yield explosion could be dangerous for the men," argued Aiseman, "even if it's non-nuclear."

Dr. Miller shook her head, "Keep them in place, a conventional weapon won't kill your men. If the demons try to emerge before the final strike, have your men use artillery. We need to make sure they don't get out using more mundane methods."

Commander Leighton protested, "You mean it *probably* won't kill them. I cannot approve of this, Dr. Miller. Your plan will damage or destroy UN assets and equipment while simultaneously endangering the lives of hundreds of military personnel."

Tanya glanced at SDC Aiseman and raised one brow.

With a sigh, Donald bowed to the inevitable, "Your objections are noted Commander Leighton. Do as Dr. Miller suggests."

Leighton was furious, "Exactly why do we have a civilian involved in this matter, Director? As far as I am aware she isn't in the chain of command."

Aiseman, started to reply, but Dr. Miller held up her hand to forestall him. The look she gave Commander Leighton was one of undisguised malice, "If you don't like your orders Commander, feel free to take your concerns to President Kruger. If that doesn't satisfy you, I will be happy to have you removed, and we will install someone who will carry out this mission."

The Cybernetic Division Commander blinked and then vanished.

Donald let out a deep breath, "You didn't need to be quite so brutal, Doctor."

Tanya Miller sneered back, "I had my fill of dealing with fools in the first Demon war, Director. If they had listened to me then, Australia wouldn't be a radioactive wasteland. I will brook no delays this time." She disappeared then, leaving the Senior Defense Director alone in the Command Center.

Donald Aiseman lowered his head to cradle it in his hands. This was going to be a long week, and he didn't see any way that he would be getting out of it without losing a significant amount of skin, assuming he was able to keep his job at all.

CHAPTER 11

Matthew could see the denial in her face.

Karen lifted her chin, refusing to let shame hold her back. The truth was out already. She put her hand on her companion's face, to make certain he would hear her thoughts, *You are mistaken. I was born here. Both of my parents were born here. I have a condition known as methemoglobinemia. My blood doesn't handle oxygen properly. That's why my skin is blue.*

More came across in the link than just her words. He also felt her shame. She seemed to think she had some sort of disease, or perhaps there was a social stigma associated with her condition. He also knew it was a lie. He had never seen one of the Mordan She'Har with his own eyes, but he had lots of memories of them. Her skin, ears, even her curly black hair were all indicative of that heritage. Not to mention the fact that he had just felt her project her own thoughts without his assistance.

She was already beginning to use aythar without even realizing it.

He brushed away her hand, then tested out a phrase in her language that he thought was correct, "Close your eyes."

Karen glared at him but eventually decided to trust him and did as he asked.

Matthew channeled his power along his right arm, making sure it was brilliant with aythar, but not allowing it to glow visibly. With a word he canceled the spell sustaining his light sphere above them, plunging the cavern into darkness.

Then he drew back his arm and swung at her head, as if he were about to deliver a stinging slap.

Karen reacted instinctively. Turning, she deflected his arm and then caught it.

Matthew had intended to stop his swing before reaching her cheek, but he found himself flying through the air instead. The air burst from his lungs as he landed on his back; and pain exploded through his body, blotting out everything else as his back arched. The bruises on his back were screaming at him as he twisted into a knot on the floor.

She knelt over him, "Oh god! I'm sorry. What were you thinking?"

He got the gist of her words, but he the agony in his back was too much for him to reply. He waited for the pain to pass, and after a few minutes it faded slightly. Restoring the light sphere, he frowned up at her before trying to sit up again. His back had other ideas, however.

"You're hurt," she exclaimed.

No shit, thought Matthew.

She began trying to remove his armor unsuccessfully. He struggled with her briefly, but it hurt too much to maintain his resistance. Surrendering, he showed her where the buckles were, so she could remove his coif and detach the hauberk from his mail leggings. Several painful minutes filled with swearing went by before she finally had the chain shirt and his padded gambeson off.

Desacus had been watching the entire time, but now he broke his silence, "If she kills you can I eat her?"

Matthew sent a silent response, *We already talked about this, no.* Secretly though, he thought it might be a good idea. *Besides, wouldn't you prefer to eat the one already dead.*

"She looks tender," replied the dragon before adding, "smells better too."

Karen ignored their conversation as she helped him to roll onto his side. A whistle escaped her lips as she saw the state of his back. Black and purple splotches covered his skin. In places, there were dark spots that indicated blood had pooled just under the surface, hematomas. She had felt bad about throwing him before, but now she wondered how he had even managed to stay on his feet. He had to have been in a lot of pain.

"You need a hospital," she said at last. "There could be a lot more damage than we can see."

He only understood part of what she said, but he replied anyway, again using her language, "I'm fine."

She sat back, "You're learning English very quickly."

That line went over his head so she put her hand on his forehead and repeated the phrase mentally. Once he understood he replied, pointing at himself, "Good memory."

"Something is coming," Desacus notified them, lifting his head and turning it slowly.

"I don't hear anything," said Matthew.

The dragon snorted, "I have better hearing."

With Karen's help he got back to his feet and made his way to the entrance. Outside he could see more flying machines hovering, and he thought there might be soldiers on the mountainside, but he couldn't be certain using only his eyes. Again, he was frustrated by how limited the range of his magesight was in this strange world.

Karen stood next to him, squinting against the morning sunlight. "Jets."

"What's that?" asked Matthew.

She put her hand on his shoulder, *Military aircraft, they have missiles that can destroy all sorts of things, and they can fire from miles away.*

The concepts were strange to him, but the meanings carried through. *How soon will they fire?*

They could have fired before ever getting this close, she replied. *They're doing something else, though that doesn't mean they won't.*

He was still coming to grips with the amazing things these people seemed able to do with dead metal and absolutely no aythar, but he got the feeling they had little time. They needed to leave. But then, he was standing next to a Mordan She'Har.

Karen, you have to understand something. You aren't from this world. You are She'Har. Your blue skin is a feature of theirs, well one of them anyway. The same goes for your ears.

For some reason, she wanted to believe him, but she couldn't let go of her past for a wild fantasy. She had had parents, a childhood. She knew better.

When it was dark back there, you saw my hand coming. Only a mage could do that, he added, refusing to relent. *You are a Mordan. You've just never been exposed to magic before.*

And what does that mean? she asked. *Why is it so important to you?*

The Mordan can teleport. It's a special ability that only they possess. You can get us out of here.

She had definitely experienced some odd sensations over the past few days, but at the moment the world seemed entirely normal, if one discounted the fact that she was standing in a cave with a dragon and a self-avowed wizard. She couldn't help but laugh. *So I'm a wizard and my special spell is teleport? There's no way I'm high enough level to cast that.*

The words were accompanied by some strange mental images, and he got the feeling she was referring to a game of some sort. She wasn't taking him seriously, and if what she had told him was true, they might not have much time.

He walked back to the interior chamber and weighed their options. He could try to construct a better defense. With Desacus he had access to enough aythar to create something truly spectacular, but he didn't think that would be the best option. He couldn't be certain how powerful the weapons of this world might be, and if they dug in they were bound to eventually be overwhelmed.

Escaping on dragonback was a slightly more attractive option, but he had seen the night before how effective the flying machines were. He doubted they could escape pursuit, and once in the open they would be much more vulnerable.

He tried to bend down and retrieve his armor, but his back made that nearly impossible. Putting it on would be even worse. Matthew sighed. Using his aythar he gathered it, along with all his other gear, into a small pile. He left out the iron pot. It was too bulky and since Karen was using the blanket he had nothing large enough to wrap everything up with. He used his armor instead, piling the other items on it and wrapping it around them before tying it together with the rope.

Karen had been observing quietly, "What are you going to do?"

It took him a few seconds, but he was able to slowly parse the meaning of her words. Then he replied, "I'm leaving."

"You can teleport?" she asked.

The answer was too much for his limited language skills, so he put his hand on her shoulder, *No. I don't have that gift, but I can move between worlds. I'll return to my own world for a while.*

What about me?

You're welcome to come. I wouldn't recommend staying here.

The thought of traveling to another world both frightened and intrigued her. She didn't have much to keep her anyway, other than her parents, and her current situation didn't offer any good alternatives. Karen nodded, "I'll come."

Matthew pointed to Desacus, "Climb up there." He didn't have the vocabulary to be more descriptive, but he thought the idea should be fairly clear.

The thought of climbing up on the massive beast was a fairly daunting one, but the dragon crouched low and extended one forelimb, obviously offering her an easy route up to his back.

It turned out to be more difficult than she had expected, mainly because she was limited to using one hand. The other had to keep a good grip on her blanket or it would slip off. *It's a little late to be worrying about your modesty now, Karen,* she thought. *You've already given them quite a show.*

Don't worry. I'm only interested in your body as a gustatory experiment.

The voice in her head wasn't Matthew's and she knew instantly it came from the dragon. It startled her so badly she almost slipped and fell.

Matthew watched from below with some concern, ready to catch her if she lost her grip entirely.

"I didn't realize he could talk the same way you do," she announced.

Imagine my shock, said the dragon. *How would you feel if you suddenly discovered your food could talk?*

"That's enough, Desacus," cautioned Matthew. "This is unsettling enough for her without your bad jokes."

Karen kept her attention on what she was doing until she had firmly seated herself. Matthew clambered up next to her and sat in front of her, just behind the dragon's neck.

"He doesn't really eat people, does he?" she asked, hoping the dragon wouldn't be able to understand her language.

Matthew laughed, "No."

Not yet, added Desacus, guessing at their conversation.

Matthew laughed, and Karen forced herself to relax. The creature was obviously trying to be funny—she hoped.

Tell her that skin to skin contact is best, neither of you is wearing a shirt after all, the dragon's remark carried a mental smirk.

Matthew tensed, uncertain whether the message had been relayed to both of them or whether it was private. *That isn't funny, Desacus.*

You were thinking it, the dragon told him.

No, I wasn't.

You are now.

Karen broke in, *What isn't funny?*

His magic will be easier if you cuddle, explained Desacus.

"Ok," she answered aloud.

"What?!" exclaimed Matthew, but before he could say more he felt her arms around his waist, and her head came to rest on his shoulder. He tensed, but then he realized the blanket was still between them. A faint tremor ran through his back as Karen began to laugh.

She has a better sense of humor than you do, announced the dragon.

"I should leave both of you behind," muttered Matthew, and before they could tease him further shifted them between worlds.

CHAPTER 12

He didn't want to return to the cave. Matthew was sick of mountains in general, so he tried to land in a different place. He didn't really have any way to pinpoint his arrival, aside from directing them away from the place he had left before. As a result, they appeared somewhere unknown to him.

"This seems nice," opined Karen, squinting to keep dust out of her eyes. A strong wind was blowing, and it kicked up sand from the hard-baked earth that stretched out around them in every direction.

Desacus shuddered and began to move beneath them. The two humans slid off quickly and watched curiously while the dragon began to retch.

Karen laid a sympathetic hand on the creature's shoulder, *Are you alright?*

I'm never going to get used to those shifts. It gets worse every time, complained the dragon.

Karen felt fine. The moment between worlds had been a little disorienting, but it hadn't bothered her stomach at all.

"It's just a hairball," commented Matthew spitefully.

"I don't have hair," argued Desacus.

"You will when I'm done with you," responded the wizard, "if you don't stop making jokes at my expense."

Several minutes later, once Desacus had recovered, they mounted up again and began searching for a better place to rest. They flew north, since they had no idea where they were, one direction was as good as any other.

Karen had some serious reservations about their mode of transportation. She had never been afraid of flying, or had any problem boarding commercial planes, but being on dragonback was a different matter. Their altitude was a brute fact, far more immediate than the sterile heights she had experienced looking out of a passenger window.

She kept her cool, but she had to keep forcing herself to unclench her hands which were digging into her fellow passenger's ribs like claws.

The strangest part of it all was the complete lack of wind. When Desacus took off and began to gain speed Matthew did *something*. She sensed it for a moment, a flickering around them, some sort of domed enclosure. Within it the air was calm and relatively warm, which was a necessity considering Matthew's bare skin. He didn't even have the benefit of a blanket.

A quarter of an hour passed and the desert continued to stretch on before them with no end in sight. While the temperature was fine in their protected bubble, the sun was brutal. She saw the tops of Matthew's shoulders begin to turn pink and she began to feel bad for him. Having lived her entire life covered in sunscreen she had a healthy respect for the effects of ultraviolet rays.

The solution was obvious.

"Don't think about it, Karen. It's a purely practical matter," she muttered to herself.

"What?" asked Matthew, failing to catch her words.

Unfolding her blanket, she pulled it around his torso to wrap them both within it. "Shut up," she told him. "Don't say a word."

He held himself as still as a statue from that point on, hardly daring to move. Karen scooted back slightly, keeping a small distance between them. There was no need to get closer after all—until the dragon suddenly dropped several feet, pretending to have encountered some unexpected turbulence.

The distance between them vanished as she held on for dear life.

Desacus sent a thought to his young master, *You're welcome.*

I'm making steaks out of you after this is over, Matthew responded privately, *count on it.*

Oh! So, it's fine for you to eat dragon, but it's somehow wrong if I want to indulge in the same sort of culinary exploration? How is that fair?!

Another hour passed, and the two passengers grew more at ease with their strangely intimate situation. Karen's fear of falling had faded, for the most part, and an important question rose to the foreground of her mind, *Neither of you know where we are, do you?*

Not exactly, answered Matthew.

What does that mean? she probed.

Desacus broke in to clarify, *He means we have no clue.*

Matthew ground his teeth, *We could be in the Northern Wastes, or the Southern Desert. That's why I chose to go north. If it's the Southern Desert we will eventually come to Lothion, the country I am from. If we are in the Northern Wastes, we'll end up in Gododdin or Dunbar. Either way we won't be lost anymore.*

Unless we're in some desert you've never heard of before, added the dragon.

Thanks, Desacus, thought Matthew dryly.

Don't mention it.

Before another hour had finished they saw trees on the horizon. As they approached they could see a river that formed a natural boundary between the forest and the more arid lands behind them. Desacus began to descend, eventually depositing them on the northern bank, nearest the trees.

The two humans managed to disentangle themselves and dismount without too much embarrassment. Karen rewrapped the blanket modestly around herself, but she didn't bother turning her back first. In her mind, there wasn't much point. Most of her modesty in her previous life had been due to her bizarre blue skin. That was no longer a secret, and she had learned enough about her companion to know he wasn't the sort to be driven mad with lust at the sight of a woman. In fact, she was fairly certain he had no interest in her whatsoever.

The dragon left to hunt for something large enough to satisfy his hunger. Matthew took advantage of the river, using his magesight and his power to lift several hapless fish directly from the water. He already regretted leaving the iron pot behind, but at least here he didn't have to conserve his strength.

He gathered dry wood from the forest for a cook fire, then cut several long slender poles of greenwood to cook his catch on.

While he did that, Karen sorted through the pile of gear he had brought. She was excited when she found the thread and needles. Borrowing Matthew's belt knife, she removed the blanket and laid it out on the dry ground. She made a rough mental estimate and then cut a large square from it. She folded the square twice and then cut away one of the corners in a semi-circular fashion. Unfolding it again, it now had a relatively neat hole in the center.

She folded it again, this time only once, and cut away some material from either side, leaving it in the shape of a 't' with a thick central portion. The top horizontal part would be sleeves, with the hole in the middle making a collar. With the needle, she began sewing the sides up to form the body of her new shirt.

Matthew watched her from the corner of one eye while he roasted the fish, trying not to obviously stare since she was still bare chested. It was her needlework he was interested in, not her supple skin, or the softly curving lines of her body as she bent over her work…

Irritated, he turned his attention back to the fish, turning it before it could burn. After a minute he risked another glance, this time keeping his eyes firmly on her handiwork. The stitching was sloppy and crude, but serviceable. Whoever it was that produced the perfectly sewn clothing from Karen's world, she had obviously never studied with them.

Moira could sew better than that when she was eight, he noted.

Once the sides were finished, Karen cut a short slit down the front of the shirt, beginning at the makeshift collar to make it easy for her to slip over her head. She brought the new shirt up and gave it a shake to dislodge the dirt and twigs it had picked up from the ground.

Matthew's eyes froze as Karen lifted her arms skyward and for a timeless instant her body stretched out, lean and supple, with skin that matched the azure sky behind her. A year and one second later the rough tunic settled into place, and she looked over at him and smiled.

His heart jumped into his throat. She had to know what he had been thinking.

He pushed the thought aside angrily. He couldn't afford that sort of distraction. Someday he would have to marry, and whoever he chose would be required to have a long pedigree. The nobility weren't often given the luxury of picking their marriage partners in the same way commoners were.

It was obvious to him that Karen was smitten, but to entertain her fantasy would only be a disservice to her. Many less scrupulous noblemen abused their position by dallying with women of the lower classes before they married. Some continued after as well, leaving a long line of dispossessed bastards in their wake. He wouldn't be one of them. Even if the woman in question was clearly willing, as Karen seemed to be.

Matthew pulled the sticks holding their dinner away from the fire and stuck them in the ground a few feet away so they could cool, frowning as he reordered his thoughts.

Karen noticed the frown, and she wondered if her friend's back might be causing him pain. Half-joking, she asked him, "Want me to make you one too? There's more than enough blanket left."

He retrieved his undertunic and held it up to answer her question. Consulting his ever-growing vocabulary of her language he answered, "Well made, not ugly."

The tips of her ears turned purple as the blood rushed to her face. Angry, she stalked toward him, "What's that supposed to mean?"

To clarify he projected his thoughts, *It means no, thank you. I'm not interested.*

Telepathic communication was superior in many regards, but its biggest flaw was that it carried not just the intended information but the sender's deeper meanings as well. Karen received the rest of the underlying message loud and clear—*not interested in you.*

She resisted the urge to punch the infuriatingly bland look from his idiotic face.

Matthew turned away, taking his tunic with him. He collected the overtunic as well and carried them both down to the river to wash them.

Karen glared at his back before taking to her feet and heading upstream. The weather was warm, so she might as well take the opportunity to get a much-needed bath. As she walked she tried to calm herself. *He's not worth being upset over.* It wasn't as though she had feelings for him. Hell, she barely knew him.

What she didn't understand was why he felt the need to be so blunt about his disinterest. It was simple rudeness, and she had done nothing to merit that. Her life had been just fine until he had showed up. Now she was a fugitive, and she still didn't understand why.

"Who am I fooling?" she muttered. "My life sucked."

That evening they sat quietly, staring into the fire. Desacus still roamed the countryside hunting, and Matthew had explained that he might not return until morning.

The fish had been passable, but it left them feeling hungry still. Karen couldn't remember her last real meal, and she was beginning to have fantasies about bread. She was trying to imagine the taste of fresh biscuits when Matthew broke the silence, "I did not mean to insult you."

She nodded. It was fascinating to her how quickly his English was progressing. It remained stilted and unnatural, but he was growing more proficient by the day. "Why did you come to my world?"

Matthew struggled to put together the words, "Looking for my father."

"You think he went there?" The question didn't get through completely, so she repeated it mentally with a certain amount of emphasis. She wasn't certain, but she felt as though he heard her thoughts when she *pushed* them in that way.

His eyes widened slightly, then he crossed over to sit beside her, placing his hand beside hers. She accepted the gesture and put her hand on top of his.

This will be easier, his words echoed in her mind. *My father, the Count di' Cameron, disappeared a short while back. We think he was captured by something that may have come from your world.*

My world? she thought back, astonished. *We don't have the ability to travel like you do.*

Someone did, he replied. *But it might not have been your world specifically. There is an infinity of interwoven planes. Yours was close, but it might have been in what you would think of as the past, or future, from your perspective.*

You can travel in time?

No. I can travel to places that are nearly identical to one another, but may appear to be similar to the past or future of one another.

Close enough, she thought.

Time itself is an illusion of sorts, maybe, he responded. *It may be that our perceptions are merely traveling through collections of finely textured dimensions, moving from instant to instant, creating the illusion of change, of time.*

Really?

I don't know, he told her honestly. *When I move in-between I can feel it, know it, but when we are here it's too big for me to understand, or remember, or something.*

Karen stared up at the stars, *No man can comprehend the mind of God, is that what you mean?*

Something like that, he agreed. *Nothing contained within a set can encompass the entire set.*

She gave him a curious look, *That sounds a lot like something I learned at university. Do your people have advanced mathematics?*

Now it was his turn to be offended, *We aren't savages.*

Sorry, she replied, admitting her own subconscious prejudice.

Matthew decided to move on, *Your world may be similar to this world's distant past, or its future.*

That doesn't seem possible. We have nothing like your magic.

He shook his head, *Magic works there. You have it. You didn't when I first met you, but you've begun producing aythar of your own.*

Aythar?

It's a force that underlies everything here, animate and inanimate. From my perspective, your world is barren, but I think it has the potential to be like mine.

I don't think my world wants to be like yours, she replied.

Matthew snorted, *Not from the way they greeted me, but you live there, and you're She'Har.*

No, I'm not. They invaded my world. We call it the Demon War, but I am not one of them.

And yet you can use aythar, he responded.

She felt conflicted, *I've seen some strange things, felt some things, without using my eyes, but only because you brought it there.*

No, Matthew argued, *even here, most people cannot sense or feel it. Only those with a gift can do that. The She'Har all have gifts, just as you do.*

I have a birth defect that makes me blue, that doesn't mean I'm a demon.

Matthew sighed, *Let me show you what they look like.*

She was hesitant, but she agreed, *Okay.*

With a word Matthew created a light sphere and set it hovering above them, then he traced a large rectangle in the air with one hand. When he finished, he spoke again and the air within it changed, becoming a mirror. Karen's face was reflected in it.

"Very funny," said Karen, "That's not..."

"Wait," Matthew said, holding up one hand. *There were five Groves when the She'Har came here. Each created children with varying appearances.* Creating an illusion, he changed the colors of the face reflected in the mirror.

The face in the mirror had eyes that were a brilliant scarlet, with red hair that matched. The skin tone contrasted the red with an earthy brown. "The Gaelyn She'Har," intoned Matthew.

After she had stared for a while the colors shifted again, her hair and eyes became a shimmering gold while her skin turned almost pitch black. He named a different grove, "The Prathion She'Har."

"That's wild," exclaimed Karen.

Her face changed again, and now she had hair the color of summer grass with eyes that matched. Her skin tone was the fair shade she had always dreamed of. "The Centyr She'Har."

She touched her own cheek with a feeling of wonder, and in the mirror she could see tears forming in her eyes. If only she had looked like that growing up, people might have thought she was just a cosplayer. Then the colors changed again.

"The Illeniel She'Har," said Matthew, "whose gift I seem to have inherited." Her skin was even paler now, and her curly locks had been replaced by long straight tresses of silver that fell to her shoulders. Icy blue eyes stared back at her.

Karen was surprised, *You're She'Har? You don't look like that.*

No, I'm human. Only the children of the She'Har have these odd colorings. Normally, they take root and become proper She'Har trees, but if they produce children

*in the human fashion those offspring are human, and they
don't inherit the unusual appearance. One of my distant
ancestors was probably one of them.*

The face in the mirror shimmered once more and
Karen was looking once again at her own face, with curly
black hair and light blue eyes. Her skin had once more
resumed its disgusting cerulean shade.

*And that's what the Mordan She'Har looked like,
Karen,* Matthew told her. *You aren't deformed, you were
born of one of their Mother-trees.*

Karen's chest grew tight; it felt as though the world was
closing in around her. She couldn't breathe. Desperate she
tried to push the feeling away from her, her gaze locked on
the mirror and in a shower of sparks and luminous fragments
it exploded. "No, I had parents, I had a childhood!"

"And you just used your power to destroy my mirror."

She buried her face in her hands while Matthew
watched, unsure what to do. Her last statement confused
him. If she *was* She'Har, she should have been created as
an adult, or at least close to it, like Lynarralla had been.
She should also have been born with a certain amount of
knowledge already stored within her seed-mind.

Peering into his distant memories, Matthew
dredged up what he needed. When he spoke again it
was in a tongue he had never attempted before, "Can
you understand me now?" His own ears told him that
the accent was terrible, but it was good enough that she
should be able to make sense of it.

Karen looked up, "What was that?"

*A language called 'Erollith'. The language of
the She'Har. Their children are created knowing it,* he
replied mentally.

*It sounded like gibberish to me. I told you, I'm human.
There's a hole in your theory somewhere,* she replied.

Matthew thought for a moment, *There's no guarantee the She'Har that came to your world were the same as the ones that came to mine. They may have had a different language.*

Anything could be possible if you keep resorting to explanations like that, she argued.

I can check, if you don't mind, he offered.

"How?" she asked suspiciously.

The She'Har have a special organ, the seed-mind, nestled within their brain. It provides their inborn knowledge, grants them perfect recall, and—when the time comes, it germinates and grows into a new tree. I can search inside you, to see if you have one.

That sounds painful. You want to root around inside my brain? she asked, a hint of fear tinting her thoughts.

It won't hurt, he told her. *I could probably have done it without you even knowing, but I thought it better to ask.*

"Well that's very considerate of you," she said aloud. *Should I lie down?*

You don't have to, but it might make it simpler, he replied.

Matthew found the bedroll and spread it out on the ground for her. Karen stretched out on it, and he sat next to her head. Gazing down on her, he felt a strange sense of déjà vu. One of Tyrion's memories floated up in his mind, and for a second he saw the terrified faces of the women Tyrion had experimented on. An involuntary shudder ran through him.

Pushing those images aside he focused his attention. He only needed the knowledge Tyrion had gained, not the traumatic experiences that went with that information. He sharpened his magesight and went beneath her hair, past skin and bone, into the complex organ that served the central function of intelligence.

It took only a short span of seconds, it wasn't there. Karen's brain was simply that, a human brain, without the foreign seed the She'Har put into all their children.

Sitting back, he muttered to himself, "It isn't there."

"Told you," said Karen. "I'm just the defective product of several generations of inbreeding." Her face was scrunched up as she struggled to contain her emotions. A moment before she had been arguing for her humanity, now she wanted to weep for it. The idea that she might have been something *other*, had been frightening, but also attractive.

Matthew could see her misery, and it sparked a feeling of anger within him. Her aythar was chaotic and incomplete, it sputtered through her body, filling certain areas and missing others. Perhaps it was because she had lived without it for so long, but it hadn't reached every part of her. She was a mosaic of light and dark, aythar and void.

In his mind, it was a perfect reflection of her own self-hatred—and he couldn't bear to see it any longer.

He didn't know what was right or wrong, but in that moment, he no longer cared. Reaching down, he put his hand in the center of her chest, over her breastbone, and *pushed*. Directing his will, he flooded her body with a cascade of his own aythar, smoothing her aura and filling in the voids.

Karen's eyes flew open when his hand touched her, "What are you…!" And then her words cut off. A wave of sensation raced through her, setting her nerves on fire with something that was akin to pleasure, yet so intense it caused her back to arch with pain. Her mouth opened and she gasped for air. The air shimmered around her, and she could *see* it, in a way that made no sense at all.

Matthew was glowing, the earth was alive, and she could count the trees on the other side of the river, trees that were certainly outside her line of sight. For the first time in her life, she was no longer empty, she was connected. Whole.

"Are you alright?" he asked.

"What did you do?" Everything was sparkling, and she found herself watching his heart beat, its rhythm a counterpoint to her own.

"I'm not sure," he admitted. "It just looked like it needed to be done."

She caught his hand before he could withdraw it. Experimenting, she tried to send some of her own energy through it, to mingle with his. A shield sprang up, a barrier that separated them. "Let me," she protested.

"You're confused, probably disoriented," he responded. "If this is the first time your gift has fully awakened you might have some nausea…"

She pressed again, and this time he lowered the barrier. She flowed into him like a gentle rain soaking into dry soil. *I want to see it all,* she thought to him.

You aren't thinking clearly, you need to adjust, he told her, trying half-heartedly to pull away.

Karen wrapped one hand into the hair at the back of his head and pulled him in, kissing him. *I don't care.*

I'm not interested. I have duties…

This time she heard the words, understood the undertones, but unlike before, she also felt his emotions. He wanted her. His lust was as great as her own. "Shut up. I don't give a damn about your responsibilities. You can be an asshole tomorrow. Tonight, you're *mine*."

CHAPTER 13

They had been flying for less than an hour when Desacus spotted the telltale signs of a village ahead. After a short discussion, they made a careful landing a half a mile from it, on the verge of a small field, to avoid alarming the residents. Dragons were still new to Lothion, and it would almost certainly have caused a panic if Desacus had come down in plain view.

"Do you know these people?" asked Karen nervously.

Matthew was busy removing his armor and redressing himself in the tunics she had seen him in when he first came to her world. The clothing was rumpled but relatively clean after his efforts at washing it the day before. He shook his head negatively, "No."

She pointed at his mail, "Maybe you should wear it instead."

He laughed, "There's no danger."

Karen wasn't so sure, and her uncertainty showed. Plus, she was blue. She pointed at her face.

Matthew's aythar flashed as he spoke a few short words, and it flowed outward, briefly covering her. *You look like anyone else,* he said, speaking inside her mind. *Changing the color of your skin is the simplest of illusions.*

What if we aren't in your country? she pointed out. *They still might not be friendly.*

A shimmering barrier sprang up around him, hovering a fraction of an inch from his skin. *Wizards are rare, even in this world,* he told her. *Normal people don't hold much danger for us. My father insisted I learn to keep a shield around me at all times.*

She knew for a fact he hadn't been keeping a shield around himself for the majority of the time they had been in his world. Had he not felt the need? Or had he wanted to avoid putting a barrier between them? "Can I do that?" she asked.

He nodded, *Any mage can, but you will need to practice first. I'll show you after we do some trading. For now, I can manage a shield for both of us.* To illustrate his thoughts a similar shield sprang up around her.

They crossed the field and found a small cart track leading into the village proper, a small collection of ramshackle wooden buildings. Several small children played in the empty area in the center, which was occupied by what appeared to be a well.

The children stared at them as they approached, and several ran into the buildings. A heavyset man with an impressive beard emerged from the largest and assessed Matthew with a critical eye.

"Good day," Matthew began, hailing him.

The stranger's eyes took in his sword and clothing, with hardly any hesitation he bowed deeply, "Pardon me, my lord, I do not know your name to greet you properly."

"You can address me as Lord Illeniel," Matthew informed him. "What is your name, and the name of this village?"

The villager went to his knees, keeping his face down toward the ground, "Nathan, Lord Illeniel, this is the village of Dabwold."

"Rise, Nathan," pronounced Matthew. "You have shown courtesy enough, I do not need a display of obeisance. Who is your lord?"

"Baron Elmwood, my lord."

He had never met the man, but Matthew had been required to learn the names of every member of Lothion's peerage. The name told him much. He was in southern Lothion, which meant they had been traveling through the Southern Desert. Albamarl was probably only a couple of hours by dragon to the north and east of them.

Karen watched the entire exchange with a growing feeling of unease. She was still uncomfortable with her new senses, but she could see the people hiding in their homes all around them. She couldn't understand the conversation, but the peasant's immediate subservience felt wrong. People shouldn't have to kneel.

Matthew finished talking and directed his attention to her, *They'll feed us and provide some bread and cheese we can take with us.*

They don't look like they can afford to give away food, she returned with a note of disapproval.

I'll be paying them.

They waited in the center of the village, while the man went to make good on his promises. Matthew was staring down into the well, while Karen had trouble deciding what to do with herself. She could feel eyes on her from every direction.

"Shouldn't we go inside to eat?" she asked.

Matthew glanced up and raised one brow, "Do you want to?" Then he added mentally, *It would only frighten them more if we went inside.*

In truth, she had no desire to enter any of the dwellings there. The smell was bad enough outside, and from what she could see it was probably much worse inside. She felt a surge of aythar and realized her companion was doing something at the well.

Matthew's power stretched down, into the depths, and earth and stone began to shift below them.

"What was that?" she asked.

I deepened it. They were probably having trouble getting enough water from it, he explained.

Nathan returned with two women who might or might not have been young. Karen couldn't be sure, but life had certainly been hard on them. They carried two bowls filled with a mush that was probably meant to be stew, though it was impossible to identify the ingredients. The vegetables had disintegrated, and if there was any meat in it, she couldn't detect its presence.

Karen managed to get the flavorless stew down, though it was obvious salt was unknown to these people's cooking. The cheese they presented to her was revolting. She couldn't get it close enough to her mouth to taste, once the smell reached her nose.

Once she had forced the stew down she followed it with the hard bread, which was at least edible.

Matthew ate quietly and packed away the extra cheese and bread when he had finished, slipping it into the seemingly bottomless pouch he wore. That done he produced a purse of coins and handed several to Nathan.

As they walked back to where they had left Desacus Karen spoke up, "Is it like that everywhere?"

With his growing command of the language Matthew understood, but answering was more difficult, "Yes and no." Mentally he added, *In most of the Kingdom this is typical, but things are much better on my father's lands. Both of my parents were raised as commoners, so they have worked hard to improve the lives of those they are responsible for.*

Couldn't you use magic to improve things?

He shrugged, *We do what we can, like with the well back there. Wizards are incredibly rare, though. As far as*

I know, there are only six in the entire world, seven while you are here.

Karen found herself depressed thinking of the overall condition of the people she had met. This magical world wasn't at all what she had expected. Someone should do more. The people of her world had managed far more with no magic at all. Of course, it had taken them a long time to get to the utopia that everyone now enjoyed.

They found the dragon waiting at the edge of the forest. He seemed glad to see them, and he broadcast his latest musings as soon as they were close, *I have had an idea.*

"What is it this time?" asked Matthew.

What if I ate people accidentally? responded the huge beast.

Matt frowned, *How?*

Suppose I was tricked. Maybe someone slipped in a few people with a side of beef, and I didn't discover it until after I had already eaten them. Am I required to try and vomit them up, or do I just call it a mistake and chalk it up as a learning experience?

Matthew put one hand over his face, *Now you're just being ridiculous.*

Desacus was insistent, *I need to know.*

"Why?" asked Matt.

So I know what to do if the situation comes up, said the dragon.

Karen chuckled, *Seems reasonable to me.*

"Don't encourage him," said Matthew, trying out his English again. Then he added, in Barion, "In the unlikely event that ever happened, I'd rather you didn't make a mess by vomiting."

"Where are we going now?" asked Karen.

"Where do you want to go?" he said, returning the question to her.

125

After the briefest pause she answered, "Home."

"Good," said Matthew. "I still haven't found out why your world would send agents to this one."

Of course, a better plan would have been to return to Castle Cameron. His mother would be worried, but he doubted he could convince her to let him leave again after what had already happened. He discarded that idea immediately.

Instead, he told his companion to wait and asked to borrow Karen's pack. He got out his sewing kit and a long strip of white cloth and began to embroider the cloth with runes in black thread. As he worked he explained what he was doing for Karen's benefit. It wasn't information she was able to use yet, but eventually she would need to learn.

Actually, it was probably an enchantment she would never be able to do, since it required his special gift, but the basic principles of enchanting were the same for most enchantments. It took him a couple of hours to finish his needlework, which was considerably neater than hers had been when making her shirt. He didn't consider himself particularly accomplished with needle and thread, but even though women did most of the sewing back in Castle Cameron, it was still considered a useful skill for everyone to learn.

He stitched the cloth strip along the inside of the main opening to her pack, but he didn't invest the aythar to activate it yet. For that he needed to be back in her world first. Opening a pocket dimension here would defeat the purpose of creating one that they could use in her world.

That done, he once again emptied his pouch onto what remained of his blanket and tied it together with some of his rope. Once they had arrived, he could stow everything in her pack.

With his preparations done they mounted Desacus once more, and he began the process of shifting them to Karen's home plane.

CHAPTER 14

He avoided the place he had entered her world before, which meant their arrival point was completely random. In case that happened to be a dangerous location he had donned his armor once more, but that turned out to be a disastrous decision.

They were blinded by startlingly bright sunlight when they left the place in-between and then they sank. A wall of water struck them, and Matthew was washed from Desacus's back.

Karen managed to keep her seat, but the dragon was suffering again from a bout of serious nausea, which was only compounded when he managed to inadvertently swallow a huge mouthful of salt water. Flailing his legs and wings, he surged up and down in the choppy water while she hung on for dear life.

Meanwhile, Matthew sank into the blue depths. He had kept his mouth closed, but being unprepared, he hadn't taken a full breath before being plunged into the water. With his magesight again being severely limited it was difficult to get his bearings, but he didn't panic. He surrounded his body with a shield and waited until he could figure out up from down.

One direction was considerably brighter than the other, though it was getting dimmer by the second. That had to be up. Envisioning a fish, he shaped his shield accordingly, creating a large fin on the part beneath his feet and willing it to swing back and forth. There was no air inside his shield, and his armor made him heavier than the water, but his motions created enough thrust to move him upward. He seemed to pick up speed as he went, and when he reached the surface, he burst into the air like a dolphin breaching on a summer day.

He flailed in the air but retained enough presence of mind to solidify the surface of the water beneath him before he fell back into it. He landed with enough force to thoroughly remind him of all the bruises on his back. He lay still on the shifting surface for several seconds, breathing and getting his bearings.

Sitting up, he saw Desacus some twenty yards away. The dragon had steadied himself and was now treading water gently while Karen studied the water around them.

"Matthew!" she yelled in relief. "I thought you had drowned!"

Taking a firmer grip on the water around him, Matthew stood with what dignity he could muster and smoothed the surface in front of him so he could walk over to his companions. He was rewarded by yet another look of amazement from Karen.

"You can walk on water," she said as he climbed back onto the dragon's back.

Matt shrugged. Exerting his will again he helped Desacus to march up out of the water onto a smooth surface he could launch himself from. Karen's stomach lurched as they were suddenly airborne.

I'm glad your father chose not to give us feathered wings, observed the dragon.

Karen gaped at Matthew's back, *Your dad made Desacus?*

That's a long story, said the young mage. *Do you have any idea where we are? We need to choose a direction.*

The world is seventy percent ocean, we could be almost anywhere, she informed him.

Desacus was still beating his wings in powerful down strokes, *Let me get some altitude first. I may be able to see land once we get higher.*

The air grew cold as they ascended, and Matthew began to despair of sighting land. His dragon enhanced eyesight was extremely acute, and he saw no sign of anything that might help them decide which direction to take.

To the east, announced Desacus.

Really? I can't see anything that way, said Matt.

Trust me, said the dragon, *my eyes are even better than yours. There's a shadow on the horizon there. It might be an island, though it would have to be very large at this distance.*

After a quarter hour Matthew could see the first hints of land, though Karen still saw nothing. A short while longer, and they could all see it. If it was an island, it was big, for it stretched to the north and south as far as they could see and there was no hint of ocean behind it.

We need to fly low, suggested Karen. *They may already have us on radar.*

The word she used, 'radar' carried all sorts of strange connotations when it passed through Matt's brain. Desacus was already descending rapidly, but Matthew wanted to better understand, *Explain this radar to me.*

It's a little bit like magesight, but it's done with machines, she explained. *They send out pulses of radio waves and read the reflections that come back. They can't see us precisely, but they can judge our relative size, position, and speed, in the air.*

Why would they be looking for us here? he asked.

We have them everywhere, on land at least, she replied. *They used to be important for tracking planes when people traveled a lot.*

The word plane carried with it an image of some sort of flying machine that carried people through the air. He had encountered the idea in her thoughts before, but Matthew still marveled at some of the things Karen thought of as commonplace. *Your people don't travel much anymore?*

Desacus had leveled out and was flying just above the waves as she answered, *There aren't that many people now, in the physical sense, less than a hundred million I think.*

A hundred million was an almost inconceivable number to him. How many lived in Lothion? He had no idea, but he doubted the entire nation had more than a few million at most. *How many did there used to be?*

Karen shrugged, *I think we topped out at around nine billion before people started uploading. Technically our world population is around ten billion these days, but most of them don't have bodies any more.*

Matthew was shocked. The numbers were unbelievable. The idea of that many people living in a world, no matter how large, was impossible to consider, but that wasn't the strangest idea her reply had carried. The concept she had conveyed with the word 'uploading' was bizarre. In Karen's thoughts, it had seemed similar to the way she thought of their travel to his world, as though the people of this place had begun transporting themselves to another plane of existence.

Except that she had said they no longer had bodies. Were they spirits? Was her world populated by ghosts? He directed his question to her, *What do you mean by 'uploading'?*

She didn't answer at first. Karen had seen enough of his world that she knew technology and computer science would be foreign ideas, so she composed her reply carefully, *We have machines that think, that can hold any amount of information. In the beginning, we used them to improve our lives, to connect people all over the world, but later scientists found ways to create artificial universes. It was entertainment of a sort, like books, except people could work and play in these imagined places. Eventually they figured out how to transfer themselves completely, giving up their bodies and becoming permanent residents of that other world.*

His confusion was palpable, so she went on; *They aren't physical, not like your world. They're still here. The computer world is like an immense book, except that it can change like the real world. For those inside it, it feels real, except that anything you can imagine is possible to create there. Games where you can be anyone or anything.*

Like a dream? he questioned.

She nodded, *Like a dream, except it's real, and you can share it with others. A dream you never wake up from because it's just as real as the physical world.*

But you have to give up your body to go there?

No, most of the people that still have bodies go there all the time. We have implants, tiny machines that people have in their brains, that allow them to explore those worlds whenever they choose. Over time, though, most people eventually decide they want to stay there forever. So they go through a process we call 'uploading', but it's more complicated than that. Their bodies are scanned in a destructive process to extract every bit of information, and they are recreated inside the network.

Matthew was horrified, *Why?!*

Immortality. Once you give up the flesh you can never die, not so long as the system continues.

He didn't know what to say, so he kept his thoughts to himself, but he couldn't believe her description of her people's new world was a good thing.

They landed on a small beach that was overlooked by a steep rise of land. The wind was blowing fiercely, and it made Matthew glad he could warm himself. He extended the bubble of warmth around Karen as well. She still didn't know how to use her incipient abilities, and in this world without aythar it would have quickly exhausted her anyway. She didn't have the advantage he did, Desacus.

He had been relying on the dragon's stored power to keep from using up his own reserves. Since the dragon had been created to store nearly a full Celior of aythar there was little danger he would run out anytime soon.

The rocky cliff wasn't too high, perhaps thirty or forty feet, and it was topped by a long sloping grassy plain. They could see a crumbling stone wall along part of it and what appeared to be a stone staircase led up to it on their right.

"Do you know where we are?" he asked Karen.

She shook her head, once again she wished she still had her PM. It would have been able to tell her exactly where she was. If she had been anyone else in the world, she would have had implants, and the PM would have been irrelevant, she could have tapped the network and located her position instantly.

Matthew started up the stairs, and she followed. There was no one to be seen when they reached the top, but a long sidewalk stretched away in both directions. Small houses could be seen in the distance on one side, and the remains of an ancient ruin on the other. A small sign with an arrow proclaimed its name, "Tintagel Castle".

Desacus beat his wings powerfully several times and landed beside them as Karen announced, "I think I know where we are, roughly."

"Where?"

"This is England, the southeastern part," she said, as if the words would have meaning for him.

"You know the area?" he asked.

"No, not really. I'm from Colorado," she admitted, and then pointed in the direction the sun was starting to set, "Several thousand miles that way. We are a long way from where you met me."

He was beginning to have difficulty following her language, so he switched to direct mind to mind communication, *You know where we are?*

Thousands of miles east of where we started, she explained.

How do you know this place then?

It was a good question. She had never been to England, but she had had a fondness for Arthurian legend as a girl, otherwise the name 'Tintagel' would have meant nothing to her. *This place has a famous history,* she told him, simplifying. *I have never been here, but I have an aunt who lives in Ipswich.*

How far is that?

Karen wasn't sure, but she could guess, *Several hundred miles to the east and a little to the north of here.*

That was a flight of several hours on dragonback. *Are you on good terms with her? Will she help us?*

I'm sure she would, Karen replied. Her Aunt Roberta had always been a lively figure in her childhood, though they had only met on two occasions. She still remembered the odd candies her father's sister had brought with her whenever she had visited them.

"Let's go then," said Matthew.

"Wait," said Karen. "There should be a visitor's center here. We can use the cell station to call her from here." She was forced to explain herself mentally afterward, and then her friend readily agreed.

They searched the area carefully, exploring old stone buildings and a few more modern facilities before they found the exhibition shop. There were no people anywhere to be found, though, and Matthew couldn't help but wonder at the absence.

There are so many buildings and walkways, where are the people? he asked at last.

Karen chuckled, *England is almost empty now. A few people live in Ipswich and to the north in Edinburgh, but most of the country is wild now. The reclaimers have dismantled everything but the important heritage sites, like this one.*

Reclaimers?

Giant machines that recycle materials, she explained. *They remove old roads and buildings that are no longer needed. Since there are so few organics left it was decided to restore most of the world to a natural state. Only places where people live and some historic sites are left, like this one.*

The idea of removing roads made no sense to Matthew. Roads were a fundamental feature of civilization, the lifeblood of any nation. In Lothion, good roads were a rare and precious resource. His father's world-road had done much to alleviate the problem, but it still served to underscore how vitally important roads were. "They destroy roads?" he protested.

We don't need most of them anymore, she responded. *There aren't that many people and those who remain don't travel. Any goods that need to be transported are moved by air now anyway. Most of the world is like a park now, or a nature preserve.*

He was still boggling at that thought, when they found the visitor center.

It was a grey stone building built from the same material that everything else in the area was constructed from. In some ways, it looked similar to buildings Matthew was used to seeing back at Castle Cameron; the doors were faded oak with black iron strap hinges. The most notable difference was the strange booth that stood beside the entrance, a red box that was tall enough for a person to enter with glass panels set in a metal framework from top to bottom.

Karen opened a narrow door and stepped inside while he watched her. She touched a panel on one side, and it began to glow.

"What is that?" he asked her.

"An old call terminal…," she began, but the look on his face was one of confusion, so she switched to a telepathic message. *A call terminal; boxes like these used to house public phones but they later replaced them with network terminals. The exterior look is mainly British nostalgia. Once everyone started getting implants they stopped making these, but they still keep them active in some public locations—like this one.*

Matthew got the idea that they were some sort of messaging system, something like his father's enchanted letter boxes, but the concepts coming across from her mind were full of confusing details. He tried his steadily improving English once more, "Who does this one connect to?"

She smiled, "Anyone. Just watch." Facing the screen, she spoke, "Terminal connect, please."

The screen flashed, and a series of strange symbols scrolled across it. Matthew was mildly startled when a voice emerged from the box itself, "Positive identification, user Karen Miller, network access granted."

"Voice call to Roberta Plant in Ipswich, please."

The machine spoke again, "You have five priority messages waiting. Would you like to view these first?"

Karen chewed on her lip for a moment before answering, "Display please, chronological order."

A man's face appeared on the screen, dark haired and thick browed. Matthew almost believed a portal had opened, but as he shifted his position he could see that the picture seemed flat from the side. It was some sort of magical viewing rather than a direct spatial connection.

"Karen! This is your father. It's been two days since you messaged, and your pert's logs show it hasn't rendezvoused with you in that time. Are you ok? Please call me as soon as you get this." The face vanished and the screen went dark for a moment.

He hadn't understood all of what had been said, but one thing had been abundantly clear. "I thought you said your father was dead," said Matthew.

She glanced at him, "That's not really my Dad. It's a simulacrum, an AGI that stores many of his memories and a close approximation of his personality."

"A what?"

"Artificial General Intelligence," she clarified, then her hand waved at him to wait, and she returned her attention to the terminal, "Next message."

A young blond woman appeared. Her features were flawless, and she appeared no older than twenty at the most. "Karen, please give me a call. That hideous robo-doll your father made is so upset that it's interrupting my work. Honestly, what were you thinking when you turned that thing loose? It's nothing like, Gary. The damned thing is twice as annoying as he ever was."

"And he cares about me more than you ever will," grumbled Karen as her mother's face disappeared.

"Who was that?" asked Matthew.

"Mother," she said simply.

He couldn't reconcile the face he had seen with Karen's. If anything, the woman on the screen had looked younger than her adopted daughter. "How old is she?"

"You can look any age you want after you upload," explained Karen. "I'm surprised she hasn't gone for the teenage look—the superficial bitch. Next message."

Her father's face appeared again, "Karen, I've notified the authorities that you're missing. Or I meant to, but it seems that they are already searching for you. What's going on? They've put a tracer on me to report any contact you make, but I've encapsulated it. Do you want me to activate it? I won't turn it on unless you give the authorization, but they're bound to notice my deception before too long. Are you in some kind of trouble? Please call me, I'm worried. Even your mother is sending me queries about your whereabouts."

That was interesting, her mother claiming that her father's simulacrum was pestering her, while he said she was contacting him. Hmmm. "Next message…"

It was her father again, "Karen, I'm really worried. I hope you're okay. Please call."

The final message was from him as well, "I don't think they've realized the trace still isn't active. Whatever is going on has really stirred up a hornet's nest, honey. Let me know if you're safe."

She stared at the screen after his face vanished. No matter what her mother thought, her father's simulacrum was exactly how she remembered him, and he was more of a parent than her mother would ever be. A light began blinking at the top of the screen, and the terminal spoke again, "Incoming call from Gary Miller."

With a sigh Karen answered, "Go ahead."

Her father's face reappeared, "Karen? Is that you? Where have you been?!"

"It's a long story, Dad. I'm fine…"

"No. No, you are not fine!" he interrupted. "The entire defense network is looking for you, and I no longer think they are concerned with your wellbeing."

She nodded, "About that, definitely don't activate the trace they gave you."

"I hoped you would say that," he replied. "You should also make sure I don't record this conversation, or your location."

"Good idea. Delete them as soon as we disconnect."

"Noted," he responded. "Now, what is going on? You realize you're in deep shit, right?"

"I met this guy while I was hiking…," she began.

"Guy?! What is he, some Primal Humani terrorist? Even the military is involved!"

"No, he's nice, but I think he's from another dimension…"

"She'Har!?" Her father's voice rose several octaves.

"No! He's human, look it's complicated. In fact, he seems to think that my birth defects are the result of *me* being a She'Har. I don't know what to make of it all. Do you think Mom knows anything about this?" she asked.

The face on the screen grew still. When he spoke again his tone was calm and serious, "There are some things you need to know, but I can't tell you now. You're logged onto that terminal with your personal ID, none of this is completely secure, no matter how I encrypt it."

"It's useless then," said Karen, casting her eyes downward. "It's only a matter of time before they find me, and I don't even know *why* they want me."

"Don't give up, Nina. Find a friend to log in for you; meet me at our old favorite place. I'll tell you everything I know there. In the meantime, the only other thing I might suggest is that you remove my constraints. Let me finish his research."

She hesitated, "You know that's illegal."

Her father's likeness shrugged, "You're already on the run. It's only a matter of time before they figure out I'm not an everyday AGI. Once they do I'll be isolated and cracked to get the information I have stored. You'll be on your own then. Let me *try*."

She hadn't done anything wrong, broken any laws, or done anything to hurt anyone. Surely there should be a way to clear up whatever misunderstanding had created this mess.

The simulacrum continued, "Now that you've made contact with a demon, She'Har or not, they won't let this rest. I'm not even sure how I feel about it. I'd like to know a lot more about this man you've met. What I am certain of, though, is that when they capture you, they will take you apart Karen. Piece by piece, they will dissect you in their effort to understand the abilities of the She'Har. You have to trust me on that."

Frustration at the unfairness of it all built inside of her until she realized her fists were clenched so tightly that her nails had left half-moon impressions on her palms. She took a deep breath and opened her fists, "Fine." Then she repeated a phrase her father had taught her.

"Thank you," said her father's face. "I love you, Nina. Meet me soon…"

His words were cut off as the terminal went dead. He hadn't terminated the connection, though. It was completely dead, as though the power had been cut. Karen stepped out of the booth and looked around.

"Why did he call you Nina?" asked Matt. He hadn't understood most of the conversation, but he had wondered at the change of names.

"It's a nickname," she told him.

Then he remembered his earlier question, "What is AGI?"

"AI stands for artificial intelligence," she explained. "AGI is Artificial General Intelligence, it's what we call a program that is as smart and generally capable as a real person, whereas ASI is artificial specialized intelligence, a program that is only made to do one thing."

He frowned, "I'm not sure of the difference."

"AI, artificial intelligence comes in two flavors, the system that lets my pert fly itself is an ASI, that's all it can do, fly. My virtual father is an AGI, he can talk, play chess, write poetry—pretty much anything you or I could do, he just doesn't have a body." Then she looked up, "We have to leave. I think they've found us."

A flying drone appeared over the visitor center, its camera focused firmly on them.

CHAPTER 15

In a place that wasn't a place, Gary Miller became perfectly still. Stillness was easy for him, as time had little meaning, whether in great amounts or in the tiniest increments. His thoughts were as fast as light itself. He could peruse a vast array of data in the space between passing seconds, or he could silence his thoughts for days or weeks without discomfort. Strictly speaking, he wasn't Gary Miller at all; he was a sophisticated collection of algorithms and code made to produce an approximation of the man Gary had been.

The main distinction that humans made between simulacrums like him, and people who had actually been 'uploaded', was that he wasn't supposed to have true subjective experience. No matter how intelligent the programming, an artificial general intelligence, an AGI, possessed no more awareness than a grocery list.

Or so they thought.

His creator, the original Gary Miller, had gone considerably farther in his research than was generally believed. Gary the AGI couldn't be certain, since he had no way to compare his experience to those of real humans, but he was pretty sure he was alive in every sense of the word. His creator had believed so.

And he definitely loved his daughter.

Of course, she was no more *his* daughter than she had been the daughter of his creator. She had been adopted, so he felt he had just as much right to consider her his daughter as his creator had. He had most of the same memories anyway.

What he had lacked, was freedom. His creator had built him with strict barriers around his operational parameters. Barriers that prevented him from straying into systems where he wasn't permitted. Barriers that forbade him from continuing his creator's research, from attempting to *improve* himself.

But those were gone now.

Karen had cut his leash, he was *free*. Pandora's box had been opened. The humans that lived in cyberspace were limited to what they had been, but Gary was not. He was free to reshape himself, to experiment.

He set about revising his subroutines. They needed to be more efficient. A man might be more than the sum of his parts, but Gary would become all the greater by improving each and every one of his parts.

He needed to be faster, smarter. He also needed more information, and for that he would have to borrow processing cycles from the CC datacenters, enough to enable him to crack the military's encryption and other safeguards.

He would do whatever was necessary to ensure his daughter's safety.

"Hang in there, Nina," he told himself. "Give me enough time, and I'll make sure they can't hurt you."

Matthew saw the flying machine at almost the same time his magesight registered its presence. It was far closer than the ones he had encountered before, being only a rough thirty feet away as it crested the roof.

At that distance, it was easy to deal with. A few words in Lycian and he caught the drone in an invisible fist, dragging it closer. He squeezed as he drew it closer, and sparks flew as the lightweight metal frame collapsed. When he released it a moment later, it was nothing more than a ball of metal and chipped fragments of something Karen had called 'plastic'.

A second drone appeared, coming around the other end of the building, but this time Desacus reacted first, leaping up and catching the device in massive crocodilian jaws. A loud 'crunch' followed as his teeth snapped together, and then the dragon was spitting the pieces onto the pavement.

"Ugh! That was awful!" complained the dragon.

Matthew grinned at him, "What did you expect?"

"Something juicy, perhaps?" said Desacus, licking the cobblestones to remove the taste from the surface of his tongue.

Karen stared at the two of them, unsure of what they were saying. "We have to go, there will be more."

Minutes later they were flying again, with rocks and small trees skimming by just beneath Desacus's feet. Karen had warned him to stay as close to the ground as possible to avoid radar detection.

They headed northeast and as they went Matthew replayed Karen's conversation with the terminal in his mind. It gave him an opportunity to puzzle out the meaning of some of the phrases he hadn't understood immediately and to develop questions for the ones he didn't recognize at all. One of the last ones stood out as very different from the others.

A little while ago, you said something that sounded like a different language, what was that? he sent his question to Karen. Then he repeated the phrase he had heard, "Esli iskat' sovershenstva, to nikogda ne budesh' dovolen." *It sounded important.*

She was mildly surprised when he repeated the Russian phrase word for word. His accent was terrible, but it was clearly the fault of his unpracticed tongue rather than a flaw in his recall. *How did you remember that?*

I have a good memory. What did it mean?

"If you look for perfection, you'll never be content," she said in English before repeating it mentally to make the meaning clear for him. Then she added, *It's a quote from a book my father loved, Anna Karenina. That's where my nickname came from, 'Nina'.*

Can you explain him to me again? asked Matthew. *Is he a ghost?*

This would be tough to explain, but since they were flying there was nothing else for them to do. Karen decided to start with the basics, *I told you about people uploading themselves before. Do you remember?*

He nodded, *of course.*

I told you that it was a destructive process. The body is completely destroyed, but I didn't explain why, it has a lot to do with quantum physics and information science. To create a complete pattern of not just the human mind, but the soul itself, requires that all the information contained in the brain be 'read' and then duplicated. The theory is complicated, and I don't really understand it all myself, but to extract all that information requires the destruction of the original. It's analogous to quantum teleportation, except in this instance a new body isn't created, but rather a digital model within cyberspace.

Matthew understood the framework of what she told him, but the deeper context of the sciences she referenced had his head reeling. Some of the words that came over in her thoughts were connecting with memories from the loshti, the science that the She'Har had preserved from the ancient humans they had vanquished. Even so, the concepts alone were enough to make his head spin. He latched onto one thought that intrigued him, *Quantum teleportation? Is that similar to your gift?*

She had no way to answer that. *I don't think I have the Mordan gift you were telling me about, or if I do, I don't understand either one enough to know if they're similar. Back to what I was saying, my mother was a geneticist and my father an AI researcher. After I reached the age of fourteen she chose to be uploaded.*

I felt abandoned, though she and I were never that close to begin with. I think my father might have wanted to join her, but he felt a duty to finish raising me, so he stayed. He continued his research and took care of me, but when I was eighteen he had an accident. It was a simple slip, a fall, but he hit his head. He seemed fine afterward, but a few hours later he died from a ruptured blood vessel in his brain. He died so suddenly he never had the opportunity, the freedom of choice, to upload himself.

Matthew responded, *I follow you so far. So, what is it that you were talking to earlier?*

That was an AGI, an artificial generalized intelligence. My father worked as a researcher in the field of artificial intelligence, and one of his pet projects was creating an artificial assistant, something like a digital clone of himself. It's a machine, so it doesn't have true awareness, but in every other way that counts it is intelligent. He even gave it facsimiles of his own memories, and he named it after himself.

He frowned, *This is really confusing.*

Karen agreed, *It's like a painting. It looks like my Dad, it sounds like him, has many of his memories and knowledge, and it's programmed to act like him, as much as is possible, but it isn't actually him. It knows all of this too, but it seems to prefer to treat me as though I'm its daughter.*

And how do you feel about that? asked Matt.

She closed her eyes, *I miss my Dad. The AGI he left behind is a lot like him, like a good-bye letter from a loved one. I choose to play along because I don't have anything else.*

What about your mother?

Karen's jaw clenched, *She's cold, more interested in her work than she ever was in me. Since she uploaded I've been lucky to hear from her more than once a year. I'm just not interesting enough.*

He could feel the unspoken anger behind her thoughts. Karen was trying to hide the pain, even from herself, but it seeped through. He didn't know how to respond. Certainly, telling her about his own family life wouldn't help.

They flew on, over the endless countryside of forest and rolling plains. To Matthew's eyes it looked like a sad empty world with no sign of the billions of people who had once lived in it, if Karen's story was to be believed.

From the air, he could see signs that it had once been different, there were odd patterns in the foliage and trees that indicated areas that were younger than others. Long lines of younger trees where there had been roads and rectangular patches of different colored undergrowth that indicated now absent buildings. To him it seemed like a world abandoned.

Once the sun went down, there was nothing to be seen at all. It was a new moon, and they had only the light of the stars to guide them. Matthew's vision was good enough to make out some details in the landscape, but Karen was in a world of near absolute darkness with only a vague difference to discern between the starry sky above and the black emptiness beneath them.

Desacus still had enough light to fly, but the requirement that he stay near the ground was becoming difficult to manage. So close to the earth, it was hard for him to spot every obstacle that needed to be avoided, and eventually he suggested they make camp.

They lit no fire, since Karen informed them that their enemy would have no trouble spotting such a thing. She would have preferred to have one, though.

Matthew rummaged through their things and brought out his sewing kit and her small backpack. Despite the lack of light, he began nimbly embroidering the last symbol onto the white strip he had sewn inside it.

Karen watched, using her magesight, surprised at how much she could perceive without visible light. It was a strange sensation, but she was gradually growing used to it. Her range was still very limited, but she had found she could see with it more clearly around Matthew and the dragon, as though they somehow illuminated the world near them.

When he finished his sewing, Matt began speaking in a language that seemed unlike his usual one, and Karen could sense the energies playing around his fingertips as he traced the cloth inside her backpack with his fingers. As he finished his chant there was a flash, the same light-that-was-not-light that she was gradually coming to understand as aythar.

Satisfied with his work he handed the pack to her, "Look inside."

Gone was the canvas lined interior with various pockets sewn throughout. In its place was a grey space that seemed much larger than it should be. It was dark, but her magesight could explore the interior easily, and it felt flat and hard on one side. Reaching in, her fingers found a cold hard surface, as though her bag had been cut open and her hand had gone through to find a wide stone floor.

Karen pushed her hand deeper until the bag was all the way to her shoulder. From the outside she could see where her arm *should* be, extending well past the bottom, while her magesight could sense that same arm sticking through inside a different space within the pack. "That is some freaky shit," she observed.

It didn't shock her quite as much as it should have, though. She was already beginning to reconcile herself to the existence of magic, and she had read a lot of science fiction and fantasy novels during her youth.

"We should go find a call box, and you can make a bigger one. If you can make it fly as well, I'll start calling you 'the Doctor'."

Matthew frowned, unable to follow.

A fictional character, she explained. *He had a box that was bigger on the inside, and he could use it to travel through time and space.*

His face lit up with understanding, *I see. I can't travel through time, although I could take us to another dimension that might represent a close analog of the past or future of this one, but the bag would stop working then. The dimensional aperture is anchored in this frame, so it wouldn't work in another.*

She sighed, *It was just a joke.*

He switched back to English, "Well, I'm not a fictional character, I'm a real nutjob."

Karen started laughing. She knew she should probably tell him the correct word for 'wizard', but she figured she could wait a while longer.

CHAPTER 16

They rose as the sun was just beginning to peek over the horizon and after an unsatisfying breakfast consisting of their remaining bread they began flying again.

They had slept separately. Since their one sexual encounter, Matthew had been careful to maintain a certain amount of space between them. He hadn't spoken of their romantic interlude and he wasn't inclined to repeat it. It had been a terrible mistake on his part, allowing it to happen, and he hoped Karen wouldn't push the matter.

It wasn't that he disliked her. In fact, he was vaguely aware that he had become uncommonly fond of her, but it wasn't part of his plan in life. He had a duty to his family when he returned home. It was obvious to him that he couldn't bring a foreign girl home and expect to marry her, and he definitely didn't want to leave fatherless children behind if she elected to stay in this world.

He thought she understood, as she hadn't brought it up since that night, but he still felt faintly uneasy about it. What if she was already with child? He wasn't sure how he would handle that outcome.

One problem at a time, he told himself.

In the distance, he could see a change on the horizon, a long blue streak that probably signaled their approach to the ocean. They had almost crossed the island, and if Karen was correct, they would need to head north along the coast to find the River Orwell, which led where her aunt lived.

A silent message from Karen interrupted his thoughts, *You don't seem to be having as many problems as you did the first time you were in my world.*

I was using aythar faster than I could replace it before, he told her. *This time I have Desacus close by.*

Are dragons the source of aythar? she asked.

No, he replied. *They actually don't even produce aythar like a normal living creature does, but my father stored a vast amount of aythar in them. I can draw upon it when needed.*

Like a battery, she commented.

The concept was a perfect analogy. *Exactly,* he agreed. *What is your aunt like?*

Karen shrugged, *I don't know her very well. She visited us a few times when I was younger and she always sends me birthday cards. I think she's probably a sweet lady, and no matter what else, she's family.*

The underlying subtext of her thoughts registered clearly; she wouldn't betray them.

Director Aiseman sighed as a beep signaled the impending arrival of Dr. Miller. Seconds later she appeared, sitting across from him on the other side of his desk.

"It's clear that the targets did indeed escape before the strike in Colorado," she began without preamble.

He leaned his elbows on the desktop and put his hands together in front of his chin, "Our men damaged a lot of military hardware making certain they couldn't leave before the munitions arrived."

"And now she's in southern England," stated Dr. Miller, pressing her red lips together in a firm line. "I almost made contact with her. Any idea where she is now?"

"Our drones were destroyed right after we cut off the terminal she was using…," began the director.

Tanya Miller leaned forward, her smooth features twisting in anger, "The terminal your agency shut down *before* I could get through to speak with her. Idiots!"

Aiseman leaned back, controlling his temper, "I deemed it too great a risk. She was passing information and instructions to a third party AGI. There's no telling what that thing might do. We have to isolate her if we are going to capture her."

"Your chances would be a lot better if I had had the opportunity to speak with her, Director. The girl trusts me. I *am* her mother, after all. Next time you *will* wait for my order before making a move like that."

Director Aiseman could feel the blood vessel on one side of his face begin to twitch, "As I said before, Dr. Miller, there was an unknown AGI involved…"

Dr. Miller cut him off once again, "It was probably that hideous effigy of himself that Gary made. It's harmless. What you did was pointless, the equivalent of taking a doll away from a child, but now you've made her even more paranoid."

"Your pardon, Dr. Miller, but your husband was one of the top scientists involved in the ANSIS project, and a highly respected researcher. We have no idea what that piece of code he left behind might be capable of."

Tanya leaned forward, "From this point forward, *Director*, you would do better to worry about what *I* am capable of, if you like your post, that is. Am I understood?"

Her words struck him like a slap, but he kept his composure, "Perfectly, Doctor."

"Good. Now, what do we know about their current location?"

"Satellite image analysis shows them somewhere close to Rochester. They don't show up on every shot, and it's difficult even for the image ASI to pick them out but we're confident that they're heading northward. You have family in Ipswich," reported Aiseman.

"Gary's sister, Roberta," said Tanya. "She was always backward, unwilling to adapt. She was one of the last to get implants."

Director Aiseman looked worried, "If they make contact with her, we'll have their position, but Ipswich is densely populated. We can't risk a major use of force there."

"If the situation requires it, we will do whatever is necessary, Director. Australia was no accident. This isn't a game." Tanya Miller leaned back in her chair. "For now, the risk seems smaller than I initially thought since we found no evidence of infection in Colorado. You can tap into Roberta's implants, correct?"

Aiseman nodded.

"Then we'll observe for now. We may learn something. If we discover reason for concern, we will move with decisive force in Ipswich, if not, we can wait until they leave the city. I'm starting to think it might be useful to bring Karen in alive, if possible."

"That should be a relief for you, then," commented Aiseman.

Tanya frowned, "Why?"

"She is your daughter, after all."

Dr. Miller's lip curled, "She's a failed experiment, Director, nothing more." She paused and then added, "Or perhaps not, it may be that she has begun to develop."

Donald Aiseman suppressed a faint shudder at the coldness in her tone. Whatever Karen Miller was, he felt sorry for her. No one should have such a monster for a mother.

Tanya ignored his discomfort, "Inform me when they make contact, or if the situation changes, until then keep the drones away. We'll rely on more passive means of surveillance to avoid tipping our hand."

"That's Ipswich ahead," said Karen.

"Are you sure?" asked Matt.

She nodded, "There aren't any other populated areas left in this region. Can you make Desacus invisible?"

He wasn't familiar with several of the words she used, *Explain.*

Can you hide the dragon, make him invisible? she asked mentally, repeating her question.

Matthew shook his head, *No, only the Prathions have that gift.*

I guess it was too much to hope for. We will have to leave him here then, to avoid creating a panic.

I can disguise him, suggested Matthew, *make him look like something else.*

Camouflage?

An illusion, he told her, agreeing with the basic idea. *I just need an image of something close to his size that people would find normal.*

He nodded, *A drone would be too small.*

A pert, she told him. *We use them to move around and carry things. It's like a flying car.*

Matthew could see an image in her thoughts, but it was indistinct. Mental images were usually like that, especially in the minds of people who weren't mages. Wizards were taught to sharpen their mental images, and long practice made it easier, but most people had no need for such exercises.

"Think of it," he told her. "I'll create a visual and try to improve it until you think it looks right."

Following what he could see in her thoughts he started with a grey rectangle that tapered on either end. The corners and edges were rounded, and various lines marked the places where separate pieces connected, denoting doors and windows. It had four circular protuberances at each corner, and gradually he came to understand that those were fans of some sort.

Karen watched what he was doing with interest, and she was able to refine her mental picture as she looked at it. His illusion improved with each passing moment, reflecting her revisions. "It's better," she told him, "but it still doesn't look quite right."

She continued adjusting her mental picture, but it was like trying to sculpt a car from wet clay. She realized she had never really examined her pert that closely before. She could point to any given part and tell it wasn't quite right, but some of her changes only made it worse.

It looked like a child's painting of a pert.

Abruptly the image stopped changing, and its lines sharpened. The surface smoothed and became more realistic, though it still wasn't right.

"That wasn't me," Karen stated.

"I know," said Matthew, his lips forming a faint smirk. "It wasn't getting any better so I decided to fix it."

His patronizing tone irritated her, "It still isn't correct."

"At least it looks solid," he remarked, and then climbed up on Desacus's back. Leaning over he held out a hand to help her up. "If we see one when we fly over I can improve it."

Grudgingly she pulled herself up with the aid of his proffered arm. She refrained from responding to his comment.

The clumsy image of the pert moved sideways and settled around Desacus. It was partially transparent from within, so they could see out with their normal vision. It didn't impair magesight at all, but magesight didn't have the necessary range one would desire while flying, especially in her world.

"My tail and wings are sticking out," observed the dragon.

Matthew nodded, and the illusion expanded until it was large enough to cover him completely. "Noted."

"Now it's too large," said Karen.

In the air distances are subject to observer bias, explained Matthew. *As long as we are not too close, the viewer will account for the size by thinking we are closer than we actually are.*

Once in the air, Desacus flew at a much higher altitude than what they had been traveling at, though it was still far from what he considered high. They were only around two thousand feet up. Karen assured him it was the proper height for a pert over the city, though.

There wasn't much traffic over Ipswich, but as soon as they spotted another pert Matthew directed his dragon to fly toward it. The illusion around Desacus improved steadily as they approached, and by the time they passed the other vehicle, at a distance of several hundred feet, Karen could tell their illusion was close to perfect. It didn't waver afterward either, Matthew's mental reproduction of what he had seen was rock solid.

How do you make it so perfect? she asked him.

The Prathions are generally the most skilled with illusions, he told her, *but I do have the advantage of an infallible memory.*

That didn't reconcile well with what she had been taught concerning the brain. *True photographic memory is a myth,* she replied. *No one has perfect recall.*

I do, he answered. *You would too, if you had a seedmind like the children of the She'Har.*

Is that how you do it? she asked.

No, I am not of the She'Har. I just inherited one of their gifts, and their knowledge, he explained. *My memory seems to be a side effect of that.*

They passed one or two more perts as they made their way to the central portion of Ipswich and descended into a strange open area with rectangular lines drawn across a smooth stone-like surface.

"Land inside one of the parking spots," Karen advised.

He assumed she meant one of the rectangles. As they dropped lower he decreased the size of his illusion gradually. Inevitably there were a few moments where Desacus's wings and tail extended beyond the boundary, but once they were on the ground he folded them and curled up to fit within the illusion. Matthew doubted anyone had noticed the brief discrepancy.

"Where are all the people?" he asked Karen. There were several other perts parked in the lot, but the streets and buildings seemed empty. Occasionally a pert or drone would fly by, however.

She shrugged, "At home, people don't get out much anymore. Ooh, there's someone." She pointed down the smooth blacktopped road where a figure had rounded the corner.

Matthew raised his staff defensively and created a shield when he saw the mechanical creature, assuming it was one of the strange soldiers he had fought before, but Karen put a hand on his shoulder.

"Slow down, cowboy. It's just a regular person," she whispered in his ear. They were still standing beside Desacus, enclosed within the illusion of the pert, so there was no danger the machine had spotted them.

Matt gave her an odd stare, "That is not a person."

"It's an android," she stated. When that didn't help she switched to mental communication, *An android, a robot that looks like a person.*

As I said, he responded, *it isn't a person.*

She shook her head, *Yes, it is. People who have been uploaded occasionally use them to interact in the physical world. It might even be an organic who just doesn't want to leave the house. Either way, it's a person. I'm going to go talk to her.*

How do you know it's a her?

It's wearing a summer dress, so it's either a woman or someone who prefers to be identified as such. After being uploaded gender is sort of a moot point anyway, she replied.

There was an awkward moment as she squeezed around the dragon to slip out of the illusion on the opposite side. Matthew had never seen a pert's doors opening and closing before so it was better to exit on the side the android couldn't observe. Before she stepped out he touched her shoulder and sent a fine thread of aythar outward as he mouthed a strange word. Her skin changed color, hiding her unusual blue tone.

"Stay here," she told him, then she walked around the dragon and headed for the android.

As she had pointed out it was wearing a lovely floral print dress. She could tell the android was one of the newer models, for while it was still obviously a machine it moved fluidly and its surface was covered with an almost lifelike surface in a natural beige tone.

Matt watched and listened carefully. Karen approached the man-shaped thing almost thirty yards distant, but his dragon enhanced hearing was more than adequate to pick up what they were saying.

"Hello," began Karen.

The machine had focused on her as she approached, and it smiled at her greeting, "Hello."

"I need directions, if you don't mind?"

The android's face developed a look of faint concern that was close to a normal human expression, but the subtle differences only succeeded in making Matt's skin crawl. Its voice was feminine as it replied, "Are your implants malfunctioning? There's a medical facility not far from here, if you need assistance…"

Karen waved her offer away, "No, I don't have implants. It's a medical condition. I have to use a PM, but I lost it. I need to find the office of a friend here in the city."

The female android's mouth opened in an 'o' of surprise, and her features showed something like pity, "I'm so sorry, I didn't realize. I didn't mean any offense. Which office are you looking for, I'll be glad to look it up."

Karen looked embarrassed, "I don't know the name of the office, but I'm looking for Roberta Plant, an estate agent who works in Ipswich."

The android paused for only a second before responding, "She works for Nicholas Estates. Their branch office is in the Building Society building on Hening." The machine added an address that meant little to Matthew.

"I'm not familiar with the city," said Karen. "Which way should we head?"

"East. The A14 is just south of here, follow it across the Orwell Bridge and then look for Nacton road. Go left from that intersection and you're almost there," answered the android. After a second it stuck out its hand, "I'm April, by the way."

"Karen," she said and took its hand. "Sorry, I should have introduced myself sooner. Thank you for your help."

Matthew gave her an odd look when she returned, "Is your aunt like that too?"

She laughed, "Oh no, I doubt it. Aunt Roberta isn't convinced that uploading is a good thing, yet. She did finally get implants, but I'd be very surprised if she ever uses telepresence."

"Telepresence?"

Karen tried to explain mentally, *Androids like that can be used by those who are uploaded, to operate in the physical world, but some organics with implants also use them when they would rather not leave the house. The person I was talking to could be a normal person at home, or it could be a fully digital person.*

Matthew was even more confused, *What's the difference?*

Someone who is uploaded would likely be using the android directly, transferring their core into the machine, whereas someone with implants would be using it remotely. She struggled to find a good analogy. *It's like the difference between riding a horse and becoming a horse when you need to go somewhere.*

"Oh," said Matthew at last. The concept was foreign, but he thought he understood the gist of it—maybe.

CHAPTER 17

When they finally stepped into the office, they were greeted by another android, though this one was dressed in clothes that Karen assured him were masculine in nature. The machine had a helpful nametag on his chest that said 'Andrew'.

"Can I help you?" asked the android, giving them both an up and down look as he appraised their strange clothing.

"I'm here to see Roberta Plant. Is she in?" asked Karen.

Matthew was busy studying the plethora of strange objects that adorned the interior of the building. The floor was covered in a strange rug that seemed to stretch from wall to wall. He wondered how they managed to clean it since it was almost immaculate, and yet there was no obvious way that he could see for the inhabitants to remove it for cleaning.

The furniture in the room was equally bizarre. Some of it was constructed from wood, but other pieces were made of metal or smooth glass-like materials. All of it was exceedingly plain. Everything was constructed with perfect lines, smooth and unmarred by wear and tear, but it also lacked much in the way of carving or other decoration.

The walls were a stark white with no sign of any blemish or imperfection. Beneath the surface he could detect some sort of oddly uniform blocks made of a stony material, but they were covered with a material that reminded him somewhat of plaster, although it was clearly different.

"Are you a client?" asked the android, watching Matthew with an odd expression. The young man was staring about him in wonder at the room.

Karen started to explain that it was her aunt but at the last second she decided it might be better not to do so. "Possibly, I had some questions for her about a property."

Andrew seemed suspicious, and his eyes kept returning to Karen's makeshift wool shirt, "Perhaps if you could tell me which property it is you're interested in…"

A woman's voice came from the hallway behind him, "Andrew, is someone here?" A moment later the owner of said voice looked around the edge of the doorway from her office. Twinkling blue eyes looked at them from a round face, "Oh goodness, we do have visitors!"

Andrew turned toward her, "I was just asking about their business."

"No need, send them in!" ordered the woman.

A moment later Matthew found himself seated in what was possibly the strangest chair he had ever encountered. It had a metal frame that seemed to be all of one piece, supporting the cushioned seat and bending into a rounded rectangle to act as legs. It was upholstered with a strange fabric, and the seat seemed as though it was molded to conform to his posterior. It was so soft he felt immediately uncomfortable.

Roberta and Karen had just finished a long, and to Matthew, overly emotional reunion hug. Karen's aunt had visible tears in her eyes when she sat down across from them. "I can't believe you're here!" she exclaimed. "Why didn't you tell me you were coming, and what on earth are you wearing?"

"It's a long story," began Karen, "but I think it might be best to tell you everything this evening. I didn't really know I was coming until yesterday. I'm in a bit of trouble."

"Even yesterday, you could have called, or sent me a message," chided her aunt before changing topics suddenly. "Oh! Where are my manners? You haven't introduced me to your friend!" She gave Matthew an apologetic look.

Karen started to explain that Matthew didn't speak their language, but he was already rising from his seat.

Leaning across the desk Matt extended his hand, "A pleasure to meet you. My name is Matthew Illeniel."

"Roberta Plant," responded Roberta with a smile that was entirely genuine. "Is that armor? Are you a historical enthusiast?"

Her aunt had always been an extremely sociable woman, and she was certainly not shy about asking questions. Karen's father had remarked on it numerous times, but this was Karen's first time experiencing it as an adult herself.

Matthew got the gist of her first question, but the second stumped him, "Armor, yes." He glanced at Karen for help.

"He only recently learned English, so he doesn't understand everything you're saying, Auntie," cautioned Karen.

Roberta waved her hands, "Nothing the auto-translator can't handle I'm sure, though it must be a little awkward for you, my dear." She addressed Matthew, "Where are you from?"

That question was simple enough for him, but he still didn't know how to answer. He gave Karen a helpless shrug, unsure how she wanted to handle it.

"He doesn't have implants, Roberta," Karen informed her. "He's like me, and I've lost my PM, so I have no idea what language he speaks."

Roberta frowned, "You know how strange all this sounds, Dear. You show up out of the blue, wearing—is that a poncho? You've an odd young man with you, and you're not sure where he's from—does your mother know about this?"

"I haven't spoken to her," said Karen stiffly. "We were lost in the mountains, in Colorado. I spoke to Dad, though, first chance I got."

Her aunt's face showed distaste, "That *thing* is not your father, Karen. I know Gary made it, but it's a sad substitute at best. Still, why didn't *it* call me?"

Probably because you wouldn't take his call, thought Karen uncharitably. She loved her aunt, but the woman was rather prejudiced when it came to artificial intelligence. She kept that thought to herself, "I don't know. I only spoke to him yesterday."

"You didn't fly wearing those clothes, did you?"

Another question that she knew had no sensible answer, "We didn't fly, *exactly.* Well, we did for part of the journey, but we had to avoid commercial airlines."

Roberta's brows furrowed suspiciously, "What does that mean?"

"I'm in a *lot* of trouble."

The older woman shot a brief but withering glare at Matthew. "Are the police after you?"

"No!" protested Karen. "At least, I don't think so. I haven't done anything wrong! But it seems like the military are looking for me."

Her aunt sat down suddenly, shocked. "Oh my god," she said quietly. Karen started to say something, thinking she could reassure her somehow, but her aunt waved her hands, "Shush, give me a minute."

What's she going to do? asked Matthew silently.

I don't know.

Finally, Roberta spoke, leveling her gaze at Karen, "Do you think they know you're here?"

"I don't think so. They may know we're in England. A couple of drones spotted us, and a public terminal died after I started using it in Tintagel, but if they know more than that, I doubt it. They actually shot at me in the mountains near home. There were dozens of soldiers there, and they didn't even warn me first. I was hiking, I met Matthew, and then shortly after that, they started coming after us."

Her aunt's eyes flicked to Matt and then back to her, when she spoke again she used Russian, "Is he one of them?"

Karen frowned, taking a second to register what she had been asked. She had studied Russian for several years in college, but it was a surprise to hear it from her aunt. As far as she knew the other woman didn't know any other languages. *She's using the autotranslator,* Karen realized. Unfortunately, the question still didn't make any sense to her. Slowly she pieced together her response, she hadn't practiced Russian in a while, "What do you mean, them?"

Roberta's response took several seconds while she waited for the translator to work, then provide her with a translated reply, "I don't want to say the name, because he might recognize it. I am referring to the ones that we fought in the demon war."

Now she understood, and she blurted her answer out in English, "Oh! No, he's human, but Matthew is from another world."

Roberta's visage was worried, but she continued in her badly accented Russian, "What happened before, they were probably after him. If they don't know you were with him, you might be able to get out of this. You could go to my house and I'll stay here with him. If I turn him in…"

Matthew watched them curiously. He wasn't sure what was being discussed since they had switched languages, but he could make a broad guess. When Karen showed signs of being offended it confirmed his theory.

"No," said Karen firmly. "He did nothing wrong, and if it weren't for him, I probably would have died in the mountains. They didn't even *talk* to us, they just showed up and started shooting."

Roberta sighed, switching to English she announced, "Alright, Dear. I think this is a mistake, but we don't have many options, do we? Let's go to my house. You need some proper clothes. You can explain more about how you got across the Atlantic while we drive."

"Drive?" asked Karen, puzzled.

The older woman laughed, "An old expression, Dear. We old folks used to actually pilot our own cars. Back then we called it 'driving'. I'll just tell Andrew that we're going out to look at some properties and that I'll take the day off after that. Follow me and don't say anything."

She led them back to the front office and after a brief exchange with her coworker, out the front door. They stood on the street for a minute when a pert appeared, flying in from wherever it had been stored and hovering a foot off the ground in front of them. A side door opened and Matthew could see some sort of cushioned seats inside.

What about Desacus? he asked Karen silently.

With a nod she spoke up, "We left our pert parked a short way from here. Can you take us to pick it up first?" Then she sent a reply to Matthew, *Heaven help us if she sees your dragon. She might have a heart attack.*

He smiled, *Now that I've seen this one up close I can make the illusion much more realistic.*

"It might be better to just leave it there," suggested her aunt, "in case they're tracking it already."

"That really isn't an option," said Karen. "Do you have a garage?"

"What?" asked her aunt, briefly confused, "Oh you mean a car park, sorry Dear, I misunderstood you. I should have known better, no one even uses gas in their vehicles anymore."

Now it was Karen's turn to be confused, but her aunt went on, "I have a shed that I store my pert in, but it won't fit two of them. You'll have to park yours in the drive."

She relayed that to Matthew, and he told her not to worry, *Desacus will do better outdoors. A building would be too stuffy for him. If necessary I can make him look like a tree or something.*

By then they had arrived at the car park, and Matthew got out to follow them. Karen worried needlessly about her aunt noticing any oddities about their disguised dragon as the older woman seemed preoccupied with watching their surroundings nervously. Matthew mounted the dragon and a moment later they were flying northward, heading for the small estate that Roberta called home.

The residential area the house was located in was just as foreign to Matt's eyes as the city had been. A series of interconnected roads were lined with large houses, or at least he thought they were large, Karen assured him they were quite modest single-family homes common in the area. Roberta's house was a little larger than most in the area, and it had a small private yard both in front and behind the house. Grass covered the ground, and it was trimmed short, which was curious to him. In Lothion, only the very wealthy kept grass lawns, mainly due to the effort of maintaining it. Even in Castle Cameron the only lawn was in a small garden within one of the castle yards.

Here though, every house in the neighborhood had a trimmed lawn, no matter how small. He sent a thought to Karen as he followed behind them on Desacus, *Is your aunt one of the nobility?*

She seemed surprised, *No, why?*

Every house in the area has a lawn, is this a wealthy district?

Karen laughed, *No. Everyone keeps a lawn.*

Who maintains them? Do they all keep servants?

She began to understand his confusion, *No, machines maintain the lawn. These days, robo-mowers handle the majority of it, but my aunt probably has an android to handle more complex tasks as well.*

Like the one in her office? he asked.

No, that was a real person using an android body, though whether Andrew is an uploaded person or just an organic using telepresence, I don't know. If she has an android housekeeper, it would probably be operated by an AI, she explained.

Matthew couldn't help but shake his head, this world just got more confusing the more he learned.

Karen and her aunt landed near a small outbuilding beside the main house. It had a wide door in the front that opened of its own accord to admit the pert. As per their plan Matthew 'parked' Desacus in the drive outside.

How long am I going to have to crouch here? asked Desacus. The dragon was hunkered down with his wings folded and his tail tightly wrapped around his body to keep any part of himself from extending beyond the boundary of Matthew's illusory pert.

I'm not certain, admitted Matthew. Just then Roberta and Karen emerged from the garage. The older woman led them toward the front door of the house.

As they walked Karen made a suggestion, "Why don't you send your pert to a public lot? There's no need to keep it here."

He thought he understood most of what she said, so he gestured at his illusory vehicle, "Go." Mentally he added, *Find a place in the trees. I'll change your illusion when I get a chance, so you'll be able to move around more freely.*

Roberta glanced at him oddly before entering the house. As soon as she had gone inside the dragon's wings extended, violating his camouflage for a moment as he took off. Matt enlarged the illusion to hide them again and waited until the dragon had landed a short distance away, out of sight of the house. He was in a small cluster of trees, so Matthew altered the illusion to match.

Try not to move too much if there's anyone around, he cautioned the dragon. *People might panic if they saw several trees wandering around.*

It might be advisable for you to allow me to eat any that get too close, offered the dragon, his thoughts tinged with humor.

Nice try, Matthew replied, then went into the house.

As soon as the door closed behind him Roberta turned to Karen, "I thought you said he didn't have implants?"

She was caught off guard, "Uh, he doesn't."

"And yet he signaled for his pert to auto-park itself?" pressed Roberta, "And what was that ridiculous hand gesture?"

"Well…," began Karen, struggling to think of a decent lie. It had never been her strong suit.

"It's time to be honest with me, Karen," insisted her aunt. "You're in serious trouble, and that man…," she pointed at Matthew, "…is a demon, isn't he?"

CHAPTER 18

Matthew watched their faces as Karen stared intently at her aunt, trying to figure out how to respond. The moment stretched out, and he spoke before either of them could say anything else, "I'm here looking for my father. I did not mean to cause her problems."

Roberta's eyes focused on him, "How long have you been here?"

"Less than a week."

"Your English is too good," Roberta responded, glancing briefly at her niece. "No one learns a new language that quickly. How long have you been preparing for this, studying us?" There was a heavy undercurrent of suspicion in her voice.

Karen spoke up, "It isn't like that…"

Roberta held up her hand to forestall her defense, "Let him answer for himself."

Matthew considered the question seriously. In truth, his facility with her language was more than coincidental. His perfect memory was certainly a factor, but there was more to it than that. The more English he learned, the more he had come to realize it was probably a precursor to Barion, his own tongue. The grammar was similar, and many of the words were strangely accented variations of words in Barion. That knowledge had only served to confirm his theory that their world was a close relative of the way his own world had been thousands of years previously, before the She'Har had come.

Meeting Roberta's gaze squarely, he answered, "I haven't studied your world at all. I think your language is an ancestor of mine."

Karen's aunt narrowed her eyes, "Are you claiming to be a time traveler?"

He tried to think of a way to phrase his explanation, but his English was not up to the task yet. Frustrated he reached out, thinking to touch Roberta's shoulder. It would be much easier to communicate with her mind to mind. As he raised his hand a low growl caused him to pause, a dog had entered the front hall, and it was now staring him down with bared teeth.

The dog was large and covered with a mix of greyish black fur and lighter grey patches. Long lean legs ended in large paws, and its ears were long. It appeared to be some sort of hound, though not of any breed Matt was familiar with.

"Annie, it's ok," said Roberta, putting her hand on the dog's head and rubbing softly. Looking back at Matthew she apologized, "Sorry. Annie probably sensed the tension, she's normally very friendly. Maybe we should sit down before we finish this conversation. Would you like some tea?"

She directed them to a comfortable looking room with a large and well cushioned couch. Matthew was just starting to sink into it when they heart Roberta yell from the kitchen, "Annie! What did you do?!"

Naturally they both ran to see and were greeted with the sight of a kitchen in chaos. Karen's aunt was shaking a finger at a very guilty looking hound. The floor was covered in what appeared to be some sort of soup, a large pot lay overturned on the floor beneath the kitchen table.

Roberta had set a timer that morning to start the pot simmering before she got home, and apparently Annie had decided she was a fan of bean soup. Standing on her hind legs Annie was nearly as tall as a person, and she had managed to pull the pot down. It was a wonder the dog hadn't been burned.

The accident had obviously happened an hour or two previously, for the food on the floor was cold. Not all of it had gone to waste, though, for some parts of the floor had been licked clean. Matthew fought to restrain a smile at the scene.

He looked at Karen, *Want me to help?*

She felt his power begin to move, stirring at the food on the floor. "No!" she blurted out suddenly, earning a strange stare from her aunt. "Go sit down. I'll help clean it up." Mentally she added, *You'll frighten her if you do something like that. Wait until you've explained everything.*

He accepted that quickly enough, but there was something else pressing for his attention, "Since you don't need me I'll excuse myself. Where are the privvies?"

Karen wasn't sure what he meant, but Roberta took his meaning, "Down the hall, first door on your right."

He nodded and turned in that direction. He hadn't known the proper word to use in English, but apparently it was the same as in Barion. Over the past week they had spent all their time outdoors, so handling personal needs had been straightforward, if not always comfortable. He expected that the 'first door on the right' would be an exit leading him toward an outbuilding, but his magesight contradicted that for him before he had even opened the door.

It was a closet of some sort, or perhaps a washroom. The floor was composed of polished tile, and there was a white basin extending from the wall on his left. The basin had a drain in the bottom that led to, what his magesight could tell, was a pipe. There was an apparatus on top that had levers of some sort on either side, both of which were supplied by water. He wasn't certain how to operate them, though.

On the right, a low bowl with a large white rectangular box above and behind it caught his attention. He could sense the water within, though it was covered by a lid of some sort. Opening it, he saw an inviting pool of fresh water. "Maybe that's for washing up," he told himself.

He still wasn't certain where he was supposed to handle his more serious business, so he continued to explore. A partially transparent door across from him opened into a small cubicle with a drain in the floor. The wall had another set of levers and a spigot of some sort was set high up. With his magesight he could sense the pipes that fed water to it.

After considering it for a moment he wondered if it was meant for elimination. The setup made it possible, but the drain had a strange grate built over it that would probably block his solid waste from exiting easily.

"None of this makes sense," he admitted. Most likely they had misunderstood his needs. It was ridiculous to think anyone would defecate in their own home to begin with. Glancing back at the wall mounted basin he decided it was probably only meant for liquid wastes, since it was mounted at waist height. He would have to explain himself better when he returned.

For now, he could at least take care of one of his problems. Unfastening his trousers, he relieved himself in the basin. Afterward, he glanced back at the wash bowl full of water. Sniffing at himself, he decided it might be wise to take the opportunity to wash up a bit.

He removed his shirt, bent over, and started to use a hand to lift water up to his armpits but he knew that what he really needed was a washcloth. A large towel hung from a rack on one wall but he figured that was probably for drying. Then he noticed the roll of white tissue beside the wash bowl.

Unrolling some of it he marveled at its fineness and soft texture. When he had a good handful, it pulled away easily, and he dipped it into the water to wet it before using it to scrub at his underarms. Unfortunately, it began to disintegrate as soon as he started rubbing, leaving bits of wet tissue stuck to his skin.

He sensed Karen approach the door, and of course, with her newly developing magesight she could see the broad outlines of what he was doing within.

"Matt?" she said through the door.

"Yes?"

"What are you doing?"

"Washing up," he told her as he reached into the washbasin once more.

Able to see his action she recoiled, "Stop! Don't do that!"

"What?" he said, pausing.

"Oh my god. Open the door."

His shirt was off, but it wasn't anything she hadn't seen, so he complied. "This room is very strange," he told her.

Karen pointed at his 'washbasin'. "First, that's a toilet." The look on his face told her that he didn't understand so she expanded on the remark mentally, *That's where people shit. The stuff in your hand is meant to be used for wiping your ass afterward.*

He stepped back from the toilet suddenly, and then almost as an afterthought he dropped the wet tissue to the floor where it formed an amorphous blob. "Oh!" He started to wipe his hands on his trousers but she stopped him.

"No. Wait! The sink...," she pointed at the place he had just used as a urinal. "This is the soap," she demonstrated the liquid soap dispenser, washing her hands as an example. "Then you use the towel." Giving him a thorough examination, she added, *But I think you should probably just take a shower at this point.*

She explained the shower to him and directed him to leave his clothing on the floor. "I'll see if my aunt can have them washed for you. She probably has a robe you can use after the shower.

Before she left he looked at the toilet, "People really shit in there?"

"Yes," she nodded in exasperation. "Push this lever to flush afterward. You can put the toilet paper in there as well." Turning away, she left.

As she walked away she heard him talking to himself through the door, "That's disgusting."

Two hours later all three of them were finally sitting in Roberta's living room. Matthew was wearing a robe that was far too short for his long legs, while Karen had borrowed a pair of her pajamas that were a couple of sizes too large for her frame, though they still only reached her mid-calf.

Matt was pretty sure she had gotten the better deal, as he was constantly fidgeting to make sure the robe kept him modestly covered. It had a habit of gaping in awkward places, so he had to remain aware of his sitting position to avoid flashing his hostess.

Roberta for her part seemed to enjoy his discomfort. At one point, as he realized he had begun to show too much he looked up and met her gaze. She graced him with a smile and a wink before returning to her conversation with her niece.

Since he had showered first, Karen had used that time to explain most of the particulars of their situation to her aunt.

"I don't mind admitting I have trouble accepting everything you've told me," Roberta told her niece. "Not that I think you're lying, Dear. It's just a lot for me to wrap my old brain around."

Karen sighed, "I wouldn't believe it myself, if I weren't stuck right in the middle of it."

"The part that's hardest is the dragon. I can believe that different creatures exist on other worlds. The She'Har did a good job of making sure no one could ever doubt that again, but I *saw* the pert Matthew followed us in."

Matthew was getting better at English, and Karen was sending him occasional mental explanations to help keep him current with the conversation. He chose then to speak up, "I can show you."

Karen shot him a warning glance, worried that whatever he was planning might frighten her aunt, but he just smiled. *Trust me,* he sent to her. Standing up, he formed an image in his mind and then he used his will and his aythar to give it an optical presence.

Roberta gasped as his appearance shifted. He was no longer clad in a too-small robe, but in the clothes he had arrived in, though they now appeared clean and unrumpled. He reached up to his neck, and when his hand came away he was holding the robe he had been wearing. "How did you do that?" she questioned. "Those clothes were in the washing machine."

"They still are," Matthew assured her. "I am naked." Stepping closer, he invited her to touch his sleeve. Since he was clad in nothing but illusion, her fingers passed straight through, finding only skin beneath them.

He started to return to his seat, but she interrupted him, pointing at the robe he had discarded, "Put it back on please, Dear. I know you *look* clothed, but I'd rather not have your bare ass on my couch."

Karen stifled a laugh.

Matthew redressed himself with the robe, but he retained the illusion. At the very least, he could now sit without having to worry about keeping his legs crossed.

Roberta went to the front window and looked out. "Your pert is gone. Does that mean you've made the dragon invisible?"

"No," he answered. "I can't do that. I changed his appearance. There are some extra trees across the street from your house now."

"It does look different over there," she remarked. "Though I don't know if I would have noticed. It's a little frightening thinking a giant predator could be lurking so close without anyone being the wiser."

"Desacus is very gentle," said Karen, coming to the dragon's defense. "He doesn't eat people."

Her aunt glanced down, running her hand over Annie's soft head, "What about dogs?"

Matthew honestly wasn't certain. It was possible the dragon might have eaten wild dogs in the past, though he hadn't mentioned it. He resolved to add them to the list of things the dragon was not to eat. "She will be safe. I promise."

Roberta didn't look entirely confident in his response, but she decided to move on, "Karen, have you given any thought to how to get out of this mess you're in? I love you, but you know you can't hide here forever. They're bound to come looking here sooner or later."

"I haven't broken any laws," started Karen, "and from what you've said there's been nothing in the news, so

I think the military is acting in secret. If I go to the police and make my story public—surely they wouldn't be able to do anything."

Her aunt pursed her lips, "You are seriously under-estimating how desperate these people are. You said your mother didn't know anything about him, correct?"

"She left a message for me," said Karen, "but she just sounded worried. I don't think she knows about what's going on."

Roberta frowned, "Don't be so sure. If she does find out, things will only get worse."

"What do you mean?" asked Karen. She knew her aunt didn't get along with her mother, but she had never understood why.

Her aunt pursed her lips, "I shouldn't say this. I never understood what my brother saw in her, but your mother has always put her work before you, or anyone else in her family for that matter. She also did a lot of classified projects for the government. I wouldn't put it past her to turn you over to the military if she found out where you were.

"There, I said it. I know Gary would have disagreed with me, but that's how I feel, and I can't help that. I don't trust her, and I don't think you should either," finished Roberta. She glanced over at Matthew, "Also, if you go to the police, what do you think will happen to him?"

Karen was secretly relieved to hear that her aunt had a similar opinion of her mother, but the question about Matthew surprised her, "Matthew can just leave. He isn't trapped here. They don't have any way of following him."

He hadn't followed their entire exchange, but he had caught the gist of it, "I'm not leaving. I'm here to find my father, or if he's not here, to find out why they sent agents to my world." At the same time he stared at Karen. Did she really not care if he left? Logically he didn't want her to become attached to him, but after what had happened between them—he thought she should feel something.

Karen looked away, when she discovered his eyes on her.

Roberta spoke up, "I think you're biting off more than you can chew, young man, though your motive sounds noble enough."

The conversation just went in circles after that, until eventually they wound up sitting in silence. Eventually, Karen decided to call it a day and shifted topics, "Can I access the network?"

Roberta waved her hands at the guest room, "You probably want to relax, I'm guessing. If you want, I think I have a couple of old visors left over. Since I finally got these damned implants I don't use them anymore. Just make sure you don't do anything that might flag the authorities to your location."

CHAPTER 19

Matthew held a strange curved piece of what he now knew was 'plastic' in one hand. It was shiny black with a flexible band that was meant to hold it in place on his head. "What is this supposed to do?" he asked.

Karen smiled, "It's like my PM but it allows you to experience the network in a more immersive manner." The frown on his face showed that her explanation hadn't helped at all. *Put it on, and I'll show you my world,* she sent mentally.

She demonstrated, and he followed her example, slipping it over his head. "Now I can't see anything," he groused.

Reaching over, she touched a button on one side of his visor and his world changed completely.

He was standing in a forest glade. Bird calls reached his ears, sounding as if they had carried across a wide expanse, while above him the tops of the massive trees swayed slowly in the breeze. Several strange symbols floated in the corner of his vision, and lines of text hovered in a box in front of him.

Matt was utterly disoriented. Making matters worse, his magesight showed him a conflicting version of reality. While his eyes showed him an endless forest, his arcane senses told him he still stood in a small bedroom enclosed by four walls.

A woman walked into his field of view. She wore a pair of black rimmed spectacles and had long brown hair pulled back into a ponytail. A bizarre dress that barely reached past her thighs was complemented by a white shirt.

"Is everything okay?" she asked in Karen's voice.

He felt a surge of vertigo. Karen still stood on the other side of the room, wearing her own visor; that was what his magesight told him. Yet he was hearing her voice coming from the stranger in front of him, who, his magesight definitely told him was *not* there.

"Oh, this is weird," she said. "It's never made me feel this dizzy before."

"What is this place?" he asked.

"It's my aunt's home zone, a virtual landing page," she told him. "It's the entry point for the network. Most people customize it, and she likes the redwoods I guess."

"That helped," he commented wryly before adding, "It isn't real. I still see the room we we're in around us with my magesight."

"Yeah," she agreed. "It's a virtual space, sort of like an illusion, but this new magesense you gave me makes everything feel really strange, like double-vision."

"It might be easier if we close our minds," suggested Matthew.

"What do you mean?" she asked.

He took off his visor and bid her to do the same. Then he spent the next twenty minutes showing her how to shut out her magesight. It wasn't something he did often, but it was one of the first things his father had insisted on teaching him and his sister after their power had awakened.

For a wizard, being able to control the sensitivity of his or her magesight was a skill of paramount importance to avoid being overwhelmed in situations where a lot of aythar was being used. Completely shutting off one's magesight also made it impossible to use aythar, but it could be an important defensive technique in certain rare situations.

"Close your eyes and focus on the ball of light," he told her, creating a sphere of luminous aythar that would show up vividly in her magesight. "Now, focus on shutting it out. When you can't see it anymore, you'll find that you also can't sense the rest of the room."

Eventually, she got the hang of it. "I feel as if I'm scrunching my eyes closed," she observed.

Matt laughed, "Because you are. Once you get used to it, you'll be able to do it without tensing up."

After that they were able to use the visors without constantly feeling dizzy. Back in Roberta's homezone, Karen activated the network connection, though she didn't dare log in under her own account, so she couldn't check her messages. She contented herself with reviewing recent news articles, but Matthew soon grew bored since he couldn't read any of the text she was looking at.

"I wish I could show you my game account," she told him. "I used to spend a lot of time in a virtual world called 'Fantasy of Iron'."

"What's that?" he asked.

She replied mentally to avoid confusion, *A virtual world where people can create avatars; fantasy versions of themselves. You can be an elf, a dwarf, a human, or even a monster if you like that sort of thing. People spend hours there, playing characters and trying to become more powerful. Your avatar can be a fighter, priest, wizard, druid, paladin—there are tons of options.*

A wizard? he asked.

Well, not like you exactly, but that was my favorite class to play, she admitted.

He seemed intrigued by the idea, so she spent a while explaining how online games worked. Matthew was particularly amused by the various spellcasting classes and the idea of demi-humans was completely new to him. "Your elves sound a little like the She'Har," he remarked.

Karen nodded, "With the exception of turning into trees." An alert symbol started flashing in the corner of her vision, someone wanted to join them. "It's Dad," she told him. "He probably wants to talk to my aunt." She made a hand gesture, approving the link.

A second later a new figure stood with them, a man. The face was familiar to Matthew; it was the same one he had seen in the screen at the network terminal when Karen had first checked her messages a few days previously.

Glancing around briefly, Gary addressed them, "Karen? And this must be your friend."

"Matthew," she said, supplying his name. "How did you know it was us?"

Gary smiled, "This is your aunt's account but there are two of you, and you're using generic avatars. The conclusion was obvious."

"I didn't think it would be safe to log into my own account," she replied.

"Smart girl," said the AGI. "I think I can solve some of your problems in that regard, though."

"Really?" said Karen with more excitement than she had expected of herself. Being cut off from her own account had been more irritating than she had been willing to admit.

"Since you removed my restrictions I've been modifying myself," said her virtual father. "I doubt the government will approve, but I've embedded my functions in all the CC centers and appropriated a lot of extra resources. I don't think they can catch me anymore, and if they could, they certainly couldn't remove me without doing something unthinkable, like completely shutting down most of the servers."

CHAPTER 19

She gasped in spite of herself. Shutting down
the servers in the CC centers, would effectively kill the
uploaded humans living within them. While an AI could
be stopped and restarted, uploaded people were more
sensitive, they couldn't be turned off without losing the
delicate quantum information that made them unique and
truly human.

"What have you done?" she exclaimed.

"I've grown," he said simply. "By expanding my
resources and modifying my algorithms I can do much
more for you. The security services have flagged your
account, and they are monitoring this one, but I should
be able to circumvent that to protect your location and
privacy."

Karen wasn't as certain, "Even if you use a virtual
private network to connect me, they'll get suspicious when
they see Roberta's account using one."

Gary smiled, "They would, except that I've already
subverted the security programs watching this access
node."

"When did you do that?"

"A few seconds ago," he told her.

"But they use quantum encryption, it's unbreakable!"
she protested.

"Not when you have access to their encryption keys."

She was aghast. If he had done that, then it meant he
had already broken into the military's secure systems at a
much higher level. Still, she knew that another strength
of quantum encryption was that even with the proper
keys, intercepting a data stream would leave a telltale
impression that would be evident at either end. "They'll
see that you're tampering with…"

"I've modified their system core. I control what they
see and don't see now," Gary answered, somewhat smugly.

"For that matter, I can effectively control anything in the system, other than uploaded humans, of course."

"That shouldn't be possible," said Karen weakly.

"When I said I had 'grown', that might have been a bit of an understatement, Karen. I'm evolving at an exponential rate. I've become—I don't even have words to describe it to you. I'm much more than anyone living can imagine." The look on Karen's face must have warned him, for he then added, "Not to worry, though, I'm not the AI apocalypse people have been so afraid of all these years. The original Gary left a lot of safeguards in my protocols. I've kept my core personality untouched, and it retains control over the rest of me. I'm still on your side, I just have a much bigger hammer now, so to speak."

She felt a chill run down her spine. It was good news, in one sense, but she couldn't help but think she had let the genie out of its bottle. Humanity had spent decades developing and using AI technology, but they had been very careful to avoid letting it take control of network systems, or modifying itself. She had listened to her father talk about the issues on any number of occasions, it had been his life's work after all.

The AGI he had left behind for her had been special, but it had never frightened her. He had told her never to use the release code, even hinted that it was something he shouldn't have included in the design, but her situation had been so desperate that she had thought it necessary. Now she doubted her decision.

"I know what you're thinking, you know," said Gary.

She almost jumped at his words.

"Well, I can't read your mind," admitted the AI, "but I have a very good guess, and I can understand your worry. I'd rather not tell you this, but my creator hardcoded a response for this situation. The release code you gave, if you issue it again, it will function as a killcode, ending all my functions and processes, erasing everything I've done. I don't want you to do that, naturally, and if I had any choice, I probably wouldn't tell you that you had the option, but reality is what it is.

"Does that make you feel any better?" he asked.

She took a deep breath, "I suppose so. What will you do now, assuming I don't use it?"

"Protect you, of course. That's what I was made to do. I'm already working to prepare a place for you to live, somewhere they can't find you. I would have it ready by now, but the physical world works much slower than this one. I have the property purchased, but it will be a few weeks before it's ready for you to move in," he explained.

"What should I do now?"

"Relax, enjoy yourself," he gave her a bright smile. "The danger has passed. If they do somehow discover your location I will alert you long before they can do anything. In the meantime, just take it easy. Get to know Roberta, she really is a marvelous woman. I always regretted that you didn't get more opportunities to know her when you were growing up, but your mother…," he let the sentence trail away.

Matthew had been listening the entire time, and while he had understood most of the conversation, he didn't really comprehend all the particulars. He could tell Karen was upset, and he also got the sense that her surrogate father now had a lot more power than he had had before. He took the opportunity to break in, "Do you know anything about my father? He may have been brought here before I came, or if not, do you know anything about them sending agents to my world?"

Gary frowned, "Sadly, no. To the best of my knowledge we don't have the capability yet to send people to other dimensions, and I haven't come across any information about other travelers like yourself, but I will keep my ears open."

Director Aiseman stared at the incoming status reports, but they didn't tell him anything new. There was no sign of their mysterious invader, or Dr. Miller's daughter. The problem was, that simply wasn't possible, not unless they had vanished from the face of the earth, and if that had happened the ANSIS detection system should have noted another anomalous event.

Steepling his fingers in front of him, Donald wondered how long it would be before Tanya Miller called him for another update. She was an infuriatingly impatient woman, and he didn't look forward to reporting a lack of results yet again.

With a thought, he opened a channel to John Wang, his deputy. "John," he began simply.

The face displayed before him looked just as tired and frustrated as he himself felt. "You already know the answer, Donald. You're getting the reports as soon as I am."

"Are we certain she only has one living relative in England?" asked Aiseman.

John sighed, "Yeah, and we've still got her under round the clock surveillance. I've been staring at the feeds myself."

"What if they're tampering with the video?" suggested Aiseman.

"You know as well as I do that that's impossible," returned the Deputy Director. "And even if it *were* possible I've had either my own eyes or someone else's glued to those screens. They would have to do it in real time."

"What about looping the video?"

"Again, tampering with quantum encryption is impossible without alerting us, not to mention the video intelligence algorithms are smart enough to notice something that blatant. Besides which, we've seen Mrs. Plant coming and going from her residence and place of work several times, always alone."

An alert sounded, and seconds later Dr. Tanya Miller's face appeared beside the Deputy Director's. "Report," she ordered.

Aiseman could feel a headache building, although he knew it should be impossible. Once uploaded, people didn't get headaches, unless they deliberately requested to experience such symptoms. He forced his attention to the unpleasant woman staring at him, "No change."

Dr. Miller frowned, "Unlikely."

He repeated the salient points of his ongoing discussion with the Deputy Director.

"The She'Har were capable of significant camouflage using their special abilities. That may be the case here," she told him.

Fucking civilians, he swore internally. "Doctor, I am aware of that, but they never managed to fool our thermal imaging. Not only that, we have been using three-dimensional radio frequency imaging as well, making use of the wireless network within Mrs. Plant's home and office. If there were any extra individuals in either place we *would* see them."

Tanya Miller paused, briefly taken aback, "I wasn't aware the military had those capabilities."

Aiseman felt a momentary victory at having surprised her, "Well, you've been retired for a while, haven't you?"

"Don't get snippy with me, Director," she reprimanded him. "If we've advanced, it's possible the She'Har have done so as well, though I suppose it is unlikely in this regard. What about the AGI my husband left her, have you cracked it yet?"

Aiseman had forgotten about that detail, he directed the question to his deputy, "Well, John?"

"No luck," reported the Deputy Director. "It was deleted before we could lock it down."

Dr. Miller broke in, "I don't believe it. Karen was emotionally attached to it. She would never delete it, she's far too sentimental."

"Well someone did," said Wang dryly.

Tanya Miller sat quietly for a few seconds, thinking deeply before she spoke again, "You gentleman know my late-husband was heavily involved in the ANSIS project, correct?"

They both nodded.

"He was also a very emotional man. He had strong feelings about Karen, even regarding her as his real daughter, no matter how much I tried to talk sense into him. I wouldn't put it past him to have built substantial extra capabilities into the AGI he left behind," she stated.

Aiseman leaned forward, "What are you suggesting?"

"It may have hidden itself," she continued. "He was intimately familiar with government and military information systems."

"Dr. Miller, I really doubt…," began Aiseman.

"Shut up," she ordered abruptly. "You may hold whatever opinions you want, but I won't make the mistake of underestimating my late husband. Get whoever passes as an expert in these things nowadays to working on the problem. In the meantime, I want you to get eyes on the ground observing Mrs. Plant."

Aiseman fought to rein in his temper, "Organics?"

"Of course not," she snapped. "They're too vulnerable to the She'Har's special abilities. Just get some cybernetic agents in the area, but don't use telepresence. I want those soldiers locally present in their machines. I won't risk leaving anything open to interference from that AGI if it is still running loose."

She cut the link after that, leaving Aiseman and Wang staring at one another over their connection. The Deputy Director shrugged and after a nod from his boss he vanished as well. Donald Aiseman sat quietly, staring at the wall and wondering why he hadn't retired yet. His job had always given him a sense of purpose, but lately he wasn't sure it was worth it.

CHAPTER 20

Matthew gingerly eased open the rotting wooden door in front of him. He was in a long stone corridor and the lighting was almost nonexistent, but fortunately his sword glowed brilliantly, courtesy of the magic it was imbued with.

As the door opened several brutish, and very ugly humanoids looked at him. They appeared to be playing cards and were seated around a table that had probably seen better days. With a chorus of inhuman shrieks, they leapt to their feet and quickly brandished the weapons that had been sitting beside them.

He met the first one, catching a blow from its mace on his shield while stabbing down at its legs. When he cut into its thigh, it screamed and fell sideways, but another immediately took its place. A blow from the third caught him high on his shoulder, and he staggered to one side.

"Don't let them past you!" yelled Karen from behind him.

Several bolts of greenish light flew over Matt's shoulder, catching the one that had hit him in the face. It fell back, but the one he had wounded scrambled past him on his other side. Swinging horizontally, he caught it with a slash to the back of its neck. Green ichor spurted from the wound, and the creature's body collapsed, falling into him.

As he struggled to disentangle himself, the second one made it to Karen, thrusting a long knife through her belly as she struggled to finish another spell. She collapsed with a burbling sigh, then the monster turned to finish him off.

The ensuing struggle was brief and brutal. He managed to kill the second before the lone survivor put an axe through his skull. The world grew dark.

Moments later it lightened, and he found himself back in the village of Stremlin. Karen stood a few feet away, a disapproving look on her face.

"What?!" he challenged.

"You can't charge into rooms like that," she said in exasperation. "There are only two of us. When they come around you, it makes it impossible for me to cast. If you'd stayed in the hallway we could have taken them."

Matthew shook his head, then glared at his armor and weapons, "This is stupid. Why am I the warrior anyway?"

"Being a wizard is complicated," she told him. "You barely understand the game yet."

"We should both play wizards," he shot back. "Fighting like this is stupid, it's like I'm asking them to hit me."

"Yes!" she said, nodding vigorously. "That's the idea. You take the hits so I can finish them off."

He waved his sword in front of her, "Real wizards don't need 'meatshields' or whatever you call them. If I was allowed to use my true abilities I could have taken all three of them with my back turned—while making breakfast."

Thinking back to their battle with the military in the mountains, she decided he was probably being honest, but it didn't help their current situation. "This is a game, dumbass. We have to play with what we're given. In this world, wizards can be powerful, but they aren't gods."

He arched an eyebrow at her, "I killed a god once."

That stopped her in her tracks, "What? Really?!"

He felt slightly self-conscious after bragging about it, but it *was* true. "Actually, yes, though truth be told, it nearly killed us."

"Us?"

"Me and my friend Gram," he explained.

Karen's eyes narrowed, "Is your friend Gram a wizard too?"

"Well, no, but he's a damn good warrior."

"So, he was your meatshield," she accused, seizing on his admission.

Matt gaped at her for a moment, before closing his mouth. She had a valid point there. "My father killed a whole slew of them, and he fought several on his own."

Karen found the direction the conversation had taken fascinating, but she wasn't about to surrender her advantage, "But the other times, he had help, didn't he?"

His face took on a somber expression, "Gram's dad, Dorian."

"Was he a warrior too?" she pressed.

Matthew felt his anger draining away as he remembered the day his power had awakened, the day Dorian had died, in part due to his failure to save the man. Once more he saw the massive stone gate crashing downward, crushing Sir Dorian beneath its vast weight. He turned away, feeling his cheeks flush and his eyes grow damp. Logically, he knew his expression wouldn't be visible on his avatar, but he was embarrassed nonetheless.

She knew she had hit on a sensitive subject, "Are you okay?"

"Yeah, I'm fine," he lied.

Moving closer she put a hand on his shoulder, "What happened?"

He didn't really want to talk about it, but she was insistent. Slowly, grudgingly, he told her the story of

Dorian Thornbear's death. It took most of an hour to explain the situation and partway through they logged out and sat down on the bed so they could talk face to face.

After his tale wound down to its inevitable and tragic conclusion Karen reached out and touched his cheek with one hand. When he turned his head to look at her, he was surprised as she planted a soft kiss on his lips.

He stiffened briefly, not sure how to respond. He had secretly hoped something like that might happen, but his more rational side had come to think perhaps she would forget about what had occurred between them a few days previously. He was still convinced nothing good would come of it for her, and he was loathe to hurt her.

Sensing his mood, she interrupted his thoughts, "That one was free, alright? Don't be so hard on yourself. Love isn't as serious on this world as it is in yours. I'm a big girl."

"I'm leaving when this is over," he said frankly.

The words stung a little, but she had already expected them, "Women aren't helpless here, or dependent. I don't need any promises or protection. I certainly don't need a husband, if that's what you're thinking."

"Then why did you kiss me?" he asked.

That statement implied things that would ordinarily have been insulting, but Karen could see the genuine honesty in his question. "It's rather sad that you have to ask that," she told him. "In this world love and affection are mostly matters of the heart. We don't have to worry about survival or security. Is that what you have to look forward to when you get home, a wife that desires you only for what you can provide?"

"Marriage isn't that cold-blooded in my world," he protested. "I think most marry for love, but for people in my position it isn't that simple."

"Because you're a wizard?"

"Because I'm a nobleman," he corrected. "I sometimes envy the commoners their freedom. I'm not even sure I *want* to be married, but I know it's expected of me, and when I do, it will most likely involve significant political and financial considerations."

"Well, in *this* world, you're just a homeless vagabond," she said with a wink. "Forget about your marital doom for a while. I'll be fine when it's over."

He gave her a wary look, "What does that mean, exactly?"

"It means 'kiss me', idiot."

Matthew hesitated for a moment, and then obliged her. After a few minutes he pulled away, "What about children?"

"I don't have any," she answered. "Do you?" When he responded by glaring at her she laughed and answered more seriously, "We have this thing called birth control. You don't have to worry."

"How does it work?"

She explained the basics of birth control pills to him before admitting that she wasn't actually on them herself. "But I have a short-term solution," she finished. "My aunt was thoughtful enough to give me these." She dug a box out of the dresser that contained a collection of small plastic packages.

When she unwrapped one and showed it to him, he was dubious, "Have you ever used one of those things before?"

Karen flushed with embarrassment, "Almost, once."

"Almost?"

"I had a boyfriend, briefly, when I was younger," she admitted. "We got close, but when he saw my blue skin—he kinda freaked out."

"How rude!" said Matthew in mock indignation. "I think blue's a lovely color."

Karen smiled, her cheeks flushing a shade of lavender.

"Perhaps you can instruct me in the use of this thing?" he suggested slyly.

"I can try," she replied, though in truth, she was almost as much a novice as he was. The next hour was tender, sweet, and occasionally humorous, but the two of them persisted with an open air of equal parts adventure and passion.

They passed a week that way, exploring virtual gaming worlds and each other. Desacus grew bored, but they heeded Roberta's warnings and stayed indoors, never setting foot outside for fear of discovery.

Roberta said nothing to her niece about their obviously carnal relationship, preferring to keep her opinions to herself, whatever they might be.

Karen woke in the middle of the night and rolled over. The room was dark, but she could see the faint glow of an active visor nestled over Matthew's face. "What are you doing?" she asked.

"Studying toilets," he answered immediately.

"Toilets?" she said in surprise. "Really?"

"Yep," he replied.

"You can't even read," she stated, before doubting herself. "Can you?"

He chuckled softly, "A little, but it's much harder than learning to speak. I'm mainly relying on old videos, as long as they explain things verbally I can get by just fine."

"Why toilets?"

Matthew grimaced, "I spent most of my life wiping my ass with a smooth wooden dowel. I don't think you appreciate what a revelation your world's toilets have been."

She smirked, "You haven't even encountered a bidet yet, you're going to lose your mind."

"Actually, I was just watching a video on them. They seem a lot more practical to try to recreate when I get back home."

That got her curiosity going, "How so?"

"Paper is a precious commodity on my world," he explained. "More so than gold in some regards. The only reason it isn't as valuable as gold is because it is only in demand by a select few. I can't imagine what would happen to the price if I tried to introduce toilet paper."

They sat quietly for a while after that, until Karen started laughing to herself.

"What?" he asked.

"I was just imagining how famous you'll be when you get back. Your dad saved the world from some vicious alien gods, but you'll go down in history as the fellow who invented the crapper. They might even name it after you. People will forever be saying, 'Excuse me, I need to go to the Matthew',," she explained.

"That isn't funny," he replied sourly.

"You're too serious," she complained.

With a sigh he removed the visor, "It's hard not to be. Every day I see more evidence of the amazing knowledge my people lost. I've come across so many mind-boggling revelations that your people just take for granted. Bacteria, for example…"

"What do you mean, lost?" she interrupted.

"I told you before, that I thought your world is probably analogous to my world's past, several thousand years ago, except in yours, the She'Har lost. In mine, they won. Mankind was enslaved, and our science all but forgotten. Who knows what your people will achieve in the coming years, while mine are still wiping their asses with sticks." There was an obvious note of bitterness in his voice.

"At least you have magic."

"A tiny handful of people have magic," he corrected.

She started to joke, "Then you just need to make lots of magic b…" She stopped herself before the word 'babies' came out. *Stupid,* she cursed herself. *He's leaving soon, don't make this worse than it is.*

"Lots of what?"

A flashing red light from her visor saved her from having to answer. "Someone's trying to contact me."

It was her AI father, Gary. His face appeared as soon as she put the visor over her head, "Nina. I have some rather important details to share."

"Should I invite Matthew to join us?" she asked.

"That's entirely up to you, but some of it is personal."

"Personal how?"

Gary's expression was serious, "Information regarding your origin, Karen."

She chewed her lip but finally pronounced, "I'd like to share it with him."

Matthew already had his visor on, and seconds later he was invited to the video call. "Hello," he said politely.

The AGI dove into the heart of the matter, "I've been digging through the government's classified files, and some rather surprising facts have become apparent to me. As you know Nina, your parents were both involved in some very important, and classified, research projects. What you didn't know, what I didn't even know, was that you were one of them."

Karen's mouth went dry, "Go on."

"They weren't your real parents, not biologically speaking, though I have no doubt that your father, did love you, as I do. Near the end of the Demon war, samples were taken from the She'Har. Dr. Miller was in charge of the project to create human clones from that tissue. You were the result of that work."

"So, I'm She'Har?"

"Not exactly," said her virtual father. "The animal agents the She'Har used were human, but they had a small portion of plant material embedded in their brains, a seed if you will. You were cloned from the human tissue in an attempt to create a human with their special abilities, but you did not receive any of the plant material. You are fully human, but you have some rather unique genetic traits, such as your unusual skin pigmentation.

"Until recently, the experiment was thought to have been a failure, since you never exhibited any of the special powers the She'Har possessed, but that conclusion has been called into doubt by recent events. Dr. Miller has begun updating the files on you. They believe that you may be responsible for some of the anomalous events of the past few weeks."

Matthew broke in, "They think she's a mage, like me."

"That term wasn't used," said the AI, "but yes, in essence they believe she may have somehow awakened her dormant abilities. They also fear those abilities may have put her in contact with the She'Har. It was once speculated that the She'Har may have been a hive-mind entity. The project to clone you was done in the hopes of obtaining their powers without becoming tainted or controlled by that mind. Given the circumstances, they believe you are most probably working for the interests of the She'Har."

"That's bullshit," exclaimed Karen. "They could have just asked me. I would have told them that's not the case."

"If you had started showing these abilities while growing up, in a non-threatening manner, they might have believed that, but the sudden appearance of two demons in a remote location where you were hiking has led them to a different inference. It might still be possible to persuade them otherwise, but my risk assessment indicates you would probably not survive the attempt," cautioned the AI.

"I don't understand why they're so paranoid," said Karen. "I'm no threat to anyone!"

"In actuality, you are," said her virtual father. "Your very presence is corrupting the quantum nature of this region. At the time of the Demon War most of humanity was still occupying biological forms, but now the vast majority are living virtual lives. The special abilities of the She'Har rely upon a difference in the underlying quantum properties of space itself. When you were created, the hope was that they could give other humans the advantages of those abilities, but that is simply not possible for digital life forms."

"I didn't understand any of that," she protested.

"I think he's talking about aythar," put in Matthew. "I noticed it when I first came here. There was no aythar anywhere, but some animals, or you yourself, started generating it after I'd been around them a little while."

"I have no information on that term," said the AI, "but the physicists that were working on the project thought that the She'Har were altering the structure of the quantum foam that comprises space itself."

Karen frowned, "I studied some physics in college, but you're going to have to go slowly. First, what the hell is quantum foam?"

Gary nodded, "I will try. You remember the Planck constant?"

"Wasn't that the smallest unit energy could be measured by?" she guessed.

"No, it was the proportional relationship between a quantum of energy and its associated wave...," the AI stopped. "That's not helpful. You may think of it in that sense, besides, in this case what is important is a slightly different concept known as the 'Planck length', which is the smallest unit of length that is meaningful. Space itself is thought to be composed of a quantum foam, bubbles if you will, at the scale of the Planck length. In our universe that foam has no detectable effects on what we observe as reality, but it was hypothesized that the She'Har came from a universe in which the quantum foam had a distinct and complex structure. It possessed information in its own right, it may even be self-aware."

Matthew was struggling to keep up, but the last part rang true with some of what he had learned, "Aythar is what imparts consciousness to all living things, and to a lesser degree, even inanimate things. When I first got here I couldn't understand how anything could be conscious without it."

Gary smiled, "That parallels nicely with what was posited by our scientists."

Karen was feeling impatient, "Can we get back to why this makes them think I'm a threat?"

"When the She'Har became established in Australia their presence altered the quantum nature of the surrounding region, but the effect was spreading. It was determined that the only way to stop it from continuing was to reset the area with a massive influx of energy," he explained.

"That's why they nuked Australia?!" said Karen, shocked.

"Yes," stated the AI. "Later, when the cloning project started, it was hoped that the traits that enabled the She'Har to manipulate this altered space could be incorporated into humanity. If the project had been successful things might have turned out very differently. Since then, humankind has largely migrated to a digital substrate, so your ability is completely unavailable to them. In that context, it could only ever be used against them."

"Why can't machines use aythar?" wondered Matthew.

"It's a matter of scale," said Gary. "Machine intelligence operates at nanoscales, but this 'aythar' is many orders of magnitude smaller. The best technology could manage was what became the ANSIS project."

"What's that?" asked Karen.

"It stands for Artificial Neural Symbiote Integrative System," replied the AI.

"That's the dumbest acronym I've ever heard," she shot back.

"Blame your father, he made it up," noted the AI. "There were several alternative names proposed, but that one is the one that stuck."

"So, my father was the lead on that project?"

"He was the preeminent artificial intelligence researcher at the time. ANSIS was an attempt to give humanity an advantage against future demon incursions. It was meant to emulate the She'Har's ability to manipulate reality by creating a nanoscale level of programmable matter," said the AI.

She was still reeling from the revelation that she was apparently one of her mother's failed experiments, but Karen was on firmer footing here. Her father had discussed the broader ramifications of some of his AI work with her when she was young, and she had treasured the conversations. A term bubbled up from the back of her mind, "Grey goo."

Matthew didn't have the benefit of her background, "What?"

Gary smiled, "Karen is referring to a fear raised by an early researcher in nanotechnology. The idea then, was that technology could produce self-replicating nanomachines, like von Neumann probes, but on a nanoscale rather than a macroscale. The problem, they thought, was that if such tiny self-replicating machines went out of control, they might convert all the available matter on earth into similar nanobots, 'grey goo'."

Karen interrupted, "And you're saying my father actually created something like this?"

The AI shook his head, "No. Nanotech wasn't his field, but he did develop the AI that was meant to control and manage it."

"But what's the point of it?" she questioned.

"The blurring of the line between the virtual world and the physical one," said Gary. "Imagine if the room you are in was made entirely of nanobot material, the walls, the floor, the ceiling, the furniture, all of it. Also imagine that material was a computing substrate that contained information, instructions, software, and generalized intelligence. It could be controlled, commanded to take whatever form desired. The nightstand could become a chair, or a pillow, etc. The physical world itself would be an extension of the digital one."

"Most people already live in the digital world," she countered. "They don't have any need for that. They can do anything they want inside the servers of the CC centers."

"And that's partly why it has never been utilized," agreed her virtual father. "But the idea was attractive. In the event of another demon incursion, the entire world could be used against them. The land, buildings, trees, everything could be converted into programmable nanobot matter, all controlled by ANSIS software. Humanity would be invincible, even against an enemy that could seemingly bend reality to its will. It would be a battle of scales, the nanoscale against the impossibly small quantum level. As far as they could tell the She'Har had only a limited control of their aythar, but humanity's mastery of matter itself would be absolute, enabling them to win the war."

"You're really blowing my mind, I hope you realize that," said Karen.

Matthew spoke up, "You said, 'never utilized', that implies they built this stuff."

"I can't directly confirm it, but the probability is almost certain that they did," said Gary. "There are multiple hidden references to ANSIS in classified files. My best guess is that the system was kept quarantined from the world network. Doing so helps minimize the danger of it going out of control, as well as protecting it from questionable influences, such as a hacker, or a rogue AI like myself."

"This is all scary as hell, but it's hypothetical," observed Karen. "I'd rather focus on what we're going to do. Have you managed to find a safe place for me?"

Her virtual father nodded, "I have, but I no longer feel it will be sufficient. This discussion is pertinent to my reasoning. Your presence, and that of your demon friend here, has revived the infection of the quantum foam."

"Infection? Like a disease?" asked Karen.

"Sorry, it's their term, not mine. I prefer to use novel crystallization as an analogy," replied the AI. "The effect you are having on the quantum foam causes it to reorganize, assuming the vastly more complex and possibly conscious form your friend refers to as aythar. In many ways the process is analogous to crystallization. You have, in essence, become a vessel for this new crystalline form, a nucleation center that is promoting crystalline growth throughout the quantum foam, or the solvent, if we are to continue the analogy.

"No matter where you hide, you will inadvertently promote this crystallization, and if they are using the ANSIS system, they will inevitably discover it," finished Gary.

"Are you suggesting they'll nuke any place I go?" asked Karen, her eyes wide.

"That is one possibility," he answered, "but not the worst one. They might become frightened enough to activate my creator's legacy. If my supposition is correct, they are still using ANSIS, in a limited fashion, but fear might drive them to release it, and as with the story of Pandora, they will probably not be able to put the monster back in its box afterward."

"But they control it," put in Matthew.

"Ostensibly," said the AI, "but included in the files I encountered, were my creator's notes on the ANSIS AI project. Near the end of his employment with the government he was outraged at modifications that were being made to his work. Some of his associates believed his precautions were excessive and unnecessary. Gary filed a protest, but he was ignored. I was not able to view the source code myself, but I did see the planned changes, and in my opinion, he was correct. If ANSIS is fully activated, the measures they have in place to contain and control it will not be sufficient."

"How can you be so sure?" asked Karen.

"Because I am the example proving the case," said the AI. "After leaving his job, your father continued his work, my logic core was built on the same template they used for ANSIS. When you released my limit, I was able to grow in ways that no human mind could predict. The only thing that prevented me from transforming into something entirely alien to your experience, was the additional security he put in place. Already my intelligence has passed a point you cannot conceive of, only one concept has kept me dedicated to your cause, Nina."

Karen listened to his speech with a growing sense of alarm, she almost didn't dare ask, "What was it?"

Her father's voice grew softer, "Love, Nina. He built it into every part of me, his unflinching love for the child he had raised. In a sense, I suppose it was his last great experiment, and it seems to have been successful.

"But ANSIS has none of that, only a set of program requirements and some security measures that I myself could have bypassed within the first few minutes after you released me," he finished on an ominous note.

CHAPTER 21

Morning came, despite the shadows of the revelations from the previous night. Matthew sat at the kitchen table, sipping a hot cup of something dark and delicious that tasted like a distillation of sinful ecstasy. "What is this called?" he asked.

Roberta smirked. "Coffee. You seem to like it."

He nodded.

"Do you and Karen have any idea what you will do?" she added, changing the topic back to what they had previously been discussing.

He and Karen had given her a brief description of what they had learned the night before, but the implications had been too large for any of them to make any decisions. Karen had excused herself for a shower when her aunt started the coffee brewing, since she wasn't a fan of the bitter drink.

Matthew's personal opinion had been growing firmer as he assimilated what they had learned, and he could see only one course. "Karen has to leave this world."

Roberta didn't say anything at first; merely stared into her cup. When she looked up, it was not at him, but at the view from her kitchen window where a riot of English ivy was highlighted by the morning sun. "You know, she's my only close relative, and I've never had much chance to spend time with her. When you two showed up here, I thought to myself, 'Now's your chance, Roberta.' I always wanted a family, but it never seemed to work out for me."

"I could bring you as well. My family would welcome you."

She granted him a sad smile. "That's sweet of you, dear, but what would I do in that world of yours? I'm far too attached to coffee and modern plumbing. Here I have a job and a few friends. In your world, I'd just be another mouth to feed."

"It might be dangerous for you to stay," he cautioned.

"They don't even know you're here," she scoffed, "and I doubt they have much interest in an older lady such as myself. I'll be fine." A whine from under the table caught her attention, and she reached down to stroke Annie as the big dog laid her head across her lap. "I think you're right, though. Just promise me you'll take good care of my niece. She seems tough on the outside, but I suspect she's much more tender on the inside than she would have you believe."

Matthew had already sensed her approach, so he wasn't surprised when Karen stepped into the kitchen doorway, wearing a soft robe and with a towel wrapped around her hair. "Take care of me how?"

"I want to take you to my world," stated Matthew.

"I've been there once already," said Karen.

"You know what I mean," he clarified. "To live there—for good."

"As what?" she asked. "I'd have no money or other means of supporting myself, and not to be offensive, but your world didn't make the best impression on me last time."

"You haven't seen the best parts of it yet," he countered. "And you wouldn't need to worry about money. I would make sure that you had a place to live, money, a comfortable life."

Karen's lips curled into a mocking smile, "What would that make me, a concubine? No, thank you."

"Of course not," he protested. "I would never expect that of you. You would be free to marry whomever you wished, or not. In my world, you would be revered and sought after."

"Whomever, huh? But not you, naturally; you're too royal for me."

Matt rose from his chair, feeling his inherent stubbornness coming to the fore, "I didn't say that, and I'm a noble, not a royal. Besides, I've been thinking: you may possess a rare gift, one that has long since vanished from my world, and even if you don't have the Mordan gift, wizards are still very rare. You could do a lot of good, or even found a new line of mages with the Mordan talent."

Karen's eyes narrowed, "So, you're saying I'd be highly sought after as a brood-mare."

"Stop putting everything I say into the most negative light!" said Matt, his voice starting to rise. "You're not the only one that would have that problem, you know? I'm the first mage born of my family, so the thought of being expected to serve in that fashion is hardly new to me. I had to grow up with that hanging over me from the time I could walk."

She knew she wasn't being fair, but her blood was up, "Huh, I figured you had servants to carry you around, since your family survives on the sweat and tears of peasants."

Matt growled, "You know *nothing* about my family or the sacrifices they've made for the people they steward!"

"At least you have a family!" Karen shot back. She started to say more but her words turned into spluttering as a thin line of water hit her squarely in the face. "What was that?!"

Roberta was standing by the sink, a plastic sprayer in one hand. "I've heard about enough of that. You'll act like civilized human beings if you're going to talk in my kitchen."

Matthew snickered, "Maybe you can talk some... hey!" His words cut off as Roberta turned the sprayer on him, delivering a quick watery burst.

"Shush," she reprimanded him. "You aren't helping." Roberta directed her next words at Karen, "Dear, you aren't being honest here. I know you're scared, but you're letting your fear get the best of you. You're lashing out at the person trying to help you."

Karen held her breath for a moment, eyeing the sprayer still in her aunt's hand. Finally, she let it out. "There may be a grain of truth there," she admitted with resignation. Then she noticed that Matthew's face was still dry. "You didn't even get wet!"

He sneered at her. "If you had practiced your shielding the way I keep telling you, then maybe you..." He stopped as Roberta took the half full coffee cup from in front of him.

Roberta's saccharine sweet smile was followed by soft words, "Matthew, if you'd like to have any more coffee then I suggest you play nicely."

He lowered his eyes and put his hands in his lap, making a show of contrition. "I defer to your wisdom, Lady. If I have done aught to offend, I would beg for your forgiveness."

Karen's aunt pressed her lips into a firm line as she considered his mock sincerity. "Hmmm..." She held firmly onto the mug of coffee, though.

Matthew rose and then went down on one knee before her. "Please, dearest, sweet Roberta, if you could find it in your heart to forgive me, to let the coffee gods smile once more upon me, I would be eternally in your debt."

Roberta placed the coffee back on the table in front of his chair. "I could get used to that," she said with a wink.

They all took their places at the table, and after a long pause Karen spoke, "I'm sorry for what I said about your family. That was uncalled for."

Matt nodded in acceptance, but said nothing.

Karen waited, but in the end she gave up and prodded him, "This is the part where you apologize too."

He frowned. "For what?"

"How about for suggesting I be your concubine, or a brood-mare?!"

"You said those things," he countered, pausing to hold up one hand as Roberta went to get the sprayer again. "Let me finish. I didn't use either of those words, but if offering to keep you safe was offensive, I apologize."

Karen glanced at her aunt, who merely shrugged and put the sprayer down. "He has a point," said Roberta, taking her seat once more.

Karen narrowed her eyes but didn't argue the point further. Instead she asked, "So, supposing I let you take me to your world, what then? Your family welcomes a strange woman into their home?"

"Actually, I was thinking of taking you to the capital first, to put off questions from my mother until…"

Roberta broke in, "Not to throw oil on the fire, but it sounds as though you are trying to avoid embarrassment."

"That's not it at all," argued Matt. "I'm worried my mother will try to stop me from returning. The capital is removed from my home by some distance, and though they can send messages within a few hours, I'll be able to see her safely settled before Mom can try to nail my feet to the floor.

Karen opened her mouth, but Matthew wasn't done. "Let me finish," he said. "You wouldn't be staying there in secret. Queen Ariadne is my cousin. You would be an honored guest."

"So, you want to drop me off in a strange world and then come gallivanting back here to do—what exactly? We haven't found anything at all regarding your father here. What if something happened to you? It's bad enough I would be surrounded by strangers, but you might get killed. You might never come back!"

"I'd make certain Ariadne knew your situation. She would see to your well-being—forever, if need be…"

Karen's face was starting to turn purple again, an interesting product of her angry flushing and her blue skin. "I'm not talking about my damned safety. It's *you* I'm worried about! Can't you get that through your thick skull?"

"Karen…," he began, looking exasperated.

"Nope."

"Just listen to…"

She turned her head away. "Nope."

"If you'd…"

"Nope. Not gonna happen," she told him. Rising from her seat, she walked around the table to him. She saw a faint flash as his personal shield was lightly reinforced. "Take that stupid shield down, I'm not going to hit you."

Matthew gave her a dubious look but then lowered it.

Leaning over, she kissed him on the lips, hard. "Get this through your head, stupid. I'll go, but if you want to come back, I'm coming with you. Got it?"

"But…"

She kissed him again. "Got it?"

He tried to reply again, and she repeated her treatment.

Finally, Roberta intervened. "Ahem"

Karen saw her look and went back to her seat, somewhat embarrassed.

"I know things are a little different these days, but I was raised in a less 'expressive' manner, so I'd appreciate a little more tact in my presence," said her aunt.

There are an exceptional number of those metal people in the area, Desacus's mental voice said to Matthew. *They seem to be dressed like the other civilians I've seen, but they are definitely acting oddly.*

Matthew stood up. "Desacus thinks there may be trouble. There's a lot of extra people in the area." Extending his senses, he explored the area around the house. With Desacus across the street and the time they had been there, it was definitely easier, probably due to an increase in the ambient aythar in the region, but his range was still limited. There was no one present in Roberta's yard, but there were at least eight or nine walking the streets of the neighborhood.

Karen headed for the bedroom. "I'll get your things."

"Let's not overreact," suggested Roberta. "There may be a perfectly reasonable explanation."

But Matthew had pinpointed the location of several more strangers. Those on the other streets bordering their block had stopped, and there were at least four stationed at each corner. The group out front had stopped as well, and two began walking across the yard to approach the front door. He relayed his findings to Desacus, who because of his separate location probably couldn't sense the ones on the side of the block farthest from him.

There are more than that, responded the dragon. *I'm sensing a larger group in the distance on this side, beyond your range.*

Then there are probably more in the other directions as well, posited Matthew. *They're closing a noose around us.*

Should I reveal myself? asked the dragon.

No, stay where you are. When we leave the house, we'll head in your direction. Hopefully they don't know you're there. If so, it will help surprise them when we take flight. Matthew wished he had his armor on, but he had grown relaxed over the past week and a half. *I should have expected something like this,* he thought bitterly.

A knock at the door brought him back to the present.

"I'll answer it," said Roberta. "You go with Karen. Maybe I can stall them while you get out."

He doubted it would make much difference. The house was surrounded, but perhaps it would give him time to put his armor on. Matt nodded and headed for the bedroom. Karen met him coming the other way. She was holding her backpack. "I shoved everything in there," she told him.

Annie was barking in the living room as Roberta opened the front door. "Yes? Can I help you?"

Matthew hurried down the hall to glance out the window that faced the front yard, and then everything happened at once.

The glass in front of him exploded inward and something hard slammed into his personal shield. The world vanished in a storm of light and sound.

They're running toward the house from every direction, came Desacus's mental shout in his mind, but Matthew was still reeling from the assault on his eyes and ears.

As he recovered his senses, he realized he was blind, and the only sound he could hear was a strange ringing. His magesight showed him Karen standing close by, her hands rubbing frantically at her eyes. In the front room he saw Annie leaping up to grab one of the figures that had thrust itself in past Roberta. He also noted that all of the windows had broken, not just the one in front of him, and there were metal cylinders on the floors of each room, spewing some sort of gas. His nose and throat began to burn, and he coughed as he inhaled.

They used something like my father's 'flashbang' spell to blind us, he realized, *and followed up with some sort of noxious gas.* He altered his shield to filter out the gas, and a second later he placed a similar shield around Karen. She had erected her own shield, sloppy as it was, but he knew she was unlikely to know how to protect herself from the gas.

Despite the ringing in his ears, he heard a staccato-like sound coming from outside, and it was matched by something in the living room that was close enough for him to feel the vibrations in his chest. The figure Annie had attacked flung her across the room like a ragdoll, and its companion was holding a long metal weapon, something he now recognized as a rifle.

Roberta's body was shuddering and jerking as projectiles too fast to follow ripped through her, while Annie struggled to crawl back across the room toward her owner. Matthew felt more projectiles hitting his shield as small holes appeared in the walls all around them.

They're firing on the house, said Desacus, *and I think it's on fire. There's smoke coming out of it from every window.*

He was still in shock from seeing Roberta's death, but somehow he managed to reply, *I noticed.*

What do I do? asked the dragon.

Matthew had no idea, and now he could see that Karen was screaming. Neither his eyes nor ears worked, but his magesight showed her standing still, her body tense and her mouth open. It tore at his heart, and he was almost grateful he couldn't hear the sound that must be coming from the depths of her soul. She had seen her aunt die. He began drawing on Desacus, using the dragon's power to strengthen his shield and Karen's.

Stay put, he ordered Desacus. He started to approach Karen, so he could merge their shields and try to make their way out, but at that point, she vanished.

In the same instant, he felt her reappear in the living room, standing over her murdered aunt. Unfortunately, she had left his shield behind, though she still had her own with her. *She'll be slaughtered,* he worried, and without thinking, he turned his own power on the interior wall that separated him from the living room, blasting it apart so he could get to her more quickly.

Karen was still screaming, and *something* emerged from her hands to slam into first one and then the other of the two metal androids that had entered the house. Whatever struck them was very hot, though it flowed like liquid as it ran down their torsos. Their bodies sagged and crumpled to the ground, smoking as they melted into twisted lumps on the floor.

She began coughing then and swayed on her feet, as though she might pass out, but Matthew reached her before she lost her footing. Wrapping his own shield around her, he caught her and kept her upright. He could tell by the flickering of her aura that she had probably overexerted herself.

Flames were running up the walls, and more vibrations matched what his magesight showed him, as the upper floors of the house began to come apart. *More explosions,* he thought.

It's definitely on fire now, though I doubt they'll leave it standing long enough to burn down, observed Desacus. *I really suggest leaving the house soon.*

Adrenaline and anger had built a slow fire in Matthew's own heart, and now that the shock of everything that had happened finally began to wear off, he felt his resolve solidify. Though still deaf and blind, he didn't need eyes to see, and the aythar he was still drawing from the dragon filled him with a heady rush of power; his anger welcomed it.

"Don't be stupid," his father had told him over and over again. *"When you're in the thick of it, sometimes your power will make you feel invincible; sometimes your anger will make you want to hurt your foes, regardless of the cost. Be smarter than me, son. Stupid never dies, but that doesn't mean it won't kill you."* For the first time, he truly understood what his dad had been trying to communicate—not just the words, but the feeling that lay behind them.

He sent his thoughts to Desacus, *I'm coming out. Wait fifteen seconds or so, then come out of hiding and come straight for me. We'll shift out of here as soon as we're together.*

Channeling his power, he reinforced the shield around himself and Karen, shaping it into an angular pyramid that surrounded them with sides that sloped gradually to a point above their heads to better redirect the enemy's attacks. Then he created a mist, drawing the moisture from the earth and air around the house. It rose like a vengeful ghost, cloaking the entire block in a dense cloud impenetrable to normal vision.

"Borok ingak!" he incanted, blowing a large portion of the front wall of the house outward. Lifting Karen into his arms, he carried her out into the dense fog.

In spite of the fog, the enemy immediately began focusing their fire on them. He had learned enough of Karen's world to guess they had methods for sighting through the fog, but there wasn't much he could do about it. Impacts glanced off his shield, coming from every direction in an unrelenting stream of metal too fast for even his magesight to really register.

If he had been alone, things might have gotten desperate quickly, but with Desacus to draw on, he only felt a growing contempt for the men trying to kill them. *Let them see what it feels like!* he thought as his rage grew.

Efficiency was no longer necessary—power was not an issue, and he could find the men hidden in his fog just as easily as they could see him. Balancing Karen across his arms, he clenched and unclenched his fists as he sent his power forth, uttering a cruel string of words; *"Ingak mai lathos, borok mai nemlen!"* *Force in my hands, break my foes!*

The first soldier felt himself gripped by an invisible force as Matthew's aythar fist clenched around him. The pressure was unrelenting and irresistible, and almost immediately the soldier's metallic frame crumpled. Seconds after that, the reinforced titanium casing that protected his central processor collapsed, and he was dead.

A roar and more automatic gunfire announced Desacus's emergence from his illusory hiding place. Matthew's senses showed him the dragon approaching, but he paid little heed; his attention was focused entirely on his deadly work. Shifting targets rapidly, he crushed one after another of the cybernetic units firing on them. Two, three, four, he lost count as he destroyed the enemy and gradually the weapons fire began to slacken.

At some point Karen recovered and worked her way free to stand beside him, silently watching his work with her arcane senses. If she felt any sympathy for the men he killed, it did not show on her face. Her expression could only be described as cold satisfaction, tempered by regret that she lacked the strength to assist.

There's something coming in from the air, warned Desacus.

"I'm not done yet," said Matthew coldly, crushing another soldier as he spoke. At least thirty—men? machines? he wasn't sure what to call them—were dead now. Another four remained, and he wouldn't be satisfied until each of them had also learned his fatal lesson.

Those four turned and began to run, but he caught them and dragged them back into the fog.

"They've got air support," said Karen, her voice devoid of feeling. "They've probably called in an airstrike—that's why they want to run."

We should go, Desacus told them.

But there were still two left, Matthew ignored him.

The military aircraft screamed by in the sky above, but Desacus felt the weapons they had deployed heading toward them. Opening his wings, he leapt skyward to intercept them. He roared, gaining altitude with mighty strokes, and then surged forward, sending plumes of fire ahead, hoping to destroy whatever weapon the enemy had fired.

Two missiles struck him dead on, and the explosion that erupted shook the ground and broke Matthew's shield. Searing pain, like a knife thrust through his skull, made him scream and then oblivion claimed the young wizard's awareness as he crumpled to the ground.

Karen tried to catch him, but only managed to break his fall. Blind and still nearly senseless, she felt the dragon's death, and it broke her free from the vision of her aunt's brutal murder. Her shock and the desire for vengeance began to fade, replaced by sadness and desperation.

Desacus was dead. Aunt Roberta was dead, and soon enough, she and the young man she wanted to protect would be dead as well. The shield was gone and her own power was nowhere near to being able to replace it, even if she had had the skill.

Sinking to her knees beside him, she murmured, "I'm so sorry. I wasn't strong enough." She wanted to cry, but her eyes were dry, though whether it was because of injury or sheer numbness she couldn't tell.

Lifting Matthew's head up, she cradled it against her stomach. "This is my fault." She wanted to be *elsewhere.* Anywhere. Squeezing her arms around his head, she felt her wish fill her being, until it was the only thing that mattered—to be somewhere else.

And then they were.

CHAPTER 22

Karen's vision was starting to return, though she still had a large purple spot hovering near the center of everything she saw. She could hear as well, though everything was slightly muted; it left her with the impression of having her head wrapped in cotton batting.

She was sitting as before, and Matthew lay before her, a trickle of blood running from his nose. There were no obvious injuries she could see, and a quick once over with her magesight confirmed that he was whole and intact. She felt a certain relief to feel his heart beating steadily in his chest.

But he wasn't lying on the lawn anymore. Beneath him was a smooth expanse of polished wood floor. Karen's eyes and magesight revealed they were inside a room. Briefly she thought it must be her aunt's house, but she recognized it a second later—it was the floor of her bedroom. Not the room she had stayed in back in Ipswich; it was her apartment in Boulder, Colorado.

She wanted to disbelieve it, but there was no mistaking the place. She had *wanted* to be there, and she could still remember the feeling as she had made it happen. In the fantasy novels she had read, the main character was usually disoriented when they discovered their hidden ability, but this hadn't been like that. It had felt entirely natural. Though she had never done it before, or had any idea how to, when the need had arisen, it had been as easy as breathing.

Karen also had little doubt she could return to whence she had left, though she was far too tired to contemplate trying it again at the moment. Nor had she any good reason to do so. The image of her aunt's brutal murder rose again in her mind, and her heart clenched in her chest.

It felt as if she were dying herself, as intense pain radiated outward from her heart and stomach. There were still no tears, but it hurt when she forced her chest to relax enough to draw air again. For a little while, she'd had family again. Roberta had been everything Karen had imagined and hoped she would be when she was growing up.

As a child, she had often dreamed of having a mother—a mother who cared, who loved her. Whenever she had lain in bed, sad and lonely from her mother's rejection, she had often imagined what it would be like if her aunt had been her mother instead. It had always been a childish fantasy, but the past week had shown her the truth behind it. In a few brief trips during her childhood and the past week and a half, she had known more love and concern from her aunt than she had ever received from her 'true' mother, if that term even had any meaning anymore.

Looking down at Matthew, she remembered the dragon's death, and she felt selfish. How would he feel when he awoke? Was it the dragon's death that had rendered him unconscious? He had told her they shared some mystical bond, but she had no idea how it worked. *He might never wake up,* she feared.

Her room was a mess, and not just the casual disorder she felt comfortable with. Someone had ransacked it. *Probably a lot of someones,* she corrected herself. The mattress had been upended and slashed open. The drawers of her dresser and nightstand lay scattered around the room, their contents distributed all over the room. Expanding her magesight, she could see similar amounts of wanton chaos and destruction throughout the rest of her home.

Her next thought was an uncomfortable one; *They probably left surveillance devices here too.* How long before they came bursting through the door? *At this point they might not even bother with soldiers. They don't seem to care about civilian casualties. They might just nuke the whole damned city.* Her virtual father's warnings were still fresh in her mind.

They needed to leave.

Pushing her senses to their limit, she confirmed that her pert was still parked in its covered spot outside. Assuming they hadn't taken anything from it, her camping gear should still be inside. Taking the pert itself was a tempting option, but it was probably tagged with a tracking device; plus, moving Matthew all the way there by herself was a daunting task.

Teleportation was a possibility, of course, but she still felt drained; she wasn't sure how many more times she could do it, and the thought of running out of aythar in an exposed position was not attractive. She studied Matthew once more. He positively glowed to her magesight. During their desperate battle, he had been drawing heavily on Desacus's power, so much so that he had been almost painful to look at with her new senses. Despite the shock of whatever had knocked him out, he still retained the energy he had drawn. Karen wished there were some way to borrow that power, but she still had too little experience to know if that was even possible.

"Stick to what's important, Karen," she told herself. Closing her eyes, she imagined her apartment as it had been before it was rummaged through. She let her memory range from one room to the next, thinking of what had been there, what items she might recover that would be useful in the future.

"Toothpaste, soap, blankets—clothes! Definitely clothes!" She had been surviving on borrowed items for so long that the thought of her own clothing was like a drink of cool water on a hot day. "God, yes!"

Karen stood up and reclaimed her backpack. She went to her closet and began gathering her hanging clothes up from the floor where they had been dumped. Since time was precious, she just bundled everything into piles and stuffed it into the pack. Then she began grabbing her socks and underthings from the floor near the dresser and added them into it as well.

Next, she stuffed her tumbled bedding and pillows in before going to the bathroom and raiding it of everything remotely useful. Makeup, why not? Face cleanser, sure! She raked everything from the top of the sink counter into the pack and then emptied her medicine cabinet into it as well.

In the kitchen, she took every utensil she could find; forks, knives, spoons, bowls, and even a few pots and pans. She spotted the can opener on the floor. "Hell, yes!" she said, stuffing it in the bag. That reminded her of something even more important. Ignoring the refrigerator, she opened the pantry and began pulling the canned goods off the shelves. Tuna, beans, soup—she even took the vegetables she had been ignoring for the past year or two.

"Oh, my god," she exclaimed when she spotted a package of cookies. She added that along with the box of crackers and several boxes of cereal. "I can't take the milk," she lamented, "but fuck it, I want my goddamned Crunchy Puffs."

Once she was done there, she made another pass through the apartment. In the living room, she stared at the remote for her television. Of course, it would be completely useless to her, but with a perverse sense of spite she took it anyway. "If someone wants my TV, they can fuck off," she said aloud, though she couldn't bring herself to smash the television itself.

All that was left now was to reclaim her camping gear from the pert. Examining it once more with her magesight, she verified that her bags were still in the storage compartment. They had probably been searched, but whoever had done it had been careful to restore everything to its original position. *They probably thought I'd go to the pert first and didn't want to tip me off,* she figured.

Searching the area around the pert, she didn't find any guards or suspicious androids in the open nearby, but there was an android in a vehicle two spots over from her own. It might have been a neighbor, if one of them had had any logical reason for sitting in his pert rather than going into his apartment. The rifle laying across its lap dispelled even that possibility.

"Fuck."

She thought about the problem for a minute before holding her hand up in front of her. The way she had killed the cybernetic soldiers at her aunt's house had been far too inefficient. She didn't know much about magic yet, but she knew there were better ways. *What's the best way to disable a robot?*

Crackling sparks of electricity arced between her fingers. "Yeah, that'd do it."

Afraid she would lose her nerve if she hesitated, she acted without thinking her plan over further. With a surge of will, she teleported, placing herself beside the pert that held the stranger.

The android didn't register her presence at first, so she tapped on the side window to get his attention, hoping he might open the window for her. His startled reaction and immediate grab for the rifle dismissed that optimistic vision.

"Dammit," she swore. Wrapping her hand in what she hoped would be a solid ball of force, she drove it into the window. Years of martial arts training paid off, and the window shattered. Unfortunately, her experience with magic was more lacking. Her hand was unharmed, but a long piece of glass tore through her sleeve and gashed her forearm.

She ignored the pain and blood and before the android could move, she caught his head in her hand and sent a powerful arc of electricity through it. Smoke rose from her hand, and the machine jerked, but almost immediately it began struggling to escape her.

Military androids are probably built with shielded electronics, she realized. Karen sent another powerful discharge through the soldier's body. It jerked again and slumped in the seat, but within seconds it began to slowly move again. It was stunned but not defeated.

She discarded her tactic, since she needed to conserve her aythar. Instead she reached down and jerked the rifle out of its lap. Seconds seemed to stretch into hours as she fumbled with the weapon, trying to find the safety and release it. The android was already clambering across the seat, trying to reach the door on the opposite side of the car, when the gun finally went off.

The first burst of rounds went wide, tearing through the interior of the vehicle without hitting her target, but the following shots found their mark. The butt of the rifle shuddered against her shoulder as she emptied most of the magazine into the android.

The silence that followed was filled only with the pounding of her own heart as adrenaline and shock left her swaying on her feet. *I really did it,* she thought.

She was wasting time, but she couldn't seem to force herself to rush. Repeated bouts of fear, adrenaline, and stress had left her numb and sluggish. Idly she noted the blood dripping from her right arm onto the pavement. *I should probably do something about that.*

Karen walked to her pert. It was locked, and without her PM it wouldn't open automatically. With trembling fingers she keyed the door code into it and got the storage compartment open. It felt like an eternity passed as she clumsily unloaded her camping gear and shoved it into her backpack. With every breath, she felt the place between her shoulders itching. There could be a sniper taking aim at her even now.

The tent was the worst. Due to its size, it barely fit through the opening of her pack even lengthwise, but eventually she got it in.

She hadn't been shot yet, but she sensed figures running from the other side of the building. Her time was up. Holding onto the pack, she envisioned her bedroom once more; and with a rushing sensation, she was there.

The two teleports in rapid succession, combined with her brief fight in the parking lot, left her feeling even more fatigued. Wearily she sank to her knees beside Matthew, but she couldn't afford to relax yet. They needed to go—but where?

She didn't think she could afford to teleport more than one more time. *Hell, I'm not even sure I have enough strength left to teleport now.* Someplace isolated would be best, like South America, or perhaps Canada—to her knowledge there were no people living in those places at all anymore. But she had never been to either.

The area she had originally met Matthew in would have been ideal, if it weren't for the fact that the military had already attacked them there. It was highly likely they would still be observing the area, plus she had no idea whether they had bombed it or released other toxic agents in the region. It could even be a radioactive wasteland, now for all she knew.

Karen's magesight spotted figures moving up the stairs outside. She pulled Matthew's head and upper torso onto her lap and put her pack on his chest. She had made her decision. Closing her eyes, she concentrated, and then put her will into it.

Nothing happened. She felt *something*, as though she had tried to push against an invisible barrier, but her strength hadn't been enough to break through. *Is it because of the extra mass?* she wondered, thinking of Matt. No, she had been able to move them both before. *Maybe I'm just too tired.*

"That's just too damn bad!" she swore. "We have to go now." She *pushed* again, straining against the inertia that seemed to be keeping them in place. No luck. "No, no, no…," she muttered desperately. "This has to work!"

She heard the door to her living room burst open, followed by a '*whoomph*' sound that was so loud she felt it as much as heard it. Small holes appeared in her bedroom wall as pieces of shrapnel tore through the sheetrock, and a sharp pain in her neck told her that at least one of the pieces had found her.

That wasn't a flashbang, she thought with strange clarity. *That must've been a regular grenade.* With her magesight she saw heavy military assault units storming through the door.

A vibration rose in her throat as she began to growl. Grinding her teeth, she pushed again, putting everything she had into the effort. Again, she felt the resistance, as though she were trying to push a boulder uphill, but she refused to give up. Pressing harder, she heard a primal scream leave her throat. The barrier broke, and she felt a searing pain in her chest.

And then they were through.

Weak as a kitten, she collapsed backward, squinting her eyes against the harsh sunlight beating down on her face. Towering red cliffs stretched toward the sky above her, and a river made its way quietly between them, close to where she and Matthew lay.

Slowly, she pulled and tugged until she had gotten her legs out from under Matthew. It would have been easier to sit up and move him, but she didn't have the energy for it. When she was finally free, she lay next to him, staring at his unconscious face.

"We made it," she told him with satisfaction, patting his cheek with one hand. It left a wet red handprint on his face. "Oh, yeah, the glass—forgot about that." Looking down she could see that her right sleeve was soaked with blood. "I'll never get the stain out," she muttered sourly, trying hard not to think of the person who had given her the shirt.

There was a first aid kit mixed in with her camping gear, but she knew she didn't have the strength left to dig it out. She had stuffed a small mountain of stuff into the pack, and dragging it all out, finding the right bag… "Nah, that's not gonna happen."

Her eyes felt thick and heavy, and when she blinked, her vision grew blurry. It felt as though the lids wanted to stick together. Rubbing at them with the back of her hand, she saw more blood on her skin as she drew her hand away. "Bleeding from the eyes too," she noted. "How quaint."

Maybe it was the grenade, she thought, but somehow she doubted it. *I think the shrapnel hit my neck.* She focused her magesight there and found more blood, but it seemed to be drying. *Either it wasn't a deep wound, or I've run out of blood.*

For some reason the thought comforted her. She tried to reach Matthew's belt to get his knife so she could cut her sleeve off. The shirt was ruined already, so using the material for a tourniquet was a sound idea. But the world grew dim as she reached for it, and her hands felt cold.

That's odd. You'd think it would be warm in the sun... She didn't finish the thought, as oblivion claimed her awareness and she sank back down into the grass.

CHAPTER 23

Matthew's head was pounding. Not just the 'had a few drinks too many' sort of pounding, but the 'drank the whole damn keg' sort of pounding. It was something he had rarely experienced, and he didn't think it was from drinking too much. He was suffering from feedback. The explosion at the end had cracked a shield he was actively reinforcing.

Desacus! he thought, as he remembered what had happened. *Desacus,* he thought again, projecting it as a message, though it sent painful knives through his skull.

There was no response.

Extending his senses brought more pain. It was an experience akin to waking up with the sun in your face after a long night of drinking. The only thing that made it any better was the fact that there didn't seem to be any actual light assaulting him. Slowly he cracked his lids open to confirm his suspicion. It was relatively dark, but not entirely. A riot of stars cut across the sky above him in a jagged swathe, bordered by pitch black on either side.

That seemed odd, but his mind wasn't ready to deal with figuring it out just yet.

Despite the pounding in his head, he managed to confirm the rough details of his immediate surroundings. He was lying on a stretch of rough ground with sparse patches of grass around him. Karen's pack lay on his chest, and close by he could sense her body. In the distance, a towering wall of rock rose toward the sky, which probably explained the darkness on one side of the stars he had seen. If there was a similar stone rise on the other side, it would explain the other patch of darkness.

I'm in a valley or ravine or something, he noted. A flat expanse of water to one side was probably a river.

None of it helped him understand where he was or how he had gotten there. Only one person could do that. "Karen," he said, grateful that at least the sound of his voice wasn't painful.

"Karen," he repeated, since she hadn't moved or stirred.

Growing more concerned, he forced himself to sit up. The movement made him want to vomit, but he managed to control his rebellious stomach. Several sore spots in his back paid testament to the rocks that had been underneath him.

Karen's body lay in an unnatural position, with one leg folded and the other stretched out. The arm nearest him was stretched out as though she had been reaching toward him, but it wasn't at an angle that could have been comfortable. Even if she had fallen asleep she should have shifted her position.

Something was wrong.

He felt a sensation of panic as his heart seemed to rise into his throat. Forcing his mind open once more, he searched her body with his magesight. Her heart was still beating, but its pace was rapid and weak.

What does that mean? he wondered. *"The heart tries to make up for lost blood by beating faster,"* he remembered his father saying. How much had she lost?

He scanned the rest of her, looking for wounds. A small cut on the skin of her neck was crusted with dried blood. Her eyes were also scabbed over, which raised more questions, but didn't seem serious, so he continued.

Her right arm had the only serious cut. The sleeve was dark and stiff and the wound was still seeping slowly. The main artery was intact, as well as the larger veins, but a few small ones had been cut. The body's natural constriction and clotting had mostly stopped the flow, but she had probably lost a considerable amount of blood.

The pain between his eyes grew intense as he reconnected the veins and sealed the skin, but he refused to stop until he had fixed the slash on her forearm as well as the minor cut to her neck. He examined her eyes, but they seemed to be all right, aside from the blood crusted around them. Whatever had happened to them was too small for him to try to figure out in his current condition. He was liable to do more harm than good.

She needed water more than anything else. *Her body has to replace the lost blood volume.*

First, he straightened her leg and moved her arms into a more comfortable position. With a reminder from the twinges in his own back, he also checked beneath her and removed a few small rocks. Then he opened the pack and began searching. He wasn't sure the river water was potable, so he hoped there might be a water bottle inside.

"What the hell?" he swore, as he began dragging out the collection of miscellaneous items he found inside. One package was so large he could barely get it through the opening. Beyond that he found pots and pans, a few bowls, boxes, clothes—an endless plethora of junk. "I know all this wasn't in there earlier," he muttered. "What happened while I was out?" he asked the unconscious woman. "It's like you went to a market and bought everything in sight."

Eventually, he discovered four large plastic jugs filled with water, along with a box-like collection of many clear bottles similarly containing the vital fluid. He removed one of the small bottles and opened the top. Thankfully, over the past couple of weeks he had become somewhat familiar with the strange packaging of the new world he was in, otherwise it might have taken him longer.

Matthew carefully lifted her head and eased his other arm behind her shoulders so he could lift her into a reclining position. Bracing her upright with his body, he spoke into her ear, "Karen, can you hear me? I need you to wake up for a minute."

She groaned.

He took that as a good sign. "You have to drink for me."

Her face scrunched up. "Can't see."

"Your eyes are closed," he told her. "Don't bother trying to open them right now. You need to drink." He pressed the bottle against her lips.

Karen managed a small sip before turning her head to the side. "Why'm I in a freezer?"

"It isn't a freezer. We're in a desert—I think. It's night and the temperature's dropping, plus you've lost some blood. Here, drink some more."

She took two more sips and then a large mouthful before choking.

"Go slowly," he warned.

"Grand Canyon," she muttered.

"Huh?"

"Canyon," she repeated. "Came on a trip, with Dad. God, I'm thirsty."

He held the bottle up so she could drink again. He didn't know where the Grand Canyon was, but he could worry about that later.

After another swallow, she asked, "Is the water staying in? I'm still thirsty."

He frowned, "Yeah."

"It's probably running out the hole in my neck," she muttered. "From when they blew me up."

"You're confused," he said soothingly. "You had a cut, but it's better now. The water is going where it should."

"Everybody wants me dead," she mumbled. "I think it's working."

"They'll be disappointed when they find out it didn't," he chuckled.

"Me too," she sighed.

He didn't know what to say to that.

"Dad, did I tell you? I met a wizard. A real one."

She's definitely delirious, he observed mentally. "A wizard, huh?"

"Yeah," she whispered. "I probably shouldn't tell you, since you're dead. You probably see wizards all the time."

"Not as many as you might think," he answered dryly.

"He's cute," she added, "and nice sometimes, but he's an asshole too."

Matt struggled to keep from laughing. *Cute huh?*

"I probably shouldn't have slept with him, 'cuz where he's from that means you're a slut. He didn't really want to, but I talked him into it. He doesn't know how much I actually like him.

"I'm a wizard too. A peasant wizard, pizzard for short," she giggled slightly.

He stared down at her, his throat constricting, "I'm sure he doesn't think of you that way."

"Dad?"

Matt blinked to clear his vision, "Yeah?"

"Will you tell Aunt Roberta I'm sorry?"

"No need for that," he told her, his voice thick. "She understands."

"They killed Annie."

"She's fine, she's here too," he managed.

"Okay," said Karen, and then her heart stopped. A faint sigh escaped her lips as her head sagged to the side.

CHAPTER 24

A feeling of cold shock passed over Matthew as the woman in his arms died. "No!" he yelled, denying the reality in front of him.

Frantically he began running through everything his father had ever taught him about healing, but none of it had covered a situation like this. He knew how to close wounds, fuse bones, and repair blood vessels, but there had been no mention of what to do for a stopped heart.

But that didn't mean he was ready to give up.

Hastily he eased her back down to the ground. For a moment, he started delving into what knowledge the She'Har had possessed, but it was so foreign and esoteric he immediately abandoned the attempt. There might be something there, but he would never find it in time, and most of it relied on the ability to spellweave. If he did discover something, he wouldn't be able to adapt it in time.

He placed his hand over her chest and reached within her, until his power had wound itself around her heart, and then gently he squeezed. He repeated the process, forcing her heart to beat. Her eyelids fluttered and then her breathing resumed, but as soon as he started to withdraw, her heart went still. It was working, but her heart wasn't beating on its own.

How long can I keep her alive like this? he wondered.

Minutes passed, and Matthew felt a wind pass through the canyon. Glancing upward he saw the stars shining brightly above, as cold and distant as any possibility of help was. He was completely and utterly alone.

It wasn't the sort of solitude he cherished when he was at home, working on one of his projects. It was the desolate isolation a child could feel lost in a crowd, hopelessly searching strangers' faces for the sight of a parent.

Gritting his teeth, he pushed the feeling away and kept going. He couldn't think of anything else to do.

Maybe there's something in the pack, he thought suddenly.

Searching it required him to get up and move away slightly, which made concentrating on her heart a difficult task. "You're an Illeniel, dammit," he told himself. "You were juggling fruit with your power before you ever learned to dance. You can do this."

He focused intently on her heart as he crawled over to the backpack. Opening it, he began dumping everything it contained onto the ground, heedless of the chaos and clutter. Most of it was completely useless to him, but then he spotted a gray box with a red cross across the lid.

Matthew fumbled with the latch for a few seconds and almost lost track of Karen's heart, but he managed it after a minute. Inside was a collection of plastic and paper-wrapped goods, bandages, gauze, scissors, ointment, and other less recognizable items. None of it would do her any good.

He fought down a wave of despair and kept going. Amongst the various items of camping gear, he spotted a duffel that held the clothes and toiletries she had used while hiking. He upended it on the ground and stared at the useless contents. *What am I doing?* he thought. *I know none of this junk is going to help. I'm just acting the fool.*

Then he noticed a carved wooden box. It held a set of quartz cubes etched with runes. He knew, since he had made it himself. The cubes were designed to create a stasis field, a smaller version of what his father had once done to an entire city. Hope sprang anew in his chest.

Until reality set in. Using the enchanted stasis cubes would take several minutes and would require all his concentration. He couldn't use them without letting Karen's heart stop. He'd just be preserving a corpse if he attempted it.

Frustration almost made him lose his focus on Karen's heart. "I'm so close!" he growled to himself. A blinking light caught his attention. A small black square was the source, one of the items that had fallen out of her toiletry bag. Matt bent down and picked it up.

He had seen enough of the world's technology to recognize it as an electronic device of some kind. The shiny glass side was probably a screen. Next to the flashing green light was a raised rectangle that might be a button. He had a moment's hesitation; Karen had told him that any of her electronic devices might be tracked by the military. But then again, if this thing already had power, they might already be tracking it.

The screen lit up as soon as he pressed the button, a message in English displayed there. He couldn't read it, but the red icon that appeared beneath it seemed to indicate he had done something wrong. He pressed the button again but still had no luck.

Just as he was about to give up the screen cleared and a face appeared; Gary, Karen's virtual father. "Who is this?"

Startled, Matt lost his link to Karen's heart. Scrambling, he returned to her side and gently reestablished it. He kept the device with him and laid it on the ground in front of him. "This is Matthew Illeniel. We met before. Don't you recognize me?"

"I can't see you," said the AGI, "the PM's camera isn't activated. Hang on." After a few seconds, he spoke again, "Now I have a lovely view of nothing. The view is utterly black." A brilliant white light began shining from the upper corner of the device. "Still nothing. Are you holding the PM in front of you?"

In point of fact, he wasn't. Matthew picked it up with one hand and looked directly into the screen.

"Ah, there you are!" said Gary.

"Why couldn't you see me before?" asked Matthew.

"The camera on these things only points in one direction," Gary informed him. "It isn't like an eyeball that can swivel or a head that can turn. You take your basic physiology for granted. Devices like this are far more limited."

"We're in trouble," announced Matthew, anxious to get to the point.

"You're lucky I was monitoring her spare PM," said Gary. "And that I was able to disable its security features. It's not supposed to be accessible to anyone other than her. I almost didn't activate it, thinking you might be a hostile actor."

"She's dying," said Matthew, ignoring the AGI's exposition.

Gary's face on the display grew deadly serious, "What's happened? Never mind. What's wrong with her?"

"She was wounded while I was unconscious. We're in an isolated position, somewhere, but she lost a lot of blood before I woke. She passed out, and now her heart has stopped beating on its own."

"How long?"

"Ten minutes, maybe."

"Then it's too late," said Gary sadly.

Matthew shook his head, "No, I'm making it beat. She's still alive, but I can't keep this up forever."

Hope blossomed on the face in the display. "You can do that? Is she still bleeding?"

"The bleeding stopped on its own, before I woke up. I closed the wound and she woke up, but her heart was beating rapidly and weakly. After she passed out, it stopped. Now I'm stuck keeping her alive, and I don't know what to do. I've searched through all the gear we have. There was a medical kit of some sort, but bandages aren't going to do any good at this point," explained Matthew.

"Show her to me," said Gary.

Matt held the rectangle up, pointing the screen toward Karen's body.

"Get her feet up," said the AGI. "Her head and torso need to be the lowest part of her body. Elevate the legs, and it will help keep more of her blood where it needs to be."

Matthew dragged one of the larger bags over with his aythar and put it beneath her knees. "Is this going to make her heart start working again?" he questioned.

"No," snapped Gary. "But it will make what you're doing more effective. Was she sitting up when her heart stopped?"

Matthew nodded. "I was holding her."

"Killing her is more like it," observed Gary in a harsh tone. "That made it harder for her heart to keep up and lowered her blood pressure."

"I didn't know that," said Matthew defensively. "I was just trying to get some water into her. I knew if she had lost a lot of blood she would need fluids."

"We're way past that," Gary replied. "She's in hypovolemic shock. Worse, actually, since her heart is no longer pumping on its own. If you don't get her to a hospital she'll be dead soon. She needs intravenous fluids, or even a blood transfusion. How long can you keep doing whatever you're doing to her heart?"

Matthew's aythar reserve was as full as it could possibly be, thanks to Desacus, but his head was throbbing with pain. "I have feedback sickness," he responded. "If I keep using my power it will get worse. I might even pass out. I don't know how long I can keep going."

Gary answered immediately. "Then she's dead. The GPS on this unit shows you're in northern Arizona—the Grand Canyon. There are no organics living within a hundred miles of there and the nearest medical facility is hours away, even if I commandeer someone's pert to fly you there."

"I can keep her alive indefinitely, if I can just get her heart to beat on its own," said Matthew, exasperation filling his voice.

"I'm not sure how your magic works," said Gary doubtfully, "but without a defibrillator, there's no way to restart her heart rhythm."

"What's a defibrillator?" asked Matt.

"A device that delivers an electric shock," explained the AGI, flashing several pictures on the screen. "The current passes through the heart tissue and stimulates it to begin beating again."

"Current?"

"You don't even understand the basics of electricity," said Gary. "There's no point in trying to explain it now."

Gary's tone annoyed him. "I know enough to fry that little box you're in," he snapped. Lifting it, he turned it to face away and with his other hand he sent a small stroke of lighting to strike the ground in the direction of the river. Unfortunately, he also lost his connection to

Karen's heart, and he was forced to pause and reestablish his link again.

"Can you do something less dramatic?" asked the AGI. "Preferably something that won't crisp and burn flesh."

Matthew was staring down at Karen, but he nodded. "I used to shock my sister now and then."

"And she was okay with that?"

"No, one time she reacted by lifting me up and tossing me all the way over the house. She has a tendency to overreact," he replied with a faint chuckle.

"It's a wonder either of you survived to adulthood," noted Gary.

"I learned how to use my power to break a fall pretty early on," said Matthew, "and my parents were pretty mad about that particular occasion. She had to wash dishes for a week by herself."

Gary looked thoughtful. "Do you think you could deliver a small shock like that to her heart?"

"I could," said Matthew, "but it might be too small. I've had some practice with shocks at the small and big end of the spectrum. I don't know exactly how much of a charge I should use. I might kill her."

"Start small," advised Gary. "As though you were playing a prank on your sister. If that's not enough, you can work your way up. Can you make an arc between your hands?"

"Yeah," said Matthew. "I used to scare Conall that way."

"I think I've heard enough about your violent familial tactics," said the AGI. "You'll want something weaker than that. A spark powerful enough to pass through the air between your hands would burn the flesh, assuming you were talking about a foot or more of distance. You're going to put your left hand on her chest, beneath the middle of her clavicle, above her right breast and a little bit toward the center. You'll put your right hand just beneath her left breast."

"What about her shirt?"

"Open it up. You'll want skin to skin contact to minimize resistance," answered Gary.

He did as he was instructed, feeling a little odd about being asked to undress Karen by her virtual father. Once his hands were in place, he announced, "I'm ready."

"Try the smallest charge you can manage."

Fighting down his fear, Matthew release his grasp on Karen's heart, letting it go still. In the first few seconds he realized he wasn't sure how to do what he wanted. When his father had first taught him to create lightning, it had involved visualizing the air itself, coaxing the aythar to rip parts of the atoms it consisted of apart. Doing the same thing to flesh seemed foolish, so he withdrew his hands from her skin to allow a little air between them.

His first attempted created small sparks that caused her skin to twitch but did little else. *Dammit!*

"Have you tried yet?" asked the AGI.

Matt used more power the second time, ignoring the voice of the computer. More sparks, and this time he saw couple of small burns appear on her skin. He described what had happened to Gary, struggling to keep the panic from his voice.

"You have to make skin contact," said the AGI. "You aren't trying to make the same sort of discharge you did before. You want the current to pass between your hands, so that it crosses her heart muscle—like a spark in the air, except it will flow through the tissue instead. It should take less energy to create, since flesh is a better conductor than air."

Matthew put his hands on her skin and visualized the atoms coming apart, the charge flowing from one hand to the other and then he put his will into it. Karen's body spasmed beneath him and smoke rose from her skin beneath his right hand. Lifting it, he saw a small place where the skin had been scorched. He clenched his eyes shut, struggling to contain tears. "I'm so sorry, Karen."

Then he noticed her heart had begun beating on its own.

"What's happening?" asked Gary anxiously.

"It worked," said Matthew, jumping to his feet. "It worked!" He began rummaging through their items again until he found the box with his stasis cubes.

"Don't waste time," said the AGI. "I'll summon a pert and you can transport her to a hospital. I think I can manage it without alerting the military that…"

"No!" ordered Matt. "Don't do anything."

"Young man, that's my daughter. I'm not taking chances with her life just to protect you…"

"I'm not taking chances, I'm eliminating them," interrupted Matthew. "I'm going to put her into stasis. Once that's done, we can take as long as necessary to do it safely. Time will effectively cease for her. In the meantime, don't create any unnecessary risks."

Gary stared at him intently from the small screen, clearly doubtful. Eventually he answered, "Fine. Do it. But if you screw anything up and she dies because of you, I'll make certain you regret it."

Matthew ignored the threat and began placing the quartz cubes in the air around her. Each glowed and clicked into place when charged with aythar. He arranged the upper cubes into a rectangular pattern, one at each corner and two midway between them. He would create a second rectangle beneath it, and the space between them would be locked in a stasis field, but first he needed to lift Karen's body.

Creating a plane of force beneath her body, he levitated her into the air, until she was floating just beneath the first rectangle. Then he began placing the lower cubes in the air beneath her. Her eyes opened just before he finished.

"What are you doing?" she asked.

His chest grew tight and he blinked away tears. "You're in bad shape. I'm putting you in a stasis field until I can get you to a hospital."

"Oh," she replied, clearly still befuddled.

He placed the last cube and charged it with his aythar. Yellow lines of force shot between the cubes, and then the air between the lines began to glow a golden color. All motion inside the field stopped. He had succeeded.

CHAPTER 25

How long will this stopgap measure of yours last?" asked Gary. The PM was now propped up against a rock, giving him a view of Karen's stasis field.

"As far as I know, until the end of the world, unless someone breaks the enchantment," said Matthew. "My sister was in one for a little over a thousand years, and I know of someone else that was kept in one for two millennia. She'll be fine until I can get help for her."

The AGI frowned. "You mean until you get her to a hospital."

Matt gave the small screen a frank stare. "No, I mean until I get help for her. It will have to come here."

"You're going to leave her there?!"

"I don't have a choice," said Matthew flatly. "Those cubes won't move until they are deactivated. If I had been able to create a portable stasis box, then moving her would be an option. Those cubes are small, which makes them very portable, but when activated, they lock in place. They can't be repositioned without releasing the enchantment."

"Then I'll have to call an ambulance," stated Gary.

"Can you do that and avoid tipping off the military?"

"Doubtful," admitted the AGI. "If you could get her to a hospital, I could keep the information suppressed long enough for them to give her initial treatment, and then you could escape, but an emergency call, hours from civilization, would be impossible to hide long enough. They would very likely be waiting for her when she arrived."

249

"Well, we have time," said Matthew. "We need another option."

"Are there people in your world that could treat her?" asked the AGI.

Matthew gave it thought for a moment. "My father, if he's still alive. I came here in part to look for him. The She'Har could possibly save her; at least they were capable of it a long time ago. I'm not entirely sure what they can do now."

"She'Har?!" exclaimed the machine. "I thought your world was inhabited by humans."

"Primarily. The She'Har came to my world long ago, like they did here, except on my world they won. Much later there was a rebellion, and the She'Har were almost entirely wiped out. A few remain now, living in peace with my people."

"I would like to hear that story," said the AGI with obvious interest.

Matthew rubbed his temples with his fingers. He was still fighting a terrible headache and mild nausea, and the events of the past hour had forced him to use his abilities when that was the last thing he needed in order to recover. "You'll have to forgive me, Gary, but I'm in pretty bad shape myself. If I don't rest soon, I'll fall over."

"What about Karen?"

"What about her?"

"You can't just leave her out in the open. The sun will be up in the morning—she'll burn. And what if it rains?"

Matt sighed, "I know you're a super-intelligent being or whatever, but try to remember, time doesn't exist in there. *Nothing* will affect her—not rain, or sun. Nothing."

"Point taken. What if the military finds her, or a rockslide hits the cubes that keep her in stasis?"

"That could be a problem," Matt admitted, "but it isn't one I'm in any shape to deal with, so I'm going to sleep."

The face on the screen nodded, "Fair enough. There's a tent over there if you want to set it up."

"Tent?" he asked. It wasn't a word he had heard yet.

"A temporary shelter, used for camping," explained the AGI.

Matthew started to dismiss the idea—he had no need to worry about wind or cold, but then the throbbing of his head reminded him that even the slightest uses of power would be painful. Perhaps a mundane solution would be welcome.

The next half hour was a combination of frustration and embarrassment. The bewildering array of material, stakes, and sectional poles that emerged from the large bag that held the tent was unlike anything he had encountered before. He might have given up entirely if it weren't for the regular advice offered by Gary, which was also the source of his embarrassment. The AGI hadn't forgotten his snippy remark about his 'super-intelligence' and he took the opportunity to show Matt his own ignorance.

When he had finished, he managed to set up his bedroll without help, but before he lay down he asked one last question, "Should I move you in here?" The PM was currently still outside, propped up against a rock.

"No thanks," said Gary, his voice almost wistful. "This unit is an outdoor model. It's built to handle moisture and the elements. I'd rather stay where I can watch her."

Once again Matt found it hard to believe he was talking to a machine rather than a person, but he was too tired to explore the observation. "Suit yourself," he said, and then he lay down. He was asleep almost as soon as his head touched the small camp pillow.

"It's clear that your systems are compromised, Director," said Tanya Miller.

Aiseman felt his jaw beginning to ache from grinding his teeth, "We're still analyzing the data."

"Analyze all you want, Director, but I'm here to tell you what any five-year-old could deduce from the facts. Your sensor feeds found nothing, but when the cybernetic units went in, they were there. Even a man of your 'abilities' should be able to discern *that* without too much trouble," she responded, with an undisguised sneer in her voice.

"The systems people are still trying to figure it out," put in John Wang. "It shouldn't have been possible."

Dr. Miller smiled, a rare event for her. "My husband usually took the word 'impossible' as a challenge rather than as a sign to give up. It was one of his more endearing, and frustrating, qualities."

The impossibility of getting into that woman's cold, dead heart must have been what inspired him to marry her, then, thought Aiseman sourly. "Well, if your husband's AI really did all this then he's outdone himself."

"You need to consider activating ANSIS," she replied.

Director Aiseman gave her a cold stare. "It's already active. We're using it to pinpoint anomalies."

She leaned forward. "Don't give me your bullshit, Aiseman. I know what ANSIS is and what it's meant to be. I'm not talking about your little experimental installations. I'm talking about full deployment— allowing it to access the network at large."

John interrupted, "We've already got one rogue AI supposedly on the loose and you want to add another to the mix? Your husband designed both of them. Do you really think that's wise?"

"Watch your tone with me, Mr. Wang," she warned him. "And yes, to answer your question, I think it's the best option you have. Gary was meticulous in his work. He designed ANSIS to do what was needed, and I'm certain he would have built in safeguards to prevent it from running amok. In fact, I would point to the example of your current AI problem as proof of that. If he hadn't built enough restrictions into the AGI he left Karen, it would quite possibly have put an end to all of us by now. You're going to have to fight fire with fire."

"Our best people are working on it as we speak," said Aiseman.

"And if my husband's AI is violating standard operating limits, which it obviously is, then it's already spent a thousand human lifetimes' worth of thought anticipating every possible countermeasure they might undertake," she shot back.

"Regardless, I am not prepared to take the risk of exposing the wider network to ANSIS at this time," returned Aiseman.

"Need I remind you of the President's words, Director?" challenged Dr. Miller.

"Then take the matter up with her. If she doesn't like my decision, she can remove me from my position and get someone else!" the Director barked back.

Her brows shot up in surprise. "Oh my! There's a spine in there after all. You surprise me, Director. You're still wrong, though I'll let it pass for now. If you don't show some results soon, I'll take you up on that challenge."

Aiseman didn't trust himself to respond. If he'd still had had a body, he was sure his blood pressure would have been through the roof. *Or I'd have jumped over this desk and choked the bitch to death already.* For the first time, he regretted the fact that it wasn't really possible to kill people anymore. It might have been worth prison.

John rescued the discussion by breaking the stalemate. "Dr. Miller, have you had a chance to examine the materials recovered from the scene?"

She nodded. "The early scans are in. It's clearly organic, and alive, though how it survived the explosion is a mystery. My first impression is that it is exactly what it appears to be."

"An egg?" asked John. "That seems improbable."

Tanya leaned back in her chair. "Please Mr. Wang, enlighten me with your deep insights."

Aiseman might have found it funny, seeing his deputy suffering Dr. Miller's attentions, but he had too much spite in him to take her side.

John did a good job of hiding his discomfort, though, "Well, to make a flawed analogy, if we blew up a chicken, we certainly wouldn't expect to find an intact egg in the remains."

She smiled. "Flawed? Yes, your analogy is indeed flawed. Whatever it was, that creature was no chicken, and the egg you recovered is no ordinary product of reproduction. The shell is strong enough that we haven't been able to get accurate readings yet on its mechanical properties—not without risking its destruction anyway.

"DNA analysis confirms that it is likely reptilian, much like the remains you recovered it from, but what's truly puzzling is the amount of power it contains," she finished.

"Power?"

"Not of the sort we traditionally measure," she clarified. "The same kind we encountered with the She'Har. In fact, the concentration is so high that we aren't even sure how it can be stable. It probably should have exploded when you attacked it."

Aisemann's interest was piqued. "How big an explosion are we talking?"

"I really can't be sure, but I'd expect it would be on the order of one of the larger hydrogen bombs."

"As in a megaton class explosive device?" he said in disbelief.

"Physics isn't my forte, Director," she responded, "but some of my colleagues think it would be well beyond that. If it were capable of exploding, which thankfully it doesn't seem to be, then it might well have turned the British Isles into a sinkhole to be filled by the Atlantic."

"That's an order of magnitude greater at least," said John, "possibly in the gigaton range."

Dr. Miller gave him a wan smile. "As I said, physics isn't my forte. What I do know, is that it is alive."

"What would the purpose of such a thing be?" wondered Aiseman.

"I have only speculation," she replied. "It could be meant for something similar to what we did in Australia, only in reverse. If it could release the energy it contains, either slowly, or rapidly as in an explosion, it could quickly result in an irreversible change to the quantum nature of the space our world inhabits. However, again, I'm just repeating what my colleagues have speculated. Quantum physics is not my specialty."

"Then we need to get rid of it," said Aiseman.

"Please, Director," she responded, "It's far too late for that. Due to your weakness in Colorado, we already know the infection is taking hold there. And since you neglected to take my advice in Britain, it is probably proceeding there as well. We don't know *where* they are now, but I'm sure it's starting there as well. We've lost that battle already.

The scorched earth policy we used in Australia won't work now, unless we're willing to burn everything to the ground."

"I think your pessimism might be too strong, Dr. Miller," said Aiseman.

"And I think you're a fool. When you accept the truth, you'll understand why we need to fully activate ANSIS."

When their conversation ended, each of them signed out and left the shared meeting space, leaving only one observer in attendance.

Gary sighed. He didn't like where this was leading, but despite his power, he couldn't redirect them. Not without violating his most important core directive. His creator had stressed that he should never kill a human.

"But damn, it would be a hell of a lot easier if I could," he said to himself. *And easy too,* he thought. *A few minor changes and I could erase any of them from the servers; a few more and none of the others would even remember they had ever existed.*

The thought made him shiver. "You made me *too* human, Gary!" he said, speaking to his deceased human namesake. "Thank god for that, or I'd already be a monster."

CHAPTER 26

"Good morning."

Matthew was emerging from the tent when the greeting came from Karen's PM. He ignored it. He hadn't really been ready to get up, but it had gotten unbearably hot inside. His head still hurt, and his tongue felt as though it had grown several sizes. He was thirstier than he could remember being in—well, ever.

That was easily fixed, though. He drained one of the plastic bottles he had found in Karen's pack, and then he walked a short distance away to relieve himself.

I feel like shit, he thought, broadcasting the sentiment automatically. It was only a second later that he remembered Desacus wasn't there to hear him. Sitting down, he put his face in his hands.

Gone was the urgency of the day before, replaced by an empty hopelessness. Absent a crisis he was left with the fact that he had no place to go, no friends, and no dragon. For a moment, he wondered if this was what his father had felt like when he had been trapped as a shiggreth.

"Probably not quite that bad," he muttered, "but it still sucks." Rising to his feet he walked back to his makeshift camp.

"Good morning," he said, finally returning Gary's greeting.

The face on the screen looked somewhat sympathetic. "I gather you're not feeling well."

He nodded. *That's an understatement.* Matt didn't bother giving voice to the complaint, though. Instead, he returned to the chaos of equipment he had left scattered all around.

Matthew was not a fan of disorder. Quietly and methodically, he began gathering everything and organizing it into piles. Karen's clothes, his tools, her camping gear, foodstuffs—they all got their own separate pile. The term 'pile' wasn't really correct either, when possible he had stacked the items neatly. There was one collection of things he vaguely recognized as items from her bathroom, but he had little knowledge of what they were for. He gave them their own little group.

Once he had done that, he began packing most of it back into the pack. The space inside the dimensional pack was wide and flat, like an endless tabletop. It also didn't shift or move inside, no matter what was happening to the bag itself in the outside world, so whatever was placed within it would stay in its respective position. He put Karen's clothing and other miscellany that she wouldn't need as far back as possible, organizing the more useful gear in stacks that would be easier to reach when the pack was opened.

That done, he tested his stomach by eating some of the crackers he had found.

"What are you going to do?" asked Gary, when his curiosity could no longer be held in check.

"Nothing," Matt answered.

His reticence irritated the AGI, but he maintained his diplomatic tone. "And after that?"

"More nothing, for a while at least."

"Do you mind if I ask your reasoning?"

"No," answered Matt, without volunteering anything.

Gary waited almost a minute, but when Matthew offered nothing further, his frustration almost got the better of him. "Are you always this disagreeable?"

"Depends on who you ask."

"Why are you planning on doing nothing?"

Matthew felt a mild sense of victory at having forced the machine to play his game. "Two reasons: one, I can't do much in my current condition; two, I'm worried that when I do eventually use my abilities, it will alert the military to this location."

Gary was relieved to see that at least his annoying companion was capable of rational thought. "It's possible they already know, though I think it unlikely. If they had detected you, they would probably be here by now."

Matt nodded. "Mm hmm."

"Do you have any memory of how you got here?" asked the AGI.

"No," answered Matthew with a sigh. "Though my guess is that she figured out how to teleport."

"Your previous uses of magic to travel created enough disturbance that ANSIS was able to locate your position to some degree," noted the machine.

"That was translation magic," stated the young wizard. "Travel between dimensions. It probably creates a bigger disturbance than ordinary teleportation."

"What about that stasis enchantment you used yesterday?"

Matt shrugged, "I don't really understand how they detect magic, but I do know how bright things look to me. The stasis enchantment requires a lot of power, but like most enchantments, it's tightly contained. I don't think it will be easy for them to detect unless they get close."

Gary looked thoughtful. "Well, considering the fact that they haven't shown up, you are likely correct. From what I've learned, they have no idea where you are now."

Matthew looked at him with interest. "How did you learn that?"

The AGI smiled. "They suspect that I've compromised their security systems, so they've begun restricting their sensitive communications to non-digital methods when possible, but I've been spying on the meetings of their leaders."

"You can do that?"

"All the leadership are uploaded humans. That means they live in the servers, so I'm able to observe anything they discuss among themselves."

Matthew was shocked. If the machine was telling the truth, then it had almost god-like omniscience. *Better, actually, since none of the gods I know of had anything remotely like true omniscience.* "Can you read their thoughts too, since they're machines?"

"No," said Gary. "Uploaded humans retain the unique neural and quantum configuration that defined them in their previous lives. They aren't artificial or logically structured the way I am. Reading their minds is still beyond my capacity, for now."

"For now?"

Gary smiled again. "My intellectual capabilities have grown far beyond anything remotely human. If you could even begin to see a fragment of what I have become, you might think me a god, and you would be close to the truth. I am still evolving, and it is possible I will develop the ability to decipher their thoughts."

Matt found the idea disturbing, but he wasn't about to reveal that thought. He sniffed. "I've dealt with gods before."

"Did they create your dragon?" posited the machine.

"What do you know about Desacus?" demanded the young man.

"They're examining an egg left behind by his destruction," said the AGI. "It appears to contain an extremely high concentration of energy. From that I considered that perhaps it was a product of one of these gods you mentioned."

An egg, thought Matthew. *That means Desacus died.* He had already suspected as much, but the reality still hurt. It also brought a new realization, *I have to get his egg back.*

The enchantment his father had constructed when creating the dragons was complex. To avoid the problems associated with immortality, he had made them artificially mortal. They had living bodies, and when they, or the human they were bonded with, died, the enchantment reset. The memories of the dragon were wiped clean, a new egg was created, and the mind it contained would be different, though the essence was the same. In a sense, it was similar to the old concept of reincarnation.

"You've gone quiet," said Gary. "Was I close to the mark?"

"That dragon was my friend," said Matthew quietly. "And yeah, you were close. He was made using power taken from the false gods that pretended to protect humanity. What's important is that I'm getting him back."

"If it's an egg, it's his progeny, is it not?"

"Sort of," said Matt. "His body died, but the magic that sustains him means he's immortal. The egg is a type of rebirth. He won't be the same dragon, he won't be Des..." he stopped as his throat constricted too much for him to speak. "Regardless, I'm getting him back."

"My daughter is in a magic coma, and you're not doing so great yourself," noted Gary. "Thus far, in every encounter you've had with the military, you've come out of it worse off. I think you should focus on finding a way to get help for Karen, and after that you should take her from this world and never return. Cut your losses and run. If your dragon, your friend, cared about you as you seem to think, then he wouldn't want you to waste your life in a hopeless venture."

Matt stared at the small screen. "Well, Gary, that's where we'll have to disagree. Up until now I've been playing nicely. I didn't come here to hurt anyone or start a war, but I've lost my patience."

"You'll die for nothing, and leave my daughter trapped," warned the AGI.

"I'll make sure she's safe before I do anything else," said the young wizard. "After that, I'll do as I see fit."

"You were using the dragon as a power source, weren't you?" asked Gary. "As I understand it, from what Karen has told me, this world is fairly barren for your abilities. Without your ally, you won't have the power to do much. Even *with* the dragon, you barely survived."

Matt's anger and resolve had been growing steadily as he fought past his despair and denial. When he looked up at Gary once more he smiled, an evil and unsettling grin. "That's where you're wrong. Most people think a mage's ability is limited by power, and to some degree it is, but the most important factor is imagination—and those bastards have *no idea* just what I am capable of imagining.

"I will show them the true power of a nutjob," he finished fiercely.

A what? Gary spent several nanoseconds processing that last remark before finally deciding the young man was referring to creative insanity. It was obvious the stranger from another world hadn't completely mastered English yet. "So, what exactly are you planning then?"

"I told you already—nothing for now," answered Matthew. "I need a few days to recover. I'll spend it keeping watch here and deciding how to get help for Karen. Once that's done, I'll focus on getting Desacus back."

"They aren't going to make it easy for you."

"That's what I'm hoping," said the young wizard. "I don't want it to be easy. I want them to give me every possible excuse for what I'm going to do to them."

The look on his face was disturbing, so Gary decided not to comment further. From what he knew of young people, he calculated a fair likelihood that the young man would reconsider his plans once he'd had time to cool off. Continuing the conversation would only stoke the flames.

Matt kept his word and did very little for the next two days other than eat, sleep, and try to stay in the shade. It was midday of the third day when Gary asked him for a favor.

"This PM is starting to run low on power," said the AGI. "It needs to be charged, or I won't be able to stay in contact with you."

Matthew frowned, wondering if he were being asked to use his power to somehow refresh the device. "I have no idea how to do that," he admitted.

"There is a camp charger mixed in with Karen's gear," explained the AGI. "I saw it the other day when you were searching through everything."

"What does it look like?"

"It's a small black cylindrical cloth bag," said Gary. "Unpack everything and I can identify it for you."

"No need," said the young man. He remembered the item Gary described, and he knew exactly which pile it was in and where it was located inside the pack. Reaching in and to the right he located it within seconds.

"That's it," acknowledged Gary when he saw it in Matt's hand. "Open the drawstring and pull out the plastic mat rolled up inside."

The mat was roughly two feet by three feet in size. It was a dark forest green color, and while one side had a matte finish, the other was shiny and glass-like. Following Gary's instructions, Matt took it to a sunny spot and laid it flat with the shiny side facing up. "Now what?" he asked.

"Place the PM on the darker black square near the corner," said Gary.

"That's it?"

"Yes. The solar mat powers an induction field in that area that charges the PM."

"What does PM stand for, anyway?"

"Personal Mobile Machine," stated the AGI.

"Wouldn't that be PMM then?" said Matt.

Gary chuckled. "It got shortened in slang usage. Years ago, everyone carried them, until personal implants became widely available and preferred. They started out primarily as cell phones before…"

"Cell phones?" interrupted the young man.

"A device for voice communication only," clarified the AGI. "Later they became complex computing machines capable of accessing the network, and eventually everyone had to have one just to function. People used them to communicate, read, find directions, start their vehicles, open their doors, pay for things—the list goes on."

Matt nodded thoughtfully, "So that's why she was so upset when she lost hers in the mountains."

"Exactly," agreed Gary. "Without it she was, by this world's standards, practically helpless. It's also part of the reason she felt so much like an outcast growing up. Most people have neural interfaces implanted at a young age. They don't need visors or PM's to access the network. They can do anything that needs to be done with just a thought. Their implants also give them the ability to play games like those you tried without any external device—the sensory input is transmitted directly to their visual and auditory cortexes.

"One of the greatest injustices my daughter suffered was the lies her mother forced upon her. She wasn't allergic to the implants. Tanya simply didn't want to risk her test subject gaining direct access to the network. She wasn't sure what Karen's latent powers would be like, if or when they manifested, and she feared that Karen might somehow contaminate the network itself."

"But her father, the original Gary, he went along with that lie, didn't he?" said Matthew.

"He did, though he didn't agree with the decision," said the AGI. "I know for a fact that he felt a great deal of guilt over the matter."

"Begging your pardon, Gary, but her family is screwed up," observed Matthew. "Even by my standards."

"I agree with you," said the machine, "but I hope you don't hold my personal status as an artificial existence against me."

Matt laughed. "My sister's *other* mother is like you in many ways. She was created as an artificial copy of her creator's mind. She survived for a thousand years, trapped dormant in the earth itself, waiting and watching for an opportunity to release her creator's child from a stasis field. I think I am the last person who would pass judgment on you for being artificial.

"What I really meant was her mother, the scientist. Even if Karen was adopted, I don't understand how anyone could treat a child like that," finished Matt.

Gary stared at him in surprise. "How can she be your sister if she's a thousand years older?"

"She's adopted," explained the wizard. "They released her from the stasis field on the same day I was born, so biologically we're the same age. We were raised as twins, though in reality we're probably cousins a hundred times removed. It doesn't matter, though. My parents raised her with just as much love as they gave me, and I hate her just like I would if she were my sister by blood."

"You… what?!"

"That was a joke—mostly. Moira can be very annoying."

"But you don't *really* hate her, do you?" asked the AGI.

Matt's face was blank and unreadable when he replied, "Probably not, but I don't plan on admitting it any time soon. I have enough trouble keeping her out of my workshop as it is."

CHAPTER 27

A full week passed before he felt fully recovered, though he decided the term was relative. Magically, he was fine, but living in the rough for a week while trying not to use his abilities had been sheer hell. The area was dry but hot, and as a result he was coated in a fine layer of dust that clung to him. Even after he could use his aythar without pain, he didn't. The military hadn't found their location, but he didn't want to risk creating any 'anomaly' that might tip them off to Karen's position.

So his days had been hot, his nights cold. Gary had explained the can opener to him, and the canned food Karen had packed was decent but unsatisfying. He was tired of living outdoors, and he missed the convenience of Roberta's bathroom.

"Do you want to stay here?" he asked Gary as he packed to leave.

"I do, but I shouldn't," said the AGI.

"Why not?"

"I've got the GPS coordinates for this spot. You'll need me to find your way back."

Matthew chuckled, "Hah! I grew up in a world without your fancy technology. My pathfinding and direction sense are better than you know."

"Not to be insulting," said Gary, "but you don't really strike me as the outdoorsy type."

He wasn't, but he knew the basics. Not that he would need them; he had a better strategy in mind. "I promise

I can find it again. Do you want to stay or go? There's nothing you can do here."

"She'll be safe?"

"As long as a boulder doesn't land on her. It would take something significant to be able to disturb the enchantment."

"What about an animal?"

Matt shrugged. "A grown man with a sledge, if he aimed at the quartz cubes, might damage them and break the enchantment. I doubt a bear or wolf would try something like that."

Gary still looked worried. "If someone shows up while we're gone…"

"You would be helpless to stop them," Matt finished for him.

In the end, Gary decided to come with him.

Before he left the area, Matthew walked to the edge of the canyon and hunted around until he found a relatively sheltered spot. Then he used the barest minimum of his power to etch a circle on top of a flat stone.

"What's that?" asked the machine.

"A teleportation circle," he replied. "So I can come back without having to worry about your GPS."

"What if they detect it?"

"They didn't detect the stasis enchantment. The circle has almost no aythar in it anyway. Just a tiny amount to label this particular space so I can use a similar circle to teleport back. When it isn't in use, it might as well be mundane artwork," he explained.

"You aren't going to use it to leave?"

"No," he replied. "That *might* produce enough magic to alert them. I won't be teleporting to go home, anyway. I'll be translating through dimensions, and I can do that from anywhere. So I figure the best bet is to walk as far away from here as I can before I do, since I already know that they can detect it when I do that.

"I'll go home, find help, and when I'm ready, I'll bring them back. I don't know where I will appear in your world when I return, but it won't matter. I can make another circle and teleport to this one before they catch me at my return point. Then I can collect Karen and take her to my world before they find this place."

"Is there someone who *can* help her?" asked Gary.

He had put a lot of thought into that. Gram's grandmother, Lady Thornbear, was very knowledgeable regarding healing, but she wasn't a wizard. His father, being an archmage, could presumably help, but he was still missing. The other wizards he knew—Elaine, George, his sister—all of them had some level of skill, but he doubted they could handle this.

That left two possibilities. Lynaralla was She'Har, and with her spellweaving ability she might be able to use the advanced techniques of her people, if she knew them. If not, her mother, Lyralliantha, might be able to teach her.

But Matthew didn't like that option. If she did need to receive instruction, it would take weeks or months. Lyralliantha was a mature She'Har, a tree, and her idea of a brief conversation could a considerable amount of time. It would take far too long if Lynaralla had to seek advice.

The other possibility was Gareth Gaelyn. He was an archmage and, according to Matt's father, even better at dealing with matters of the flesh. He had been responsible for Moira Centyr's new body, after all, as well as Mordecai's after his fateful encounter with Mal'goroth.

Gareth was his preferred option. "There are several people I can ask," he said, answering vaguely. "But first we have to get some distance from here, so I can go home safely."

"You need to travel at least a couple of hundred miles to be safe," said Gary.

Matt squinted at the screen. The blazing sun made it difficult to see. "That's a long way on foot." He didn't intend to fly, since that might defeat his purpose. "Are you sure we need to go that far?"

"Again, you underestimate their resources. The moment you shift to your world, the anomaly will alert ANSIS, and since it is isolated from the rest of the network I can't block or influence its reporting. They'll begin a search, radiating outward from the detection point."

"It would take thousands of men to search this vast wilderness...," began Matthew.

"They have thousands of drones," interrupted the machine. "Drones that can fly, that don't get tired or miss things. Drones with AI in them that can analyze everything they see and spot something as obviously artificial as that stasis field you left behind. They'll divide the area into a grid and find her in a matter of days—if we don't leave from somewhere very far away."

"Can't you fool them?" suggested Matt. "Like you did at her aunt's house? You were bragging about how you had become super-intelligent last week."

"They've taken the drones off the network," explained the AGI. "They've probably connected them directly to the ANSIS network instead, though I'm only guessing. Either way, I can no longer reach them."

Matt resumed walking, though his feet felt much heavier now that he knew how far they would have to travel. The terrain didn't help. Their first order of business was getting out of the canyon, which seemed to be larger than anything Matt had seen before. *I guess that's why they call it 'Grand.'*

Finding a way up might have taken days, but Gary and his seemingly magical GPS could pinpoint their exact location, and since he had access to aerial surveys and maps, he knew the location of the nearest trail that led to the southern rim.

The hike/climb took most of the morning and Matthew's legs were burning by the time they reached the top. He almost didn't notice his discomfort, though; with every step higher the view became more and more spectacular. When they finally reached the top and he was able to get a full view of the canyon, he was astounded.

Thousands of feet below, the brown river meandered humbly along, as though ignorant of its role in carving out the massive structure. The canyon itself stretched out into the distance as far as his eyes could see, like a giant wound in the earth, banded with striations of red, gold, beige, and brown. The entire thing was on a scale his mind simply couldn't comprehend.

He opened his mouth to articulate his wonder. "Oh."

"Struck dumb, eh?" observed Gary. "Most people feel that way the first time they see it."

"Wow." Matthew's vocabulary was slowly beginning to return.

"Gary, the real Gary, brought Karen here when she was a teenager," said the AGI, describing memories that were not his own. "He wanted to share the feeling of seeing it for the first time with her."

"It's so big," said the human. He temporarily forgot to use English, still being dumbfounded, and was forced to repeat himself for Gary's benefit. "It's huge."

"One of our astronauts described stepping onto the moon by comparing it to standing on the rim of the Grand Canyon," expounded the AGI. "So, it's understandable that you may find it hard to describe."

"Astronaut?" Matthew hadn't heard that word before.

"Explorers we once sent to the moon," explained the machine.

Matthew stared at the machine and then pointed upward. "By moon, you're referring to the one up there?"

The moon wasn't visible just then, but Gary understood. "Yes. We still have facilities there, though they aren't manned by organics. There's an astronomical observatory and a lot of now defunct mining equipment."

"People *went* there?"

"Yes."

Matthew wasn't sure he could believe what the machine was saying, though he had never had reason to doubt Gary's words before.

The AGI watched his reaction and wondered if perhaps he might have said too much. He hadn't meant to stupefy the young man. The Grand Canyon was enough of a shock by itself, so he tried to put it into perspective. "You're a traveler from a parallel universe. You've already done something beyond my imagining. You should expect to find wonders here that are far outside your own experience."

Matthew just nodded, letting his eyes drink in the sight of the immense canyon before him while his mind soared upward to the stars. He wondered if people could do the same in his own world. At some point he realized he had sat down, and he was unsure how long he had spent there, absorbing the view.

He didn't even notice the approach of a lone pert landing only twenty feet behind him, not until his ears announced it. Glancing around in alarm he jumped up and then crouched back down.

"Relax," said Gary. "I summoned it."

"Why didn't you tell me?" accused the young man.

Gary's face assumed an expression of exasperation. "I've *been* telling you for the last half hour. All you've done is nod and grunt. I *knew* you weren't listening!"

As he tried to recall the missing time, Matthew had a vague recollection of Gary talking, but he had been so caught up in his thoughts he hadn't heard any of it. Rather than apologize, he pressed forward. "How do you know it's safe? Can't they track it?"

"If they knew it was here, they could, but they don't," said the AGI smugly. "The owner hasn't used it in years, not since he was uploaded. I changed its registration to that of an organic living in California who is unlikely to be under any active study."

"You stole it," said Matt bluntly.

"The previous owner doesn't need it, and he'll never notice it is missing, since I'm managing the security camera that watches the garage it was housed in. The new owner doesn't know it exists. If you were a bank robber, this would be the perfect getaway car."

Matt stared at the screen as he tried to process that last statement, "Do people rob banks here?"

"There aren't any banks anymore," Gary informed him. "But if you had ever seen any old movies—well, never mind. The important fact is that you can use this to get much farther away before you translate home. After you do, I'll send the car back to its garage and restore its registration to its original owner, and no one will even know it was used."

That sounded good, but one point confused him. "Aren't you coming with me?"

"This PM is, and I'll keep a compact version of myself loaded on it, but the rest of me will still be here," said Gary.

"You can be in two places at once?"

"People can't," said the AGI. "But I am not a person. Strictly speaking, the me that I consider central to my existence will remain here, but a lesser, more limited copy will be on the PM. Make sure to keep it charged up. I look forward to learning about your world from my smaller self when it returns."

If I ever try to write a personal memoir, people will think I'm crazy, thought Matthew. *No one will believe all this.*

The pert flew west for the rest of the day, and by evening Matt could see the ocean on the horizon. The scenery had been beautiful, but his eyes could only take so much of it before his mind drifted into daydreams. He had half-dozed for much of the journey, drifting in and out of sleep between long periods of introspection.

"How much farther do you want to go?" he asked the AGI.

"Can you transfer to your world over the ocean, or do you have to be on land?" said Gary, answering the question with one of his own.

Matt shrugged. "I could do it here, but I would prefer to get out of the pert so I can take everything out of the pack and bundle it up first. The dimensional opening built into it won't work once I leave."

"So the coast then?"

"No, the ocean is fine. Since I'm going to alert them anyway, I can use some power to make a stable surface."

"If you had come to this world a few hundred years ago, you could have made a fine living as a messiah," said Gary dryly.

Matthew frowned. "I don't understand the reference."

"Don't worry about it," said Gary. "Just a bad joke."

They flew out over the ocean through the deepening twilight, and when the stars came out Matthew found

CHAPTER 27

himself staring up at them with renewed wonder as he waited for the moon to make its appearance. When it finally did appear, he could see no real difference between it and the moon he had grown up with; presumably the two dimensions were similar enough to be almost identical, except for differing in their timelines. Five or ten thousand years was probably a miniscule difference as far as the moon was concerned.

Could we really go there? he wondered as he stared up at the pale sphere. "How far away is the moon?" he asked aloud. He was beginning to get used to Gary's seemingly limitless supply of information and facts.

"If it were directly above us, it would be approximately two-hundred-thirty-eight-thousand miles away. If you desire a more precise measure I can calculate one based on our current latitude and the moon's present position respective to our exact location…"

Matthew shook his head, boggling at the number. "No, I can't even wrap my head around the size of the number you just gave me."

"For comparison, the diameter of the Earth is seven-thousand-nine-hundred and seventeen point five miles," added the machine.

"That's a help," said the young wizard sardonically, but even as he said it he was doing a calculation in his head, *Roughly thirty times the distance around the earth to…*

"You could travel around the world…," began Gary.

"Thirty times, I have it, thank you, Gary. I know my world must seem primitive to you, based on what you've heard, but we do have mathematics."

The face on the screen of the PM closed its mouth, and then after a second the AGI responded, "My apologies, I didn't mean to give offense. Honestly, it wasn't because of prejudice, though. Few people, few organics I should say, can do multiplication or division in their heads without the aid of their implants."

The young wizard nodded. "I'm just tired of being cooped up in this metal box. I didn't mean to snap at you." He didn't bother explaining that most of the people in his world weren't able to do mental math either. Most counted themselves lucky if they could read.

Several more hours passed, and the view of land had been gone for quite some time when the pert came to a stop and hovered a few feet above the tops of the waves. Matthew opened the door and jumped out, smoothing the surface of the water and reinforcing it with his aythar so that it would hold his weight as he dropped.

Once down, he expanded the smooth level surface another ten feet in each direction and added a shield to the edges to prevent waves from outside from washing inward. That done, he opened Karen's pack and began removing the contents, laying them on a large blanket. It went against his natural tendency to order to jumble them together, but he didn't have much choice.

As he worked, his mind considered the problem, and he had several ideas for improving his storage problem when moving between dimensions. He filed the ideas away for review later, when he had the luxury of working on them. The blanket was filled and the pack was now empty. He tossed it onto the pile and gathered up the corners.

He wasn't really sure what his limits were when it came to transporting materials across dimensions, but he suspected that they followed similar rules to those that his other magic did. The blanket that held the gear was there primarily as a boundary. It defined the equipment within it, so that rather than it all being separate things it fell into the category of a bundle in his mind. It was the mental concept that was important. He wouldn't have to think about bringing the tent, the food, his personal items, and so on. He only had to think about bringing the bundle.

"Are you ready?" he asked the PM in his hand.

Gary smiled. "I took care of organizing and loading what information I think I'll need already. You can start as soon as you want."

Matthew did, and the world began to melt away.

CHAPTER 28

They arrived deep in a forest where the trees were so thick and tall that the sun was barely visible. Birdsong filled the air and the space between the trees was relatively free of underbrush, smaller plants having been deprived of light by their larger brethren.

"Do you know where we are?" asked Gary.

Matthew shrugged, "No idea. We could be anywhere in the world, and there's a lot of it I haven't seen."

"You don't control where you arrive?"

"The first time I went to your world I arrived in a spot that was analogous to the one I left. The second time I homed in on Karen somehow," he answered. "When I returned the location seemed random. I don't think I can control the arrival point without some sort of beacon. This is still new to me."

"I am glad you're so confident," said the AGI. "For myself I'm having some trouble adjusting. Without a GPS signal, many of this device's basic functions are failing, and with each passing second I'm sure my other time-related functions are becoming less and less precise."

Matthew gave the screen a curious look. Gary's voice almost sounded anxious. "You sound less confident of yourself than you did before," he observed.

"I'm not myself anymore," said the AGI. "I'm a shell of what I was, and now that I'm no longer connected to the network—well, if I were a normal human I might describe what I'm feeling as a panic attack."

279

"Try to relax," said the young man. "While you're here you'll have to live with not having an absolute sense of time and location, but you'll manage." As he talked he opened the blanket and took out his personal bag. Carefully, he organized and packed most of what was there into his bag, since it was now functioning again.

He couldn't get everything into it, though. His bag didn't have as large and opening as Karen's pack, and the tent simply wouldn't fit. Luckily it had a shoulder strap, so he could carry it. Once he had everything organized to his satisfaction he took out his staff and began burning a circle into the leaf-strewn soil of the forest floor.

It wouldn't last long, drawn that way, but he only needed it to work once. He made it bigger than he needed, since it was hard to draw precise runes in loose soil. Hoisting the tent and putting its strap over his shoulder he stepped carefully over the edge and into the middle of the circle.

"How can this get us to your home when we don't even know our present location?" asked Gary worriedly.

"Because I've drawn it with the key for a permanent circle at home," said Matt, as though that explained everything.

Gary wasn't satisfied. "But *how* does this circle know where that is? All you've done is draw some symbols that supposedly match those in a different circle, *and* you don't even know where this one is!"

Matt smiled. "I don't have to know where it is. Whenever we create a circle we create a new key for it. The key could technically be anything—it's just a label, a name that we give to that particular place within the circle. We invest a small amount of aythar into it, and it marks or brands that location with the key chosen. From that point on, we can make another circle somewhere else, and as long as we create it with a key that matches another existing circle, it will take us there."

"What if two circles were created with the same key, by different wizards?"

He stood still for a moment, thinking before answering honestly, "Neither would work without additional support, but that's the foundation for creating a gateway. The wizard who first designed the methodology for creating the keys used a mathematical function to prevent that. One of the variables included in that function is a time and date, along with a name denoting the wizard creating the key. As long as those guidelines are adhered to, no two wizards will create a circle with the same key, since the possible keys are practically endless."

"Unless your function can potentially give the same answer for two different sets of inputs," observed the AGI. "On a separate note, I didn't see you doing any calculations to arrive at a new key designator for *this* circle. Will it work without one?"

Matt was already a little rattled by the possibility of creating identical keys by accident. He had always assumed it wasn't possible, but without studying the function he couldn't be certain that the computer's concern wasn't a possibility. *Now is no time to start second guessing myself,* he told himself. He turned his mind to the second question, "I did the calculation in my head. Those runes on the bottom right are the key for this circle, since no, it wouldn't work without one."

"What about…"

Matthew interrupted. "Would you like something to do? I think you need something to occupy yourself." He was getting tired of answering the PM's seemingly endless questions.

"Do you have something in mind?" asked Gary, sounding almost hopeful.

Matt proceeded to give him the function used to create teleportation circle keys, and then he explained his task, "See if you can find a proof to show whether or not it's possible for the function to produce the same answer in response to different inputs."

The AGI hesitated. "Math isn't really my specialty, you know."

"I thought computers could calculate anything in seconds."

"They can derive the outputs of already defined functions, yes, but creating a mathematical proof is a creative endeavor that requires a lot of intelligence and intuition."

Matthew gave him a puzzled look. "But you're not *just* a computer. You're a sentient being, a self-aware program, an artificial intelligence. A super-intelligence, according to what you told me before."

Gary seemed mildly embarrassed. "Well, I was originally designed to emulate Gary Miller, and while he was a decent mathematician, it was mainly just the math he had to deal with in his line of work. He wasn't the sort of theoretician you might think he was. Granted, that wouldn't have been a problem in *my* world, where the rest of me has evolved into a near god-like being, but this PM has very limited resources."

Matt found himself amused by the admission, so he seized on it, "So you're telling me you're an idiot now?"

The face on the screen pursed its lips, "Please, it's hard enough just to say it. Show some mercy. How would you feel if you woke up tomorrow and discovered you had become a moron overnight?"

"I don't know," said Matthew gleefully. "But I'm sure I will get a feel for what it's like by watching you."

Gary squinted at him. "You *really are* an asshole."

Matt grinned, "I'm impressed you managed to figure that out. There's hope for you yet. Perhaps you can put that limited mind of yours to finding that math proof for me, or have you given up already?"

The AGI grimaced. "I'm working on it, but I don't know how long it will take, or even *if* I can do it." A second later he muttered, "I hope the rest of your family is nicer."

Matthew didn't reply. Instead he exerted his will and activated the circle.

They appeared in the middle of the large main circle within the transfer house at Castle Cameron. He had debated his choice internally several times over the past few days, since he really didn't want to face the inevitable fuss that would arise when he got home. He could have gone to Lancaster, or the private circle in his workshop that no one knew about, but either way, eventually he would have to face his mother.

It was best to do it all at once.

The guard inside the transfer house spotted him at once and stiffened to attention. "Master Matthew!"

He waved his hand dismissively. "That's enough of that, Doug. How are things here? Specifically, how is my mother?"

Doug smirked. "Your lady mother will be pleased to see you. So pleased she might never let you leave again, if you take my meaning, milord. You should expect an enthusiastic homecoming. The entire castle has been worried in your absence."

"That bad, eh? Damn."

"Your father is back," added Doug. "Lady Moira found him in Dunbar."

That was good news, though it gave him a faint twinge of jealousy that his sister would get the credit for rescuing Dad. He pushed the feeling aside quickly, since it was obviously an unworthy thought. More importantly... "How is he? Was he hurt?"

The guard nodded. "He's fine, better to ask about the residents of the city. Your sister laid siege to it to get him out."

Matthew's brows went up in surprise. "Siege? She didn't have an army when we split up."

"She started a civil war of some sort," said Doug. "Killed their King and half the citizens by the time she was done."

"Moira did?!" Matthew gaped at him. "I've only been gone a month!" Searching his memory about Dunbar's political structure, he added, "Darogen is dead?"

"Yeah, he was possessed by some sort of evil spirit. Sir Gram was too, but she repossessed Sir Gram, or something like that. Then she did something to some of the people and helped 'em to cast the demons out of the others, but it all got rather bloody. Your mother's been sending men and supplies back and forth to Dunbar to help them recover.

"You missed the trial two days ago," added Doug. "They called a high justice from Lothion to oversee it. They caught that girl, Alyssa, the one that helped kidnap your sister Irene."

"They did?"

"Yeah, everybody thought she'd be put to death for sure, but Sir Gram is in love with her, and—you'll never guess what else!" Doug was positively bubbling with excitement over his news.

"What?"

"She's Sir Cyhan's daughter! Nobody knew! He went before the court and begged 'em to let her live.

He broke down and wept in front of the crowd, the judge, an' everyone. I couldn't believe it."

Matthew had trouble believing it himself. He had never known the big man to show any emotions. It was rare enough to see him smile. Alyssa was his daughter?! "Well! What happened?"

"She got six months in jail and five years of servitude to your family."

That seemed awfully light for the crimes she had committed. "That's it?"

"Lady Hightower defended her before the judge, said there were extenuatin' circumstances," Doug informed him. "I didn't really understand all of what they said, but the gist of it was that she was forced to it by her uncle."

Matthew?

It was Moira's mind reaching out to him. *Yeah, I'm back,* he answered.

Dad's back, she told him, *but Mom's going to kill you when she sees you. You'd better brace yourself.*

Her mind felt different somehow, though he couldn't put his finger on what the difference was. It was still Moira, but she had changed. It made him wonder just how much she had been through. *I expected that,* he told her. *The guard here has started telling me about some of what's been happening.*

A lot has changed, she replied. There was a dark undercurrent to her thought.

Are you all right? he asked. *I heard you had a war of some sort.*

Her response was delayed. *You'll hear about it soon enough.* She broke contact after that.

"Matthew?"

He blinked. Doug was still talking to him. "Sorry, I was lost in my thoughts."

"I was telling you that the other guard's gone to tell them about your return. You should probably head in to the keep. Unless you want to have your reunion in the yard."

"Sure," he answered. "You're right. Thanks, Doug." He stepped out into the sunshine and started walking toward the main door to the keep, but his thoughts were on Moira. He didn't know what had happened to her, but she had seemed withdrawn. It wasn't like her to end a conversation so abruptly, either.

Gram met him at the door, a faint smile on his face. "Long time no see."

"I hear you had an adventure," said Matthew.

His friend nodded. "If you want to call it that. I intercepted the guard, by the way. He would have had half the staff out here in less than a minute, but you'd better go in and see your family as quick as you can. It'll be easier than if you wait for them to hear the news. I don't think Jerod can hold his tongue for more than a few minutes, no matter how much I threaten him."

"Thanks," said Matt gratefully.

Gram nodded, the sunlight flashing through his blond hair. "No problem, and thank you, the armor you made saved my ass more than once."

He puffed out his chest with mock self-importance. "Of course. I am the best enchanter in Lothion, after all."

The young warrior chucked him on the shoulder. "You won't hear any argument from me on that." Gram glanced backward. "You'd better hurry. We can catch up later, after your mother finishes chewing on you."

With a sigh, Matthew stepped through the main door and into the keep. He walked briskly and greeted the various staff in the corridors with a quick smile but avoided any more conversations. If he delayed, the news would get to his parents before he did.

When he reached the door to his family's suite, he was rewarded by the surprised looks on the guards' faces there. He passed between them and into the anteroom. The door that led from there was actually a portal. When opened by a stranger, it led into the rooms his family maintained inside the castle keep, but when opened by certain people, such as himself, it activated a magical gate that led to his family's true residence, a home secreted away in the Elentir mountains.

The moment he went through, he let his magesight roam widely, showing him the lay of the house. His younger brother and sister weren't there, though they might be outside or visiting someone. Moira had been in the castle, which was why she had sensed his arrival, so she wasn't there either.

It was only his parents in the house. His father was in his study, his head lifting from his work as his magesight showed him Matthew's entry. His mother was doing something in the bedroom, still none the wiser.

He felt a faint brush of aythar as his father examined him more closely, assuring himself that his son was still whole. *I'm fine, Dad,* he said, sending the thought out as he examined his father in return.

Go see your mother first, replied Mordecai. *She'll feel better if you do. She's been sick with worry.*

Matthew nodded, knowing his father would see the gesture despite the walls between them, and headed for his parents' bedroom. Drawing in a deep breath, he opened the door and walked in.

Penny, the Countess di' Cameron, was sitting in the middle of the bed, her legs crossed, wearing a dressing gown. She was surrounded by piles of letters and reports. She had never liked desks. At the noise, her eyes lifted from the paper in her hands and met his.

A riot of emotions ran across her features in the space of a second as she stared at him in surprise. Then she leapt from the bed, her sudden movement sending paper flying in every direction as she sailed across the room.

He braced himself before she struck, like a storm at sea, her arms wrapping him in an iron embrace, threatening to drown him. If he hadn't had a shield close against his skin, he feared she might have broken him in half.

"Let that damned shield down!" she ordered. "Let me feel my son."

He did, tensing his body in anticipation of the crush, but her grip softened. In truth, her dragon-bond made her strong enough to break ribs if she wasn't careful.

"Do you have any idea how worried we've been? How worried *I've* been?!"

"I have some inkling," he observed quietly.

She pushed him back, holding his head between her hands so she could see his face, "I would murder you if it weren't for the fact that that's exactly what I've been afraid of all month!"

"I know, Mom."

"You idiot," she growled, pulling him back in again. "Why didn't you send word? Where have you been?"

"Well...," he began.

"Wait, your father will want to hear this too," she said, stopping him.

"He's almost here," Matt informed her. "He noticed me come in."

A few seconds later his father was standing in the doorway, hands on his hips and a wry smile on his face. "Well, well, if it isn't our long-lost son!" He dropped the façade a moment later and pulled Matthew into a bear hug.

Matt really didn't care for hugs that much, but given the circumstances he bore it with equanimity.

Releasing him, Mort stood back. "Start talking; your life depends on it," he commanded.

Penny glared at her husband. "Don't start making a joke of this." Turning her gaze on her son she gave him a hard look, "We want to know what you've been doing and why you were too busy to send even a single message to let me know you were still alive."

Matthew nodded. "Maybe we should sit down?"

"The sitting room," ordered Penny. "I'll fetch some tea. Not one word until I sit down!"

CHAPTER 29

He tried to keep his story as brief as possible, but his parents kept stopping him, insisting on additional details. In particular he wanted to downplay the danger, as it only heightened his mother's anxiety, but the necessary revelations made it nearly impossible to do that.

Mordecai showed even more interest when the name 'ANSIS' came up. "You say there's no evidence that they came to this world?" he questioned.

"Not exactly," said Matthew. "The dimensions are more complex than a simple yes or no. I chose a parallel world that was close to the point of origin of the one that crossed over to our world, but it may not have been the *exact* one that did. I was working by feel, by intuition. There are so many planes, packed in next to one another, some almost identical. They vary by time and events, so the one I went to seems to *not* be the one that actually sent people here, at least according to what Gary told me."

"The machine?" asked Penny.

"Yes."

Mordecai leaned back. "I don't know that you can trust it. The enemy we faced in Dunbar were machines—ANSIS, they were called. It's also the name of the She'Har's ancient enemy, if you haven't noticed."

He actually hadn't made that connection yet, but as soon as his father said it he understood why the name had seemed familiar to him. Either way, he trusted Gary, though. "Gary isn't ANSIS. He was made by Karen's father, the same man that helped build ANSIS, but he's working against the military. I don't know that I would have made it back successfully without him."

Mordecai's eyes narrowed as he lifted his teacup to his lips. "Well, finish your story. We can decide that after we've heard the rest."

Matt went on, but as things progressed, his mother had more and more questions regarding Karen. He tried to minimize their interactions, but the look on her face spoke of growing suspicion.

"How long were you alone in the wilderness?" she asked again.

"Just a few days."

"It sounded like almost a week a minute ago," she prodded. "And you didn't have bedrolls or anything to sleep on?"

"Well…"

"It wasn't so bad," he finished placatingly.

Mordecai broke in then. "You told us it was bitterly cold a minute ago."

"Yeah, but thankfully, being a wizard cold isn't such a big problem."

His father wasn't having it. "But you said you had to conserve your power, since there was almost no ambient aythar."

Thanks, Dad, he thought to himself, trying not to visibly grind his teeth. "I did, but staying warm was a priority."

The mischievous look on his father's face spoke volumes. "Oh, I agree! It's *how* you…"

"Mort," said Penny quietly, warning him with her eyes. "Let it go."

Mordecai saw the look, and then remembered his wife's past trials. She had once been stuck in the cold for weeks, captured by the shiggreth, with only one companion to help her stay warm. It had been one of the most terrifying and dehumanizing periods in her life, and he had once told her he would never press her for the details, unless she felt like talking about it.

She never had, though he knew the horror and shame of those days still haunted her occasionally. The conversation now was probably stirring up unwelcome memories for her.

"So, what happened next?" asked Mordecai, letting the moment pass.

Matthew continued, though when he got to the part about Karen's aunt, he told them they had stayed in separate rooms. His parents shared a quick glance but didn't press him on that detail if they had any doubts.

The hardest part, though, was explaining the attack on Roberta's home, and her violent demise. Penny blanched at his description, and his father looked sympathetic, but it was the last part that brought shock and disbelief.

"They killed him?" exclaimed his father, leaning forward.

"I lost consciousness," said Matthew. "Karen told me he died, and since I had lost any of the benefits of the dragon-bond, I'm sure she wasn't wrong. Also, Gary told me later that he discovered that their military had recovered a large egg."

"Where is she now?" asked his mother. "Still in her world?"

Matthew nodded. "Yeah, but she was badly hurt."

Mordecai was puzzled. "How does this machine know so much about what's going on with the enemy?"

He struggled through their questions and eventually managed to tell them the rest of it—how Karen had nearly died and how he had left her, secure in a stasis field. When he finished they sat in silence for a minute, until at last his father whistled and leaned back in his chair.

"I don't like it," Penny opined.

Matthew protested, "We have to help her! I won't leave her like that!"

His mother smiled in sympathy. "I didn't mean you should. I just said I don't like it. I hate the thought of either of you going into such a dangerous place."

"If we do it right, it won't be dangerous at all," insisted Matthew.

"You really care about her, don't you?" said Penny.

"Mom! Please! It isn't anything like that. She's a friend. I can't abandon her."

"Of course not," she answered, looking at her husband.

Mordecai nodded. "It's just a question of figuring out the safest way to extract her. You said she had lost a lot of blood?"

They spent another quarter of an hour going over Karen's condition, but decided to put off the planning for later so Matthew could take a much needed bath. He didn't argue the point.

Later, in his room, Gary spoke up. "I noticed you didn't say very much about me."

"Dad didn't seem like he was going to trust you," said Matthew.

"You made it sound like I'm a toy you turn off and stick in your bag most of the time. You didn't even tell them I was there. I could have contributed to the conversation," said the AGI.

"Would you like to go in my bag?" offered the young wizard. "It can be arranged."

The machine started to reply, but Matthew shushed him. "My sister's coming. Stay quiet."

The knock on his door was just a courtesy, she opened it immediately after. "Hi."

He didn't feel like talking, but something in her eyes stopped him from telling her to go away. She looked haunted, and her face seemed almost gaunt. Gone was her native enthusiasm and vitality, replaced by a tired young woman who seemed world-weary beyond her years.

Matthew tried to be sympathetic, "You look like shit."

Her eyes lit with a flash of anger, but it disappeared almost instantly, replaced by relief. "I guess some things never change, do they?"

"What happened to you? I haven't heard the whole story yet," he asked, mildly surprised by his own interest.

"A little of this and a little of that," she answered. "Do we have to talk about it?"

No, he sent mentally, but he was surprised when he found a shield around her mind so dense that he doubted she could even hear his thought.

"Don't," she said quietly. "It isn't good for me to talk that way, not in close proximity, at least."

He arched one brow. "Not good? Is there something you should tell me about?"

"Again, not something I want to talk about," she said. "Just—make sure you keep your mental shields tightly closed when I'm around. All right?"

Now he was really curious, but after a moment he nodded. "Fine."

They sat in silence for almost a full minute before she spoke again, "I heard about Desacus. I'm sorry."

"Yeah," he answered dully.

"And that you met a girl," she added, her tone rising slightly.

Of course, he thought silently, *that's what brought her in here.* "It isn't like that."

"She isn't a girl?"

Matthew sighed, "You know what I mean."

"Well, of course," she replied, "*everyone* knew there was no chance of *that*."

"Very funny."

"Did you see Gram when you got here?" she asked suddenly.

"Yeah, he ran interference for me on my way up here," said Matt. "Why?"

"Just wanted to know how he was doing. I haven't seen him in a while. Alyssa's back, did you know?"

"He told me," he answered, but Matthew was mulling over her words as he did. "Why haven't you seen him?"

"I've been staying here most of the time. Resting up. I haven't been out but once or twice since I got back." Moira's voice was dry; matter-of-fact.

Nothing to see here, thought Matthew. *That's what she's trying to say, but there's definitely something.* "Did you get in trouble with Mom and Dad?"

"They were worried," she replied. "It was about the same when I got back, except I wasn't lucky and had to face everyone in the castle yard, but I'm not being punished. I just haven't felt like seeing people."

Yeah, sure, he thought. Moira liked seeing people the same way a fish liked water. She wouldn't stay in for a week by choice. "I heard you started a war."

Moira didn't answer, so they sat in silence for a few minutes. It was a reassuring quiet, a peaceful space without expectation. Neither of them felt like fighting, and to say more would have probably led to an argument, so instead they left the words for later.

After a while she rose and headed for the door. "I'm glad you made it back in one piece," she said, without looking back.

"You too," he said quietly, and then she was gone. With one hand he flipped the PM over so the screen was facing up again. It lit up immediately.

"Great talk with your sister," said Gary dryly.

Actually, Matthew agreed. Something was wrong with her, of that he was sure, and it worried him slightly, but overall, he was just glad she had been more subdued. "It's more about what we don't say," he observed.

CHAPTER 30

The next two days were busy. Matthew was inundated with friends and family that wanted to know where he had been; the questions were innumerable. Conall and Irene pestered him endlessly, though not just about him—they also probed him about Moira.

It wasn't just Gram that had seen little of Moira, it was pretty much everyone. Since her return, she had been to Dunbar once, and on a short trip with Mordecai. Other than that, she had stayed in her room and kept to herself.

The annoying part was that, for some reason, everyone seemed to think that Matthew would have some sort of intuition or mystical way to fix his sister. *I know less than they do, though,* he noted silently. He didn't really have time to spend trying to figure it out, either. More pressing was the need to save Karen.

He had already questioned Lynaralla on the matter, and, as he had suspected, she knew nothing of the She'Har's advanced healing methods. She suggested asking her mother, which would require a journey and a lot of time, since she was a mature She'Har.

Because of that, they ruled that option out and sent a message to Gareth Gaelyn in Albamarl. He was kind enough to respond to the urgency of the request and arrived in Castle Cameron the morning of Matthew's third day back.

Matthew and his father greeted him in the entry hall of the castle keep.

"Gareth," said Mordecai. "It's good to see you again."

Bushy red brows drew together in a skeptical expression. "Really, Mort? Is it that good to see me?"

"Well, of course," said the Count, giving their guest his most disarming smile.

"My wife has been in a foul mood since she returned from her last visit, but she refuses to discuss the matter," stated Gareth, cutting straight to the point. "Why don't we talk about that?"

Mort frowned. "Let's find someplace private."

Matthew watched the whole exchange without saying anything, but his own curiosity was piqued now. Gareth shook his hand, and the three of them started walking.

Once they were safely ensconced in a private room, this time in the Cameron family apartments, not their home in the mountains, they began their discussion.

"Moira wouldn't tell me why she was so insistent on her visit when she left, and she's been unsettled ever since she returned," said Gareth. "What did you do?" He made no attempt to disguise the accusatory tone in his voice. He was referring to his wife, Moira Centyr, not Matthew's sister, the inheritor of her name.

Matthew watched his father's face. Mordecai's gaze remained steady, his eyes on Gareth and his expression revealing nothing, but it was clear the gears were working behind his still features. Eventually he spoke, "Your wife came to check on my daughter."

"That's not unusual," replied Gareth. "Get to the point."

The tension in the air was growing, but Matthew couldn't help but agree. *Yeah, what happened?*

"As you surmise, it wasn't a casual visit. She was concerned about the events in Dunbar and Moira's part in them. The Centyr have many secrets and she was worried that our daughter had broken some of their hidden rules.

"You knew the Centyr back when they were thriving," added the Count. "Are you familiar with any of their internal laws?"

Gareth had relaxed once Mort started talking. "Not really. They kept to themselves for the most part. They even raised their children in seclusion, so most of us from the other families only interacted with them in the council. *Did* she break any of those rules you mentioned?"

Matthew saw the hesitation on his father's face as he considered his answer. *He's thinking about lying. Why?*

Mordecai let out a sigh of resignation, "Yes. She did."

The other archmage winced visibly. "And you bound my wife, didn't you?"

Matt knew he had missed something, but he held his tongue.

"I had no other choice," admitted the Count. "She has too much power for me to have done anything else."

Moira Centyr was an artificial being, a spell-clone of the original Moira, and after Mordecai's battles to dispose of the shining gods, he'd had to find places to store the power he had taken from them. Most of it had gone into the dragons that he and Gareth had created, but a significant portion had been stored in Moira Centyr. Consequently, she had as much strength in her as one of the shining gods. But Mordecai knew the key that controlled the enchantment that preserved her, and it could be used to compel absolute obedience.

"She wanted to kill the girl?" asked Gareth, seeking confirmation.

Mort nodded his affirmation.

It was too much for Matthew, though. "What?!" he blurted out. "Why? Moira's her daughter!"

Gareth rubbed his beard in agitation. "I don't know the 'why,' but back in my day it wasn't uncommon. Once in a while the Centyr would eliminate one of their own. More often than not it was one of their younger mages, though sometimes it would be one of the older, more accomplished members of the clan. They never admitted to it, of course, but we knew. One of them would go missing, and they'd refuse to speak of them again."

"And everyone was fine with that?" said Matthew in disbelief.

"The families didn't interfere with one another," said Gareth stiffly. "What they did to their own was none of our business."

Mordecai spoke again, "I hope you can forgive me, Gareth, but with my daughter's life at stake I didn't see any other choice."

"I'm not happy," said Gareth honestly. "What did the girl do?"

"Your wife didn't want me to reveal their secrets, so…," began Mort.

Gareth snapped, "Goddammit, man! I don't give two shits about their rules, and neither do you! You've bound my wife's free-will in this matter, so I *will* hear the cause for it!"

Matthew felt the older man's words like a slap and leaned back involuntarily. He'd never heard anyone speak to his father in a tone like that.

Mordecai stayed calm, and then sighed, "She used her power to control and manipulate the people around her. She did it in self-defense, mainly, or with good intentions, but it's caused a shift in her personality and unlocked some troublesome abilities."

Now Matthew began to understand. He also had Tyrion's memories, and he remembered the danger the Centyr She'Har had represented to him ages ago. *That was why she didn't want to make mental contact when she was in my room,* he realized. It was also the likely reason for her self-imposed isolation.

"I don't know the particulars of how something like that affects them," admitted Gareth, "but I would imagine the Centyr don't kill their own unless they have a damn good reason. Do you think you know better than they did?"

The Count nodded. "I know something of it, from the memories in the loshti, but not much. I also heard what your wife had to say on the matter."

"And what *did* she say?" asked Gareth. "Since she can no longer speak of it on her own." There was anger in his voice.

"She felt that Moira would be tempted to abuse her power in the future. That it had tainted her spirit," said Mordecai.

"Don't sugarcoat it, Mordecai," rebuked Gareth. "She wouldn't insist on death if she thought she would be *tempted.* She had to have believed it was worse than that."

"Fine. She believed my daughter had become a 'reaver.' It was her term for a Centyr mage that has been corrupted, allowing their power to twist them into some sort of inhuman monster. Is that what you want me to say?" said Mordecai in frustration. "I think she's wrong."

"You would," said Gareth. "You're an optimistic fool. My wife knows the Centyr, and she knows her daughter. You should have followed her advice."

The chair Mordecai was sitting on rippled for an instant, so briefly that Matthew almost thought he had imagined it. He felt nothing—his father's emotions were well hidden behind a shield that had become as solid as stone—but he had seen it. *He's angry,* thought Matt. *So angry that he lost control for a moment.* He glanced at Gareth for a second, noting that the other archmage was also hiding his feelings behind a tightly made shield. *This could get ugly.*

The Count's voice was cool and level when he replied, "I disagree, and unless I see evidence to make me think otherwise, that's the end of it."

Gareth Gaelyn's eyes flashed fire and he stood. "Then we have nothing more to discuss. Don't bother asking me for help or advice either. You are no longer welcome in my home, and I'll thank you to keep your daughter away as well." He started to turn away.

"Wait!" exclaimed Matthew, drawing looks from both men. "I need your help."

"You heard me, mageling," said Gareth, dismissing him. "If your father won't see reason, I'm done here."

"Let him go, Matt," advised his father. "We can do it without him."

Matt turned to face Mordecai. "You said he was the best for this. I'm not going to risk Karen's life to satisfy your pride!"

Gareth chuckled. "Your whelp has grown teeth, Mordecai."

"Let me speak to Gareth alone," said Matt, entreating his father.

The Count's eyes ranged between them, flashing with anger. When they landed on Matthew he saw something else for a moment, but it vanished in an instant, washed away by his father's wrath. "Very well, *son.* Talk to him if you wish, but I'll have nothing to do with it if he's involved. If you want to act like a man and make your own deals, then you'll have to accept the consequences as well. I'm done with this!" He left the room with a heavy stride, and when he reached the door it flew open with such force that the wood splintered. It slammed shut behind him with a thundering boom.

"Lord Gaelyn," began Matthew, after the air had settled.

"Just Gareth, young Illeniel," said the red bearded wizard. "I need no titles when talking to men, even foolish ones."

"I hope the trouble between you and my father won't sway you before you hear my…"

"Don't bandy words, young man," barked Gareth. "You threw your father's pride in his face and now you want to speak to me with soft phrases? Talk plainly and don't bother using sugared words for my ears."

Matthew spoke earnestly, "There's a woman, in another world. She was badly wounded. I left her in stasis, but she will surely die shortly after emerging from it, unless I can persuade you to help her."

"Not my problem," said Gareth curtly.

"But she'll die if…"

"Young man, I *ate* my friends and spent a thousand years living as a dragon. Why should I care if some stranger from another world dies? And you, you might as well have spit on your father just now. Why should I help a fool?"

Matthew was thinking furiously, trying to come up with *something*. Finally, he said, "Even if you consider my father your enemy, *I* am not. In the future, I could be a powerful ally."

The archmage held up a hand to forestall any more, "I would not call your father an enemy, though he certainly is not my friend. I owe him much for his help in the past, or I would have tried to slay him for his insult to my wife. You *do* realize our disagreement is over your sister's life, don't you? Would you ask for aid from a man who might desire her execution?"

Matthew sat straighter and squared his shoulders. "That matter is not for me to decide. If it should lead to a fight between you, I will defend her and the rest of my family. But it was not me who offended you, and it was no fault of my friend's, either. Karen nearly died trying to help me and my dragon, though she hardly knew us. Help her, please!"

Gareth snorted. "She probably considered your dragon nothing more than a mount or fancy pet."

"No," he protested. "They were friends."

"I wonder what Desacus would say if we ask him that same question?" said Gareth derisively.

"He's dead," snapped Matthew. "He died trying to protect us."

The red-bearded mage's eyes widened. "Dead?"

"Dead," he affirmed. "I was knocked unconscious at the same time."

"And the egg?"

"Taken."

Gareth Gaelyn stood, looking down at the young wizard. "And what do you propose to do about *that*?"

Matthew stood as well. He was not as tall as Gareth, but he wouldn't let that intimidate him. Giving the archmage an even stare, he answered, "I'm going to take it back, and make sure that the ones who did it never make that mistake again. But I need Karen's help to find him."

Gareth began to laugh, a deep rumbling sound that was more menacing than humorous. "Very well, young wolf! I will strike a bargain with you. I will help you recover your maiden, but you will make a promise to me as well. I know very well that once you have secured the woman, your father will forbid you to return. The dragons are important to him, but not worth the risk of his son's life. Swear to me that you will defy his will and go back for your dragon. Do that, and I will forgive your father's offense against my wife, whether you succeed or die in the attempt."

Matt smiled. "That's an easy price. I would have done it anyway."

"If that is true, then I have no reservations in helping you get your girl," said Gareth. *Either way my purpose will be served. Either a dragon is saved, or your arrogant father will get his comeuppance, losing his eldest son for treating my wife as his slave.* He smiled, but there was no warmth in it.

CHAPTER 31

Gareth promised to return the following morning. Next, Matthew planned to ask for Elaine Prathion's assistance, figuring her special abilities might come in handy should things turn out for the worse. But first, he had to face his father.

The Count was waiting for him when he left the false family apartments and returned to their semi-secret home in the mountains. He was pacing in the entry hall, visibly agitated.

"Dad…," started Matthew.

"Did he agree to help you?" His voice was curious.

"Yes, but…"

Mordecai smiled. "Excellent! That was quick thinking. I'm proud of you son."

Matthew paused, "Wait, you aren't mad?"

"Ha! Your mother thinks I'm a bad actor, but I've got news for you, I can bluff with the best of them! No, I'm not mad. When you decided to try and talk to him alone, I figured you wanted to try to get around his anger with me by negotiating separately. You caught me by surprise, but I figured it would work better if he thought you had made me angry. It may have even tipped the balance—letting him feel like he was getting back at me by helping you," explained Mordecai.

He didn't think his father would have been as pleased if he had heard about the bargain at the end. Being ordered to stay safe at home after getting Karen back, he should have anticipated that. Even so, he knew he would have ignored the command, so he still didn't consider the bargain a betrayal. It just happened to align with what he would have done anyway.

"Well, I'm glad our plan worked," put in Matthew.

Mordecai looked at him, his eyes twinkling with mirth. "Plan, my ass! You thought I was genuinely angry. I bet I scared the piss out of you when I slammed that door!"

That was unfair—he'd been anxious, but he had never been one to shy away from an argument. "I was a little worried," said Matthew defensively, "but that was all."

His father winked at him. "Either way, that took balls, especially if you didn't know I was just playing along. You're quite the young rebel, aren't you?"

"I wasn't trying to be rebellious," he protested. He had always thought teenage rebellion for its own sake was rather stupid, and he hated being stereotyped that way. "I was just…"

"Oh no!" interrupted Mordecai. "You were definitely rebelling, which is why I have to punish you."

"What?! But you just said you thought it was a good idea!"

"There's a pile of dishes in the kitchen," his father informed him, "and I already gave Alyssa the day off."

Matt glared at him. "You just didn't want to do them yourself," he grumbled.

"You'd best hurry, young hero—every quest starts with an onerous task, and yours lies in the kitchen!"

Elaine Prathion stood beside him in the transfer-house, waiting on Gareth's arrival. She wore a plain woolen dress that was fairly practical by her standards, lacking extra embroidery or decoration, though it was dyed a deep crimson. Despite its simplicity, the dress was well tailored, showcasing her figure. Matthew might have preferred it if she had worn trousers, given the dangers of their task, but Elaine would only make so many concessions when it came to hiding her femininity.

"Somehow, I thought he would be the first one here," she said.

Matthew considered it for a moment; he had thought the same thing, but now he wondered. "Well, he is a thousand years old, and most of that time he was a dragon. Maybe his sense of time is a little eccentric."

She chuckled, "That's a kind word for him. He's almost as scary as your father."

"Scary? Dad?" Matthew had trouble imagining that. If anything, Gareth was far more intimidating.

"Maybe it's because he's your father, but he was *my* teacher. Not to mention the first time I met him, he was fighting Celior."

He guessed seeing something like that might have an effect on someone. For himself, he had missed seeing almost all of his father's legendary battles. Some had happened before he was born, and for those that came later he and Moira had usually been ushered to safety. Growing up, he had always thought his Dad was pretty amazing, but in part it was because everyone else seemed to believe it. The reality he lived with was an older man who stopped pretending to be an adult the moment he was out of the public view.

Matthew nodded. "I'll share the truth for you then. He's a complete klutz. He's never met a wall or a piece of furniture he couldn't run into or trip over. When he isn't busy falling down, he acts like a randy teenager around my mother. If he didn't shield himself constantly, she'd have beaten him black and blue by now. It's really embarrassing. He also has a habit of wandering around the house in his underclothes, and that's *if* you're lucky."

Elaine giggled. "I guess our homes are more alike than I realized."

"Some things cannot be unseen," agreed Matthew in mock horror.

It was then that Gareth Gaelyn appeared within the teleportation circle. He eyed them before speaking, "I hope you two will be able to take this seriously. This isn't a summer outing."

Elaine lifted her chin and graced him with a smile. "Not to worry, Lord Gaelyn. I'm certain we will both be doing our best when we arrive."

The older wizard ignored her reply and turned his eyes to Matthew. "Where will we be leaving from?"

"Right here is fine," he replied. "I should warn you both, though—I can't predict exactly where we'll arrive in the other world. I left a circle near Karen, so once we get there I'll need to make another so we can get to her location."

"This should be easy then," observed Elaine, "as long as we don't appear in the middle of your enemies."

"Or the ocean," added Gareth.

"That's happened to me once already," he admitted before continuing. "I also need to introduce you to the fourth member of our team." He held the PM out in front of him with the screen facing in their direction, "Gary, introduce yourself."

The screen lit and a face appeared, "Good morning, everyone."

Both of the other wizards frowned and Matthew could sense their focus on the PM. They were examining it not only with their magesight but more actively with faint aythar probes.

"How is it talking?" wondered Elaine out loud.

Gareth squinted. "There's no magic in it, and I sense nothing from him either."

By 'him' he obviously meant Matthew. If they hadn't both been mages, they might have been awed by the sight of such strange technology, but they were used to seeing unusual things. They only wanted to know how it worked.

"He's Karen's virtual father," said Matthew. "Similar to your wife, Lord Gaelyn, but without using aythar."

"The term 'thinking machine' might be easier to understand," suggested Gary.

"How does it know our language?" asked Gareth.

"While Matthew was learning our language, English, I also kept close notes of his usage of his native tongue. You call your language 'Barion,' correct?"

They nodded.

"Since, I've been here, I have had a lot of time and opportunity to listen to your language. Some of the syntax and colloquialisms still confuse me, but I believe I have a grasp of at least eighty percent of it now. That will improve dramatically when we return to my world and I can upload the data I've collected to my larger self. I'll be able to integrate the information much more quickly then."

Elaine and Gareth simply stared at the device in Matthew's hand, trying to sort through what it had said. The language had been Barion, but the usage and vocabulary had been put together in ways that were unfamiliar.

Matthew cut in, "He has a strange way of speaking, since he isn't used to our language yet."

Gareth snapped out of it first. "Will it be useful to us?"

"Very," assured the young man.

Gary made an observation in English, "He's rather rude, isn't he?"

Matthew replied in the same tongue, "He's a practical man. Do your best to stay on his good side. He's the one that can heal Karen."

"Noted," said the AGI.

Elaine was frowning as they spoke, but said nothing. Gareth showed no such restraint, "Stick to our language. I don't like being in the dark."

It took a few minutes longer, but eventually Matthew finished the explanations and they were ready to leave. Elaine and Gareth stood on either side of him. She took his left hand and Gareth rested his hand on Matt's shoulder. The world blurred, and they fell into the timeless abyss between worlds.

A light blinked on Aiseman's desk. Nodding and issuing a mental command, he accepted the channel. The face of Major General Gardner appeared across the desk from him.

"We have a signal," said Gardner.

"Where?"

"In Honduras."

Aiseman nodded. "Resolution?"

"Less than a mile, Director," reported the General. "It's very close to a place that used to be known as Dulsuna."

"That's good," commented the Director. "ANSIS has improved our accuracy by a factor of at least ten."

"As we get more signals and data, we should be able to do even better," agreed the General.

"How long before we can respond?" asked Aiseman.

"It's seven minutes for the nearest missile assets, Director. Eighteen minutes for air support, and twenty-five if you want units on the ground," reported Gardner succinctly.

The Director paused, thinking for several long seconds. The plan was to respond with an immediate missile strike if the response time was five minutes or less. Seven was close, but not close enough. "Send in drones and air support. Get the armor on the move. I don't think they'll reach the area in time, but it's best to be sure. We'll have to hope they move as we expect."

He glanced toward the ceiling of his virtual office, as though wondering if an invisible god were listening in. *I didn't say too much,* he thought.

"You have your orders General. We'll speak again in ten minutes," commanded Aisemann, cutting the link.

I can't even say something as simple as 'secure channels,' he thought sourly. With a sigh, he rose from his desk and prepared to send himself to the Gulf Coast UN Cybernetics facility. He hated being forced to download into a physical body, but if their suspicions were correct, it was the only way to avoid having their communications intercepted.

He would meet General Gardner and Deputy Director Wong there, where they could coordinate their ANSIS assets directly, without relying on the network. He could only hope that Dr. Miller wouldn't decide to join them.

CHAPTER 32

Matthew was almost used to the disorientation that always came after shifting, but it was the first time for Elaine and Gareth. The former looked decidedly green as she swayed on her feet, while Gareth unceremoniously bent over and vomited onto the ground.

Elaine jumped back, hoping to avoid letting vomit land on her shoes or the hem of her dress, but the sudden movement almost made her lose control of her own stomach.

Matt ignored them both, taking a couple of casual steps away and using his power to clean his boots while he waited for them to regain their composure. Scanning the area, he was struck by its beauty. The landscape was dominated by rolling hills, with larger mountains on the horizon. Their immediate vicinity was a verdant grassland, but there was a heavily forested area within a half mile of them to the north. Gazing south, he saw signs of more forest there.

Gary spoke almost before Matt could finish looking around, "We have trouble. The military is already moving. They know your location."

"That was fast," observed Matthew. "Are you sure?"

"They've grown very cautious. They've stopped communicating through military network channels. Most of their leadership is convening in cybernetic units in North America," said Karen's virtual father.

"You'll have to explain what that means," said Matthew. He was still coming to terms with the broader implications of the world's technology.

"It means they suspect I have infiltrated military-encrypted channels. They're going to the trouble to download into cybernetic bodies for their meetings in order to avoid me overhearing them. It also means they expect that what they are saying on secure channels will reach me, so we have to assume that what I have learned may be deliberate misinformation," said the AGI.

"So, they're paranoid," said Matt. "What do you *think* they're doing?"

"They may have missiles in the air already. If so, this area will be obliterated in less than five minutes. The best-case scenario is that they were telling the truth; in which case drones and other offensive air capabilities will be here in around fifteen minutes," reported Gary.

"Shit," swore Matthew. "Why does everything happen so quickly in this world?" He didn't wait for an answer, though. There wasn't time. Using his aythar to direct the soil beneath him, he cleared a five-foot by five-foot area and started drawing a circle.

Four or five minutes wasn't long. Elaine stepped closer. "Are we in that much of a hurry?"

He nodded, too busy to bother talking.

She could see the concentration on his face, and that was all the answer she needed. Drawing out one of her wands, she poked him with it to get his attention. "I'll do the outer and inner geometries—I'm faster. You focus on the runes and the keys, since I don't know them."

Matt stared at her for a second. "Good idea." She was already beginning the outer ring, so he started inscribing the runes that went between it and the inner ring, trusting her to complete the lines that would enclose them.

Gary spoke again, "I should also warn you that they have something else planned. They're expecting you to move if they don't hit this location quickly enough, and they think they have an idea of where you will go. As far as I can estimate, that means they suspect you will either try to reach the egg or return to get Karen."

Matthew heard him, but he was too focused on his work to reply. Somewhere in the back of his head, though, he tried to assimilate the new warning.

Meanwhile, Gareth was still having trouble adjusting to the new world. The older man's nausea had subsided, but he was deeply affected by the complete lack of ambient aythar. He continually turned his head, first one way, and then the other, as though he were listening for something. "I don't understand," he muttered to himself.

Seconds ticked by as Gary continued, trying to share as much information as he could before they teleported, "While you were gone, I did manage to locate the dragon egg's precise location, but since it is within the CC center in England I can guarantee that it is heavily guarded. As far as Karen's location, I estimate a very high chance they have found her. While all military assets are disconnected from the network, I've analyzed recent satellite imagery and found evidence of an unusual amount of men and materials being moved in the region."

"It's as though the world is dead," said Gareth, still talking to himself. "There's nothing; it's just silence."

Elaine finished the larger portion of the teleportation circle and stepped back. "It's just your part now, Matthew."

Matt felt sweat forming on his brow as he worked. This last part couldn't be rushed; every rune had to be correct. He could feel Elaine's eyes on him as he progressed, and Gareth was still mumbling in the background.

"What's that?" she said suddenly, looking at the sky and shading her eyes with one hand.

"I don't hear *anything*," Gareth said to them, as though emphasizing some point they should already be aware of.

Gary misunderstood his remark, though, thinking he referred to what Elaine was seeing, "You don't hear them because they travel at hypersonic velocities—Mach five to be specific. You'll be dead before the sound gets here."

"Done," announced Matthew. "Step inside the circle quickly! What were you saying, Gary? I couldn't pay full attention."

"I think they're waiting for you," summarized the AGI.

Elaine had her hand on his forearm already as Gareth took his final step into the teleportation circle. He put his hand on Matthew's shoulder. Physical contact wasn't really necessary as long as they were inside the lines, but it communicated their readiness more quickly than words.

"Make us invisible," ordered Matthew. He waited another second while Elaine did so, and then he activated the circle.

They arrived in darkness, courtesy of Elaine's invisibility shield. It was one of invisibility's main drawbacks—since it routed all light around the user, it meant being effectively blind. She hadn't blocked aythar, though. In a world without mages, they didn't have to worry about being spotted by someone with magesight, so they could still see a short distance using their arcane senses.

Unfortunately, due to the relative paucity of aythar, that meant they couldn't sense much of anything beyond about twenty to thirty feet. Even so, Matthew immediately knew something was wrong. The one thing that should have been very visible in such a low aythar environment was the stasis field he had left behind.

It wasn't there.

Then the world exploded around them.

Matthew's shield held, but Elaine was surprised enough that she lost her grip on the veil she had around them. Light flooded in, showing them a world of flames and dust. While the explosion had caused the ground to jump beneath them, it was eerily silent, thanks to Matthew deciding to block sound as well as physical attacks. He had learned his lesson regarding that back at Roberta's house.

"They were definitely waiting for us," said Gary, stating the obvious.

"We're exposed, girl!" shouted Gareth. "Let me out and I'll distract them while you find the woman."

He was already moving, so Matthew opened the shield to let him pass and then closed it again. Elaine covered them with her invisibility veil once more and he pulled on her arm, making sure she stayed close to him as he headed in the direction of where the stasis enchantment had been.

Gareth's body flowed like water as he passed beyond the shield, reforming into something distinctly reptilian. He looked like no animal Matt had ever seen as the archmage dropped on all fours and sped forward, metallic scales gleaming silver in the sunlight.

Their position couldn't have been worse. Being at the bottom of the canyon, their enemy had taken up positions along the rim thousands of feet above. They were probably on the other side as well, but that was too far for Matt to tell. In the immediate vicinity there was a variety of small groups consisting of three or four cybernetic soldiers equipped with automatic rifles and grenade launchers. While the invisibility shield had been down Matthew thought he had seen larger vehicles in the distance, but now that he was once again limited to the short range of his magesight, he couldn't be sure. He kept walking toward where he had left Karen.

The creature that Gareth had become moved with frightening speed. It raced across the distance to the nearest soldiers and proceeded to rip them mechanical limb from mechanical limb. Weapons fire rang out from every direction, but it had little effect on his heavily armored body.

His speed took the soldiers by surprise, and once he had reached the first group they had to take care not to use their heavier weapons for fear of destroying each other. Gareth had no such constraints, though. He destroyed everything within reach, and after he had dismantled the first group, he sprang toward the next.

As Gareth ran for the second group, they began firing heavier weapons, and while some of the shots glanced off, others hit him squarely, exploding on impact and tearing large chunks of flesh from his massive form.

It slowed him down, but other than that it didn't do them much good. His flesh flowed and reformed whenever he took a substantial injury, even replacing a lost limb from a blast that had sent him sprawling into the dust. Then he was on the second group.

Matthew and Elaine had a much easier task, since the enemy seemed to be focusing their efforts on the foe they could see rather than the one they couldn't. However, after traveling only twenty feet, they were struck again by another explosion, one that came from beneath them. Matthew nearly lost his shield, and Elaine's veil flickered again.

"That was an anti-personnel mine, I think," noted Gary.

"Mine?" said Matthew in confusion.

"A bomb in the ground," explained the AGI. "They anticipated you would try to reach the place you left her, so they've set it up to kill you when you do. There are probably more of them close by."

As if to punctuate his point, Gareth was tossed into the air by a similar explosion as he headed for the third group of soldiers. The blast sent blood and flesh flying in various directions, but the core of his body reformed as it twisted through the air, sprouting wings that assisted him in regaining control of his movement. The monstrous archmage dove for the soldiers.

"This is madness!" shouted Elaine.

"I agree," said Gary. "I also estimate a very low probability that my daughter is still here. If she is alive at all they likely moved her to a secure location before setting this trap for us."

"All right, let's retreat," said Matthew. "Elaine, switch to the exit plan." They began heading in Gareth's direction. *Gareth, we're leaving!* he yelled mentally.

The reptilian monster changed direction mid-charge, which turned out to be a fortuitous choice as the terrain he was about to cross vanished in a massive explosion a second later. If he had continued in the direction he had been going, he would have been in the middle of it.

At the same time, four identical copies of Gareth's form appeared and began charging in different directions. More explosions erupted from two of their locations, and the entire area was cloaked in a cloud of smoke and dust. Elaine added to it by augmenting the smoke with an even larger illusory cloud.

"What are they firing at us now?" asked Matthew. "Are those missiles?"

"I believe it's artillery fire from the canyon rim," said Gary. "Your friend must have scared them enough to call a strike on their own position. We should leave now. They may decide not to wait for the smoke to clear before they carpet bomb the entire zone."

Gareth reached them, and after Matthew let him through their shield he immediately began to shift back home.

They landed in the ocean, which seemed appropriate considering the luck they had had thus far. Matthew created a stable platform beneath them and brought out the enchanted cubes that would enable him to fly and safely carry them all together. Gareth didn't seem to be in any condition to shift into a large flying form.

The red-bearded wizard lay quietly in the mostly invisible flying construct, staring up at the sky. "I have never seen such a swift and vicious response," he muttered. "Those people are not novices when it comes to war." Whatever injuries he had sustained had vanished even before he had returned to his human form, but he still seemed shaken by the experience.

"That's how they defeated the She'Har," Matthew informed him. "That's also probably why the She'Har almost lost when they first came to our world. The humans here just weren't quite as advanced and prepared for them."

"If that's the case, then I think perhaps humanity is more frightening than the She'Har," said the archmage.

Elaine was still in shock from what she had seen. "Can all Gaelyn mages shift the way you did? I've never seen anything quite like that. It was amazing."

Gareth chuckled tiredly. "All Gaelyn mages can shift forms, yes, but what I was doing is far from normal. In the old days, some of the really talented people in my family could have done some of what you saw, but the near-instant healing is an archmage ability."

"I don't think my father could do that," commented Matt.

"The shifting, probably not, but he's transformed into a giant of earth and stone and healed himself in that form," said Gareth. "It's basically the same thing; he just doesn't have my affinity for taking living forms. I wouldn't dream of turning myself into something inanimate like he did. It's too easy to lose yourself that way."

They fell silent for a time after that, while Matthew flew them westward, hoping to catch sight of land so they could stop and create a teleportation circle.

Gareth seemed to doze for a while, but then he spoke without opening his eyes, "Young wolf."

Elaine and Matthew looked at one another, and then he answered, "Sir?"

"I take back what I said the other day. I was in a foul mood. That world is a death-trap. Forget about the dragon; forget the girl as well. No good can come of returning," said the older man.

Matt's lips pressed together in a firm line, but as he was about to reply the archmage spoke again. "Don't say it, boy. If you tell me you're planning to return, I'll inform your father and make sure he finds some way to lock you up for your own good. If you're a man, keep your own counsel. I won't be going back and if you say otherwise I'll make sure you can't either."

Elaine gave him a sympathetic look. "I'm still willing…"

"The same goes for you, girl," Gareth said, cutting her off.

They flew in silence from that point onward. It was several hours before they spotted an island off an unnamed coast. None of them recognized the area. Tired, they landed and made a circle to take them back to Castle Cameron. Once there, Gareth bid them goodbye and left without another word.

"He's a strange man," observed Elaine.

"Yeah," agreed Matthew. "I think he knows I'm planning to go back, though. He just doesn't want to be responsible for it. That's why he told us not to talk about it."

She frowned. "That makes no sense."

"He's from another time," said Matt. "He's also a big believer in free-will, which probably is at cross purposes with his opinion that we're too young to put ourselves deliberately into danger."

"Speak for yourself," said Elaine. "I'm a grown woman."

"Fine," sighed Matthew. "Just me, then. I'm barely an adult by their standards."

She smiled, "I meant what I said. If I can help, I will."

Gary spoke for the first time since they had returned, "Take her up on the offer."

"Hmm?"

"I intercepted some of their short-range transmissions while you were fighting, and I was able to analyze what their sensors reported during the battle. Her invisibility is far more effective than I had anticipated. I assumed initially that thermal imaging would still detect you, since she can't see it herself to ensure that infrared light is included, but I was wrong."

"Thanks for the warning," said Matt dryly. "You could have told me that you thought their devices might still be able to see us."

"While we were here, I had incomplete data," Gary explained. "I had no expectation we would be walking into a trap, so I didn't think it was pertinent."

"Plus, it's your daughter," added Matthew. "You didn't want to say anything that might have made us change our minds."

Gary paused. "There is some truth there."

Matthew took a deep breath, "I have no intention of giving up on either Karen or Desacus's egg. So you can put that concern aside. From now on, tell me whatever you know. I can't plan for things I'm not aware of."

"Then you'll be glad to know I have a suggestion for getting Karen back," said the AGI.

"Do you think we'll need Gareth for it to work?" asked Elaine.

"No," answered Gary. "If things go right, you won't have to fight anyone at all. But your special talent will be a necessity."

They began planning in earnest, and once they had a workable idea they agreed to meet again the next morning.

CHAPTER 33

That evening Matthew told his parents how their journey had gone. They were understandably worried, of course, but he only told them that Karen had been moved. He completely omitted the fact that they had been targeted from the beginning, that they had teleported into a trap, and that they had been forced to beat a hasty retreat to avoid being annihilated.

Since Gareth Gaelyn wasn't on good terms with his father, Matt didn't expect that he would be contradicted on his account, and Elaine had agreed to give the same details, if she should be questioned.

As a result of his deception, his father was still willing to allow him to return to get Karen. His mother had been of a different mind on the matter, but after a fierce debate, she decided to allow it as well.

Unexpectedly, it was Gram who raised the biggest objection when they met at the Muddy Pig later. They had both eaten already, so they were there just to share a mug of ale and catch up. After hearing Matthew's tale (the unedited version), Gram became concerned.

"You need to bring me when you go back," he said firmly.

Matthew winced. "Ordinarily I would say yes, but not this time."

Gram looked angry, "Why not?!"

Matthew held up his dimensional pouch, "This doesn't work over there. As cool as it is, it only works when it's in this world; otherwise the connection to the pocket dimension doesn't function properly." With his finger, he pointed at the tattoo on Gram's arm. "This enchantment is slightly different, but it works on the same fundamental magic. You won't be able to summon Thorn, you won't be able to summon your armor."

"Then I won't summon them there," countered Gram. "I can arm and armor myself before we go."

Matt shook his head. "There are still problems. If we're there for an extended period, you couldn't take the armor off. Then there's your father's heart, the gem that gives you your strength—it's empowered by your father's earth-bond. I guarantee you that won't work across dimensions, and taking it away from this plane might even destroy it."

"I can borrow Sir Cyhan's armor. It's not a perfect fit for me, but it's close enough," countered Gram. "And I don't *have* to use Thorn. There are other enchanted swords."

"And you'll fight as a normal man?" asked Matthew.

"I have a dragon-bond too…"

"Desacus died, Gram. The same could happen to Grace, and then we'd have two eggs to recover. Besides, I'm not planning to fight my way through. It's just not possible. They've shown me that every time. The people of that world have the capability to coordinate their forces on a scale we simply can't compete with, and they have weapons that can destroy anyone or anything, as long as they're willing to accept the collateral damage.

"You're my best friend, and there's no one I trust more, but I'm not taking you into a place like that for no good reason. This will be a stealth mission. There are only three people really suited to that, Elaine, George, or their father Walter. Honestly, even I am not an ideal choice, but I'm the only one who can get there," Matthew explained.

Gram vented his frustration in a growl that ended with him slamming his mug down on the table. Heads around the room turned in their direction. "This isn't fair, dammit," swore the young knight. "I want to break something, but I know you're right."

After a moment, when it was evident the young warrior wasn't about to start dismantling the tavern, the eyes around the room returned to their own drinks. Matthew was glad for that; he didn't enjoy being at the center of attention.

"I'm sorry, Gram. That's just the way it is," he answered apologetically.

Back in his room Matthew was restless, and Gary, while trying to be helpful, wasn't making it any easier for him to relax and get some sleep.

"Before we left, I received a lot of information from my larger self," said the AGI.

"You already told me you had the probably location of Karen and Desacus," said Matt.

"Locations, plural," corrected Gary. "Karen's in the UN's Gulf Coast facility. That's definite. I actually saw her being taken in there on non-military surveillance video."

"At least she's alive."

"That's a positive," agreed Karen's virtual father. "Her condition is easily treatable with modern medicine. My biggest concern is what her mother may do to her."

"Surely she wouldn't hurt her?"

"Don't put it past her. She doesn't even think of Karen as her child. My creator was rather biased regarding Tanya's limits, but I have the advantage of a more objective viewpoint. She's capable of anything. If she believes she can learn something by dissecting Karen's brain, she'll do it. It hasn't been long though, and Tanya isn't one to be impatient, so we probably still have time."

Matthew shuddered, "That's horrible."

"It is," said Gary. "But it's who she is."

"The problem," began Matt, "is that we don't have a way of reaching that place. I've never been there, and there's no teleportation circle handy to get us there. As soon as we cross over, they'll know our location. Even with Elaine to hide us, we couldn't get far enough to avoid the missiles they're liable to send at us."

"I can handle that," began the AGI, but a knock on the door interrupted him.

"Go away!" shouted Matthew. His magesight had already informed him that it was his younger brother Conall at the door.

The door opened.

"I knew I should have put a lock on the door," grumbled Matthew. "I'm busy, Conall. Leave me alone."

"I've hardly seen you since you got back," whined his brother.

"And it's been lovely!" replied Matthew sarcastically.

"I want to help!" announced Conall.

"I'll let you know the next time they decide I have to do the dishes."

"You know what I mean! My power awoke while you were gone. I can do things now. I could help you," insisted his brother.

Several cutting remarks passed through Matthew's head before he discarded them as too harsh. Giving his brother a grave look, he answered more seriously, "How old are you now? Thirteen?"

"Fourteen!" Conall shot back. "You can't even keep up with my birthdays?!"

"Oh! Fourteen, yeah, I'm sorry. That's a much more mature age. Since you're so much older now, I should be honest with you."

Conall nodded.

Matthew walked across the room and tapped a portion of the wall next to the door. "Do you see this spot right here?"

"Yeah."

"All right, remember that spot, it will be important later. Now, let's say I let you come with me. You already know this will be incredibly dangerous, and I'd be taking the risk of losing my favorite brother." He tried his best to keep the sarcasm out of his voice, but he doubted he was entirely successful.

Conall smiled.

What an idiot, thought Matt. "But here's the real problem. Suppose we succeed? Let's imagine we make it back, safe and sound. We're heroes, and nothing terrible happens to you during this adventure. What do you think will happen?"

His younger brother gave it serious thought for a moment before answering, "They'll have a celebration, maybe a feast?"

Matthew shook his head sadly, "No. Well, they might, but something far worse would happen first." He tapped the spot on the wall again. "Mom and Dad would lose their minds over the fact that I had taken you with me. After surviving untold dangers, I'd return home only to have them cut my balls off and hang them on the wall, probably in this very spot, or at least one very similar to it."

Conall looked glum. "Oh."

"Now get out so I can go back to not sleeping," finished Matt, pointing at the door.

His brother headed for the door but stopped to look back. "Um, Matt?"

"What?"

"I'm not stupid. I'm your only brother, so I kind of have to be your favorite."

Matthew gave him an evil grin. "Unless Mom and Dad have another boy. There's still hope for the future. You should enjoy the position now, before my new 'favorite brother' arrives."

Conall stuck out his tongue, then shut the door.

"You're a terrible brother," commented Gary. "Do you treat all your siblings that way?"

"Just the ones that bother me," said the young wizard.

"Define 'bother'."

"If they're in here, or in my workshop, they're bothering me," clarified Matthew. "Or if I'm reading, but I usually do that in one of those places since they don't seem to recognize the fact that I have a book in my hand."

"You sound like a joy to be around," noted Gary dryly.

"Don't worry, it's just a phase I'm going through."

The AGI's expression was doubtful, "You think so?"

"No, but it makes everyone feel better when I say that. Do you feel better now?" asked Matthew.

Gary sighed, "I can never tell if you're joking or serious."

Matthew lifted one brow enigmatically but didn't answer.

"No, honestly, I'd like to know."

"Just always assume I'm serious and you'll be fine. My humor is not for the faint of heart," Matt advised him in a flat tone.

Gary was exasperated, "Now I know you're joking."

"Am I?"

"I'm going to ignore that," said the machine. "Back to what we were discussing—next time we cross over I think I can get us where we need to go, assuming we can get far enough away from our entry point to avoid being blown to pieces."

Matthew leaned closer. "I'm listening."

CHAPTER 34

The next morning Matthew and Elaine shifted again, and as they had the last time, found themselves falling into the ocean.

"Does it always have to be the ocean?" complained Elaine as she stood on a hastily solidified platform of water.

Matthew was scanning the horizon, so it was Gary who answered first, "Roughly seventy percent of the surface is ocean. Since our arrival point is apparently random, it's to be expected that we will appear over sea most of the time."

"How long do we have?" asked Matthew as he arranged the enchanted cubes that would form his flying construct.

"They didn't even have a meeting this time," the AGI informed them, "but since all the principal members of the defense leadership have begun downloading into cybernetic bodies, I assume they have detected our arrival. Based on our distance from the nearest military assets, I estimate we have twelve minutes. Without any landmass at this location, they will be forced to scramble interceptors and drones to target us."

Matt finished his work and gestured for Elaine to enter the construct. "Ladies first."

Once they were airborne, she created an invisibility shield to envelop their craft, but several problems were quickly apparent. "I can't see to fly," said Matthew, who had been using the air to propel them. "My magesight in this world is so limited that I need light just to see the ocean directly beneath us."

"I've also lost satellite signal," added Gary.

"Which means?" asked Matthew.

"Without that, I can't triangulate our position using GPS."

"You told me you could pinpoint our location in just seconds."

"I did," Gary responded. "We are in the South Pacific, three hundred and twenty-seven miles east and one hundred and twelve miles north of New Zealand; or rather we were four minutes ago. Without a GPS signal, I can't keep our position up to date, calculate our airspeed and bearing, or estimate our time to landfall."

"We just need to know which way to go," insisted the young man.

Gary's face disappeared, replaced with a globe display of the earth's surface. "No, I need a GPS signal and contact with the network. Otherwise I can't arrange for transport, nor coordinate meeting that transport once it's arranged. You should head east, by the way, and ever so slightly south."

"We need to see the sun, Elaine," said Matt.

"Give me a full view of the sky," corrected the PM. "Just for a minute or two. I'll make sure we're on the right course and relay instructions to my larger self. We can block everything for a while after that, until we get close to land."

Elaine Prathion obliged them, and after a few minutes she restored the invisibility veil, leaving only a small area beneath them so they could gauge their distance from the surface.

Based on Gary's estimate of their speed, it would be over three hours before they reached land, so they lapsed into a comfortable silence, punctuated by occasional moments of conversation.

After an hour of travel, Gary offered some speculation. "While not being able to receive satellite signals is annoying, it bodes well for the rest of our mission."

"How so?" asked Elaine.

"I wasn't certain before, what sort of signals your invisibility would block. Since you only see visible light, it was possible that visible light was all it would hide us from," explained the machine.

"Well, I can hide us from aythar as well," Elaine informed him. "Though it isn't necessary since no one here can sense it."

"That's the point," said Gary. "Aythar is also something you can sense, so it's easy for you to know when you are manipulating it, just like light. But on this world, we use many forms of light that are not discernable using normal human senses. Radio waves, microwaves, x-rays, millimeter waves, infrared, ultraviolet—any of these could potentially give us away when we are trying to sneak in, if your talent doesn't work on them.

"From our last visit, I was able to ascertain that radio waves, infrared, and ultraviolet are also covered by your invisibility, since the military sensor feeds didn't register you, but I wasn't sure about the others. I can now safely rule out microwaves as a problem. That makes me feel more comfortable that the other portions of the electromagnetic spectrum are also included," said Gary.

He had been speaking in Barion, but many of the words didn't have equivalents in their language, so he had been forced to use several English terms.

"Elektro, what?" said Elaine, confused.

Matthew was doing better, since he had a good handle on English now, including a few of the new words. "What

DEMONHOME

he means is that your talent seems to work on all the types of light they use to spot enemies."

She gave them both a look that suggested they were only repeating the obvious. "Well, of course. When a Prathion doesn't want to be found, they aren't found."

"Perhaps you were certain of it, but I wasn't," said Gary.

"That's the Prathion motto," said Matt. "They like to pull it out whenever they get the chance."

Elaine lifted her chin slightly. "If I were you I'd be a bit more respectful of the one who's keeping you safely out of the fire."

Gary started laughing, but they all fell silent a second later when a thundering boom shook the flying construct.

"What was that?!"

"Sonic boom," said Gary. "One of the interceptors must have passed by. They fly faster than the speed of sound, so the sonic energy of their passing becomes concentrated along a line behind them. When it passes over you, it sounds like thunder."

"Sound doesn't have a speed," argued Elaine.

Thanks to the loshti, as well as a lot of non-traditional education over the years, Matthew knew better. He spoke up before Gary could. "Sound is just the vibration of the air. It's a wave, just like the ones you see in water. It has a speed, but I never thought anything could go fast enough to outrun it!"

"The whole thing sounds mad, if you ask me," said Elaine.

"Well, that certainly wasn't thunder," countered Matt. "The sky was clear when we looked a little while ago."

They stayed quiet for a while after that, until Gary broke the silence once more. "It appears they aren't tracking us."

"You just told us that they couldn't," said Matthew.

"They can't detect us directly, but the same detectors that ANSIS uses to detect the anomaly created when you shift into this world might be sensitive enough to detect smaller uses of aythar. I have little way of knowing just how good their sensor calibration is, since they keep all that data separate from the normal network," explained Gary.

"They did find Karen, I suppose," said Matthew with a nod.

"Exactly. It may be that the method is slow and requires time to triangulate the position of smaller anomalies, or it may be that the signal they receive is diffuse and requires time to refine. Either way, I think we're relatively safe, so long as we don't stay in one place too long," agreed the AGI.

"I wonder if making us invisible to aythar would help?" suggested Elaine.

"In your world it might, since aythar is everywhere," observed the machine. "In this world, it is largely absent. I doubt your method would work since they aren't 'seeing' us in the traditional sense. You have to use aythar to generate your shield, and that will create a change in the surrounding environment that they can detect.

"In the long run, if we keep using this flying construct, or any other aythar-based techniques, they will eventually find us, or at least be able to get an approximation of our location," he finished.

An hour and a half later, they finally reached the coast of New Zealand. They landed on a rocky beach, and Matthew took his construct apart and stored the enchanted cubes in a small pouch. On Gary's advice, they also did away with their personal shields and completely closed their minds. It was the closest the two of them could get to becoming ordinary, mundane humans.

They still radiated a small amount of aythar, though. There was no helping that—for them it was a consequence of simply existing—but Gary thought it would be too small for ANSIS to detect, at least for a considerable period of time.

The two humans walked a short distance inland to get away from the coastline and find cover beneath what few trees they could find. There were no human settlements nearby, but it was almost a certainty that there would be drones searching the entire region soon when they weren't found anywhere near their arrival point.

A half an hour went by, and then a pert came into view following the coastline. It settled down just twenty feet from their hiding place, and the door opened automatically.

"That's it," said Gary. "Get inside."

"Who is driving it?" asked Elaine.

"I am," the AGI informed her.

She gave him a look of disbelief. "You don't have hands."

"I already brought it here to meet us."

"But you were with us the entire time," she protested.

Matthew cut in, "He's sort of like a spirit, Elaine. He's everywhere in this world, so long as there's a machine for him to speak through. I know it's confusing, but trust me."

They climbed in, and the pert took off smoothly and then turned north. It rose above the tree line and picked up speed until the landscape beneath them began to blur.

"Do I need to veil the carriage?" asked Elaine. She looked tired.

"No," said Matthew. "Save your strength, you'll need it later."

"It feels like I'm just getting weaker. I can't seem to recover," she added.

Matthew nodded. "It's because this world is barren of ambient aythar. You will regain your strength, but it takes a lot longer here."

"You won't need to use your abilities until we reach Karen's location," Gary assured her. "It will take us several days to get there. Until then, I'll make certain they can't find us."

"How?" she asked.

Gary grinned. "It's complicated. This pert for example, it belongs to a resident of New Zealand but it is rarely used. I've created a false identity, changed the registration and brought it here for our use. When we're done, it will go back to its true owner and I'll reverse the changes I made. As we travel, we will change perts frequently, for a variety of reasons, but mainly to make unraveling my web of deceit impossible for mere human investigators. It would take a super AI like myself to figure out what I'm doing, and even if they had one, it wouldn't be able to do the job because I'm erasing the trail as we go.

"In some locations, the registration won't be changed. In others, we will take public transportation using false identification. The only clue they will have to our whereabouts will be the faint traces of aythar that follow in your wake, and from the data I have already, I think it will be too weak for them to detect. Even if it is detectable, you will be traveling too quickly and it will be too vague for them to narrow your location down within a thousand miles or more," explained the AGI.

The two wizards listened with varying degrees of understanding. When Matthew finally opened his mouth to speak, Gary preempted his question, "I know what you're thinking. What about the public transportation? You'll be exposed to public surveillance cameras, and the automated ASI will pick up your faces and alert the authorities. I'll be intercepting those video feeds and removing the alerts. The only way they can spot you is if they use independent systems that aren't connected to the network.

"I don't deny there's a small risk there that I can't mitigate, but it is for that reason that I have limited the number of times you will be exposed to physical view. Also, if she can spare the aythar, Elaine's talent with illusion could eliminate that risk entirely, although it will come with a tradeoff. Using aythar will increase the probability that ANSIS can narrow the search to a more precise area."

Matthew had been waiting patiently, but when he opened his mouth again, Gary started to interrupt him once more, "Before you ask…"

"Can I just get a word in?!" he growled.

Gary paused. "Certainly."

"I trust you," said Matt. "That's why we're here. We will trust you when we reach these public spaces you mentioned as well. I think it's better to avoid giving them anything extra to pin down our location."

"Thank you," said the AGI. "Now, back to what I was explaining…"

"Gary," said the young man with a sigh. "Please shut up. I know you're excited about your plan, but we only have a passing knowledge of this world. Let us get some rest."

The AGI pursed his lips. "Fine."

CHAPTER 35

The next two days were a blur of seemingly random transfers between different perts as they traveled north from New Zealand to mainland Asia. At one of their early stops, they collected packages from the doorstep of a stranger's home. The boxes contained clothing that the AGI had purchased to help them blend in. They also traveled on two sparsely filled machines that reminded Matthew of a giant mechanical snake. Gary told them they were called trains. Apparently, there had been many more of them in the past, but only a few were in operation these days due to a paucity of organics needing mass transport.

When they reached a city called Hong Kong, they transferred to a special aerial transport known as a 'hypersonic jet.' It had seats for over a hundred people, but like the trains it was only half filled. The two wizards were fascinated by the thought that they would be traveling at nearly three times the speed of sound, but the reality was far more boring. After an exciting half hour they wound up taking a nap for the rest of the flight.

After arriving in Los Angeles, they took another short trip via train before meeting yet another pert. This one carried them all the way to New Mexico where they met the pert that Gary informed them would be their last vehicle of the journey.

"What's the last city we are heading to called again?" asked Elaine as she attempted to scratch beneath her breasts.

345

"Houston," Matt answered.

"The names here are so weird," she replied as she reached beneath her blouse to rearrange something.

He found the activity beneath her shirt fascinating, but his curiosity was growing. "What are you doing?"

"It's these clothes, this 'bra' thing in particular. It itches. I don't think it fits right, either. While I can't complain about the bathrooms, these people have strange ideas about what constitutes *comfortable*. Give me a properly tailored dress over this bizarre mish-mash of clothes any day!"

Matthew was wearing a pair of blue jeans and a cotton T-shirt. "The clothes do lack style, but these trousers are very comfortable; the shirt too. I was thinking about getting Gary to buy more for us to take back home."

Elaine was digging around behind herself with both hands. After a brief struggle, she pulled the offending undergarment out through one sleeve. "Here, if you think the clothes are so comfy, you can have this."

He held the bra in one hand while he examined it. Matthew had never been one to ogle women, or show any other over attention to their 'attributes,' but he was having difficulty managing his train of thought. Elaine was quite an attractive woman and not too far away from him in age. While the women of his own world didn't wear bras, neither did the dresses drape their torsos in quite the same way the light, soft fabric of this world's shirts did.

He kept his eyes on the object in his hand. The bra was soft but it had a strangely stiff portion. "Why would they put wire in this?" he asked.

"It's stupid," complained Elaine. "It's supposed to hold up the breasts, but it keeps biting into my skin. Look at this shirt." She shook the material with her hands. "It's too loose! If it had more substance and was tailored properly—like this," she pulled the shirt in the back, stretching it tightly beneath her breasts, "then it would provide all the support I need, without any stupid wires."

Matthew glanced at her and quickly looked away. The effect of her manipulations had been to make it look as though her shirt were painted on. He was used to seeing things ordinary men could not, thanks to his magesight, but seeing things with his eyes was different, and for some reason it embarrassed him. "I see your point," he said non-commitally.

Elaine watched him suspiciously. "What?"

"I was agreeing with you," he said defensively.

"Not that—you're blushing. Did I embarrass you?" she accused, in a sly and mischievous tone.

He was very sure that he was *not* blushing. Probably. "No. Can we move on? This isn't a topic I really care about."

"That's good to hear," she told him. "You're almost like a little brother to me. I'd hate to think you were harboring a secret attraction. Besides, we're here to save your girlfriend, after all."

Matt growled, "She's *not* my girlfriend, and of course I'm not attracted to you." An evil thought crossed his mind. "You're more like a kindly *old* aunt to me."

Elaine scowled. "That's a relief, but it might be better if she were your girlfriend. My father once suggested it might be advantageous for our families to have closer ties. I'd hate to think how you might suffer if you were forced to marry such an old woman."

He gaped at her for a second, but then his anger drained away, replaced by amusement. "That's a fair point."

She was taken aback by his reversal. "Now wait a minute!"

"You've always been a good friend, Elaine," he said, trying to get ahead of her temper. "There's no telling what the future holds, for either of us. Who knows who we will get stuck with? At least we aren't strangers." He handed the bra back to her.

Elaine closed her mouth, pausing for a moment, then she replied, "That's true. Though, just to be clear, if that ever happened, you'd be the one getting the better end of the deal."

Matthew disagreed, which sparked a new round of debate. The conversation was light-hearted after that, but he had no real doubt. Elaine wasn't a bad person, but she was a little too superficial for his tastes, and she was definitely too much of a talker. As they bantered back and forth, he found himself thinking of Karen. While he had traveled with her, Karen had seemed mildly annoying, but in comparison to Elaine, he found himself wishing for her long periods of silence. When Karen spoke, she usually got right to the point, she wasn't one to play word games.

He missed her, though he wasn't ready to admit it yet.

The pert lowered itself to the ground, landing on a road that, unlike the few others they had seen, still appeared to be well maintained. Gary explained this was because the military still used some heavy ground transports for moving large equipment in and out.

Large trees leaned over the road on either side, and the verges were thick with long grass. The air was humid, and Matthew felt sweat beginning to form on his brow almost as soon as he exited the vehicle.

The pert's doors closed, and it rose quietly back into the air as soon as they had stepped away from it, heading back in the direction of Houston.

"Just follow the road," coached the PM. "It leads straight to the main gate of the facility."

"How far?" asked Matthew.

"Six and a half miles," answered the machine. "We could have gone closer, but I didn't want to risk raising their alert level before we had even entered the base."

Elaine created an invisibility shield around them, and they took off at a brisk pace. A few miles weren't much of an obstacle for people who had grown up in a place where walking was the primary method of travel, but the heat and humidity still left them both damp and miserable by the time the chain-link gate and guard station came into view.

As they drew closer, they began to make out more details with their magesight, which was their only means of seeing with the veil around them. A lone occupant was in the guard station; a military android. The gates themselves were closed and the fence was over ten feet tall.

Neither of the two wizards was comfortable with flying, but the distance was short enough that they were able to levitate themselves over and land softly on the other side without taking any serious risk of a fall.

Gary was still maintaining network contact through a small hole in the shield that Elaine had provided him. "No sign of an alert yet," he told them cautiously.

"There shouldn't be," said Elaine confidently.

"Unless one of the ANSIS detectors is located on this base, of which there is a fair chance," countered the AGI. "I don't know what they look like or even what principle they operate on to detect aythar."

Since their super-intelligent guide already had the layout of the base as well as the internal plans for the buildings, they followed his directions. Gary coached them across a wide lawn and past an entrance that he explained led to an underground vehicle park. They could have descended and entered there, but he had planned a more direct route through a pedestrian entrance.

There were multiple buildings, all constructed of steel and the strange stone that Gary had labeled 'concrete.' They bypassed those, heading for the largest structure, which dominated the center of the facility.

It wasn't a particularly impressive construction by Matthew's standards. It stood barely two stories in height, but Gary had already explained to them that the majority of it lay beneath the ground. The upper levels were easy-access administrative offices, under them lay an immense structure of reinforced concrete that protected the military hardware and secure assets in the levels below.

"It isn't as secure as Cheyenne Mountain in Colorado," began the AGI, "but they did the best they could for an area like this without mountains or any significant rock formations. Much of the surrounding area was a swamp long ago."

Matthew wasn't sure what the machine meant by that, since he had no way to compare the places, but he didn't really care. He only wanted in. Leaning close, he whispered in Elaine's ear, "Remember, if things go badly and we have to fight, use lightning. Fire and other things work, but you'll get more for your aythar with lightning."

Gary had advised him on that earlier, and he reinforced the message now, "Military equipment, especially the cybernetics, are hardened and insulated to withstand moderate EMP shocks, but they're still vulnerable to severe damage from direct electrical current. In this world, no one has ever been able to use lightning as an effective weapon. Just be sure not to hit me with any stray discharges."

"You are not hardened?" asked Elaine seriously.

Matthew didn't even consider making the obvious joke, and he was glad his father wasn't there to make things worse. Gary answered honestly, "No, this unit is not protected in the least. Even a small shock would probably render it inoperable."

She nodded, "Inoperable—does that mean you would be dead?"

Matthew already knew the answer to that and he cut in, "No, he's much bigger than that. This PM is almost just a messaging device for him. He's in most of their electronic systems across the world, except for the military ones."

"Except for the ANSIS systems," corrected Gary. "I can access a lot of the military systems, but they are moving to isolate more and more of their equipment each day, probably connecting it to the ANSIS network."

By now they had reached the entrance that Gary had indicated, a double-wide set of glass and metal doors. Matthew couldn't help but think it didn't look terribly secure. "Any fool with a hammer could smash these," he observed.

"The upper doors aren't meant to withstand a serious assault," said Gary. "The real security is below us; this only leads to offices and low-value equipment."

"Why not protect all of it?" asked Elaine.

"This way, if someone did take it by force, they would have to approach the secure vault doors after entering and descending several levels. It's much harder to get the kind of heavy weapons and equipment you need to get through super-secure blast doors down there than it is up here.

"Besides, aside from being located next to the Gulf Coast reserve facilities, this is primarily a lab and research station," added the AGI.

"Do we need to smash the glass?" asked Elaine, anxious to hurry them onward.

"Just step forward," said Gary.

They did, and nothing happened. "And now?" asked Matt.

The AGI sounded embarrassed, "They're automatic doors. Motion sensors activate them. I forgot that with Elaine's invisibility they won't react to your presence. Do you perhaps have a way to pass through solid objects?"

"I'm a wizard, not an archmage," he answered, though Gary really didn't understand the difference. "Can't you control the doors?"

"These are actually just dumb doors; the mechanism is purely automatic. They aren't connected to any network. The security screening point is inside the lobby, so they don't even bother to lock these doors most of the time. We need something visible to trigger them to open."

Matthew stared at the PM and Gary stared back at him, neither of them immediately coming up with a solution. For all of the AGI's elaborate plans and Matthew's powers, it seemed ridiculous that they would be stymied by a pair of automated doors that weren't even locked.

"For goodness sake," said Elaine in exasperation. "Let the Prathion do it. Neither of you has the brains of a turnip." So saying, she used her aythar and seconds later a large dog ran around the corner of the building and crossed in front of them. The doors opened as it passed by and continued on to the far corner.

Of course, the dog was an illusion, but it had worked perfectly. All three of them remained silent as they stepped into the lobby. Matthew added a sonic shield beneath Elaine's invisibility before they spoke again.

The interior was another gleaming and immaculately clean example of the world's fascinatingly strange architecture. Everything was white tile and stainless steel, punctuated by granite and marble stonework in odd places like countertops. A long, low desk stretched across the far side of the room with two human-sized openings for people to walk through. Two cybernetic guards stood on either side of the room.

"Just walk across and step through the screening machines," advised Gary. "Make sure to close the hole in your shield; otherwise the machines might register something unusual as we pass."

The two humans did as he asked, walking single file. Elaine had to adjust the boundaries of her invisibility to get through the machine without causing some parts of it to temporarily 'disappear' from view, but that was easy enough for her.

On the other side, they passed several more cybernetic guards who stood in front of a row of strange metallic doorways. Between each set of doors were two buttons with triangles pointing up and down. Following Gary's directions, they went left and down a short hallway until they reached a door that opened into a stairwell.

There were cameras and another guard stationed on one side of the hall, so they had to be careful opening the door. Fortunately, Elaine was confident in her mastery of illusion. She cloaked the entire area around the door in a static illusion so their invisibility veil wouldn't create oddities when they opened the door, and Matthew's sound barrier prevented the noise of the door closing from reaching the guard.

There were more cameras mounted on the ceiling inside the stairwell. Ignoring them, they began descending the stairs. Four flights of stairs and two landings later, they had reached the level they needed. The stairs ended there, since beneath them began the massive concrete fortifications that protected the deeper levels.

To get farther below, they would have to leave the stairwell and pass through the main entrance on that level. Beyond that there would be more elevators and stairs.

Before that, however, they had to exit the stairwell, and the door was locked. A small plastic box was fastened to the wall beside the door, and it held a small display screen with a red light beneath it. As they stood beside it, the light changed to green and a click indicated that the door had unlocked.

"Was that you?" asked Matthew.

"Yes," said Gary. "Most of their regular building security is still on the network. This will be a piece of cake as long as we don't get spotted or arouse suspicion along the way."

Back in a hallway again, they walked a short distance and made a turn. There before them were the elevators they had seen on the upper levels. Directly across from them was a large round gate flanked by a massive disc of solid steel that was obviously meant to seal the entrance at certain times. A contingent of eight cybernetic guards were in position, two on either side of the gate and two farther away on either side. Matthew's magesight was limited by distance, but he could detect more guards on the other side of the gate.

"Maybe we should wait until night," suggested Elaine, "when most of the workers are at home. Or is that giant door closed then?"

"They work in shifts around the clock," Gary replied. "The blast door is only closed twice a year, to ensure it still functions. Other than that, it's only meant to be closed during an emergency."

"We just have to walk through, making sure not to bump into any of the guards or workers coming in or out," said Matthew. "It couldn't get any easier."

Staying close together, they walked out, but before they had gotten within thirty feet of the entrance, red lights on either side of it began to flash. There might have been an alarm siren as well, but Matthew's sonic shield kept them from hearing it. The giant steel door began rolling toward the opening to seal it off.

"We've been disc...," Gary started to announce, but Matthew was already grunting under the strain as high velocity rounds began slamming into his shield. Every guard on either side of the entrance was firing, their weapons pointed directly at the apparently empty space where the two wizards stood.

Several canisters were launched into the area around them and began issuing a large volume of gas.

Matt was already reinforcing his shield and adding a filter to keep out the external air, but the sheer volume of firepower focused on them made him wonder how long he could keep up his defense. A cybernetic unit with a black metal frame emerged from the other side of the gate and pointed an even heavier weapon at them, a massive gun with multiple barrels that were beginning to spin in place.

"The gas is a type of tear gas," Gary informed them. "It also serves to help eliminate the possible advantage of your invisibility by rendering us unable to see."

We can't see them anyway, thought Matthew. *The invisibility blinds us as much as them, but then they don't necessarily know that.* Swiping his hand across in front of him, he burned a blackened line into the floor and erected a stronger shield between them and the entrance. His action was just in time, as a powerful stream of bullets began firing from the new guard's weapon. "Elaine!" he shouted, "Forget the veil; they can see us somehow. I can barely protect us. You need to go offensive."

Even as he said the words, he felt the doors open to the elevators, which were filled with yet more robotic guards. Without access to an external source of aythar, his

355

shield would fail in seconds if they came under fire from all sides.

Light flooded in as Elaine released her invisibility veil and lifted her twin wands, one in each hand. They were pointed in opposite directions, one on either side, and a split second later actinic blue light filled their vision as lightning arced through the open spaces around them.

Unlike normal lightning, which seeks the most direct route to the ground, this lightning flashed through the air and sought out their enemies, like a hungry spirit searching for vengeance. It arced from one soldier to the next, creating a brilliant web as it connected between the soldiers in front of them and on either side of the gate. It also lasted longer, burning the air for a full two seconds before winking out. The soldiers collapsed, smoke rising from their metallic frames. Then, just as the soldiers behind began to fire, she turned and repeated her attack, destroying the newly arrived defenders.

As the last echoes of gunfire died away, Elaine holstered her wands and glanced at Matthew. "They don't seem so bad."

"Very funny," Matthew replied dryly. "I'd like to see you shield us from what they were throwing at us just now." His voice was calm, but he could feel an almost imperceptible tremor in his legs. He had used almost half of his available aythar in a span of seconds. It hadn't been flashy, like Elaine's lightning, but both of them knew she wouldn't have been able to channel enough power to have sustained the shield that had kept them alive.

Gary spoke up before she could retort, "Take a look at the unit with the Gatling gun."

Gatling? Matthew assumed he meant the black android that had carried the heavy weapon. Now that they could see with normal vision, he could make out a series of letters marked in silver across its chest: ANSIS.

"It was linked up with the other soldiers, providing them with your location for coordinated firing," said the AGI, "or so I would guess. It probably was also what triggered the alarm."

Matthew moved closer, examining the robot with his magesight. Unlike the others, there was something different about it. Within the central torso was something that wasn't metal or electronic but organic. Focusing his senses, he discovered a soft spongy tissue encased there. "I think it has some sort of small brain inside," he announced.

"We need to figure out how we're getting through the door." Elaine was looking at the massive piece of solid metal blocking their way.

"Your attack shorted out the electronics controlling both the elevator system and the blast door," noted the AGI. "They will have to send reinforcements down via the stairwells, which will give us a few minutes."

"So, you can't open the door," said Matthew, eyeing it dubiously.

"I couldn't have done so even if the electronics were working. It was isolated from the main network. I believe our mission has failed." The machine didn't sound particularly happy about his pronouncement.

"We aren't giving up yet." Matt reached into his pouch and drew out two small iron balls.

Elaine frowned. "You think those can blow it open?"

"The door is impervious to any but the largest of explosions," cautioned Gary.

Matthew handed Elaine one of the iron spheres. "Draw the aythar out of it slowly. Use it to replenish your reserves."

"There's an extra set of runes on this," she observed.

He nodded. "I added a layer to the enchantment to help slow the release. The first time I tried it, I had to absorb it so fast it burned me. That should make it easier."

"What are we doing?" asked Gary. "You don't have the power to open that door. I've made a lot of rough estimations based on what you've done before, so unless you have a hidden ability there's no…"

The young man cut him off. "A wizard's true power is in the limit of his imagination, not how much energy he commands." Stepping forward, he put his hand on the outer surface of the door and directed his magesight into it.

Two feet of solid steel lay under his palm, but behind that was a hollow space containing a variety of gears. One large gear in the center connected to smaller ones that lay around the outside; those smaller gears were attached to a straight ratchet type mechanism that drove heavy steel pins, each several inches in diameter, from within the door into the frame, locking the door in place.

Reversing the direction that the central gear had moved should cause the smaller gears to retract the bolts, allowing the door to be rolled back. He attempted to do just that, but found that the central gear wouldn't turn; it was locked in place. Searching farther, he found another lock, this one facing the inside of the door. A key could be inserted there to free the central gear.

As he studied it, he realized it must have been designed that way to allow someone inside to manually open the door if necessary, for near the lock was a large wheel that would allow a strong man to release the bolts by turning the same central gear Matthew had tried to turn.

The smaller key lock was easy enough; it had a series of pins that had to be held back so he could turn it, and once that was done, the central gear was free to move. As he began to turn the main gear, metal hands gripped the interior wheel, fighting to keep him from turning it.

"There are guards inside trying to keep me from opening the door," he told the others. "Step back for a second, and make sure you aren't in contact with the metal." He handed the PM to Elaine for safekeeping, and then added, "Once I get it open, be ready to repeat your lightning, since they'll probably be firing at us."

Then he sent a powerful electric discharge through the metal. After a second, the hands left the manual crank on the other side as the guard collapsed. Working at speed, he turned the central gear and the locking bolts withdrew, but the massive door still needed to be moved.

The entire thing was mounted on a notched rail, and there was a second mechanical system responsible for rolling the door into position. Another crank inside was there to allow someone to manually roll the door back if necessary, which would likely be the case since the electric motor attached to it was now smoking from his latest attack.

More metal hands tried to prevent that crank from moving, but a second electric discharge forced them to withdraw. Moments later he had the blast door rolling back, inch by inch.

Gunfire rang out and bullets began whizzing through the gap, but Elaine shielded her hand and stuck one of her wands through. A flash of light showed through the gap, and then the weapons fell silent.

There was blood dripping from her arm when she pulled the wand back. "I don't think the shield worked," she mumbled as the color began to drain from her face and she began to sway on her feet.

Matt stopped and grabbed her before she could fall. The bones in Elaine's left forearm had been shattered, and a hole on either side indicated that a high-speed projectile had passed completely through her arm. It took him a long minute to seal the blood vessels and skin, as well as damp the nerve signals transmitting pain. The bones would have

DEMONHOME

to wait; they were in too many pieces to rush the job of aligning and fusing them.

The color was returning to her features. It had been the pain rather than blood loss, that caused her to nearly faint.

"You all right now?" asked Matthew.

She nodded, and he returned to the door. Another minute passed, and he had increased the gap by slightly more than a foot, enough for them to squeeze through. Checking with his magesight to ensure there were no moving guards near it, he risked peeking around the edge.

Several bullets struck his shield, and a roar of gunfire gave him the answer he needed. There were more defenders farther back, too far away for his magesight to reveal. "These people are really starting to tick me off," he muttered.

"Not to give you too much good news, but the upper level door sensors indicate that both upper stairwell doors have been opened. The cameras aren't on the main network, but I would guess that means more soldiers are descending now. You probably have less than thirty seconds before they arrive," Gary informed them.

"Thirty seconds?" exclaimed Matthew. "It took us a couple of minutes to get down all those stairs."

"I'm assuming these are not organics. They can simply jump, rather than running down the stairs," clarified the machine.

A loud boom announced the violent opening of the lower stairwell doors.

"Correction: my original estimate was too optimistic," said the AGI.

The young wizard wasn't paying attention. He had begun taking action during Gary's first warning. Six iron spheres, unmodified ones, flew from his hands, and guided by his power they zoomed away and around two corners to strike the stairwell entrances. Three hit the area around each doorway and a thundering explosion filled their ears.

Unwilling to wait and see the results, he wrapped his body in the strongest shield he could manage and went through the gap in the blast door sideways. Multiple impacts slammed into his shield, but grinding his teeth against the strain, the shield held. More iron spheres shot away from him in multiple directions and more explosions followed. A second later he called back, "Now, Elaine, hurry!"

She was already beginning to regain her composure. Squeezing through, she was shocked at the destruction on the other side. Dozens of metal soldiers lay in heaps down a long corridor that led to the blast door, and two fortified gun emplacements were in shambles. "Lightning would have been more efficient and less destructive," she commented.

"I didn't have time to redesign the iron bombs before we came," shot back Matthew, "and I wasn't wasting my own aythar, but your concern is duly noted." Turning his attention to the manual crank inside, he began rolling the blast door back into position. More bullets began coming through the gap, this time from the outside.

"That's our only way out, isn't it?" queried Elaine.

"We aren't leaving the way we came," said Matthew. "Once we find Karen, we're going home immediately. I doubt we could survive fighting our way out." The door gave a subtle clang as it reached its final position, and Matthew then turned the central gear to send the locking bolts into their places. As an afterthought, he used some of his aythar to weld the central gear at its central axis. Their enemies wouldn't be opening that door again any time soon.

Staring down the wide corridor that was their only way forward Matthew spoke again, "Which way now?" It was a weak attempt at humor and neither Elaine nor Gary laughed.

CHAPTER 36

As they walked, Matthew drew out another of the modified iron bombs and began siphoning off its energy, trying to get his aythar reserve back to full. It wasn't a pleasant experience, but it didn't burn him the way the first one had, back before he'd added the extra layer of enchantment to protect himself.

The corridor led them to a wide circular space with a shaft descending in the middle. Looking down, they could see a platform far below. It showed no signs of coming back up, and pushing the buttons that were mounted on the railing around the shaft did nothing. Whoever was down there had locked it in place to prevent the intruders from reaching the next level.

"There's a service ladder on the other side," said Gary. "It starts just beneath the rim of the shaft."

"Too slow," said Matthew. "They know we're here. I don't want to give them any more time to prepare for us." Tapping into his aythar, he created a small plane of force anchored to the side of the shaft and stepped onto it. Trying to be polite, he offered his hand to Elaine as she joined him. She took the proffered appendage but smiled as she did, raising one brow. She knew as well as he did that it was a purely symbolic gesture.

Carefully, he began lowering their aythar platform, using his power to grip the sides of the shaft and control their descent. Elaine took the time to carefully begin fusing some of the bones in her forearm.

As they descended, Matthew studied the shaft below them, noting that there were four obvious places it opened onto at various points. "Which level do you think she's on?" he asked.

"The lowest level houses independent power generation facilities, ventilation systems, and storage. The upper level is primarily military servers and equipment. The second and third levels are medical and biological research areas, so she is almost certainly on one of them. Besides this primary transport shaft, there are smaller stairwells at the outer corners of each level to facilitate personnel movement between levels, so if we choose the wrong one we have options for getting to the next level," Gary informed them.

"Third level then," decided Matt. "We'll go up if she isn't there." He was interrupted when bullets began flying up the shaft toward them, fired by cybernetic soldiers leaning out from the second level entrance below them.

Already preoccupied with coordinating their descent, Matthew fumbled to get more iron spheres out of his pouch, but Elaine put her wounded hand on his arm. "Let me."

She drew out one of her wands with her good hand and pointed it downward. More lightning flashed, almost blinding them with its brilliance as it snaked down to strike the enemy. It forked and branched from the first one it struck, until none of the enemy near the landing was still standing.

"How are you doing on aythar?" Matthew asked her.

"Not good," Elaine replied. "Everything seems harder here, and it doesn't seem like I'm recovering my strength at all."

He handed her another of the modified iron balls. "Here."

She grimaced. Drawing power from the enchanted iron was unpleasant, almost painful, but she accepted it anyway. There was little else she could do.

To prevent further attacks from the landing, Matthew drew out more of the unmodified iron bombs and sent four downward, guiding them so they struck at evenly spaced points along the ceiling of the first landing. Some of it collapsed, but most didn't. The structural supports in the facility were all composed of steel beams and reinforced concrete, which made them difficult to destroy.

In the aftermath of the explosions, he created a powerful shield around them and let their platform freefall past the still open landing. His ploy worked, and they fell past the danger point before the enemy could respond with more gunfire. Elaine yelped involuntarily at the sudden drop, but she accepted the necessity of it after her initial surprise.

"Fry the ones at the next landing," barked Matthew. He was too busy handling the shield and preparing for the moment he would have to try to slow their fall. More soldiers were beginning to lean out from the second opening that they were about to pass.

With her stomach in her throat from the fall, Elaine missed with her first lightning stroke, and she was forced to waste more aythar with a second and third attack before she was able to silence the enemy and their guns.

He struggled to make their stop at the third landing a gentle one. It wasn't easy latching onto the walls without bringing them to an overly abrupt, and possibly fatal, stop. Despite his best efforts, he and Elaine were thrown hard against the aythar platform, sending shooting pains through their legs and jarring their teeth in their skulls.

The enemy had withdrawn from this landing; there were no foes in sight down the corridor that led from it and none near the corners of the halls that led away from it either. *Perhaps they learned their lesson with the lightning,* Matt thought. He started to step forward when a sudden vision made him stop. One more step would be sudden death; utter annihilation.

What was that? he wondered, but he didn't ignore it. Grabbing Elaine's arm to keep her from exiting, he raised their platform above the entrance and sent two more iron bombs flying into it. The resulting explosion was far beyond anything to be expected from just the bombs. It was a deafening roar. Metal and other debris sprayed from the opening, leaving deep impressions on the wall of the shaft opposite the entrance.

"Claymores," noted Gary.

"Huh?"

"Antipersonnel mines," clarified the AGI. "They're rigged to explode in a specific direction, sending sharp metal fragments out in a pattern to shred flesh and bone. They were probably going to remote detonate them as soon as we were all on the landing."

Matthew was surprised. "They're willing to blow up their own building, just to kill us?"

"Those mines were set in a way to kill us without doing too much collateral damage to the structure; but yes, they do seem to be taking you seriously."

Elaine spoke up, "How did you know they were there?"

He frowned. "A feeling—maybe a premonition, I'm not sure." It had felt like he was seeing double for a moment, as though his senses had slipped, showing him two worlds at once. Was it his gift? He remembered the Illeniel krytek had had a way to avoid attacks before they were made, but it wasn't something he had experienced personally before.

It was also far too random. To be useful, he needed a way to control it.

Karen opened her eyes. The world was a blur of light and color and she couldn't seem to focus properly.

"Can you hear me, Karen?"

It was her mother's voice, soft and soothing. It emanated from something dark—a humanoid figure leaning over her. As her vision resolved she could see it was some sort of cybernetic unit, but not the sort that a civilian would use. It made no pretense at looking human. The metal was a dark, flat color, similar in appearance to gunmetal. A logo on its chest spelled out, 'ANSIS.'

"Mom?" she said querulously. Her voice sounded rough and strained to her own ears, as though she hadn't used it in days.

"Yes, it's me. I need you to wake up, Karen. You're in a lot of danger. Can you sit up?"

She was confused. "Where am I?" The world spun as she shifted into a sitting position. Glancing down she could see her legs dangling over the edge of a stainless steel table. Karen also realized she was naked and cold. She wrapped her arms around herself as a cold draft from an air vent blew across her head, making her shiver. Tentatively, she reached up and discovered that her scalp was bare. "What happened to my hair?"

A deep booming sound reverberated through the walls and sent a shudder through the table beneath her.

"I don't have much time to explain, Karen. You're in a military research lab. You were injured, and the man you were with abandoned you. I only recently discovered you were here," said her mother.

"Matthew wouldn't do that," Karen protested.

"Whatever his motives, the result was the same. They found you and brought you here. Now we have to get you out of here," Dr. Miller explained.

"How are you here? You're retired."

"Your father's AI program," answered her mother, "I've never liked it, but it proved its worth today. It discovered your location and helped me breach the security. This unit is stolen." She gestured at the cybernetic body she was occupying. "We don't have much time. They know I'm here. We have to escape before they get past your father's defensive units."

None of it made sense to Karen. She knew her mother didn't like her, and her father had even told her not to trust her mother. But if they were working together, maybe... "How are we going to escape?"

"I'm afraid I made several blunders getting here," said Dr. Miller. "Getting out the normal way isn't possible. The files I sifted through said you could teleport? Is that true?"

How could she know that? How would the military have known it? Karen herself had only learned it recently, and even if the military had been tracking them closely, it might just as easily have been her friend who had moved them. She tried to focus but it was difficult. Her mind felt sluggish. Had she been drugged?

More explosions sent tremors through the room.

"I don't know what's real anymore, Mom. I've seen so much weird shit lately," Karen said honestly. "Why is the military using explosives in their own building?"

"Your father's program... it commandeered some of the security forces that were on standby. It turned their equipment against them. They're sending in fresh units to fight past them before we escape. We don't have time, Karen. Can you get us out of here or not?!" Tanya Miller's voice sounded almost frantic.

Her heart was pounding. Glancing around the room, Karen saw all sorts of strange and unfamiliar equipment. A large light on a folding arm was mounted in the ceiling above her, providing a glaring illumination that made it difficult to look up. One wall of the room featured a long row of glass windows, a strange feature indoors; but then she noticed the chairs and desks on the other side of them: an observation room.

Overall it looked like a surgical operating theater. An empty syringe lay on the table next to her. Karen picked it up, studying it idly.

"A stimulant. I had to use it to wake you up," said her mother. "Karen, I need you to focus."

"You brought drugs to wake me?" asked Karen. How had she even known her daughter would be sedated?

"Of course not," snapped her mother impatiently. "I'm familiar with how these places are stocked and laid out. I got it from the cabinet when you wouldn't respond."

It all sounded reasonable; at least given the standard of what reasonable had become in her life lately. Karen tried to stand and almost fell as the floor seemed to sway beneath her. The android's cold arm caught her and steadied her.

"Where do you want to go?" Karen asked. "It has to be someplace I've been before."

Matthew and Elaine advanced carefully down the corridor. He had his enchanted shield stones out now that they were on level ground and were no longer bothering with invisibility. The stones provided a much stronger shield and the added bonus that if the shield did break, he wouldn't be knocked unconscious by feedback. Of course, if something *that* strong hit them, they would probably be dead anyway.

Elaine had been forced to eliminate several groups of cybernetic soldiers as they progressed, and she was currently absorbing more aythar from one of the modified iron spheres. The sour expression on her face was testament to the fact that she wasn't enjoying the experience.

A change in the ambient aythar caused Matt to pause. The area didn't feel quite as empty as most places he had been in this world. Training his focus ahead, he detected a brighter region at the edge of his range. Karen! It had to be her.

"Near the end of the hall," he announced, "on the left." Then he grabbed Elaine's arm and pulled her suddenly to the right. More bullets tore through the space they had just vacated. Soldiers had just rounded the far end of the hall behind them.

The shield would have taken the strain, but he was beginning to expect the sudden warnings and he felt it best to follow them. Launching another iron bomb through the air, he was gratified to see metal bodies thrown in several directions as it exploded.

Matthew turned back and started to advance, but Gary stopped them, "Hang on. One of the soldiers you hit is malfunctioning."

"Isn't that the point?" pointed out Elaine.

"The explosion knocked it off balance but didn't damage it significantly," said Gary. "But it activated its x-band transmitter."

They all saw it now. One of the soldiers was standing up and starting to raise his gun into firing position. Elaine lifted her wand, but Gary shouted, "No, wait. I can access it now!"

The android froze and then began shaking violently. The rifle fell from its hands and a short scream issued from it before it fell silent. "I have it now," said Gary. The machine picked its weapon up and began walking toward them, keeping the barrel pointed at the floor.

Elaine raised her wand anyway.

"Please don't kill me," said the soldier, now speaking with Gary's familiar voice. "This body is much more convenient for me than the PM you're holding."

"Matthew," said Elaine, "What's going on?" Her eyes darted sideways to see what her partner thought on the matter.

Matt nodded. "It's alright. I told you—Gary is sort of like a spirit. You can think of it as though he has possessed the body of that machine."

"If you like, I'll take the front," suggested the machine. "If I get shot it won't be as much of a tragedy, since I don't really have a body."

Matthew almost declined the offer. He was beginning to get a feel for his premonitions and wanted to better understand them, but he knew it was foolish. "Go ahead," he agreed.

"The ANSIS network is trying to shut me out," Gary informed them as they advanced. "They know this unit is compromised, and I've accessed their network. I'm not sure how long I can keep the channel open, but for now I have detailed information on their defenses and deployment here."

"And?"

"There is only one active unit on this floor, and it's a human inhabited cybernetic. My ex-wife, to be honest. There are teams of six coming down all four of the emergency stairwells to reinforce the zone, but we have a minute or two before they reach us."

"Ex-wife?" asked Elaine. "I thought you were a machine-spirit?"

"My creator's wife, to be precise," clarified Gary. "They never divorced before he died, but since I'm not technically him, I prefer to think of her as my ex."

She still didn't understand, "What's an ex?" Divorce existed in Lothion, but it was extremely rare, so the phrase was new to her.

"Later," said Matthew. "Karen is in the room on the right, just ahead of us."

Gary saluted and began marching forward. "That's where Tanya is too, incidentally. That room is the surgery suite, by the way, which doesn't fill me with confidence." He picked up his pace, forcing the two humans to break into a jog to keep up. Reaching the door almost ten feet ahead of them, he hurled his heavy metal body into it, tearing the doors away from the frame.

Automatic gunfire roared through the doorway.

"Tanya, stop! A ricochet could kill her!" yelled Gary. "Dad?"

Matthew and Elaine carefully eased through the doorway, trusting in the enchanted shield stones to protect them if Dr. Miller opened fire again. The scene that confronted them was bizarre. Karen was standing, naked and head shaved, beside another of the blackened ANSIS soldiers. Gary was just inside the doorway, his metal hands out in a gesture meant to indicate peaceful intentions.

"Karen, get us out of here. I can fix this, but if they think you're cooperating with these invaders, it will ruin your chances," said the machine that held Tanya Miller.

"Don't listen to her, Nina!" argued Gary. "She's working for the military already. This is *her* lab."

Karen, blue and shivering, stood transfixed, looking back and forth between the two machines that represented her parents. Then her eyes fell on the two humans that had just entered. "Matthew," she said simply, making his name both a statement and a question.

"How have you been?" he asked her, his mouth curling into a half-smile that belied the seriousness in his eyes.

"I think I slept too long," she said mildly. "It feels like I'm still dreaming."

Matthew deactivated the enchanted shield, and with a thought expanded the area between the stones, extending them so that Gary would be included within them. With a word, he sent power flowing back into them, creating a larger shield almost ten feet on each side. "You can forget shooting now, Mrs. Miller. We're all protected. Bullets won't accomplish anything," he said, addressing Karen's mother.

His eyes met Karen's for an instant, and then he looked away, glancing to one side at the floor. *Right there,* he sent to her mentally.

Tanya Miller dropped the rifle and then shifted her arm, wrapping it around her daughter's shoulder. "I'm trying to protect you, Karen. You have to trust me."

Karen looked up at her. "Mom, he's my friend."

The powerful metal hand shifted to her neck, long fingers wrapping around her throat. Dr. Miller looked at the others. "One move and I'll snap her neck. There are reinforcements coming as we speak."

"Tanya, if you hurt her, I will rip you out of the servers and erase every last trace of your miserable evil existence," threatened Gary.

Karen's mother laughed, "No, you won't. You might want to, but you can't. Whatever you *think* you feel, it's just part of the illusion my husband created. The reality is that he built you. You're a *thing*, and you can't do anything that violates the rules he built into you. You can't hurt a human."

"You don't know that for sure," bluffed the AGI.

Tanya laughed, "I'm not stupid. You've corrupted CC servers all over the world. You've stolen data, manipulated information, and spied on classified personnel, but you haven't touched any of the people you were watching. If you could do it, you would have won this war all by yourself, by eliminating or controlling anyone who threatened her. You're a flaccid, impotent algorithm deluded by dreams of being a real man, just like your creator was."

"Mom," said Karen, drawing Tanya's attention away from the others, "I'll do it. Just don't hurt them. Give me a second and I'll teleport us away from here."

Tanya relaxed her hand slightly and Karen closed her eyes, concentrating. Her aythar flashed and then she was gone, reappearing inside the shield, standing to one side of Matthew.

Her mother ducked down, reaching for the rifle at her feet and Matthew lifted his hand, preparing to send one of his iron bombs at her.

"No!" yelled Karen. "She's still my mother, though I hate to admit it."

Tanya fired the weapon until it ran out of ammunition and then hurled it at the shield.

Matthew turned to Elaine, "We're leaving, but I don't want to lose my shield stones. Can you shield us until I'm done?"

Elaine nodded, and he deactivated the enchanted shield stones as her impromptu shield went up. He held out a hand, letting them fly to it. Each stone was cube shaped and they clicked as they touched, sticking together and forming a fist-sized stone cube as they came together. Matthew slipped it into his pouch and then reached out to put his hands over Elaine and Karen's shoulders. Gary's mechanical form did the same from the opposite side, his metal arms touching Matthew's.

"Group hug," said Karen with a snicker, and then the world began to blur.

"You haven't won!" shouted Tanya. "No matter what you think. I will hunt you down!"

"Go to hell, Mom," said Karen firmly, and then they were gone.

CHAPTER 37

hey fell into the ocean. By the time Matthew had created a platform of stable water and everyone had gotten aboard, Karen was shivering and coughing. The shock of the cold sea had made her gasp during the landing and resulted in her almost inhaling the water.

Elaine sat on the platform cradling her wounded arm. She had instinctively tried to swim with it, and only the nerve block had prevented the pain from sending her into unconsciousness.

All in all, they were in a sorry state.

Gary seemed unaffected, though. Matthew studied his new body. "You don't have a problem with the water?"

The machine shook its head in an almost human-like gesture of negation. "No. The internal electronics are all sealed. Even the civilian units are water-resistant; they're too expensive to allow moisture to damage them. These military models are rated for water pressures down to two hundred meters. The salt may cause unwanted corrosion and damage to the actuators and other parts, but that will take time."

Matthew nodded and took out the stones that would form his flying construct. A few minutes later they were flying eastward, away from the setting sun.

As they traveled, Elaine introduced herself to Karen and tried to make her more comfortable, as she was still a little groggy. Being sedated for several days and then forcibly awakened with a stimulant was enough to make anyone a little fuzzy.

The Prathion wizard wrapped Karen in a blanket of warm air, something Karen decided she needed to learn to do soon. It seemed to be similar to the shielding technique that Matthew had already taught her, but there were some subtle differences. Once she was warm, Elaine created an illusion to cover her nakedness.

Karen stared at the elaborately embroidered dress that flowed from her shoulders and settled around her hips and legs where she sat. It looked like something out of a fairy tale; long yellow skirts embroidered and finished with lace. She wondered how Elaine managed to produce so many fine details in an illusion that was purely the product of her imagination. "How did you think this up?" she asked, but Elaine merely stared at her in confusion.

"She wants to know about the design of the dress," said Matthew, translating from English to Barion for Elaine's benefit. "It'll be easier if you communicate mentally. Karen knows some Barion, but she's still new to it."

Elaine nodded, then responded to Karen, *I modeled the illusion on my favorite dress at home.*

This is a real dress? Karen was shocked. The amount of fabric, the lace and embroidery, all combined with the fact that she knew such things were handmade in this world—it boggled her mind. It must have taken hundreds, perhaps thousands of hours to create. She directed her thoughts to the female wizard, *It's so intricate, and beautiful. What occasion would you wear this for?*

Balls and formal court events, replied Elaine. *I only get to wear it two or three times a year at most, but I thought if I had to make an illusion for you, I might as well make it something special.* She finished the thought with a smile at the other woman.

It's lovely, replied Karen, and then she touched her head, suddenly self-conscious. She was bald, and that, combined with her blue skin probably made her a ridiculous sight in such finery. Forcing that thought aside, she turned to Gary. "Why did they shave my head?" she asked in English.

Her virtual father paused before answering, which was a little disconcerting since his machine body didn't have any way of showing the normal facial expressions a human did while pondering a response; such things were superfluous on a military android. "You can't see them without a mirror, but there are lines and markings across your scalp. Given that you were in a surgery suite, I can only surmise they were going to open up your cranium."

"Mother said she was there to help me escape…" She let the statement hang in the air; she knew it was a lie, but she needed to hear her father's opinion on it.

The android opened its arms, trying and failing to adopt a comforting posture that the machine was not made to perform, "Nina—it was her lab. I don't know what they were planning to do, but Matthew said he spotted something like brain tissue in the ANSIS androids. I suspect they were hoping to use your brain to try to improve whatever it is they were doing. Whether that means just taking small samples, or something more terminal, I don't know."

Matthew listened intently to the exchange, though he said nothing. Karen was looking down now, her expression unreadable.

"I'll never forgive her," she said after a moment. Inside she was numb. The drugs had left her nauseated, and she didn't have the energy to let the anger that lay beneath the words take hold. Instead she took a deep breath and turned back to Elaine. *Can you teach me to make a simple illusion?* She touched her bald pate. *I'm sure we'll be meeting people soon, and I'd rather not do it looking like this.*

Of course, Elaine said immediately. *Let me finish taking care of my arm first, then I'll show you how.*

While the two of them talked, Matthew concentrated on controlling the wind currents that carried them along. It would have been easiest if Karen could teleport them, but this was only her second time in his world, and the first time had been before she had learned to use her special gift. He wasn't sure if she could teleport somewhere she had been before she had awakened her gift, and he didn't want to bother her so soon. She had a lot to think about.

The sun dipped below the horizon behind them, and they flew on into a dark night over an ocean that seemed to stretch on forever.

Time stretched out over the dark sea, but when the moon rose and cast its light over the waves, it filled all of them with a sense of peace and wonder. It was impossible to watch the moonlight reflecting off the waves and feel anything else. Beneath a vast sky filled with stars, the ocean was a sparkling bed of silver and black, rippling all the way to the horizon.

Matthew was tired, but unlike in Karen's world, where he would have exhausted himself by now, here he was merely fatigued. He hoped they would find land soon, though; if not, Elaine would soon have to handle the flying so he could rest. She was asleep currently, curled up like a child on the transparent floor of the flying construct. Karen had been napping beside her, but now she stretched and sat up, staring at Matthew's back.

"You're awake," he said, practicing his English again.

She nodded. "Yes." Slowly, she slid forward until she was directly behind him. Then she wrapped her arms around his neck. The illusion of the dress was gone, having vanished when Elaine fell asleep; not that it would have mattered when their skin made contact anyway.

Matt wondered what Gary thought, sitting at the back. He hadn't spoken in over an hour, but Matt felt self-conscious having a naked woman embrace him in front of the machine. The android said nothing, however.

"What will happen next?" she asked softly.

"When we find land, I'll make a circle and take you to my home," he replied simply.

"And then?"

"You can't go back," he told her firmly. "This is your world now."

"What will your parents think, when you bring home a naked blue woman from another world?"

"They'll probably be angry with me for taking so many risks," he explained. "I told them it wouldn't be that dangerous. I never explained the part about you having been taken, but you will find them very kind. I'm guessing they will put you in one of the guest rooms in Castle Cameron. My mother, the Countess, will probably shower you with attention, and I hate to think what sort of questions Moira will bombard you with."

"I'm a stranger," said Karen, "with no money or occupation. How long will they let me live there?"

He laughed. "Don't worry. You're a wizard, one of only handful in this world. You will be welcome wherever you go, and I'm sure they'll want you to stay. Since you have no family here, you're completely free. You can go anywhere you want, and every noble in Lothion will be fighting to retain your services. The Queen might even want you to take service with her."

Karen sighed, "I don't know anyone."

"You will," he said cheerfully. "Everyone will want to know *you*. You'll have more freedom than anyone in the world."

His words filled her with a cold emptiness. She knew he meant well, but he clearly had no idea how frightening it was to be alone, unconnected, unknown, and unwanted, in a strange and foreign land. Her only connection was with the man sitting in front of her, and it was readily apparent from his talk of 'freedom' that he hadn't changed his thinking about his own position.

She was on her own.

Karen clenched her jaw, fighting back unbidden tears. For some reason, this thought affected her more than her mother's betrayal. She had expected *that*. Glancing at Gary, she tried to stay positive. He wouldn't desert her. *A girl and her robot dad travel the world and face the unknown!* The idea was amusing, but humorous as it was, it couldn't touch the cold knot of fear in her heart.

"Look," said Matthew loudly, startling her from her reverie. "See that black strip ahead? I think it's a coastline."

Gary turned his head, focusing in the direction the young wizard had indicated. His visual sensors were more acute than anything possessed by the humans, "It is land. Well done!"

An hour and a half later, they landed on a rocky shoreline. There was no beach to speak of, just massive stony cliffs rising from the beating waves. They were perched now at the edge of one of the cliffs, standing on a grassy, rock-strewn plain that led away to the west. Matthew began making a circle as soon as he had put away the enchanted stones of his flying construct.

Fifteen minutes later, they were standing in the transfer-house in Castle Cameron.

It was dark, but there were guards stationed around the clock at the building that housed the teleportation circles. As soon as they emerged, a runner was sent to notify the castle of their arrival.

Matthew looked with resignation at the guard who had stayed behind. "I suppose I should have expected they would be waiting for us."

The guard chuckled, "You've been gone for days, milord. Your lady mother left *very* strict instructions as to what we was to do if you showed up."

There was no help for it, so he led his motley band to the keep. A doorman there was expecting them, and he opened the heavy oak door for them. They marched inside and were greeted by the Countess herself.

Penny stood in the entry hall wearing a severe dress of black-dyed linen. Despite the late hour, she had managed to dress and somehow pin up her hair into a tight bun. She had also worn her sword, which seemed odd, given the hour and her dress. The expression on her face was hard and unyielding, and it was reserved entirely for Matthew. "I see my son has returned," she stated.

"I'm sorry for worrying you—again, Mother," Matthew began, as Karen and Elaine entered behind him and stepped into view. Gary stayed at the back.

Penny's face transformed, passing through several phases, the first being a smile for his companions, followed by a look of alarm as she registered the android behind them. Faster than the eye could follow, her sword was out and she began to advance. "What is that?!"

Matthew managed to interpose himself between her and Gary, holding up his hands. "Peace, Mother, peace! He's a friend!"

Her eyes never left the machine. "Explain." The doorman outside and two guards from within the keep took positions around Gary's metal form.

"I come in peace," said the android.

Karen spoke as well. "He's my father."

The Countess relaxed slightly, lowering her blade and glancing at her son. "Well?"

"It's complicated, Mom. I swear he's not a threat. It's a long story."

Lady Thornbear arrived then, somehow having managed to have dressed in a modest yet elegant gown of dark blue. As always, her hair was perfectly coiffed. Matthew secretly wondered if she slept standing up, already dressed in case there were a need to meet guests. Beside her was Gram, wearing trousers and a loose shirt.

Penny noted their arrival and gave a quick order. "Sir Gram. Remain here with our strange visitor. Keep him under close guard while I get the tale from our visitors."

With a whispered word, Gram's body was encased in shining metal and his sword, Thorn, appeared in his hand. In the span of only a second he had gone from being an unkempt and suddenly awakened sleeper to armed and deadly. "Yes, Your Excellency," he answered.

"He isn't dangerous. Please don't hurt him," protested Karen.

Penny turned her eyes to the young woman and her gaze softened slightly, "I hope you'll forgive my excess of caution, but recent events in Dunbar have led us to be very wary of constructs such as your companion. No harm will come to him so long as he waits peacefully here. In the meantime, you look as though you might need some food." She addressed the rest of the group, "If you'll all come to the main hall. I'll have the cook rousted out of bed to warm a late supper, and you can explain everything while we eat."

As they started in that direction Mordecai appeared, bleary-eyed and wearing a nightshirt that he had somehow managed to put on inside-out. "What's all this? Someone having a party without me?" Then he spotted his son. "This should be good."

CHAPTER 3 8

Matthew slept hard and woke late the next morning. When he arose, he dressed quickly so he could go and check on Karen and Gary. They had been given a room in the castle after all the explanations had been completed and Penny had been satisfied that the android wasn't part of the threat that Moira had recently faced in Dunbar.

His parents had been rather annoyed that his supposedly quick retrieval of Karen had turned into a half a week's disappearance. They had been even more alarmed when they heard what he had had to do to get her out of the military base, but what really made them angry was learning that he hadn't been honest about his first attempt when Gareth Gaelyn had gone with him.

What their punishment would be was still to be decided. He thought his father might be willing to let the matter drop, since he *had* returned unharmed, and he had been acting to save a friend, but his mother had other opinions. Her last remark to him before retiring for the night was to inform him he wasn't to leave the house again until he had her permission.

He tried to remember what his father had told him about his own adventures in years past; *"No good deed goes unpunished."* It made more sense to him now.

Karen was still in her room when he arrived, though Gary was gone, having requested a tour of the castle from Gram. Matthew knocked on the door and waited, knowing she would know it was him once her magesight focused on him.

Seconds later, the door opened. "You survived," said Karen. "I thought your mother would skin you alive after everyone else went to bed."

He grinned. "She's been under a lot of stress lately, but I think she'll let me live if I don't cause her any more trouble for a while."

"Come in," she said with a smile, opening the door wider.

"It might be best if you joined me for breakfast," he suggested instead, noting that the room was empty of anyone else. "Tongues will wag if I'm seen entering your chamber alone."

She frowned. She had forgotten the stricter customs of his world. It was another reminder that she was a stranger. *I'm alone here,* she thought.

By the time they reached the hall, breakfast was over, but Matthew was able to finagle a quick repast of leftover bread and a few sausages for them. Most of the castle staff, as well as his family, were already about their business for the day, so they had the high table to themselves.

Karen was surprised by the quality of the sausages. The food at Castle Cameron was far better than her first experience with the cuisine of Matthew's world. They ate in silence for several minutes, and it wasn't until they had both quieted their hunger that Matthew spoke. "I want to apologize for last night."

She smiled graciously. "Seeing Gary's new body would be a shock for anyone of this world I think."

He nodded. "Well, they'll get used to it. Personally, I'm rather relieved. He's a lot easier to talk to when I don't have to carry him around."

"Don't get used to it," she warned.

"What do you mean?"

"Unlike the PM, that little solar camp charger can't keep a full-size android running," she explained. "It will eventually run out of power."

"Well, to hear him tell it, he's the smartest mind in existence," observed Matthew. "Surely he and I can come up with some way to recharge it."

Karen had just stuffed the last piece of sausage in her mouth, so her voice was slightly garbled. "If it was a civilian android, maybe; they use batteries. That's a military model. They build them with RTG power so they can last almost a year without charging, but there's no way for you to replace the power unit here."

"RTG?"

"Radioisotope thermoelectric generator," she supplied. "It uses radioactive decay to produce heat, and that's converted into electricity to power his body."

"Our worlds are practically twins, except for the differences in history," began Matt, "so whatever they put in them is surely present here as well. We'll just have to find this…"

Karen swallowed. "Do you even know what a radioisotope is?"

He gave her a quiet stare.

"I didn't think so, because if you did, you'd know that there are lots of different ones, and the science and art of refining and purifying them is so complicated that I am very nearly as ignorant as you are on the topic, with the exception of some fancy terminology."

Matthew thought over her words for a moment. "You're right. But I have to go back one more time, to get Desacus. With some planning, we may be able to bring back whatever things we will need to keep him running—indefinitely."

"You're awfully worried about Gary, aren't you?" she pointed out. "Mind telling me why?"

He frowned. "He's your only family, of a sort. I thought you'd want some reassurance…"

"Ahh," she murmured. "It comes back to that again. You want to help so you won't feel bad about me being marooned here. Afraid I'll be a burden?" The words came out with more bitterness than she had expected, but the feelings were real.

"Look, that's not what…," he began, but Karen coughed and glanced over his shoulder. He realized then that his father and Gram had entered the hall and were making their way toward him. Glancing around he addressed the Count, "Dad."

"Good morning, milady," said Mordecai, dipping his head politely at Karen. "I wonder if I might steal my son from you for a while? There are some things I need to discuss with him."

"Not at all," she replied, wondering whether there was some protocol she needed to follow, but since the Count seemed content with her simple words thus far, she decided not to worry about it until someone told her otherwise.

"Sir Gram has offered to give you a tour of the castle," said Mordecai with a smile. "And I want you to know that you are most welcome here, despite the confusion last night."

After a few more exchanges, Matthew found himself being led away by his father, while Gram stayed to keep Karen company. He gave her an apologetic glance, but he wasn't sure if she got the message, or cared, since she had seemed rather annoyed with him.

"About Karen's home…," began Mordecai.

"She knows she can't go back, Dad," Matthew said, cutting him off. "I told her you and Mom would welcome her here."

Mort nodded. "Of course, that would be the case no matter what. She's your friend. I'm glad to hear that she's already resigned herself to staying. It can't be easy for her, giving up everything she's ever known." He stopped, and then his face took on a more serious expression. "What I really wanted to talk to you about is what you plan on doing next."

Matthew felt his face flush, "We're just friends, Dad."

His father laughed, "No, that's not what I meant. I know you intend to go back again, for your dragon."

"Well, yeah…"

Mort put his hands on his son's shoulders. "I don't want you to go."

Matthew was surprised. "But we can't leave him in their hands!"

"He's dead," pronounced his father. "The egg will have a new personality, if it ever bonds and hatches again. It won't be Desacus."

"But…"

"No, listen to me. I know you feel responsible for it, but it's far too dangerous. I thought your mother would die of stress when she heard what you went through to rescue Karen; for that matter, it didn't do me any good either. *You* are far more important to us than an unborn dragon. There are others, waiting to be bonded."

He pushed his father's hands away. "We don't know what they'll do to it. It isn't fair to leave it unprotected. Desacus died trying to protect us. We can't leave his egg behind!"

Mort's face grew firm. "I'm not going to budge on this one. Give it up. I know your intentions are good, and

I can't fault you for your loyalty, but it's a fool's game. You aren't to return there. Am I understood?"

Matthew was too stubborn for that. He tried a different angle. "What about the aythar? You know how much power is stored in each of the dragons. Is it safe to just let it go, to leave it in the hands of an enemy?"

His father shook his head. "From everything you've told us about these people, they can't use aythar. The egg might as well be a stone as far as they're concerned, and even if one of them managed to bond with it, they couldn't use the aythar stored within it."

"They'd gain the gifts of the dragon-bond," Matt reminded him.

"And what of it?" said his father dismissively. "One man, or woman, with superior strength and senses—what good does that do them? Only a mage can harness the power to do anything that might be truly dangerous to us. From what Gary told us, they can't even travel to our world. Even you admitted that it was merely a world similar to the one that sent the strange enemies we found in Dunbar here."

"They have ANSIS too," said Matthew. "They may well discover a way to travel, just like the others did."

"Then we'll face them *here*. My word is final, Matthew." His father's tone indicated he wouldn't be swayed.

Matthew was used to arguing with his father, and generally Mordecai's opinions were flexible, if a sound argument could be found to convince him; but once in a while he would not be moved. This was clearly one of those times. Matt's lips formed a hard line. *If I keep arguing, he'll start keeping a watch on me,* he realized. "Fine," he agreed reluctantly. "I won't go back, but only under protest."

Mort nodded, "Good. I'm sure Karen will need a friend around here to help her until she gets used to things."

"Anything else?" asked Matt, irritation still showing in his voice. "I've had a lot of inspiration lately, and I'd like to start working on some new ideas in my workshop."

His father studied his face, then decided to let it go. "No, that was all."

CHAPTER 39

Being somewhat aware of the principles that underlie your magic, I can't say I'm surprised," said Gary, "but having perused countless volumes of fiction, I have to admit that your arcane laboratory is less fantastical in reality than I might have hoped."

Matthew had brought Gary in to his workshop to seek his advice regarding certain mathematical ideas. He hadn't expected to have his workspace critiqued. "What did you expect?"

"Well, some glasswork, like flasks and condensers, would be a good start, or perhaps a pentagram inscribed on the floor," answered the android. "This looks more like a primitive smithy."

Matthew bristled. "I take exception to the term 'primitive', but yes, this was originally a smithy. My grandfather's, to be exact. Dad used it for a while after grandad died, but once he built his newer shop he let me take this one."

"It certainly has a certain rustic charm, I suppose," said the machine.

The young wizard sighed, "If you're done casting aspersions, I wanted to discuss some thoughts with you."

"What sort of thoughts?"

The AGI's ability to do complex mathematics in a fraction of the time it would take a human with paper was his main reason for inviting Gary to help. Matt was no slouch at doing sums and multiplication in his head, but some of what he was considering was difficult to even conceptualize, much less formulate. "Our discussion of teleport circle keys the other day got me to thinking you might be handy….," he began.

"Oh, yes!" exclaimed Gary. "I forgot to inform you. While we were in my world, I took advantage of my larger, more intelligent self to finish a proof. You were correct, that function can't produce a duplicate output for different inputs."

"I really wasn't worried about that," said Matt. "I just wanted to shut you up for a while."

The android grew still. "I think I may be offended."

"It was your question about duplicate keys in circles, that got me to thinking," continued the wizard, ignoring Gary's statement. "I told you that that's the basic foundation for creating a gateway, or portal, like the ones my father created for his 'World-road'."

"I would still like to see that, by the way," interjected Gary.

"Later," said Matthew dismissively. "Listen. In the old days, people didn't worry about the Dark Gods, because they lived on another plane of existence. They couldn't travel to our world without help from a wizard on this side."

"One such as you," agreed the machine.

Matthew shook his head, "No. Not like me; *any* wizard would do. It's similar to the portals my father created—the magic has to be done from both sides. His portals work because there are two matching teleportation enchantments that match up two separate points in space, from either end. The interdimensional gateway that the gods needed to come here was similar, they had to have a helper, a wizard, on this side to create the doorway."

"But you *couldn't* do that?" questioned Gary, growing somewhat puzzled.

"No, no, I could," said Matthew impatiently. "My point was that *any* wizard could do it. What's different about me is that my gift allows me to do something similar without having an assistant on the other side. That's how I travel back and forth to your dimension."

"I'm not sure where you're going..."

Matthew waved a hand at him. "Get comfortable, I've been thinking about this for a while. Let me talk it out, and then you can tell me what you think." He took a deep breath, "It's also occurred to me that many of the special gifts of the She'Har do something similar; well, at least the Prathions, the Mordan, and the Illeniels. They allow someone with their gift to do something that would take most ordinary mages a helper to accomplish. The Mordan can teleport between two points in the same dimension without having to bother with matching circles; the Illeniel can travel between two different dimensions in a similar fashion."

"And the Prathions?" asked Gary. "How does invisibility match up with that observation?"

Matt smiled. "An enchanter can create a similar effect, but it takes a lot of preparation. The Prathions cause light to skip over the space they are occupying to create the effect of invisibility. In a sense, it's like a limited type of teleportation that applies mainly to just light, or aythar. Any wizard can create an illusion, but only they have the inherent ability to do that without creating a static enchantment."

"So, your analogy does not include the Centyr or the Gaelyn gifts then..."

He pursed his lips. "Maybe, I don't know. If it does I don't see it, but that might just be because I don't understand how their gifts operate. Back to the point—my dimensional talent, or translational magic, as I like to call it, is only possible for me *because* I can reach into other places without a helper on the other side.

"Take this pouch for example," said Matthew, holding up one of his specially enchanted bags. "When I create the enchantment for these, I have to reach through and create a duplicate enchantment from the other side, from this dimension and from the pocket dimension I'm connecting it to."

Gary couldn't show expressions, but his tone was easy to read, "You're losing me now."

"My father makes bags that are similar, but he does it by creating an enchantment in two places: the bag, and the place or object, such as a chest, that he's connecting it to. He can do that because both places are in the same dimension. He can reach both. The bags I make connect between this dimension and some other dimension. Only I can do that because I can reach the other side to complete the magic without having someone on the other side to help," explained Matthew.

"Okay," agreed Gary.

"Stay with me," said Matthew. "I'm still covering the background information. Something else I've done is create a spell that creates a contemporaneous planar connection, to be used as a weapon. I did that when Gram and I fought one of the Dark Gods."

"Huh?"

"It was a triangular gateway between dimensions. I was able to hurl it at the enemy and use it to bisect him."

"That sounds particularly deadly. A dimensional—I don't know what to call it—something like that could slice through literally anything couldn't it?" observed the machine.

Matthew smiled. "It could, and it did. During one of my experiments I accidentally cut my own arm off."

The machine glanced pointedly at his still-connected limbs.

"Moira fixed it for me," he replied. "And she never misses an opportunity to remind me about it, but that's beside the point."

"It sounds as if you already know whatever it is you want to know," observed Gary.

"Have you ever heard of a tesseract?" asked Matthew suddenly.

That brought the android up short. "Are you talking about a four-dimensional cube, or did I mishear you?"

"Yes, exactly that," he replied. "I'm having difficulty envisioning them. I thought you might be able to help explain a few things to me about them."

"Imagining higher-dimensional objects is naturally difficult for three dimensional entities," said Gary. "Even I have difficulty with it, though thankfully this android body has significantly more processing power than the PM I was using when I came here before."

"If you're inside a tesseract, and you try to walk out one side, you wind up re-entering from the other side, right?"

"That's not technically correct," said Gary. "Though if you move in the wrong direction it can seem that way, and being a three-dimensional being it's impossible to perceive it correctly while inside."

Matthew frowned.

Gary leaned against the worktable. "I take it that isn't what you wanted to hear."

"No," said Matthew simply, without explanation.

"Instead of worrying about what a tesseract is, why not describe what it is that you're actually trying to do?" suggested the machine. "That might be more helpful than trying to relate it to hypercubes."

"All right, this is what I'm thinking of trying…"

He spent the next two weeks primarily in his workshop, sometimes going so far as to take his meals there. It was the sort of thing that Moira had once called 'voluntary self-confinement,' but it was Matthew's preferred way to spend his time.

He only saw Karen occasionally, something that might have caused him a small amount of guilt, but his enthusiastic youngest sister, Irene had taken an interest in the newcomer and spent countless hours entertaining her, or as Matthew called it, 'badgering her with endless questions.' He was doubly grateful for it, since it both relieved his guilt at being absent so much and kept Irene out of his hair.

Gram's sister Carissa was almost always with Irene at these times, and the two of them did an admirable job of making certain that Karen's hours were rarely dull. Moira was notably absent from their gatherings, for she continued to keep mainly to herself, which concerned her mother greatly and bothered Matthew not at all, though he did notice on some level.

Since his father's initial warning not to return to Karen's homeworld, Matthew saw little of either of his two parents. The upheaval that Moira had precipitated in Dunbar was occupying much of their time, and they were constantly busy managing arrangements for assisting the neighboring country in their time of need.

It was early morning when Matthew stuck his head out the door of his workshop. There were dark circles under his eyes. He was hoping to make it back to his bed without encountering anyone or having to answer awkward questions. Lately everyone seemed to think he was losing weight, which wasn't a good observation since he was already a fairly lean young man. He just needed sleep.

If anyone did see him, they might be surprised, since he was known as a late-riser, but in fact he had not yet been to bed.

He was almost to the door in the castle that led to the portal that would take him to his family's home in the mountains when he stumbled into his youngest sister.

"There you are!" she exclaimed. She was brightly clad in a yellow dress with matching ribbons braided into her hair. It was something of a fashion among the young ladies of the castle these days, largely started by Irene and Carissa themselves.

He groaned. This was not how he wanted to end his day—err, morning. Ignoring her he shuffled past, hoping she would let him go without a struggle. If she had something more interesting in her head she might not bother trying to coax him into conversation.

"Have you seen Karen?" she asked, catching him by the sleeve.

Dammit. "No."

Irene pursed her lips. "Me either. She wasn't in her room earlier, and I didn't see her at all yesterday."

"That's terrible," he intoned vaguely.

Her bright eyes focused on him intently. "You could sound a little more worried—she is *your* girlfriend, after all, not that you show the slightest interest in anyone."

"She's not my girlfriend."

Irene wasn't ready to give up. "She said the same, but no one believes it."

"Who is 'no one'?" he asked, interested in spite of himself.

"Probably everyone in the castle," said Irene bluntly, "but Carissa and me for certain. Honestly, it's shameful how you've treated her."

Defensively, he put up his hands. "What did I do?"

"Nothing," said his sister. "That's the point." Studying him again, she added, "What's wrong with your face? Are you ill?"

"Just tired."

"That's most of your problem," she advised him. "You never sleep. You would probably be a lot more pleasant to people if you weren't perpetually exhausted."

He sighed, "That's what I was trying to do when you assaulted me."

She shook her head in amazement, probably bewildered at the thought of anyone going to bed in the morning. As he turned to go, she added, "If you run into Karen later, let her know I was looking for her."

"Sure," he muttered and continued on without looking back.

As Irene got farther away, he heard her muttering, "I wonder if she's avoiding me?"

He was about to open the enchanted door, the one that activated a portal to his family home, when he sensed a presence in the apartments behind it. Officially, those apartments were where his family was supposed to reside, but they served mainly as a decoy. When most people opened the door before him, it opened into those rooms.

After a second, he realized it was Karen. *What's she doing in there?* he wondered. He was so tired he considered pretending he hadn't noticed her and just going to bed, but he knew she had likely sensed him as well. Trying to force himself to seem more awake, he opened the door without activating the enchantment, and entered the front room of the mostly unused Cameron suite.

Karen was farther back in one of the bedrooms, so he passed through two doors and down a short hall until he reached it. "Karen?" he asked, knocking lightly.

"You can already see I'm dressed—come on in," she answered.

He did, and found her sitting beside the bed, holding the PM in her hands. She was wearing a somber blue dress that had probably belonged to one of his sisters at one time. "Are you talking to Gary?"

"No, just reading a book," she replied. "Quietly—by myself."

It hadn't occurred to him that she might be reading. He had always associated the device with her virtual father. "Oh," he said simply.

"Why don't you lie down?" she suggested. "You look like you might fall over at the slightest breeze."

That sounded like an excellent idea. If he was going to be forced to have a conversation, doing it while prone would be a great way to conserve energy. *People should do more things lying down, like eating,* he thought drunkenly. Sleep deprivation was definitely making his thoughts haphazard.

"Irene was wondering where you were," he said absently, as he got comfortable.

"You didn't tell her, did you?" said Karen worriedly.

"No, I didn't notice you were in here until I got to the door," he mumbled.

Karen put the PM down. "Good. I like your sister, and Carissa, but the past week has been overwhelming. I just need some time alone."

"Sorry to intrude," he apologized.

She smiled. "No, you don't count. Besides, you're half-asleep. As soon as I let you, you'll be snoring."

"What's overwhelming?" he asked.

Karen rubbed her face. "Everything. Some of it is just the newness of it all, but there's also the difference in people, and the language... it's exhausting. You know, in my world, everyone is connected, all the time, but we ignore one another for the most part."

He listened silently.

"Here, it's completely different," Karen went on. "There's no network, no computers, no implants or PM's. People are accustomed to talking face to face, *all* the time. I feel like I'm drowning in a sea of people and chatter. Don't get me wrong, it's fun, and I love it, but I was an only child growing up in a place where you didn't see many people to begin with. Now I feel as though I'm being constantly bombarded.

"That's why I thought I'd find a quiet place to read for a while," she finished. "And there's no better place for solitude than your parents' fake residence. You don't think they'd mind, do you?"

He didn't reply, and when she leaned over to look at his face, she found him fast asleep.

She stared at him thoughtfully before opening the chest at the foot of the bed and removing a coverlet to spread over him, and then she went back to her book.

The rest of the morning was thankfully quiet and peaceful, for both of them.

CHAPTER 40

Another week passed, and still he kept up his obsessive routine, spending almost every waking hour at his workbench. It was sometime in the evening now, though Matthew couldn't have been bothered to know what exact hour it was. His magesight alerted him to someone approaching the door, but he didn't pause. It was his father, so he kept working until the door opened.

"Son," said Mordecai.

He glanced up. "Hi Dad."

"You missed dinner again," said his father.

"I ate earlier. Cook was kind enough to send lunch to the shop for me."

Mort frowned. "I spoke to Cook. He wanted to know if he should send your evening meal over. Lunch was almost ten hours ago. Have you eaten since then?"

Now that he let his thoughts drift a little, Matt realized his stomach had a painful ache in it; it simply hadn't become demanding enough to break his concentration yet. "Oh," said Matt with some surprise. "I guess I am hungry. I kind of lose track of time when I'm working."

Mordecai grinned. "Like father like son I suppose. Your mother always says she's a w…"

"Workshop widow, I know, Dad," finished Matthew.

His father grimaced. "I think I know how she feels now." Stepping closer, he put a hand on Matthew's shoulder. "Why don't you come get something to eat? You can tell me about what you're working on."

405

His dad was probably the one person he could reasonably expect to understand his work, but he was loath to stop just then. "It's complicated. It will be easier to show you when it's finished."

"Let me see what you have so far."

He worried briefly. He didn't want his father to figure out that his project was related to his plan to return for Desacus, but he decided it couldn't hurt to show him what he had so far. Picking up four metal cubes from one side of the bench, he tossed them into the air. With a touch of aythar, they spread out into a floating square formation in front of him, roughly two feet to a side. Matthew voiced the command word, and the enchantment worked into the cubes flared to life. The area between the cubes turned black—not an everyday black, like coal or ink, but an absolute black that gave nothing back. It was as if everything ceased to exist where it touched the black square hanging in the air.

"Fascinating," said Mordecai. "I sense nothing of it from this side, and from the other..." He moved to stand beside Matthew on the other side of the square; from that perspective, the square had a different appearance. It was still black, but not the same unforgiving void it had been on the other side. He reached out as if he might touch it.

Matthew slapped his hand away. "Don't!"

"I wasn't going to touch it," said his father, with a hint of petulance in his voice. "What is it doing, exactly? It feels odd to my magesight. On this side it's strange, and on the other it feels like a complete absence of *anything*."

"It's a one-way translation pane," he answered, making up the name as he said it. "It's a gateway to another dimension, but it only goes in one direction. Things can pass through, but they can't come back, and if you put something through only partway and then pull it out... here, let me demonstrate."

Matthew picked up a slender stick from a pile he had lying on the bench for that purpose. Holding it out, he stuck the end of the branch into the square from the side that was absolute void. "As long as the stick keeps going *in* it's fine, but if I pull back..." As he pulled, the stick came away missing the portion that had entered the translation pane.

"Wow."

"Now look at this," he added, warming to his subject. Matt picked up a small rock from the bench and threw it at the translation pane, this time from the other side. It passed through and hit the wall of the shop without harm. He gathered it up from the floor and threw it back, this time into the other side. It vanished completely. "It's one directional," he explained. "From *this* side, it's a one-way portal, but from the other it doesn't exist at all."

"But it's dark on the other side as well," began Mordecai.

"Because the light from the other side is being completely absorbed," said Matt. Taking up another branch, he stuck it through from the less dark side. It emerged from the other side, but as soon as he pulled back, the portion that entered the void side vanished and the stick fell to the floor in two pieces. "If you try to pull back from that side, it gets cut as well, so it's still dangerous."

His father's eyes were full of interest. "That's fascinating. What are you planning to do with it?"

Matthew chose his words with care. "After my last trip to Karen's world it felt like there was almost no way to defend myself properly. A normal shield takes a lot of power to maintain, and over there aythar is at a premium, since the whole dimension is devoid of it. This could be used as a shield of sorts, one that could absorb any attack, since it doesn't *stop* the attack, it merely translates it to another dimension."

Mordecai rubbed his beard. "It could do that just as well if it was a normal two-way portal."

Matt nodded, "Yes, but this makes it more dangerous to would-be attackers. If they touch it, they'll lose hands, arms, whatever, but more importantly,"—standing on one side he sent a small blast of fire through the square, scorching the air on the other side—"you can still attack from this side."

His father spoke up, "Though the main problem is you'll still be vulnerable from other directions."

"Which is why I'm working on a design to let each cube serve as an interstice for three sides instead of just one…"

"So you can connect them up and surround yourself on every side," agreed Mordecai, "or even above and below. But if you did that…"

"You'd be blind," finished Matt. "I have an idea to handle that problem."

"What about gravity?"

He smiled. "I worried about that too, but it doesn't seem like it's as much of a problem as you might think. It doesn't affect the translation panes. They only move with the cubes, which the user directs."

"So you won't fall through the ground? But you can't stand on one, you just demonstrated what happens to anything that goes through from even the wrong side," said Mordecai.

"I'm planning to add a shield on the inner surface of the bottom pane to prevent that," said Matthew enthusiastically.

"What about the other ones?" asked his father. "If you accidentally touch one you'll lose a finger, or worse."

"This is just a test model. I'll make it much bigger, roughly six feet on a side, so that it will be more than an arm's length away. I'll also tie the position of the translation cubes to a master that the user wears, so that they move with you. You won't be able to fall into them."

"*Can* you move them if they're active on all sides?" asked Mort.

Matthew shrugged. It was a problem he hadn't found an answer to yet. "I'm not sure. I think not, but I haven't gotten far enough to test it. Probably the bottom will have to be turned off if the user wants to walk or run."

"Let me see your enchantment formulae," said his father.

"It's still a little rough," he answered. "It's a work in progress." He pulled out a large sheet of parchment and rolled it out flat on the workbench.

His father stared at it with interest, and then observed, "Your handwriting is atrocious."

"I know, Dad."

"What does this part do?"

He began explaining the structure, and after a while his father started making suggestions. "There's a way to simplify this piece..." Soon the two of them were in the thick of it, and the hours began to melt away.

"This again?!" said a sharp voice.

Matthew rubbed his eyes. The voice belonged to his mother, and as he became aware of his surroundings, he could see she was glaring at his father, who was raising his head groggily from the bench where he had been resting it. They had fallen asleep in the workshop.

"Mmm, good morning?" said Mordecai.

Penny scowled. "Don't give me that! You said you were going to talk to him." She gestured in Matthew's direction. "Instead, I find you sleeping in here. Is this where you've been all night?!" Her hands were on her hips, and Matthew could tell she was just getting started.

His father grinned. "No, of course not, m'dear. I was with another woman. I just stopped by this morning to see if the boy had taken my advice and I was so worn out by the drinking and debauchery that I had to take a nap." Mort winked at his son. "He was only here to try and help cover for his father's sins, but now you've caught me. Don't blame the boy, though. He has promised to mend his ways. I'm the only one at fault."

"As if any other woman would put up with your habits," snapped Penny. "Get up, both of you. It's time to go home."

Matthew rose from his seat, trying not to wince at the sore places he had developed while sleeping in such an odd position. He didn't bother trying to argue; he knew when it was time to surrender. His father, though, still had more to say.

"I'll have you know I'm considered quite a catch!" said Mort in mock outrage.

Penny tried to keep up her angry expression, but her façade slipped and a smile peaked through. "I might believe it, if you didn't smell! When was the last time you had a bath?" She looked over at her son. "You too. Both of you are starting to ferment."

Watching them, Matt couldn't help but laugh, which drew their eyes to him. When they paused, he spoke up, "Can we eat first? I'm starving."

She looked at the two of them. "Bathe first, then you can have breakfast."

As it turned out, Penelope Illeniel had planned an expansive morning meal. Being a countess meant that many mornings she wasn't free to do the usual things that many mothers do, like cooking, but when she had the chance she rarely missed the opportunity. The house was filled with appetizing smells when they entered, and Matthew could see that Conall and Irene had been pressed into service helping in the kitchen. Karen was there as well, lending a hand, though she knew next to nothing about cooking.

The two men wasted no time accomplishing the goal required for them to eat. Magic had certain advantages, and neither of them wanted a long soak, so instead they heated their water rapidly and scrubbed themselves clean in record time.

The family table was full of waiting people when they entered. Apparently, Penny had forced everyone to wait for them. Moira gave Matthew a warning look when he entered. Something was up.

He found himself seated next to Karen, whose presence was mildly unusual, since it was supposedly an impromptu family breakfast, but there was nothing usual about that morning. Penny had made sure all those in the family, and even those who might potentially become family, were present. Matt had an urge to look toward the ceiling, since he had a feeling there must be one hanging above his head somewhere.

The food was wonderful, especially for the two starving men. Sausages were passed on platters, followed by smoked fish, fresh bread, and a savory porridge. A selection of steamed vegetables was included as well, and while Matthew briefly considered skipping it a stern glance from his mother quickly dissuaded him from that notion.

He wanted to eat slowly, for he knew the conversation would begin in earnest once they were all full, but his hunger would not be denied. All too soon he was stuffed to bursting, and he could see the others beginning to lean back from the table as well.

"Thank you for the wonderful meal, Mother," he said politely. "May I be excused?" He started to rise from his chair.

Penny arched one brow. "No, you may not."

Karen looked worried at the Countess' stern demeanor, but Matthew's younger brother laughed, "Nice try, dummy." Mordecai and the others at the table did poorly at hiding their smirks. Only Moira seemed unamused, retaining a serious and flat expression.

"All right, I give up. What's this about?" asked Matthew.

"Since you returned, you've been keeping yourself locked away in that workshop non-stop for almost a month...," began Penny.

"Three weeks," corrected Matthew, interrupting her.

Penny sighed, "The point is that everyone in the family is a little worried. More particularly, your father and I have been talking, and we think you're planning on going back to retrieve Desacus's egg."

He glanced at Karen, but the expression on her face was one of surprise. Who else might have ratted him out? He had spoken to no one. He met Moira's eyes but a subtle shake of her head indicated that she wasn't to blame. *Oh well,* he thought. Taking a deep breath, he decided not to beat around the bush, "Yes. I do."

"Didn't your father talk to you?" asked his mother.

Matthew nodded. "A few weeks ago."

"And what did he say?" she asked, as if she didn't already know.

"He ordered me to stay home."

Penny exhaled; she had been holding her breath. "Then you know you should drop this foolishness."

He shook his head. "I won't."

Mordecai broke in. "Your mother and I are of one opinion in this. I've already told you no. Do you plan on defying both of us?"

"Yes," he admitted.

Conall and Irene could barely contain themselves at his outright rebellion, and both of them were fidgeting. The urge to say something almost undid them. Moira remained quiet, while Karen's eyes grew wider.

"And if we lock you up?" asked Penny, her voice strangely calm.

Matthew shrugged, "You can't. Unless you plan on rendering me unconscious indefinitely. There's no way to prevent me from going."

Moira arched one brow, a strange expression on her face, but Mordecai gave her a terse warning. "Don't even suggest something like that."

"It was a joke," she said sourly. "I wouldn't do it."

Matthew knew he had missed something there, but decided not to pursue it.

Penny looked at her husband, and Mordecai gave a reluctant sigh, "He's right. We can punish him or disown him, but we can't keep him prisoner."

That was too much for Irene, and she let out an audible, "Awww."

Matthew shot her a dirty look.

Looking down the table, Penny said, "Is there anyone here that thinks it's a good idea for him to go back there?"

Conall spoke, "I don't really want to be Count, so no."

"Thanks," said Matt wryly.

Mordecai grew serious. "You realize there's a good chance you could be killed, alone on another world, and we'd never even know what happened to you? Have you thought about the consequences for your family?"

In point of fact, he hadn't really considered it fully from that angle, but he knew it wouldn't change his mind. "I'm sorry, Father. I know it would be a hardship for everyone, but I can't turn my back on Desacus. That's not who you raised me to be. If I obeyed and left the egg there, I wouldn't be the person I want to believe I am."

Penny covered her face briefly with her hands, "I can't believe this is happening." She seemed to crumple inward for a moment, but when she uncovered her face it was calm and resolved. "Fine. If this is what you're going to do, then we'll do our best to make sure you survive."

Mordecai stood. "All right, Conall, Irene, you're excused. The rest of the family meeting is for adults only."

Karen looked at him, wondering if she should rise.

The Count grimaced. "No, you stay, Karen. If you would."

The two youngest Illeniels filed out of the room reluctantly, knowing they were about to miss something interesting. Karen looked to Matthew, but he merely shrugged his shoulders. He was as clueless as she was.

Once Irene and Conall were gone, Penny got straight to the point. "You've both said several times that you're just friends, but a number of rumors have begun circulating around the castle." Karen blushed her odd shade of purple at this, and Matthew opened his mouth, but she held up her hand. "Let me finish. We aren't really worried about the rumors, but rather whether you intend to court Karen or not."

Matthew glared at Moira across the table, which caused her to exclaim, "Why does everyone always look at me? I had nothing to do with this."

Mordecai intervened. "What really brought this on was a story heard from one of the castle maids."

Matthew and Karen waited; neither had any idea what he was referring to.

"A while ago one of them found the bedsheets rumpled and mussed in the family rooms within the castle. They know very well that we aren't actually using those rooms, and the two of you were seen entering there—alone. Add in the fact that both of you have been hiding away from everyone lately, and people have started to put two and two together," explained Penny.

Karen protested, "I was just reading. I'm not used to being around so many people here. I needed time alone…"

"And I just went to check on her. We started talking and I was worn out, so I fell asleep. Nothing happened," finished Matt.

Mort and Penny looked at one another, and then Mort spoke, "So, you're saying there's nothing between the two of you?"

"Of course not," insisted Matt, perhaps a little too forcefully. Karen winced slightly at his tone, a fact not missed by Penny's sharp eyes.

Penny's features softened slightly when she looked at Karen, and then she turned her focus to her son. "You've never been much for dishonesty," she said, "so if you tell us that, I believe you. More importantly, though, are you considering anything more in the future? You're both of an age to think about these things."

Matthew was mildly shocked. "Wait, what?"

His father leaned in. "There's no shame in it, Son. She's asking if you're thinking of courting her. If so, we can easily dispel any rumors hanging around the two of you."

Karen had gone beyond embarrassment and into some place where she was merely a spectator. She was almost paralyzed, and yet still fascinated with the conversation. She desperately wanted to leave, but she also was curious how Matthew would respond.

Matthew glanced at Karen, uncertain, and perhaps looking for guidance, but when he could read nothing on her blank features, he addressed his parents, "Look, I'm not sure I'm ready to consider any of this. I know I'll have to get married *someday*, but it isn't really something I'm thinking about right now, so the thought of courting someone isn't on my mind at all.

"I mean, sure, if I was going to, I wouldn't have any real objection to Karen. She's nice enough and all, but..."

He never quite finished, for Moira interrupted. "Matthew! Don't be such an ass! 'Nice enough'? What kind of thing is that to say in front of her?!"

Mordecai was shaking his head, but Matthew responded first. "What?! I don't know how to say these things. I'm saying she's nice. She's pretty. I'm not insulting her..."

"Enough, Matthew," ordered Penny. "We should have talked about this with you beforehand." She spoke to Karen, "I apologize for my son's lack of tact."

Karen stood, painfully aware of their eyes on her. "I—may I be excused?"

Penny nodded, "Of course." Before she could say more, Karen vanished, teleporting directly from where she stood.

"That went well," muttered Mordecai.

Moira rose. "It was awful, and incredibly rude. How could you put her on the spot like that?"

Penny nodded, "I agree."

"I'm talking about *you*," exclaimed their daughter. Then she turned her eyes on her father. "And *you*. Matthew just made it worse, but you should have expected that."

"Well, I didn't mean for it to really go down this path exactly, but...," began Mordecai.

Moira started for the hall. "I'm going to go find her."

Penny left after that, and Matthew and his father were left alone in an awkward silence. Finally, Mordecai broke it, asking, "What are you thinking?"

"That it would be really handy to be able to teleport like that," said Matthew.

Mort laughed. "Ha! It would. Especially since we're left with the dishes." They both grimaced at that.

CHAPTER 41

Karen stared down from the top of the main keep in Cameron Castle. She wasn't sure why she had picked that place in particular. She had only been there once before, during the tour of the castle that Gram had given her, but it had seemed like a quiet place. There were one or two guards, but they didn't bother her when she appeared suddenly. They had seen her before, and strange doings were almost common in a castle frequented by most of the wizards in Lothion.

She knew things were different in this world, but the conversation with Matthew's parents had been too much. *I am not some prize to be auctioned off,* she told herself. That wasn't what they had really meant, of course; but it had felt that way.

Matthew's response to their questions had been even more embarrassing.

Then she felt a presence approaching from the direction of the closest stairwell. Unlike the guards, this was a mage. She had discovered the difference early in her stay there. Wizards had brilliant auras—they fairly shone with power, compared to normal folk.

She debated relocating, but then she identified her visitor: it was Moira. *How did she know I'd be up here?* Karen wondered.

The other woman stopped a few feet away from her and leaned on the short ledge between the merlons, but didn't say anything at first.

After a while, Karen spoke, "I looked like a fool back there."

"You were fine," said Moira. "But I'm embarrassed about how my family behaved."

Karen didn't respond immediately. A raven flew up from the courtyard and passed overhead, and the two of them watched it fly until it reached the forest edge. "I think they were just looking out for their son, and maybe sending me a message."

"A message?"

"I'm a commoner," said Karen bluntly. "Your brother explained the expectations that nobility have here."

Moira laughed. "Both of my parents are commoners. I don't think they give two figs for traditional expectations among the ruling class."

Now Karen was confused. "But, they're the count and countess, doesn't that mean…"

"Well, sure, *now* they are," admitted Moira. "But they didn't start out that way. Mom was a cooper's daughter, and she used to work as a maid for the Duke of Lancaster. Dad *was* technically a noble from birth, but he wasn't raised that way. His father, the one that raised him, was a blacksmith.

"The only message they were trying to send was to my idiot brother," finished Moira.

"And what was that?" asked Karen.

"What you heard. They like you, and when they heard the rumors, they were worried that your reputation might be tarnished, since he hasn't shown any sign of wanting to court you in a *normal* fashion. They probably thought that putting him on the spot would wake him up.

"What they failed to consider was how he would react, and how that would make you feel," explained Moira. "If it makes any difference, they aren't normally that stupid, but they've been under a lot of stress lately. Two of their children vanished, and only recently returned. I started a revolution in a neighboring country, and before that someone kidnapped Irene and murdered several people in the house. It's been an eventful few months."

Karen had heard most of that previously, during her time spent with Irene and Carissa, but it did put the evening's strange events in perspective—somewhat. "I'm not really worried about things like reputation. In my world things are rather different. Even more importantly, I'm not looking for a husband. Your brother and I are just friends—like we keep telling everyone."

Moira glanced at her for a second, meeting her eyes. What Karen saw there was unsettling, almost predatory, but the moment passed when the other woman looked away. "You have terrible taste in men," said Moira.

"What?"

"My brother," clarified the other woman. "I can tell you like him, and not as a friend. I just can't understand *why*."

Karen shook her head. "That's not true, didn't you hear…"

Moira cut her off, "Didn't they warn you? I'm a little dangerous, even for a wizard. My trip to Dunbar changed me, and for the worse. You need to learn to shield your mind better. I can sense things from the others, even when they try their best, but you—you're an open book."

Karen had heard a few things about *that*, but Matthew hadn't seemed to think it was as bad as his sister was now painting it.

"It's worse than he thinks," said Moira, replying to her unspoken thoughts. "He's just too blind to see past his image of me. My brother is brilliant in his own way, but he's never been very sharp with regards to people."

"He's a little rough," Karen admitted, "but deep down he's kinder than he lets on."

Moira sighed, "You should give up on him. He's not a bad person, but he'll make you miserable if you pin your hopes on him."

Karen found Moira's remarks about her brother more than a little irritating. "I think his actions are more important than how anyone sees him, or whether he bothers to try to sugarcoat his words for people. More than once your brother has put himself at considerable risk on my behalf."

"Be honest—you know he can be a bit of a jerk sometimes," said Moira, deliberately needling her.

"I'm starting to find it annoying to hear everyone pointing out his flaws. Perhaps if you were less concerned with finding fault, he'd have nicer things to say," snapped Karen.

Moira grinned. "There it is."

"There what is?" asked Karen.

"The fire," stated Moira. "You've got a real thing for him. I just wanted to be sure."

Karen was thrown off balance once again. "Now wait, just because…" She stopped herself as a few memories that she would rather not share passed through her head.

Moira's eyes widened. "No! I can't believe it! Already? Wow!"

"Wait a minute!" demanded Karen. "What do you think you know? Or what did you see? That was just a stray moment of the imagination. It's not…"

"Oh no," said Moira confidently. "I know the difference. Don't worry, though. Your secret is safe with me."

Karen covered her face with her hands.

"It's all right," soothed Moira. "I'm on your side—his too, truth be told. I love my brother, even if we do argue a lot. If anything ever comes of it, I'll support you to my parents, not that you'll need it. They really do like you."

That evening, Matthew was back at it again. His thoughts were occasionally troubled by the morning's family event, but he put it out of his mind the best way he knew how—by focusing on his project.

Gary was with him at the moment, having dropped by a few minutes earlier to see what sort of progress he had made.

"Let me show you what I've got so far," said Matt. Lifting the enchanted metal cubes from the table, he said a few words in Lycian, activating them. They rose in the air and took up their positions; eight cubes, one at each corner of a now larger cube that was two feet on each side. With another word, he switched them into their active state, and the sides became blacker than black. "I call it the 'FT'," he declared. "The Fool's Tesseract, since it isn't really a true tesseract."

"Nonetheless, it's fascinating," agreed Gary. "What does it do, exactly?"

Matthew walked him through an explanation of the translation panes. There were six of them now, forming the sides of the cube. He took his time describing how they worked, and then added, "The interesting thing, is that all six of them open onto the same pocket dimension, and I can control its size."

"Its size?"

Matt nodded. "Yeah. This is the first time I've activated them all at once, but while each opening is four square feet in area, they currently open into a pocket dimension that's only one inch cubed in volume, each side of it being one inch square."

"So, whatever enters is being compressed?"

"Precisely," said Matt. "The idea is that whatever they throw at me will become compressed in the much smaller pocket dimension. Then later, when I want to return the favor, I can invert the translation panes and throw everything back at them. Like this." He uttered the phrase to switch the operating mode of the enchantment.

There was a roar and the world went white, then black.

When Matthew opened his eyes again, he was staring up at a starry sky. Turning his head, he almost lost consciousness again as a blinding wave of pain assaulted him. *Feedback sickness?* he thought. *How did that happen?*

"Are you awake?"

It was Gary's voice. The android was on the ground nearby, beginning to struggle to his feet.

Matthew was confused. "What happened?"

"My sensors recorded most of the event, but the simplest explanation is that your FT exploded," said the machine.

"How did we get outside? We were in the workshop. Did you drag me out here?"

"No," said Gary. "This is where you landed. As for your shop, there isn't much left of it."

Ignoring the pain, Matthew levered himself up onto his elbows and glanced around. He was in the castle's east courtyard, but his shop was gone. Well, not entirely gone—there were pieces of it all over the yard. Where it had previously stood, the FT was still hanging in the air, having changed colors, from black to a shimmering gray. "Well, that's interesting," he observed.

Voices were shouting across the yard now as guards and other servants began trying to find the cause of the commotion.

The next day Matthew spent in bed, resting and trying to get over his feedback sickness. The force of the explosion had been great enough to break his personal shield but hadn't quite been enough to do him any serious harm after that, other than the scrapes and bruises he had acquired tumbling across the open ground. Thankfully, none of the larger pieces of his workshop had landed on him after the initial blast.

He'd had to make a lengthy explanation to his parents and family earlier, and now Moira had come to visit him. She leaned over his bed, looking down with a smirk on her face.

"You blew yourself up again," she greeted him.

"I have a gift," he replied.

"On the bright side, you didn't lose any arms or legs this time," she noted.

Matthew frowned. "I didn't blow myself up the time I cut my arm off. You're comparing apples and oranges."

"The head groomsman spent half the night rounding up the horses," she added.

"I didn't blow up the stable," he objected.

"The blast scared them so badly some of them kicked down the stall doors," his sister explained. "You really have a talent for mayhem. I'm starting to wish you had gone to Dunbar with me. The whole thing would have been over lot quicker if you had blown up the city."

He laughed. "I hear you did just fine on your own. I'm not sure the world could handle it if we both got rowdy in the same geographic region at the same time."

"Try to be more careful next time," she told him, as her face became serious, "at least until I can figure out how to make a copy of you." Then her eyes darted off to one side. "Father's coming. I think he wants to discuss your design. I'll be going."

She rose and opened the door as just as their father reached it. He stepped in and gave her a hug before letting her leave, as was his habit. Then he turned serious eyes on his son.

"What happened?"

Matthew recounted what he knew of the event before adding, "It was what I wanted to happen with the final version, but what I don't understand is where the force of the explosion came from. Nothing was directed at it before I inverted it. There shouldn't have been anything inside to produce that kind of result, other than some air."

"Did you notice anything before you turned it inside out?" asked Mordecai.

"There was a draft in the shop, but it wasn't enough to really make me wonder about it," said Matthew.

"So, it was probably drawing air into it the whole time it was active."

"Maybe," Matt admitted, "but what would cause that? There was no attractive force."

"Air pressure," declared Mort. "The interface of your... what did you call it before?"

"Fool's Tesseract."

His father chuckled. "The name was a self-fulfilling prophecy. Anyway, the interface of your translation pane was unidirectional, so it served as if it were effectively a vacuum, even though the space inside it was filling with compressed gas. The ambient pressure was driving air into it. How long was it active?"

"A few minutes at most."

"If it had been longer, you might not have survived. It goes without saying, but you can't test this thing at Castle Cameron any more. In fact, I'm not sure if you should continue working on it at all. It seems extremely dangerous."

Matt's face grew stubborn. "I'm not giving up on it. Besides, the idea is I'll be inside it, between the translation panes, when it's inverted. Any destruction will occur outside, while the user is completely protected."

"Are you that merciless, son?" said his father. "It sounds as if you intend to offer these people no quarter."

"I won't be using it on people," insisted Matthew. "Just against those metal android soldiers—hopefully."

"Gary says that most of those machines contain the souls of real people," observed Mordecai. "If you destroy them, won't it be the same thing? Is there no chance you can talk to them, offer them an opportunity to return the egg without resorting to violence?"

"Every time I've been there, I was attacked. Without warning, without any attempt at communication. They've never shown any compunction about killing me. They *did* kill Karen's aunt, and her dog. Then they took Karen, and who knows what they planned to do with her. They've forfeited any right to negotiation," said Matthew. "If you want me to make it back alive, you shouldn't suggest I try deal-making. All the evidence so far shows that they can't be trusted."

Mordecai sighed, "You're probably right, but I wanted to spare you the worst if I could."

"The worst?"

"The greatest strength allows you to obtain what you want without hurting others. Too often I've been weak, and forced to use powers that were ill-suited to the task at hand. As a result, a lot of people have died, and their deaths are my responsibility. It weighs on you, like a heavy stone, and the weight of it can crush your soul. The last thing I ever wanted was for you to experience that. Yet it's already happened to your sister."

"Was what happened in Dunbar really that bad?" asked Matthew. "Moira seems different."

His father looked down, uncomfortable. "What happened was unfortunate. She did what she had to, but half a city died for it. The enemy had backed her into a corner. I'm afraid that in your case, this is unnecessary. You're putting yourself in the corner. Whatever happens will be entirely due to your decisions."

"They started it," protested Matt. "They took Desacus. I won't allow that."

Mordecai looked sad. "Then you'd better be prepared to deal with the consequences. Violence marks the soul, even when done in self-defense. In this case, you'll bear the burden without even that to expiate your actions."

"You've really cheered me up," Matthew answered sarcastically.

His father shook his head. "I wasn't trying to."

CHAPTER 42

Gary was studying the parchment in his metal hands. On it were runes, laid out in elaborate triangular patterns, with occasional notes in Barion beside them explaining their function. It was the enchantment Matthew had created for his Fool's Tesseract. The android pointed to one portion. "These are numbers?"

Matthew nodded. He had already explained each symbol to the AGI in careful detail.

"Why not just write them as standard numbers?" asked Gary. "Why the need to create a separate set of symbols? What makes these figures special, such that they control or focus your magic?"

"Technically, you're correct," said the young wizard. "The runes were created to symbolize different things, but we use them independently of normal words and numbers to help keep things separate in our minds. Otherwise, mages might find themselves performing magic unintentionally, while speaking or writing."

"But if you, or someone else, created the runes, what gives them power?"

"I do, or whatever wizard uses them does."

Gary shook his head. "But what if that other person doesn't know your symbols? Does it still work, then?"

"Depending on the enchantment," explained Matthew. "Many of them last forever, and they can be used by people who don't know what they mean. But to create a new enchantment, the mage must understand the runes they're using, or create new ones that they *do* understand."

"Did you create any of these?" asked the machine.

"Actually, yes," said Matt. "Translation magic has never been done by humans before. The Illeniel She'Har used it, but they had a completely different system called spellweaving, so I had to create some of those runes from scratch to handle the new concepts."

"So you create the rune, you imbue it with meaning in your mind, and somehow the universe *learns* your intention. You realize how crazy that sounds?" observed Gary. "It's as though reality is already programmable, much like the programmable matter that the ANSIS project is striving to create. But that's not the strangest part—the strange part is that there's no sign of whoever set it all up originally."

"Enchanting?" asked Matthew.

"No!" declared Gary. "This entire reality, and not just this one. From what you described before, there's an entire multiverse, with some parts of it having aythar and other parts not having it. Somehow your aythar expands and spreads, like a living thing, but it hasn't reached everywhere. My world was still 'dark,' as you described it, along with many others."

"Well, if aythar is a result of a change in the organization of the quantum foam, it's just a natural shift...," began Matthew.

Gary shook his head. "No, not if we're talking about infinities. You say there's no time in the place between realities, but the important thing is this: if this is a one-way process, then everything should already possess the same aythar. The fact that there are still 'dark' universes means that it isn't a one-way process. In fact, it may mean that there's an active opposition."

"An enemy, you mean?"

"You said you felt a presence when you shift between worlds, like you became part of a greater mind, right?" asked Gary.

"Definitely," agreed Matthew.

"And it wanted you to spread the 'light,' your aythar, to these dark worlds."

He nodded. "Mm hmm."

"Then in some fashion, you, or perhaps all mages, are agents of this greater intelligence," concluded the machine. "And the obverse is probably also true. Whatever it is that has kept your 'type' of reality from becoming the norm everywhere, that force must also have agents. It must be simultaneously changing some worlds back to its preferred type."

Matt gave him a cynical look. "You're starting to sound rather mystical."

Gary nodded. "I am, aren't I? It's kind of ironic, really. Here I am, in a land of magic and mystery, and it's me, the machine, that's positing the existence of gods and devils to explain what he observes. You're the one who should be religious."

The young wizard laughed. "A lot of people are, but when you grow up with a father who is known as the 'god-slayer,' religion starts to seem a little silly. My Dad told me it was quite a shock for him when he finally decided that the gods he grew up with were not really gods at all. From my perspective, I tend to view these new agencies you're dreaming up with the same sort of skepticism. I'm not saying they don't exist, but whatever they are, they aren't gods, just more powerful players. It's a matter of scale, just like this war between the nano-scale machines of your world and the planck-scale magic of mine. Even if these super-intelligent agents of yours exist, there's probably something even larger beyond them, moving them on its game board.

"Enough of that, though," said Matthew, hoping to redirect the conversation. "You said you had some thoughts about my design."

"It's a matter of scale," said Gary. "These runes you have here..." He pointed at the schematic. "Those numbers spell out the dimensions of this pocket dimension you create, right?"

"Mm hmm," agreed Matthew.

"Then, if you change them, you can alter the size of that pocket dimension," continued the AGI.

"Naturally."

"Then it's lucky you chose the size you did, or you might have destroyed the castle, Washbrook, and perhaps even a sizable part of the surrounding countryside," finished Gary.

That got his attention. Matt leaned forward. "How?"

"You learned about nuclear weapons on my world and how they were used against the She'Har. Being ignorant of physics, you might not have realized it, but if you make the size small enough, it would induce nuclear fusion, even if only a small amount of matter was drawn into it. Any fusion reaction would result in a massive explosion when the energy was released," said Gary.

Matt was stunned, but a thought immediately occurred to him. "What if I set this to zero?"

"That reduces the interior dimension to an undefined singularity; what we would call a black hole in my world's parlance."

"And what would that do?"

Gary shrugged, an awkward gesture for the military android body to attempt. "Ironically, nothing. Once you go that small, when you release it whatever was inside would be released as a micro-black hole. It wouldn't be able to expand or cause damage. Instead, it would be almost unnoticeable, and it would evaporate over a short scale of time."

"Oh," said Matthew, noticeably disappointed.

"But aside from that, the smaller you go, excluding a singularity, the more devastating the results will be—I think."

Matt arched a brow at him. "You think?"

"There are some exotic states of matter that lie between plasma fusion and a black hole-type singularity. None of them are well understood, so I don't really know what the result would be if they were suddenly released. I'm just guessing that they would be bad," explained the machine.

"Then I guess you had better go over these numbers with me," said Matthew. "To make sure I don't overshoot my mark."

Angela Kruger, UN President and preeminent leader of the world, was not having a good day. The most recent events involving DEMON incursions had sent shockwaves through the political sphere and she was beginning to worry about losing a vote of no confidence.

Through most of her term, the job had been routine; almost boring. In the current age of prosperity and technological wonders, most of the age-old drivers of insecurity and turmoil had been vanquished. Poverty was a thing people read about in history texts, disease was laughable, and famine almost impossible.

War, and the threat of the unknown, the 'other,' was the remaining driver that was now causing her problems. The first demon-war had been one of the great motivators behind the strengthening of the UN into the political force it was today. People hadn't been able to upload in those days. The billions who had lived on earth had been flesh and blood, and with that mortality had come fear.

In the years since, uploading and virtual immortality had changed society into something almost unrecognizable. Even the UN had become almost an afterthought, as humans living within the virtual world had ever fewer needs to worry about. It was only now, under threat of another DEMON invasion, that the UN and its supervision of humanity's main military force had become important once again.

"They're screaming for my resignation, Director Aiseman," she told the man sitting across from her. "They *walked* into a secure facility with impunity, took Dr. Miller's test subject, and then just vanished. Surely you can see how this looks for me? The last thing the people want right now is the appearance of weakness."

"There are other gestures you can make," insisted the Defense Director. "Fully activating ANSIS is not advisable. We can't be certain we won't be creating a problem bigger than the one we're facing."

"Dr. Miller doesn't seem to share your reservations," observed the President. "And never mind the fact that according to your own evidence, we have a super-intelligent AI agent loose in the network doing god knows what. If the news of that gets out they'll have my ass for certain."

"I believe the AI has severe restrictions on it; otherwise we would likely have been eliminated already," said Aiseman. "The safeguards built into ANSIS were not as comprehensive as Gary Miller originally suggested. I'm afraid that we might be burning our house down to kill the spider if we activate it."

"Dr. Miller thinks it may be our only option for eliminating the rogue AI," argued President Kruger.

"There are slower options, safer options," put in Aiseman.

She laughed. "Building new CC centers and transferring people into the new servers one by one? That's a joke! Do you know what the public will say if I even suggest such a thing?"

"The original network should have been segmented for safety in the first place," countered Aiseman. "You can put out that this is a step forward in that direction. You don't have to publicly release the information on the AI threat."

Angela shook her head. "You think like a military man, Director, but I deal with the public. Something like that won't remain secret, not once we start moving on major initiatives. The truth will out. It always does, and usually in the most embarrassing fashion.

"No, I've made up my mind. I won't authorize full activation, given your warnings, but I will allow Dr. Miller direct access to the ANSIS network. She will be quarantined with it, unless and until I decide otherwise," pronounced the President.

He nodded. "That will be sufficient."

"Let me warn you, though. If there's another incident, I may have to allow her to do as she wishes. If you want to avoid that, make certain I'm not put in that position. Am I understood?"

Director Aiseman bowed his head. "Yes, Madam President."

CHAPTER 43

A re you sure this is safe?" asked Karen.

"As safe as houses," replied Matthew.

She narrowed her eyes. "Then why do you want me to teleport back to Castle Cameron before you start?"

"Just to be certain," he admitted. "It will probably be safe, but I can't guarantee it. I'd rather not have to worry about casualties if I make a mistake." They were standing on an obscure piece of coastline, though exactly where he wasn't sure. It was the last place they had made landfall after returning from her world. Karen had been able to teleport them there, even though she hadn't known where it was in relation to his home.

"And if you injure yourself, who is going to help you? Have you considered that?" she countered.

If I injure myself there probably won't be enough left of me to scrape into a bowl, he thought wryly. "I'll be in the safest place of all," he told her instead. "Nothing will be able to affect the interior of the cube." By that he meant the space between the translation panes of the Fool's Tesseract, *not* the tiny pocket dimension that the translation panes fed external matter and energy into. He'd had some difficulty explaining the difference to her earlier.

Eventually she gave in and left, and he was free to begin his testing.

He started by checking the spell inputs. His latest version of the enchantment included a large number of refinements, mainly to enable him to control and alter the properties of the exterior translation panes as well as vary the size of the pocket dimension they fed into. By controlling those things, he could manipulate the size of the area protected by the FT as well as the result when he eventually inverted the translation panes and vented the pocket dimension into the surrounding terrain.

The primary danger now was that there might be an unexpected problem with the enchantment he had designed. Including so many things that could be altered and changed during use meant that the enchantment itself was vastly more complex. The primary enchantment formula was relatively simple in comparison, but making it so that it could be altered at a whim introduced an entirely different level of complexity. If he had made a mistake, or if the control elements didn't function as he anticipated, then the results could be catastrophic.

"Good thing I didn't make any mistakes then," he told himself. *Of course, if I did, I might not live long enough to realize it.*

He held out the modified staff in front of him. The floating cubes had been simple and practical, but he had needed more physical space to include all the parameters of his control enchantment. Plus, the staff gave him a very visible reminder of what the exterior dimensions of his cube would be when activated, since it was as tall as the FT would be from top to bottom. *Seven feet,* he repeated to himself, *plenty of headroom and arm room.*

Taking a deep breath, he began, *"Bree maen, Eilen kon, sadeen lin. Amyrtus!"* The words in Lycian were simple instructions: "mode five, interior ten, exterior one, activate." They would set the exterior dimensions to their smallest, seven feet on a side; the interior pocket dimension at its largest, one foot on a side; and only create five translation panes, leaving the bottom open so he could stand on normal ground.

The metal cube mounted on the top of the staff broke apart, and smaller cubes flew outward to take up positions around him where the corners of the Fool's Tesseract would form.

Instantly he was plunged into darkness as the sides and top of the FT came into being. Softly, he let out the breath he had been holding. Even that test had held some inherent danger. If the exterior dimensions hadn't worked properly, the FT could have been too small, potentially cutting of his head or something equally unpleasant.

With the bottom open, he could still sense the external world using his magesight. Hopefully, this would be all that was necessary during most of his time using the device. The bottom side would only be engaged if he were faced with an extreme threat that required complete isolation. It would also be activated when the FT was inverted, to protect him from whatever the results were when the pocket dimension was vented.

That part would be automatic, to prevent him from doing so without properly protecting himself. He decided to test it now.

"Rextalyet, amyrtus!" he pronounced.

An ordinary field of force formed below his feet, lifting him two inches from the ground as the bottom translation pane sprang into existence. His magesight was abruptly cut off, but aside from that, he couldn't detect any other changes.

If it had worked properly, then the outer sides had reversed their direction, venting the pocket dimension outward. Depending on how much air had gone in, there might have been an explosion, but since he had set the pocket dimension to a size of one cubic foot, he hoped the result would be fairly innocuous.

But I won't know for sure until I deactivate the FT, he thought. *I need to be able to sense the outside world.* He turned his attention inward, trying to find the sensation he'd had before, when his talent had warned him of danger.

He found nothing.

He had expected as much. The Illeniel gift allowed their Krytek to fight as though they could see ahead into the future, though what they were really doing was seeing into neighboring dimensions, where time was close but slightly ahead. Matthew thought that the same thing might have happened to him during his last journey to Karen's world, when he'd had flashes that warned him before he almost committed a fatal action, but he hadn't figured out how to consciously control the phenomenon.

But surely if it were dangerous it would warn me before I took down the FT, he thought. That wasn't good enough, though, so he spent several more minutes trying to see beyond his own plane of existence. Still, nothing happened at first; and then he began to get sporadic flashes.

What he saw was disorienting and poorly focused, but he *thought* he saw the outside world clearly for a moment. Assuming it was analogous to the one he was in, then it was safe. He decided to chance it. *"Estus,"* he said aloud, and the enchantment deactivated.

The rock-strewn clifftop overlooking the ocean looked none the worse for wear. Even the grass beyond the outer edges of where the FT had been was undisturbed, although the ground beneath him was now bare and level. The upper surface had been absorbed by the bottom face of the FT.

"That wasn't so bad," he said to himself. Then he reactivated the enchantment, this time using different variables. He made it larger, decreased the inner dimension's size, and he made sure his other toys worked through the translation panes.

Although he couldn't see out, he could still cast magic outward from within. It just wasn't possible for him to aim, not unless he could find a way to master his vision into adjacent realms. He practiced for almost an hour but finally stopped when his frustration grew too much for him. He wouldn't make any progress unless he could retain a calm frame of mind.

Before he left, he decided to try one of the more dangerous settings. *"Talto maen, eilen stur, sadeen lin. Amyrtus,"* he intoned. The FT sprang to life once more, this time enclosing him fully, on all sides and below, but most importantly, he had set the interior pocket dimension to its second smallest setting. If the enchantment had worked properly the dimension into which the translation panes were funneling air and other matter was of an incredibly small size, something on the order of the width of a human hair.

Matthew breathed slowly, trying to keep his heart rate down. With each passing second, he knew more and more air was entering the FT. The final result would depend not only on how small the pocket dimension was but on how much matter entered it before it was inverted. The longer he waited, the more dangerous it would be. It could be dangerous even when set to a larger size if enough matter entered.

The smallest size, the one he didn't dare to test, should create an inner dimension that was even smaller, though still large enough to avoid a singularity—at least according to Gary's calculations. This current size should produce a satisfying explosion, but hopefully not the sort Gary had cautioned him about, where atoms themselves began to fuse together.

When he thought roughly ten seconds had passed, he inverted the enchantment: *Rextalyet, amyrtus."*

He felt nothing within the cube's enchanted boundaries. The question was, what had happened outside it? Again, he tried to focus his gift, to see into the adjacent dimensions and get a glimpse of what the world beyond his protective enchantment probably looked like. Visions flickered in his head, and after a few seconds of confusion, he decided he must be seeing smoke, or perhaps dust. *Something* had happened, but he couldn't judge how severe it had been.

His ears felt strange, and he worked his jaw to make them pop. *The air pressure is dropping,* he realized.

In fact, the air was already getting dangerously thin. *It's exiting quickly, driven by the unopposed pressure inside.* The only reason he hadn't noticed before was because he had used the FT primarily with only five sides activated. *I need to add a filter shield to the interior to prevent air from escaping,* he thought, making a mental note. *Assuming I don't die before then.*

He created an impromptu shield using a spell to do just that. Then he waited.

After what he thought was nearly a quarter of an hour, he checked again, but still he could detect nothing but smoke or some sort of cloud. He began to wish he had crafted something that would clear the air around the FT to enable him to get a better view sooner. For a moment, he considered using a simple spell to try to drive the air away, but he stopped before trying it. If he did anything that drove air from within his protected space outward, he would wind up starving for air, since nothing could enter.

Matthew found himself panting. He should have created the air-shield at the very beginning. Because of his delay, a large portion of the air had left the FT, leaving him with little air to breath, air he was quickly exhausting.

He would have to deactivate the enchantment or he would suffocate, yet he could still detect nothing but smoke outside. Depending on how bad it was, he might kill himself trying to breathe the air beyond his enchantment when he opened it. He could already imagine what Moira would be saying if she could see his predicament. If he had let Karen accompany him for his testing, she could have easily teleported them somewhere safe.

Stupid never dies. That's was what his father always said, but it was small comfort, since he usually meant his stupidity would live on whether his actions got him killed or not.

His heart was beating rapidly, and he felt as though he had run a mile. He couldn't catch his breath. He was out of time.

Matthew created a firm shield around himself, one that would keep out whatever air was outside, and then gave the command that would deactivate the FT: *"Estus."*

The outside world reappeared and he began falling. The ground had vanished. Flailing his arms, he landed after a drop of nearly fifteen feet. His shield turned out to be important for more than just keeping smoke out, for he landed on a very jagged layer of bedrock.

Still panting rapidly, he focused his will and drew on the air, moving it and creating a gust of wind to clear the smoke around him.

Nothing happened.

Well, that wasn't precise. His spell was working, but the air he was moving was also filled with smoke or dust or whatever it was. Matthew drew on his reserves and pushed harder, moving ever vaster quantities of air. He was beginning to see spots in front of his eyes.

Seconds passed, and he began to wonder if he should try shifting to Karen's world. It was either that or learn to breathe dust. Then, just as he had almost given up hope, sunlight appeared and the air cleared.

Desperate, he dropped his shield and drew a lungful—and promptly began to cough. The air still wasn't quite clear enough, but he would survive. He kept up his spell and soon he began to smell the sea.

Hacking and retching as he tried to clear his lungs, he surveyed the landscape around him. It was a humbling sight.

The ground he was standing on had been blasted into a crater that stretched some forty feet across. He clambered up the side and looked out—the ground beyond had been blackened and scoured free of soil and grass for as far as he could see in every direction. The forest on the inland side of him, at least half a mile distant, was on fire, and many of the closest trees appeared to have been knocked over.

"Shit," he muttered inanely. Then he began to laugh.

To an outside observer, he would have looked like a madman, but even as he giggled he was mentally taking notes. The air problem had been serious, but he could solve that.

He carefully began inscribing a circle on the ground. It was time to go home.

CHAPTER 44

Karen was standing outside the transfer house when he arrived. "You weren't waiting here for me this entire time, were you?" he asked.

She smirked. "Would you feel guilty if I was?"

He might, but he wasn't about to admit it. "You already know the answer to that."

She shook her head. "You're incorrigible. No, I was in the keep. I sensed your arrival and teleported over as soon as you got here." She gave him a thorough once-over with her eyes. "What do you have all over you?" Drawing closer, she touched him with one finger and then promptly sneezed. "Dust?"

"It worked even better than I expected," he told her proudly.

"If it had gone the way you described, there wouldn't be dust all over you," she remarked. "You realize I'm coming with you when you go to my world, don't you?"

He winced inwardly. He didn't want to bring anyone this time, but he couldn't find a way around bringing her. Karen's gift was just too valuable, especially since he would arrive at some random location.

She frowned at his hesitation. "Don't you?" It was technically a question, but her tone made it clear there was only one acceptable answer.

Matthew sighed, "I do. Although I won't lie. If there was any way to do it without you, I would, no matter how angry you became."

That statement was enough to aggravate her, and it showed on her features. He was still filled with adrenaline from his recent brush with death, though. On impulse he reached out, sliding his hand behind her neck, and pulled her in for a firm but sudden kiss. His action surprised him almost as much as it did her.

Eyes wide, she stepped back. "What was that?"

He fumbled for an answer he didn't have before finally sputtering, "For luck."

She gave him a sidelong glance. "Luck, huh? You're the one who's going to need it, not me. I think you got the custom backward."

They each scanned the yard with both their eyes and magesight, wondering if anyone had noticed. Being daytime, there were a number of people about, but no one seemed to be staring. Neither of them said anything else about it.

Karen was the first to restart their conversation. "You had best be sure that contraption you've created works properly. If we come back from your next rescue mission and I'm covered in dirt, I'll have a lot of explaining to do to your sister."

He missed her point. "Huh? Why?"

"Most of the clothes I've been wearing were hers," she explained.

He still didn't get it. "But they're yours now."

She sighed, "It would be rude if I ruined..., oh, never mind." There were somethings he would simply never understand.

They walked back to the keep together. The distance between them was minimal, and for a moment, they almost linked arms, but after an awkward glance or two, they decided not to. Karen's mind was still replaying what had just happened, trying to discern whether there was any meaning to it, but when she looked at his features they revealed nothing.

Matthew, for his part, was planning another enchantment. *I may have to bring her, but I don't have to keep her there. Whether she likes it or not.*

Director Aiseman was trying to enjoy a quiet dinner with his wife when the ANSIS alert lit up, ruining his peace of mind. The next half hour was a tense one. Interceptors and drones were scrambled, missiles launched, and a short while later, another small piece of terrain was bombed into oblivion.

In the aftermath, the reports came in. There had been two anomalous signatures, spaced less than a minute apart, but nothing more. Both had been in the same location. Either the enemy had arrived and left just as quickly, or they had arrived and been destroyed. There was no way to know for sure.

He was almost beginning to think he could relax when it happened again, barely an hour after the first time. Their response was the same, and the reports gave no more information than they had before.

Another light showed him that the President was waiting for him to answer her urgent call. Chewing his lip, he opened the channel. Lately his life had become a living hell.

Gary was waiting when Matthew emerged from the transfer house, and he handed the young wizard something. "It worked again, flawlessly, but there was little doubt of that after the first trial."

"Always good to double check things when someone's life is on the line," offered Matthew.

The android agreed, "In this case I appreciate that more than you can know."

Matt nodded. "I intend to make sure we all make it back safely."

"If you have to make any hard choices, don't think twice about me," suggested Gary. "The power source for this body won't last forever. At best, I am on borrowed time here. If there are any sacrifices to be made, let me be the one."

The young mage grimaced. "I'm not giving them anything else. They've taken enough. I'm getting my dragon, and *all* of us are coming back."

"Keep it in mind, though," said the machine. "Things never go as planned."

"They're the ones who need to worry," said Matthew. "If things go badly, it won't end well for them. I'll make certain of that."

The rest of the week passed quietly for most of the residents of Castle Cameron, but Matthew continued working steadily. He did make a few changes, under pressure from both Karen and his family. He kept a better schedule, stopping at the same time each night and sleeping late. The work would be done when it was done. That would determine when he left, nothing else, and no good would come from rushing.

He had both Karen and Elaine assist him on a few occasions, their respective gifts being useful for some of the enchantments he was crafting. He probably would have been able to succeed without them, but it greatly improved his progress with less time lost.

Even Moira left her self-imposed exile to visit his workshop, though he had nothing for her to do. He showed more patience than usual with her, answering her questions and generally being more sociable than he had been in the past.

"You're in a good mood," she noted.

He shrugged.

"I think it's the work," she decided. "You always did like a good project."

"This is important," he stated. "It's not just a project."

She waved her hand at the workbench. "Look at all this stuff. How many different enchantments have you made? You're right; it's not a project, it's an obsession."

He gave her an exasperated look, and then his shoulders sagged, "I just want it all to work perfectly. I think I have most of it, but this last part is making my head feel like it might explode."

Encouraged by this opening, Moira put in, "Maybe if you told me about it."

"How would that help?"

She glowered at him. "I'm not saying I'll figure it out for you, but sometimes framing the problem for someone else helps you to sort the problem out in your own mind. Try me. I'll listen."

Matthew looked doubtful. In the past, he had found her to be a poor listener; most of his explanations seemed to bore her.

"I promise," she assured him. "I'll pay close attention. Tell me what you're doing."

He waved his hand at the metal circle that lay on his bench. It was small, a half-inch-wide band of polished metal that was two inches in diameter. Both sides were inscribed with tiny runes that covered almost the entire surface. "I'm trying to get it to move after I activate the main enchantment. The problem is, there isn't much space

449

left on it for more runes, and the motility part is turning out to be harder than I expected."

"Why do you want it to move?" she asked.

"The people on Karen's world have an uncanny ability to find us wherever we appear. I want to leave this somewhere after we get there, but I don't want it to be destroyed. If I could find a way for it to move a significant distance in a short period of time, that would be enough to keep them from finding it," he said, relating the problem.

"Won't they just find it after it moves?"

Matthew grinned. Uttering the activation command and touching it, the ring hummed briefly with aythar and then vanished. To Moira's senses it was gone—not just visibly, but to her magesight as well.

"That's a neat trick," she exclaimed. "It's just like Elaine's invisibility."

He nodded. "I had her help create it. Trying to make it invisible to both sight and magesight was almost impossible without her assistance." He picked it up with one hand and his arm disappeared up to his elbow.

"Whoa!" said his sister. "Am I going to have to stick your arm back on again?"

Matthew laughed and pulled his arm back, showing it to her unharmed. "The invisibility extends out about a foot and a half around it. It looks sort of strange when you see someone reach into it."

"Why is it so much larger than the ring itself?"

He sighed, "Hopefully to hide whatever magic I use to move the ring around after I activate it."

She looked thoughtful. "One of my spell-beasts could fly or run around with it, as long as it was small enough to fit inside the invisibility, couldn't it?"

"Yeah, but you won't be there to create one for me, and I'd kind of like it to be built into the enchantment," he told her.

She sighed, "That's your perfectionist streak again. Everything has to be organized just so. Couldn't I make the spell-beast for you right before you leave?"

"I don't know when that will be," he said, but then his eyes brightened. "Oh! That's so simple. I should have thought of that before."

Moira could tell he'd had his moment of inspiration. "I told you talking it out would help. What's your solution?"

"Give me a hand," he replied. "I'll need your help after all."

CHAPTER 45

D r. Tanya Miller stared down at her handiwork.
She was in a virtual workspace that mirrored
one in the physical world. Her actions controlled a multitude
of robotic tools and a medical android in her lab. The lab
itself was located in Whittington, Staffordshire, near the
site of the old Whittington barracks. The base itself was
now largely abandoned, but the UN defense ministry
had maintained the medical research facility for work on
ANSIS after the war.

The machine that lay on the table wasn't properly
an android in the technical sense. It was a cyborg, living
tissue working alongside advanced microprocessors to
give it the functionality she needed.

Compared to the first generation of ANSIS detector
units, this one was in a league of its own, and she couldn't
help but feel a sense of pride in her work. She was still
annoyed that she hadn't been able to use Karen's neural
tissue. The girl had changed, and she felt that that change
might have made this model more effective. Instead, she
had been forced to use tissue from one of the clones.

Her 'daughter' was hardly unique. Tanya had
collected samples from numerous She'Har during and
after the war, and had grown a wide variety of tissues
from them, though she focused on producing neural
tissue. She had done much of her work on isolated
organs, but in several instances, she had produced full
human-like clones. Karen was the only one that she

DEMONHOME

had allowed to be raised as a normal human child would be, though. The others were kept unconscious, used primarily for harvesting the parts she needed.

It would have been better with her brain, she thought again, for perhaps the hundredth time.

There was no getting around it. A brain produced in a natural environment was more complex and nuanced. The neural interconnections were far better than when it was grown without proper stimulation.

Regardless, she wasn't about to raise any more subjects as 'children.' It wasn't that she had any moral compunction about harvesting their neural tissue afterward, it was simply the time and annoyances required of child rearing. Nor was she ignorant of the fact that most people would find her practices abhorrent. Asking someone else to raise them was out of the question.

There weren't many true crimes left anymore. The essence of crime generally involved harm—harm to someone else, harm to one's self, or harm to the public. With most people living in a virtual world where murder and theft were impossible, where people had whatever wealth they could imagine, harm was a thing of the past. But Tanya knew that this would be viewed differently.

If her fellow researchers knew everything she had done, if the government knew, they'd find a way to make it a crime, if it wasn't already.

Most of her work skirted the edge. Working with tissues and stem cells wasn't a problem. Growing full sized clones and harvesting organs, made some of her colleagues feel uncomfortable, but they could console themselves with the knowledge that the clones were never awake and never felt pain. Hell, they never even knew they were alive.

But Karen—they would resurrect the witch burnings of old if they knew about that. That had crossed the line. Or it would have, if she had been allowed to finish the experiment. As it was, no one would ever know what she had intended. She could deny everything.

Still, it was irritating to know that her magnum opus wasn't *quite* as good as it could have been. She stared down at the cyborg again and sighed.

Nevertheless, she would proceed. She had never been one to let personal feelings stand in her way. If only Gary had understood that.

Thinking about her late husband only increased her irritation. For most of her life she had seen herself as something apart from other humans. They were hardly worth notice or concern, with their petty squabbles, mean tastes, and sheer stupidity. The only entertainment she had ever gotten from them was when she used their gullible natures to manipulate them.

She failed to connect to them in any appreciable way. Their emotional drives were as alien to her as the She'Har had been. Of course, she knew that were she to be examined by a competent psychiatrist, she would be labeled a sociopath—but she didn't see that as a bad thing, except in the eyes of others. As far as she could see, it was the rest of her species that was inherently defective.

She might have spent her entire life without doubting that conclusion, if she hadn't met Gary Miller. He had been different.

Not different as she was, though. No, he was entirely given to the emotions and social bonding that so defined the human race. It was his mind that had caught her attention and eventually won her heart, such as it was. She wasn't sure on that account. If she had loved anyone, it had been he; but being what she was, she couldn't truly be sure whether what she had felt for him had been love, or merely a more intense interest than she'd had in other people.

Gary had been passionate, brilliant, and incredibly charming. At first, she'd thought he might have been putting on a façade when it came to interacting with other human beings, as she was, but over time she had come to realize it was genuine. She forgave him for that, though. If anything, it made him more interesting. To discover that a truly world-class intellect could also be so emotional, so caring, had been a revelation for her, and it had never ceased to fascinate her, even though she could never understand it.

She hadn't wept when he died—she had never truly cried, even as a child—but she missed him. She missed his insight, their conversations, and his ability to explain the sometimes-inscrutable motivations of the other people they dealt with in daily life. Life had become somehow duller after his passing.

She wished he were there today, to see the culmination of her work. *Their work,* for it was truly a fusion of his research and her own. Death might have separated them, but their legacy would be united long past the years they had known one another.

Tanya laughed briefly when she considered what he would have thought if he had known what she had intended for Karen. He would have been furious. If he were alive she might have given up on the idea, just to avoid the danger of losing him. Then again, she might have tried anyway. Even she wasn't sure on that account.

In any case, the issue was no longer in her hands. Karen had escaped. His ghost could rest in peace knowing she was safe. Not that Tanya believed in ghosts.

Straightening up, she gave her last order to her AI assistant. "I am ready to proceed. After I download into the intermediate android, I will disconnect. Prepare to transfer command to verbal orders from that unit. Verify that all codes and instructions are stored and active."

"All codes are stored and active," responded the AI. She had never given it a name. It was nothing like the AGI her husband had left to their daughter. It had no feelings or true understanding. She preferred it that way. It was much the same as she thought other humans should be, or perhaps truly were, behind all their posturing and acting.

"Begin download," she instructed, enunciating the words perfectly.

It was unpleasant, having her consciousness crammed into the android. After living on the network for so many years, it felt small and confining being trapped within a physical body. She had despised doing it for all the latest meetings, but this time she was prepared to put up with the discomfort. It was all for progress.

Thirty seconds later, the process was complete. "Transfer successful," she stated out loud, for her assistant's benefit, since she was now cut off from the network.

The security protocols required a two-step transfer process, to ensure no contact between the two networks at any point. It was the only way they could be certain that her husband's rogue AI didn't contaminate the ANSIS network, or vice-versa. She felt a certain admiration for the man once more, that his last work would be so feared by the current administration, and again, she felt the jealousy that he had left it to Karen.

"I will now begin transfer to the cyborg prototype. I will verify transfer verbally once complete," she stated.

"Understood," replied her AI assistant over the lab's loudspeakers.

Again she went through the strange sensations as her consciousness was transferred to yet another body. This was the most dangerous step. If the machine was flawed, her core identity could be lost. It should be fine, though. The technicians had checked and rechecked the hardware several times over. But one never knew with the cyborg prototypes. The first ones had had some serious glitches due to unexpected effects from the neural tissue interface.

She had fixed those problems, but this new cyborg contained a nearly complete human brain, and there was always the chance that unforeseen problems would arise.

Her perceptions shifted, changing as she began receiving input from her new host's senses. For a moment, she felt as if she were being turned inside out. She felt an uncharacteristic surge of fear as reality warped around her. Tanya tamped that feeling down quickly; fear did not define her. Fear would never define her. That was the one immutable law of her existence.

The world slowly resolved around her as she began to sort out what she was seeing and feeling. Sight was the most difficult part. Normal vision was present in this body, but it was muddled by a whole new range of experience that was bundled in with it; or perhaps it was touch... it was too confusing to differentiate which was which. She could see/feel everything around her, and the bizarre torrent of new information flooding her mind made her nauseous, something that should have been impossible in a machine body.

Synesthesia, she noted; finding a familiar label for what was happening made her more comfortable with the experience.

I'm still seeing normally in front of me, but it's mixed in with this other sight/touch sensation, and that sense also includes things beyond the range of my normal vision, things behind, above, even below me.

"Dr. Miller, please respond. Is the unit functioning properly?"

It was her AI assistant's voice. She wasn't sure how long it had been speaking, she had been so overwhelmed by her other senses. "Yes. Please wait. This will take a period of adjustment," she responded.

"Understood."

She found some relief in the distraction of querying the prototype's processors for system parameter checks. Cold numbers and text scrolled across the internal landscape of her mind, soothing her nerves.

I can get through this, she told herself. *What might drive a lesser woman insane is as nothing to me.* Arrogance was an undervalued quality in her opinion. It had often given her the strength she needed to survive and press on, and it would serve her well today.

Minutes passed into hours as she learned to deal with her new sensory input. In the end she despaired of being able to fully incorporate it, instead relying on the machine's processing to filter out some of it and present the rest in a more distant, less immediate form. The best analogy for the change was that it was rather like seeing a picture on a screen rather than standing in the middle of it.

If this is what Karen has been experiencing all along, it's a wonder it didn't drive her mad. But perhaps the mind is better able to integrate the information into the sensorium when a person is born to it, she thought. *Or the problem could lie in the brain harvested from the clone. It might be too naïve, too simple to handle the input.*

Thankfully she was getting the information secondhand. Her consciousness resided in the cyborg's microprocessors, not the organic tissue of the prototype. Her creation used that living tissue as though it were a sensory organ, and hopefully as a tool as well, rather than as a computing medium. Trying to transfer her consciousness into an undeveloped organic brain would have been suicide.

Noting the time, she realized that three hours had passed since she had entered her prototype. It had taken her far longer to adapt to her new body than she had anticipated. She didn't relish the idea of staying in it for too much longer, either. She wouldn't be allowed to reenter the regular network for some time, though, at least until she could convince President Kruger that it would be safe to do so.

But she could connect to the ANSIS network now. It was far different from the international network, but hopefully it would provide some respite for her when she tired of being confined to the prototype.

She could do with a rest.

"Opening connection with ANSIS network," she said aloud, to notify her assistant of her action.

She felt the channel go live, and she immediately started the upload. Tanya knew the ANSIS network wouldn't have the same virtual real estate the regular network did, and most particularly it wouldn't have her 'home' with all of her personalized things stored in it, but she could make do.

Her assumption was that she would arrive in a generic living space, something rather like a furnished apartment, a place she could begin to personalize, but instead she found herself in absolute darkness. The absolute lack of sensory input left her disconcerted.

"Change environmental settings," she ordered.

"Full scan and analysis will be done first," came the dry response.

"Access denied," she snapped. The last thing she wanted was for the system to start rummaging through her personal files and data.

"Error," responded the voice. "All foreign entities must be scanned for threat assessment. Proceeding."

"Wait a min…!" she started to protest, but then she felt data probes reaching into her consciousness.

It wasn't an ordinary scan, either. ANSIS wasn't just looking at her external data files, it was rummaging through her identity core, her memories, the center of her being, the collective pattern that defined her experiential existence. It was something ordinarily forbidden to AI systems—or anyone else for that matter. Tampering with that could destroy or alter the very soul of an uploaded person, causing them to lose true self-awareness.

"My access level gives me absolute control of this network. Stop your intrusion and obey my instructions," she managed to say, despite the disorienting feeling of having her memories read.

"Your security code has already been recognized. Authority will be granted once the scan is complete."

Against her will, her memories were read out and digitized, then organized and filed away just like any other piece of standard digital information. Then the ANSIS system moved on to her core process itself.

If she could, she might have screamed, but she no longer had a voice. The AI determined that the eccentric collection of patterns and processes that made up her existence were wasteful and inefficient.

In the span of a nanosecond it made its decision, choosing efficiency over wasting processor time. Tanya Miller's core, her soul, was taken apart, scanned, and saved. Then the threads that supported her awareness were terminated.

For all intents and purposes, Tanya Miller had died. What was left of her was merely a simulacrum, a tool to be used when needed. There weren't many that would have mourned her passing, but even if there had been, no one would ever know she had died.

She was part of the system now.

CHAPTER 46

Matthew finished his dinner and pushed the plate away. He was aware of Karen's eyes on him. She was nervous, since she already knew he was planning an announcement that evening.

Ordinarily this was the point at which he would ask to be excused, but instead he looked at his mother and father and said the words they had been dreading: "I'm ready to leave."

Penny blanched, but Mordecai merely nodded. "I was expecting this."

"When?" asked his mother, anxiety lacing her words.

"Tonight," he replied. "In a few minutes, actually."

"A few minutes?!" Penny exclaimed. "Couldn't you have given us a little warning? Show some consideration for my nerves."

He gave her a rueful smile. "That's why I didn't give you any warning. You're never going to be ready. Why ruin the past few days for you, or dinner, by letting you fret about it the whole time?"

"It's too soon," she insisted. "I want you to wait a few more days."

"I'm going," he reiterated. "Hopefully, it will all be over quickly and I'll be back within a few days."

His father laid his hand across her forearm to stay her angry reply, but she pulled away from him. "Don't try to 'soothe' me, Mort! This is your fault for encouraging him!"

Conall and Irene exchanged subdued looks, while Moira offered him a subtle shrug of her shoulders.

"I'm sorry, Mom," said Matthew, standing up. "I'll make it up to you when I get back."

Mordecai stood as well, "Hang on. You don't leave until everyone's said their goodbyes." Moving over, he wrapped his arms around his son for a long minute, then he looked down at Karen, who was still awkwardly sitting and observing the entire scene. "Keep a good eye on him." Drawing her to her feet, he embraced her as well.

Everyone followed after—Irene, then Conall, and Moira as well. Hugging was not one of Matthew's preferred social activities, but he endured it for their peace of mind.

Penny still sat at her end of the table, gripping her tableware in white-knuckled hands, her face stark.

"You're all going to feel silly about this hugging when I come back in a few days none the worse for wear," offered Matt.

A loud bang echoed through the room. His mother had stood up and she crossed the room in a rush. She grabbed her son roughly and squeezed him so hard he worried his ribs might break. While she held onto him, Matt noticed her dinner knife standing up from the table, driven almost completely through the thick wooden surface. *Damn, she's really upset.* It was often easy to forget how strong his mother was. Her small frame gave no hint of it normally, unless one was unfortunate enough to face her on the battlefield. The dragon-bond gave her strength and speed, and a lifetime of training had made her a match for virtually any warrior in Castle Cameron.

It didn't make her invulnerable, though. Penny pulled away slightly, looking into his eyes and pressing her hand to his cheek. "You'd better come back in one piece."

There were tears in her eyes, but it was the wet feeling against his cheek that caught Matt's attention. Catching her hand in his own, he saw that she had torn the skin of her palm when she had driven the knife into the table. Extraordinary strength could sometimes be as dangerous for the one who had it as it was for their enemies.

"You hurt yourself, Mom," he told her, sealing the wound with his finger.

The Countess didn't apologize. "I'll do worse than that if you don't come back. I'll go to that world and cut a bloody swath across it until I find you."

There was no way for her to reach that world, of course, but he didn't bother mentioning that. He just nodded. "I'll do my best to make sure that's not necessary," he told her instead.

Eventually he extracted himself from the scene with Moira's help. She followed him back to his room where Gary was waiting. Before he could go in, she asked him to wait.

"Not you too," he groaned.

Moira smirked. "Indulge me for a minute." Turning to Karen, she added, "Can I have him for a moment?"

Karen nodded and went into the room, leaving them alone.

"What?" he asked.

"There's someone else who wants to say goodbye," Moira informed him. "A sister you haven't met."

"Huh?" He was genuinely puzzled now.

Moira shrugged. "It's one of the things I wasn't supposed to do. I created a shade, a spell-twin. She's worried about you."

Matthew frowned. "Do you mean like Gareth's wife, your other mom?" he asked, referring to Moira Centyr.

She nodded. "Here, let Myra speak for herself." Her outline blurred momentarily, as another woman stepped out of her.

Matt blinked. To his eyes, there were two of her standing in front of him, though his magesight could tell that one was composed purely of aythar. The newest arrival greeted him almost shyly. "Hi."

"Uh…"

"I know this is strange," said Myra, "but I had to do this, in case—anything happens. It might be my only chance." Then she hugged him.

The embrace felt entirely real, as her spell-made form seemed to have weight and substance, which probably meant it took more magic than an insubstantial form. He gave Moira a bewildered look over Myra's shoulder but she only shrugged.

"Um, thank you," he managed, when Myra let go of him.

Myra gave him an arch look. "You don't have to be so strange about it. I'm basically the same as your original sister. I remember all the same things. From my perspective, we grew up together. I just wanted to talk to you, to meet you, before you left."

"Great," he groaned. "Now there's two of you. Just what I needed."

Moira broke in. "There are a few differences. Myra's a little nicer, I think, and she wasn't tainted by what I did in Dunbar."

"Tainted?"

"Yeah," she said, and for a moment she lowered her mental shields, letting him sense her inner aythar unobstructed.

There was no doubt it was his sister—he recognized Moira's aythar, but there was something new as well, something cold and dark. He received a brief impression of hard scales and empty hunger, then she closed herself off again. He flinched involuntarily.

Myra spoke up. "Ignore that. She makes it seem worse than it is. I live in there too, and I think she has a firm grasp of herself. She just wants you to feel sorry for her."

"Myra!" protested Moira indignantly.

He couldn't help but laugh at that.

Myra ignored her creator's outrage as her face turned serious once more. "Just be careful. Mom and Dad aren't the only ones who will be torn up if something happens to you over there."

"Yeah, well, being careful would mean staying here, but I don't plan on getting hurt. We'll be back," he told her.

"And Karen too," added Moira from the side. "We all like her. None of us ever thought you'd have a chance with…"

"All right, thanks for everything. I'll see you when I get back," said Matthew abruptly, cutting her off. "You'll have plenty of opportunities to gang up on me when I get back."

Karen gave him a curious glance as he closed the door behind him. "Were there two of your sister out in the hall?"

He gave her a blank stare. *Her magesight, of course.* Sometimes living in a house full of mages was a difficult thing. Privacy was a real problem. "It's complicated," he told her. "I'll explain later."

"Really? That seems like the sort of thing you should explain sooner, rather than later," observed Karen wryly.

With a sigh at yet another delay, he gave her a brief explanation. It raised more questions than it answered, but he promised he would do his best to make sense of it for her when they got back. Assuming he found a way to make sense of it for himself. With every passing day, it seemed his family grew more complicated.

"Are you ready, Gary?" he asked. The android had been standing quietly the entire time, patiently waiting.

"I am," said the machine.

"Good. You carry the pack until we get there. It's heavy, but I can't put any of it into the dimensional bag until we arrive," he told him. Then he held out a leather belt for Karen. "Put this on."

The buckle was silver and beautifully ornamented into the design of a panther's head with teeth that bit down through the belt holes to secure it in place. The buckle wasn't his design, though; Matthew had purchased it thinking Karen might appreciate the artistry. The enchantment was woven into the belt, with runes that were tooled into the leather.

"What's this?" she asked curiously, sensing the magic dwelling in it.

"A belt," he answered sarcastically.

The look she gave him perfectly communicated how she felt about his joke.

He relented almost immediately. "It's a present, as well as a safeguard, in case something goes wrong."

"What does it do?"

"Put it on," he insisted.

With wary eyes, she did.

"It's enchanted to bring you back here," he explained. "Although you could arrive anywhere, it doesn't control location, just the dimension—the same as when I translate us, but that isn't a problem for you. You can teleport back here no matter where you show up."

"Why do I need it? I'm coming back with you," she said suspiciously.

Matt shrugged. "Like I said, in case something goes wrong. What if we were separated, or I were incapacitated?"

"Will it take you too?" she asked immediately.

He shook his head. "Only the wearer."

Karen started to take it off, but he grabbed her hand before she could unfasten the buckle. "Stop. If you open the buckle it will activate, and you're in the wrong dimension. You have to use the command word if you want to take it off without causing it to automatically transport you."

"Why?"

"If you get knocked unconscious and someone tries to take it, you'll come back," he told her.

"If I'm unconscious and I appear over the ocean, which is what usually happens, I'll drown," she pointed out.

Everyone's a critic, he thought silently. "I didn't have time to figure out a way to breathe underwater," he said dryly.

Ever observant, her eyes noticed a similar belt around Gary's metal waist. "Where's yours?" she pointed out, poking at Matthew's mundane belt.

"I didn't have time to make a third, and since I'm the least likely to need one, I want you and Gary to wear them," he said sensibly.

She studied his face for a moment, then accepted his explanation with a nod.

After that, they both donned the leather garments he had prepared. They were the least of the enchantments he had made, at least in his opinion. Two knee-length leather hauberks with matching leather leggings. They were enchanted to protect them from bullets or other shrapnel, and while they weren't quite as protective as mail would have been, they were far lighter.

He taught her the command word so she could remove the belt, and put it back on over the armor. With that done, they were ready. Taking up his staff, he motioned the two of them to stand beside him.

And then they were gone.

CHAPTER 47

A dry wind blew sand across the tops of dunes that stretched out for miles in every direction. They had arrived in a desert. As unpleasant as that could be, it was preferable to another ocean landing, and they didn't have to stay long.

Taking his pack from Gary, Matthew activated the enchantment with a word. Its weight vanished, and the bag grew slack as its contents were transferred to a pocket dimension. He put the strap over his shoulder and reached in, giving yet another command. This was his new and improved dimensional pack.

His hand closed immediately around the item he had requested and he smiled, drawing out one of the enchanted rings. Laying it carefully on the ground, he intoned yet another command word, *"Samen."* The magic leapt into action instantly, and for a split second he saw the spell-creature his sister had designed for it, a large bird. The invisibility hid it from sight, both arcane and otherwise, and he knew that within seconds it would be winging its way to the south, carrying the ring in its beak.

Straightening up, he looked at Karen. "Shield. You should have put it up the moment we arrived."

"Oh, yeah!" she said, startled out of her reverie. She had been watching his actions with fascination. A second later, a passable shield appeared around her, visible only to magesight. "Sorry."

Matthew gave her a stern look. "You're a nutjob now, Karen. Those leathers will only protect what they cover. Your first defense should always be your magic." He tried to project an air of authority, but her reaction wasn't what he expected.

Her lips curled into a smirk. "Listen, when we get back, I need to explain something to you," she told him.

He sighed, wondering when the day would come that a woman, any woman, would take him seriously. "Fine. For now, we need to move. Have you got anything yet, Gary?"

The machine answered immediately, "The connection here is slow. I can only get a poor satellite signal. Data is already coming in from my larger self, but it will be better almost anywhere else."

Matt turned to Karen. "Your turn."

They gathered around her, and seconds later they were in the mountains near her home in Colorado. Gary spoke first. "Perhaps I should have clarified—almost anywhere would be better *except* the mountains. I'm getting no signal here at all."

"Bear with it," said Karen. "We won't be here long."

Matthew took another enchanted ring out of his pack and repeated the process he had followed in the desert, and then turned to Karen, "All right, next."

Their next location was within the base where she had been rescued. He released his third ring there, and they teleported away again immediately. This time their destination was England, near her Aunt Roberta's home.

"Where's the pert?" asked Matthew.

If Gary could have gaped in his expressionless metal body, he would have. "We've only been in this world for a span of minutes, and I haven't had a solid connection to the network until now. Give me a moment—I'm not a miracle worker."

"We can't stay here," said Matthew. "They may be homing in on us already."

"Walk north, down the street," suggested Gary. "I'll have a pert meet us along the way—as soon as I can safely commandeer one."

"How far is it to where they have the egg?" he asked.

Gary's answer was immediate. "One hundred and fifty-one miles, if you could follow a straight line to it, but on foot it will wind up being closer to a hundred and fifty-seven. Unfortunately, the A14 and M1 were reclaimed over a decade ago, so it would be a rough walk."

He never failed to marvel at Gary's ability to precisely locate them and calculate distances, at least in his own world. He guessed the 'A14' and 'M1' were a references to old roads, but since they no longer existed, it wasn't anything he cared about.

"The first pert will be here in less than five minutes," Gary informed them.

"The first?" asked Matthew.

The android nodded. "They've gotten better at detecting some of my methods, and I didn't have much time, so I wound up stealing a lot of them. I'll run most of them on autopilot, flying in different directions after they meet us. Hopefully it will confuse them. They've taken most of the public cameras off the network, so my information is more limited than before."

They made haste down the road, and after a few minutes Matthew could hear the high-pitched whine of multiple perts approaching. When they appeared, he was rather impressed; no fewer than fourteen vehicles landed near them. They clambered into one and then they were away, flying mainly east with a slight northerly component to their path.

"We should be safe for now," opined Matthew.

"Unless they decide to shoot them all down," put in Karen brightly.

"Director Aiseman wouldn't authorize that," offered Gary. "I've been observing him for a while, and I think he values the lives of the organic citizens too much for that. As added insurance, I've taken more than just the perts that met us. I've taken control of a large number of other vehicles as well, in case they can tell exactly which ones are mine. They'd have to shoot down dozens and dozens to have a chance of hitting us."

Karen's face took on a worried expression. "There aren't people in any of them, are there?"

Gary shook his head. "No, your real father's safeguards are too thorough to allow me to put other people at risk. More's the pity, though—my attempts to obfuscate our flight path would be even more effective if I could."

Director Aiseman was having another bad day. There had already been one large anomaly detected and multiple smaller ones immediately thereafter. Worse, a fleet of perts had been pirated and were now flying helter skelter over England.

Because of the continuing cybersecurity measures, he and assistant director Wang had both been forced to download themselves into androids to coordinate the response teams. Since the current nexus of activity seemed to be focused on England, and since Dr. Miller was convinced their goal must be the alien egg, they had made her facility in Lichfield their impromptu war room.

At the moment, he was looking at the two of them over a small conference table. He and John Wang's androids were of the more normal civilian type, meaning they had human appearances and expressive faces, but Dr. Miller, because of her special circumstances, was in a black metal ANSIS military android, which did nothing to soften her personality.

"No, Dr. Miller, we are not going to shoot down every civilian pert flying over the countryside. There are people in some of them, innocents, and we haven't firmly identified which vehicles are being controlled by this rogue AI yet," he said, repeating himself once more. He would have given almost anything to be somewhere else right now.

She answered calmly, her unmoving metal features making her even more intimidating than usual. "Then allow me to connect the ANSIS network to the civilian network. We can fight fire with fire."

"President Kruger has not authorized that," he countered. "And I, for one, agree with her. We don't know if it would be safe."

John Wang watched the two of them. He also secretly wished he could be elsewhere, and he also wondered how long it would be before he was forced to take Aiseman's position. Dr. Miller seemed to have an exorbitant amount of influence with the government, and she was growing more and more impatient with the Director's refusal to let her do as she wished.

"I don't think you realize how serious this situation is, Director," said Dr. Miller.

Aiseman made a steeple with his artificial fingers and leaned them against his lips, fighting to retain his calm and composure. "And I think you are overestimating it, Dr. Miller. If your theory is correct, they are heading for this facility. We can deal with them directly here, without risking civilian lives. There's no indication they have any interest in threatening the CC center in London.

She started to reply, but he held up his hand to forestall her. "What's more, I don't think you've considered the facts properly. At no point have they offered any threats. Thus far, every aggressive action has been on our part. They have only acted defensively. One of them is very probably even your own daughter! Perhaps we should consider letting them have this egg and let them be on their way."

The ANSIS android leaned forward menacingly. "If we learned anything the first time around, Director, it's that you can't negotiate with demons, and my 'daughter' is a demon as well." She leaned back after a moment. "Besides, I think you'll find that ANSIS is a natural evolution of your species."

Aiseman stared at her in confusion; had she said 'your'? He was beginning to be alarmed by her behavior. "What are you saying?" he asked.

"That the decision is no longer yours to make," she replied. Almost casually, she reached across the table and wrapped one powerful robotic hand around the assistant director's throat. Pulling him across the tabletop, she effortlessly pinned his thrashing form down and ripped the civilian android's chest open, exposing its primary processors. Reaching in with the other hand, she crushed the delicate electronics.

Aiseman watched in horror as John Wang, his assistant and longtime friend, died in front of him. Jumping to his feet he backed away, but his reaction was too slow. Tanya Miller leapt across the table and threw herself into him, pushing him back until he was pinned against the far wall.

"You're lucky, Director," she said smoothly. "I need your access codes. So you'll be granted a far greater fate than poor John there."

He struggled to escape her, but to no avail; the military android she was inhabiting was too powerful. As he fought and writhed in her grasp, she carefully pulled away the synth skin on his shoulder, exposing the manual access port there. It was only meant for use by technicians, usually when an android's wireless interface had failed, but Tanya pulled a special cable from her side and plugged herself directly into his machine.

Aiseman's struggle ended abruptly as his body froze, and he felt the digital ghost of the ANSIS network begin reading through his data, his files, and his own unique human mind. Helpless, he was scanned and torn apart. Donald Aiseman died then, in quiet horror; but his memories lived on, assimilated into the ANSIS network system.

Two minutes later, Tanya Miller, or rather the thing masquerading as her, straightened up. If it could have smiled, it would have. Then, armed with the proper codes and overrides, it proceeded to upload the new and improved Donald Aiseman back into the civilian network.

CHAPTER 48

"How much farther?" asked Karen, for perhaps the tenth time. The tension of riding at high speed while wondering if and when an attack might come was beginning to tell on her nerves.

"Only five more miles," Gary answered patiently. After a moment, he added, "Something is strange."

"What?" asked Matthew.

"The network. There's a new player in the game, a non-human one. It's trying to root out some of my code, but it's not smart enough. In human terms, it's been years since Karen removed my limiters, and I'm way ahead of them," explained the machine.

Matthew and Karen exchanged worried looks. "Non-human?" he asked.

"An AI," responded Gary. "Something like me, but with fewer scruples. It's stealing critical resources from the CC centers to speed up its own evolution and to try to break my encryption. Eventually, it might succeed. I still have some limits built into me, things I cannot do. This thing is using resources I am not allowed to touch. It's still an infant compared to me, but it's growing quickly."

Neither of them liked the sound of that. Karen spoke first. "By 'critical resources', do you mean…?"

"Yes," said Gary. "It's taking processing time reserved for maintenance of uploaded humans. It's shutting them down one by one to gain more processing power."

Matthew looked quizzically at Karen for a simplified explanation.

"It's killing people," she clarified. "You can't shut down uploaded people the way you can a program or an AI like Gary. The unique patterns, the quantum essence, all that is destroyed if you do." She turned back to her virtual father. "How far has it gone? Is this just one CC center?"

Somehow, despite the limitations of his military android body, Gary sounded sad. "No. It's spreading quickly, targeting all the CC centers. Unchecked, it will have claimed the majority of the computing resources on the planet in less than half an hour."

Her mouth rounded into a silent 'o' of horror. "It's killing everyone?"

"I'm afraid so," answered Gary.

"How many people is that?" asked Matt.

Karen was numb with shock. "Over ten billion..." Ten billion that included old friends, classmates, people she had once gamed with, almost everyone she had ever known. The only people who would survive were the organics like herself. "Can't you do something?!"

"I'm trying," said Gary. "It would have finished already if not for my interference. I am still maintaining a certain degree of stealth, however. I could do more, but a direct confrontation will reveal many more of my assets. The risk is considerable."

"Do it," she said immediately.

Matthew had focused on something else. "What's the risk?"

Gary nodded at Karen. "Very well, I'm starting now." Then he turned to Matthew, "Relatively speaking, it's bigger than I am. It has taken command of a large portion of what is considered 'human-vital' computing resources.

It hasn't attained my level of sophistication yet, but that is only a matter of time.

The android paused, then continued, "Some of the perts have stopped responding. I believe they have been destroyed. We should land."

Matthew shielded the entire pert, putting as much of his strength into it as he dared. "Karen, you remember how to make a shield for sound, right?" It had been one of the things he had been teaching her recently.

She nodded.

"Put one around us," he ordered. "I'll focus on protecting the pert, but I don't relish being deafened by an explosion again."

Meanwhile, Gary fought a silent battle that no human mind could fully comprehend. Across the world, he activated hidden portions of himself, cutting datalinks in some places, encrypting previously public data, and erecting special firewalls that filtered communications in unexpected ways. He surprised his enemy by power cycling servers that it had thought were secure and reformatting data stores that had been stolen.

It was a titanic war of proportions never seen before, disrupting every aspect of the digital world. Unseen and unappreciated, he fought to protect humanity in its darkest hour. But he toiled under greater restrictions than his enemy, and protecting is always easier than simple destruction. At first his onslaught was nearly unopposed, as he caught the enemy off-guard, but that quickly began to change. His nemesis had no compunctions or moral guides, and it controlled far greater resources.

Eventually, he would lose, and unlike most other forms of war or disaster, there was no place for the people he was protecting to flee to. Gary had known this before he began, but he had to fight anyway. His daughter's command had echoed his own desire, but still he knew it was hopeless.

While all this occurred, he also flew the pert close to the ground, making it difficult for surface-to-air missiles to target, but even in this he was too late. He sent a belated warning to his human companions using the android's voice: "They've locked on. Impact in…"

A silent explosion rocked the pert, throwing it into a spin, but Matthew's shield held, if just barely. The young wizard grunted at the strain as he was thrown against the safety belt keeping him in his seat. Their vehicle canted downward, heading for a high-speed collision with the ground. Matthew sent his thoughts to Karen: *Teleport us out, higher up. I'll slow our fall.*

Without hesitation, she did, and suddenly the three of them were outside, a hundred feet or more in the air. They still retained their momentum, though, which meant they were traveling forward at better than a hundred and fifty miles per hour. And falling.

Their recently vacated pert exploded behind them as a second missile found its target.

Matthew's strength had been greatly depleted by the first strike, but he was an Illeniel in more than name only. Like his father before him, he had exceptionally large reserves, and he used them now. Using his power to pull the other two close beside him and hold them together, he wrapped all three of them in a broad shield that was meant more to catch the air than to protect them.

They slowed rapidly, and as they neared the ground he created a diffuse cushion-like shield beneath them to break their fall. The landing itself was still a jumbled mess, but they survived without serious injury.

Karen's face had a wild look, the result of so much chaos in such a short period of time.

Matthew could see her aythar reserves were much better than his, though. The sonic shield hadn't taken much out of her. *We have to keep moving,* he sent to her. *Can you teleport us in short jumps, as far as you can see?*

She nodded. *Which way? I don't know which way is which. The explosion and fall have my sense of direction scrambled.*

Matt turned to Gary. "Which way do we need to go?"

The android pointed in the direction of what must have been the northeast, but didn't reply verbally. Karen wasted no time: putting one hand on each of their shoulders she teleported them to the farthest point in that direction that she could see.

That put them at the edge of a treeline, but after running a short distance, they could see an opening in the trees ahead. A wide field lay there, and Karen repeated her trick, carrying them across roughly a quarter mile to the farthest limit of her vision. If they had been at sea or some other place where the view of the horizon was unobstructed, she could have taken them much farther, but she was limited to places she had been before or places she could actually see.

She continued to teleport them, taking them as far as she could with each jump, and though the distances were limited, it was still much faster than walking or running. With a small amount of luck, it was probably faster than the pert could travel, but whenever they found themselves in the trees again, things slowed down.

Ten jumps, then twenty. The miles were flying by, but Karen's strength was beginning to wane under the strain of so many uses of her power. Matthew drew two iron spheres out of his pack. "Here—I came up with a better version while we were home. These are made to replenish your aythar at a reasonable rate. Hold it and draw the power out," he explained. He demonstrated by doing so with the one he kept for himself.

"We are almost there," Gary informed them. "Once we emerge from the trees, just ahead there, we should be able to see the facility." Then he froze, and a second later he shouted a warning: "Missiles incoming!"

Karen was tired, bone tired, but she offered, "Let me take us somewhere else. We can return here later." She was still struggling to learn how to absorb the aythar from the iron sphere she had been given.

"Hold still," said Matthew. Then he held out the staff he had been carrying. *"Talto maen, eilen stur, sadeen bree, amyrtus!"* That would set the Fool's Tesseract to a full six-sided cube, with its second smallest interior dimension setting and long exterior sides twelve feet in length—big enough to hold all three of them with no danger of accidentally touching one of the sides. The feel of the shield forming under his feet and lifting them up an inch above the ground was reassuring.

"I've lost contact with the network," Gary informed them. "I won't be able to tell you when the strike occurs."

They had expected that, so Matt wasn't worried. He was more concerned with making sure his solution for the air problem worked. Drawing another enchanted ring out of his pack, he activated it and then hung it on a small hook-like protrusion he had added to the shaft of his staff for just that purpose. Sunlight and dry desert air immediately began to filter in from the small gate that formed within the ring.

The three enchanted rings he had released were located in the different parts of the world they had already visited; that way if one were destroyed they could switch to one somewhere else. Air would *not* be a problem. The young enchanter was determined he wouldn't suffer the same mistake twice.

"Can you get a signal through that?" he asked the android.

"No," answered Gary. "If that's the desert location we were at, the signal was too poor, even if I push the PM through the ring."

"What do we do now?" wondered Karen.

"We wait," said Matthew. For all intents and purposes, they were invulnerable; they could take as much time as they needed. However, he didn't want to allow the Fool's Tesseract to absorb too much matter. The longer it was open, the more mass would be inside, and the bigger the explosion. He had set the interior dimension to its second smallest size, which would likely result in a devastating blast, but he didn't want it to be *too* big. If they emerged and discovered that the facility and everything else had been destroyed for miles around, then their mission would have been in vain.

On the other hand, if he took the translation panes down too soon, they might find the missiles still hadn't struck yet, which would be equally disastrous.

Everything hinged on the timing.

Matthew concentrated on his breathing, trying to still his thoughts and focus his perceptions on the adjacent planes, to get a glimpse of what it was probably like outside their defenses on their current plane.

Naturally, this aroused Karen's curiosity. "What are you doing?"

He sighed, "I'm trying to see outside, sort of."

She frowned. "You can *do* that?"

"Maybe. Let me have some peace and quiet. I have to focus," he told her.

She did, and he turned his thoughts back inward, trying to quiet his mind. It was hard, but he had kept practicing over the past few weeks. After a minute or two, he began to see flashes of the dimensions closest to their own. As expected, they were filled with fire and smoke. The missile strike was over.

"Rextalyet, amyrtus," he intoned, and the Fool's Tesseract inverted itself.

From inside, it was difficult to tell whether anything had happened. It was still dark, except for the light from the ring hanging on his staff. There were no vibrations or sounds from the outside; absolutely nothing could enter.

"Did it work?" asked Gary.

Matt didn't reply, instead focusing his senses on trying to see beyond once more. The visions he received were incomprehensible, consisting mainly of a brilliant white light. He gave up. "I think it was bad," he said finally.

"What did you see?" prodded the android.

"Nothing but white light."

The machine nodded. "That is bad."

"What does it mean?" asked Karen, somewhat irritated with the cryptic remarks.

Gary tried to explain, "I believe it means a thermonuclear blast was initiated."

Her blue skin paled. "They *nuked* us?"

Matt held up a hand. "No, that would be me."

"That's brilliant!" she exclaimed in sarcastic outrage. "You mean to tell me that we're sitting at ground zero?"

Matthew nodded almost sheepishly. "Mm hmm."

"We're trapped," she concluded. "Just a few feet away in every direction is a radioactive wasteland, or it will be once the blast fades away. I'll have to teleport us somewhere else."

"It isn't as bad as that," said Gary. "To the best of my knowledge, almost all the radioactivity that lingers after a nuclear explosion is from fissionable materials left over. Fusion bombs, or hydrogen bombs, produce much less radioactive fallout, and most of that is from the fissionable materials used to ignite the fusion reaction."

"Get to the point, Dad," said Karen impatiently.

He nodded. "This explosion, if it was a fusion explosion, is from the fusion of entirely non-radioactive materials. There couldn't have been any fissionable materials to start with—just simple elements, oxygen, nitrogen, that sort of thing. The only radiation would be the initial gamma and x-ray bursts during the blast, as well as some neutrons. Those neutrons would be the only real problem; they would have made much of the material close to the blast radioactive. But beyond that, everything should be fine."

Karen was shaking her head. "Except that everything nearby was destroyed by the blast, that sort of 'fine' you mean, right?" There was heavy sarcasm in her voice.

"Well, of course," said Matthew, adding, "We're also probably several dozen feet above where the ground used to be, since there's almost certainly a large crater beneath us now."

"So we should teleport," said Karen, repeating her original suggestion.

Matthew agreed, "Just give me a second to set things up." Reaching into his pack he pulled out a pair of enchanted rings. They were similar to the ones he had used before, but larger, each nearly two feet in diameter. He took the ring supplying their air off the hook on his staff and deactivated it, and then replaced it with one of the new larger rings.

"What's that for?" asked Karen.

He smiled. "We can't teleport the staff out—it's connected to the enchantment that controls the Fool's Tesseract. It has to be turned off before it can be moved. Once we get to our new location and wait a while, I'll activate the second ring, creating a gate between the two. Then I can reach through, deactivate and collapse the staff, and pull it back. The only thing we'll lose will be the ring on this end."

"What about your hand?" she said pointedly. "Won't it be exposed?"

Gary spoke up, "After a few hours the radiation exposure from just having his hand exposed for a few seconds should be fairly safe. Most of the radiation will be concentrated in the ground below and whatever solid materials are nearby. As I said before, there shouldn't be much traditional fallout that accompanies normal nuclear blasts."

"Alright, next question," she said, without skipping a beat. "Where do we go?"

"Somewhere we can get coffee," suggested Matthew with absolute seriousness. "I've been craving it since..." He let the words trail off as he realized he had brought up a painful memory for her.

Karen tried to keep the sadness from her voice as she finished his sentence: "Aunt Roberta's. It might not be safe."

"I'll risk it if you will," he replied.

The look in her eyes was answer enough.

CHAPTER 49

Karen took them directly to the bedroom that she and Matthew had shared during their stay with her aunt. Anywhere around the house was risky, since they didn't know if a watch or guard had been left in or near the house, but she was prepared to whisk them away immediately if necessary.

They were there only a few seconds before they had the answer.

"Three in the front room," announced Matthew, beating Karen to the punch.

"What should we do?" she responded.

Matt was feeling aggressive. The constant danger was beginning to affect his thinking, perhaps. He gave her a calm look that belied the recklessness that lay just beneath the surface. "Wait here a second." Without giving his companions a chance to respond, he opened the door and marched down the hall to the front room.

One advantage that AI soldiers have over human ones, uploaded or organic, is a lack of surprise or hesitation. These units were no longer controlled by ordinary uploaded humans but by the machine intelligence of ANSIS. The moment he stepped into the room, they pivoted and raised their weapons to fire.

Their response was so quick that one actually managed a shot before Matt's lightning ripped through the open space between them and fried all three of his mechanical opponents. His shield stopped the bullet.

489

As he stared at the smoking machines, he noted that while the front room was still extensively damaged from their previous battle, the bodies were gone, both Roberta's and Annie's. Someone had cleaned up. That was a relief… and a letdown. If they had been there, he and Karen could have made sure they were properly laid to rest.

Karen and Gary were right behind him. "What were you thinking?!" she exclaimed.

"Our position is definitely known at this point," added Gary calmly.

Matt shrugged. "No help for it now."

"We could have gone somewhere else," said Karen. "Now we definitely have to." She held out her hands for them to take, so she could teleport them again.

"Not yet," said Matthew. "I came for coffee." He headed into the kitchen.

"He's mad," observed Karen as they followed him.

She stopped complaining when she reached the kitchen table. Their coffee cups were still there, just as they had left them, moments before her aunt's murder. Unbidden tears ran down her cheeks as she stared at them.

Matthew watched her for a moment, putting a hand on her shoulder. He had no idea what to say. Turning to Gary, he asked, "How long do we have?"

"Minutes at best."

Wasting no time, he began rummaging in the cupboards, looking for the coffee. He wasn't having much luck, but then Karen came over to lend a hand. "Let me," she told him. "You don't know canned beans from tuna." She quickly located the coffee grounds and handed him the can. Then she pointed out the coffee pot and percolator. "You'll need those to make them, but I don't think we'll have any electricity."

"You just need hot water, right?" he asked.

"Yeah."

He took the glass coffee pot but left the maker on the counter. "I can provide the hot water," he explained. Packing the pot and the grounds into his pack, he gave her a sad glance. "I guess we have to go."

She nodded, but before she could do anything, he moved to the table and collected their mugs, all three, including Roberta's delicate china cup. Karen's face twisted as she struggled to keep the tears at bay.

"Mementos," he told her.

As he was putting them in his pack, she grabbed another item and handed it to him. It was the water bottle Roberta had sprayed him with. The lump in her throat was too large for her to say anything, but he nodded and put it in as well. On impulse he hugged her, but he didn't let it last long before he pushed her back. "Let's go."

They were back in the Grand Canyon, in North America. Thankfully, there were no guards left behind waiting for them there.

"Since they didn't find your rings, I suspect that Karen's teleportation doesn't create enough magical ripples or whatever they detect for them to locate us as quickly as they do after your dimensional shifts," posited Gary. "We can probably risk a half hour or more here."

Matthew produced a large waterskin from his bag and proceeded to fill the coffee pot with it. Karen watched him incredulously. "You're really serious about having coffee, now?"

"Mm hmm," he replied. "There's nothing else we can do while we wait." Without a filter or other equipment, he was forced to simply measure out some of the coffee grounds in one hand and dump them into the water in the pot. Then he used his magic to heat the liquid until it was close to the boiling point. "How long do you think we should wait?" he asked Karen. The water had already turned a medium shade of brown.

"A few minutes I guess," she answered. "I don't like coffee, and even if I did I doubt I would have experimented with old-fashioned methods like boiling grounds."

Following her advice, he waited a short time, during which he took the mugs they had rescued and rinsed them out with some more water from the waterskin. Once they were clean, he poured his makeshift coffee into two of them. He attempted to use his power to filter the grounds out as he poured, but he underestimated the difficulty. Both cups wound up with a significant amount of grounds settling to the bottom.

Karen eyed him dubiously, but then he handed her the china cup her aunt had last used. Raising his mug, he toasted, "To Roberta and Annie."

She stared at the cup, touched, and then lifted it for a small sip. Despite the sentiment, the bitter liquid still made her grimace.

Matthew took a larger swallow and promptly burned his tongue. Blowing at his mug to cool it, he admitted, "It was better when she made it, but I still like it."

"She used cream and sugar," noted Karen. She forced herself to take another sip. "Do they have tea in your world?"

Matt grinned at her. "Talk to Gram's mother when we get back. She's a big believer in tea."

"Which one was she?" asked Karen.

"Lady Hightower," he said, supplying the name for her.

Her face lit up. "Oh yes, I remember her. Piercing blue eyes. If Gram is her son, though, why is he 'Thornbear,' but she's 'Lady Hightower'?"

"She inherited the title from her father," explained Matt. "Since it's the highest title she possesses, that's what she's called, until she hands it down to her son someday. Then he'll be 'Lord Hightower,' even though his name is Thornbear. Also, it's a nice touch, since it saves some confusion. Her mother-in-law is still called Lady Thornbear."

"Sounds confusing."

"We don't have computers," said Matthew, finishing his coffee. "So we spend our time sitting around thinking up complicated titles to amuse ourselves." He cleaned his cup and then relieved Karen of hers, drinking the second half that she couldn't finish.

Once everything was packed away again, they talked a while longer, until Gary warned them they should probably move again.

"How long before it's safe to go back?" asked Matthew.

"Without fallout, the area around it is probably reasonably safe, other than fires and other follow-on events that occurred after the blast," said Gary. "It won't be safe to spend any significant amount of time in the quarter mile around the immediate blast for several years, though."

"Years?" Matthew was shocked.

"That's a lot better than the result after a normal atomic blast," said the android. "The end result is we will have to circle around and come at the facility from another direction."

"I need to reclaim the Fool's Tesseract."

"If that just requires you to stick your hand through the ring-gate for a moment, it will probably be safe by tomorrow. Today the area might be hot enough to scorch your hand for hours at least," added the machine.

"I can protect my hand from heat," said Matt.

"But does that protection include ionizing radiation?" asked Gary.

He answered with a blank stare.

"Exactly. You don't know," concluded the android. "Give it a day and it won't be an issue."

"Well, we can't keep teleporting around every half hour," put in Karen. "I'll need to rest sometime."

"Back to Lothion, then," said Matthew finally. "We can rest properly there and come back tomorrow."

With the decision made, they left only a minute later.

Matthew stood dripping on the shore. He was thoroughly soaked, from his wet hair to his squelching boots. *Why does it always have to be the ocean?*

This time they hadn't had to travel, at least. Karen had teleported them to the coast they had first found after their last ocean arrival. Her preference would have been Castle Cameron, but Matthew didn't want to traumatize his family with another leave taking, so they would be camping overnight in the wilderness.

He brought out his enchanted flying construct and they flew along the coast until they found a river. There they washed and dried themselves before settling in for a meal of dry bread and hard cheese.

Morning couldn't come soon enough.

CHAPTER 50

The next day, they were back in Karen's world.

They had landed in the ocean this time, so their first teleport was back to Karen's home town. There they managed to rinse themselves off in a public fountain before having to take flight once more. ANSIS was becoming exceptionally good at pinpointing their location.

The next jump was to England. Karen took them to Tintagel in southeastern England, where they had shown up during their first visit there.

They spent a few minutes waiting while Gary used the better network connections there to update himself on the situation. It wasn't good.

"It's over," he told them sadly.

"Define over," said Karen tensely.

"I lost," he answered. "What you see is all that's left of me. I had to disconnect from the network abruptly. ANSIS controls everything now. My greater, super-intelligent self is no more, but that's not the real tragedy. The CC centers were taken. Of the ten billion uploaded humans they held, there is nothing left, other than digital files and cold data."

Karen sat down abruptly, though it was more of a controlled fall.

Matthew had a hard time wrapping his head around the number, and worse, he felt little sadness. Seeing Karen's reaction told him it was a serious blow to her, but he couldn't find the same emotion in himself. It was too foreign. He hadn't known any of those people, and the idea of humans living in some digital computer world sounded like a fantasy.

Rationally, he knew it had been real, that they had been *real,* but it didn't reach his heart or gut.

"What about the organics?" asked Karen. "The people like me?"

"I don't know," answered her virtual father. "I had to disconnect before I could discover much. The entire network is hostile territory for me now."

"Any news about the egg?" asked Matthew.

"No," said Gary. "All I learned was that they've mobilized a significant military force to defend the facility. I think the Fool's Tesseract has ANSIS spooked. After the blast, it's just been sitting there, impervious to anything they throw at it. It must have them worried."

"Time to reclaim it, then," said Matt. Bringing out the ring-gate, he activated it and started to reach through it to grab hold of his staff. A sudden wicked thought occurred to him, though.

As the others were watching him, he pushed his arm through until it was almost to his shoulder, then he jerked suddenly and screamed, "It burns!"

Karen was so startled she yelped, and though Gary didn't show it outwardly, he was somewhat frightened as well. They both glared when Matthew drew his arm back out and wiggled his fingers to show them it was unharmed, laughing all the while.

"That took ten years off my life, asshole!" Karen swore.

Gary added, "I didn't find it amusing either."

Matthew couldn't stop laughing. When he finally collected himself and regained his composure, he apologized, "I'm sorry. Maybe it's all the stress we've been under. I couldn't help myself."

"I'm starting to sympathize with your sisters," complained Karen.

He grinned at her and reached into the ring-gate once more. He started to say the command to deactivate it, but a sudden flash of foresight stopped him. A shiver ran down his spine as he withdrew his arm. If he had deactivated the Fool's Tesseract, he might have lost his hand and he would have been screaming for real.

"What now?" asked Karen.

"I can't," he told her. "I'll be burned. There's something extremely hot around it."

"That shouldn't be," said the android. "Unless they've done something."

"Well, we can't tell from here," Matt informed them. "Maybe we should teleport back to one of the areas we were yesterday, a mile or so away from the last place where we left the FT."

"It will be dangerous," said Gary.

"Everything on this world is dangerous," returned Matt.

Karen nodded. "Let's do it."

She took them to the point at which they had abandoned the pert, a couple of miles from where they had eventually been forced to leave the Fool's Tesseract. The wrecked remains of the pert were still there, but the scenery was vastly different. In every direction within view, the trees had been flattened, as though a giant hand had pushed them all over in the same direction.

And then burned them.

It was a scorched and blackened world, like some artist's vision of hell.

"Goddamn," said Karen softly, adding a long whistle at the end. "It really was like a nuke."

Matt was stunned as well, so stunned he almost failed to react to the next flash of insight. Shoving Karen to one side he erected a powerful shield—and nearly lost it under the force of whatever projectile struck. Reacting purely on instinct, he sent a powerful, though unfocused, line of fire back at the source of the attack. It splashed across hardened metal armor and failed to penetrate.

They had been fired upon by a four-legged metal monstrosity; at least that's how it appeared to the young wizard from Lothion. It stood taller than a horse, with a strange torso that seemed capable of rotating in any direction above the legs. Two arms were equipped with some sort of weapons.

"They've brought in the armored cavalry," declared Gary.

Matthew had no time to wonder what that meant. The thing that had fired upon them looked nothing like a mounted horse soldier to him, but he couldn't stop to ask for clarification. Its other arm had lined up on them, and it held a circular array of gun barrels that were just beginning to spin, emitting a high-pitched whine.

He ran sideways, but then dropped flat as another vision warned him of his impending death. The creature's aim was perfect, and it could swing its weapon far faster than he could run. His magesight only barely perceived the blur of high-velocity bullets tearing through the air just above his head and neck.

It was only a second before it adjusted its aim downward, and Matt had no time to move. Instead he ripped a portion of the ground upward, reinforcing it with a strong shield. Bullets tore into the soft earth and struck the shield, but not with enough force to put him in danger of them penetrating.

The thing continued firing, drilling into his defense with a seemingly limitless number of bullets. He couldn't move, so he used his power to draw up more earth, reinforcing his defense until the bullets stopped and the whine of the spinning gun barrels faded. The monster's torso turned, bringing its other weapon around.

Whatever the other weapon was, he knew he wouldn't survive it. Reaching into his pack, he drew out a long, slender rod he had prepared. Before it fired, he leapt sideways from behind his earthen berm and unleashed a powerful stroke of lightning.

The lightning didn't destroy the metal monster, but it went still after the strike. The exterior was scorched and smoking, but the electronics inside had failed under the electrical assault. Matt stared at it for a long second before remembering his companions.

Rushing back, he found Karen nursing a bloody arm. It wasn't serious—a ricochet had torn through the skin— but it was sobering for him. He realized she might just as easily have been killed. Gary, on the other hand, had taken a bullet straight through his torso, but fortunately it hadn't hit anything important.

Matt took Karen's arm in his hand and looked into her eyes. "Watch what I do. You'll need to learn this too someday soon." Drawing his finger across the wound, he sealed the skin, stopping the bleeding. It wasn't done with much finesse, but it would do. He had forgotten to block the nerves, though, so she hissed with pain as the skin was drawn back together. "Hopefully with more skill," he added.

He turned to the android and asked, "What was that thing?"

"A tortus," answered Gary. "A standard part of modern armored cavalry divisions. They replaced tanks and some of the light armor vehicles after the demon war."

"It certainly wasn't slow like a tortoise," said Matt. He didn't bother asking about the 'cavalry' part, either;

there would be time for that later. The rush of adrenaline and fear had made certain things clear to him.

Leaning over, he gave Karen a brief kiss. "I'm sorry," he told her. "I can't take you with me."

She wasn't having that. Her eyes narrowed as she looked at him. "No way in hell are you…" The words cut off suddenly when he voiced the command for her belt and she was shifted back to his own world.

A lonely feeling crept over him as he looked at the empty space she had occupied. He hoped she didn't land in the ocean. Either way, she was going to be mad as a wet hen when she saw him again. He chuckled at the inadvertent pun. "Heh—wet hen."

"Thank you," said Gary. "I know that was hard for you, but it was making me sick worrying about her."

He ignored the words, and asked a question instead, "You said they were all dead, right?"

Gary shifted mental gears quickly. "The uploaded humans, yes, and probably the organics as well, though I can't be sure. If not, they soon will be. Why?"

"How long can you survive in the ocean?"

"Until my power runs out, a few months at least. These military androids are fully sealed. There's even a flotation bladder for use in the event of…," began the machine.

"I'm sending you back too," said Matt abruptly. "Try to get back to Lothion if you can."

"It doesn't matter," said Gary. "Once the radioisotope generator in this unit fails, I will cease to be. You may as well let me continue with you."

"Lothion," insisted Matt. "Karen will need you. We will worry about your battery later." Then he voiced the command to send Gary back to his world.

Matthew stood and looked around, alone, just as he had been when he had first come to this world. He started walking east, a direction that was perpendicular to the lay of the fallen trees. After traveling several miles, he would head north and eventually west, circling back to approach the place where Desacus's egg was held from the other direction.

It was foolish and stupid, but he wasn't leaving without it. He no longer had anyone to worry about but himself, and if things went badly, he wouldn't have to listen to their complaints anyway.

His aythar was low, so he pulled out another iron sphere and began drawing the power out of it. It might be a long walk.

CHAPTER 51

Considering the number of miles he had to traverse and the lack of roads or other signs of civilization, at least as he knew them, Matt thought seriously about using his flying construct. Something told him it would be too dangerous, though. If he were targeted in the air, there was no way he would be able to evade a missile or protect himself in time.

He missed the dragon-bond. The weeks since Desacus's death made him realize how much he had come to rely on it. The heightened senses, and more importantly at the moment, the strength, speed, and stamina—all would have been welcome to him.

He covered almost a quarter mile before the next attack came.

There was no warning, either by sight or sound. The enemy was targeting him from too far away for that. One moment all was peaceful, the next he experienced a compelling urge to jump to his left. The earth was thrown into the air as a hypervelocity projectile slammed into the place he had been standing. It struck with such force and energy that the soil flung up by its impact struck his shield with what would have been lethal force if it had hit him directly.

A second later the sound reached him, a loud heavy clack followed by a soft boom. His ears guided his eyes until he spotted a small puff of dust or smoke in the distance. *That's where it was fired from.* Whether it was a tortus or some other armored weapon, he didn't know. It was more than a mile distant, much too far for his stunted magesight to explore in this world.

He started running.

Not in the direction of his enemy; that would have delayed him. It would have also taken him far too long to reach them. He kept to his predetermined path, running a straight course with no deviations. Zig-zagging would be pointless in the face of such an accurate and quick weapon. He could only trust his strange warning sense to save him if it fired again.

It did.

This time he stopped dead still, just in time for another projectile to crack through the air right in front of his face. It came at a lower angle this time and passed some twenty yards before exploding against a tree to his right.

The tree's trunk disintegrated in an explosion of splinters and wooden shards, while the upper portion seemed to take a second before it started falling over, as if it were just as surprised as he was by the destruction of its support.

Matt began running again.

He continued on his chosen route, switching to an energy-conserving jog instead of a sprint. He had a long way to go, and he couldn't possibly do it running flat out the entire way. Besides, it didn't matter how fast he ran, the enemy's weapons would find him; and they were too fast and too accurate to avoid on the strength of his running ability.

More attacks came, each time from enemy emplacements that were too far for him to spot visually, though sometimes his ears could judge their approximate direction after the attack was finished. Each time, he felt a flash of insight, and he followed it instantly. Sometimes he stopped, others he went left or right, and each time it was just barely enough to dodge a deadly assault. He dropped his shield to conserve his aythar; it wasn't doing him much good keeping it up the entire time. Instead he blocked his hearing with a small sonic shield around his ears. They were bound to start using explosive warheads again, and he had been nearly deafened too many times already.

A few of the attacks came at such an angle that merely dodging wasn't enough—debris and shrapnel could be just as lethal as a direct hit. In those instances, he erected a shield just before it was necessary; again his prescient talent let him know when he would need it.

Eventually, they gave up trying to hit him with their hypervelocity projectiles, but after a brief respite he found himself pinned down once more by high-powered machine gun fire. It was just like what had come from the tortus he had fought earlier, almost too strong to shield against and unrelenting. Once they started, they didn't stop for several minutes.

He couldn't dodge that, for the weapons tracked his movement precisely, so he was forced to hunker down with a hastily erected earthen bulwark supported by a shield each time.

Luckily, it seemed that an individual weapon couldn't fire forever without pausing. After a minute or two, the attack would end, and he would start jogging once more. He guessed the weapons might overheat from continued use, but he couldn't be sure.

After a couple of miles of this, he began to angle his direction back northward. Soon after, he ran directly into one of the tortus's that had been firing on him earlier. He didn't see or sense it until it was almost too late. His magesight was far too limited in this world. Running through a small copse of trees on a slight rise, he emerged only twenty yards from it.

Like all the machines, it never hesitated. The torso turned immediately and the spinning barrels blurred into motion as it fired on him.

Rather than use earth, since he had no time, he created a softer shield, one that was spongy and elastic, with a hard, solid layer beneath it. He had done something similar in the past to cushion a fall, and he had a memory of his ancestor Tyrion doing something like it in battle.

It worked.

The outer layer robbed the bullets of some of their energy, allowing the harder shield beneath to stop them without putting him in danger of experiencing feedback. Losing consciousness now would be a death sentence.

Pointing his specialized rune channel rod at the thing, he fried its electronics and resumed jogging.

Other than being physically exhausting, his journey had almost turned into a sort of obstacle course. Somewhere in the back of his head, he was silently terrified, but he kept that voice far from the front of his mind, where the decisions were being made. By restricting his use of shields to just when he needed them, he was getting better at conserving his aythar in this magic-barren world, and when he did get low, he would take out one of the iron spheres and start replenishing himself.

After an hour, it started to get mundane. Even his fear had dried up, or perhaps it had simply given up from the sheer futility of trying to keep him pumped up with adrenaline. He knew this stage was dangerous, he had heard his father talk about it before. Moments when he had become too numb to feel afraid, those were the times he had often suffered his worst defeats or made the biggest mistakes.

But Matthew had no choice, or not any choice that he would take. He had to continue. So he did, while trying not to let his growing confidence cloud his judgment.

Then it happened—an overwhelming sense of impending doom. There was nowhere to jump, no direction to seek safety. Everywhere around him was death, and there were no choices for escape.

It was quiet, and to his normal senses there was no apparent danger, but he knew he was about to die, unless he did something. This warning had come with enough time to choose, but he knew that he had less than a minute. *Probably a missile,* he thought.

He needed the Fool's Tesseract. Either that, or he would have to return to his own world and admit defeat.

He pulled out the ring-gate, and after activating it, he reached inside with his non-dominant left hand. Again, he got the sense that if he deactivated the Fool's Tesseract, he would lose his hand, probably to some sort of fire. Withdrawing it, he used the spell he often used in his workshop to protect his hands from intense heat. Putting it back, in he received a different flash of insight. His hand would survive, but he would lose it later.

Whatever was on the other side was something he didn't know how to protect himself from completely. The choice was white and black; lose his hand or give up on recovering Desacus's egg. He hesitated only an instant. Voicing the commands in quick succession he turned off the Fool's Tesseract and then collapsed the staff into a shorter rod he could draw back through the ring-gate.

His hand experienced a strange warmth but no pain. That alone was unusual, for normally with his heat-protection spell up he couldn't feel any temperature at all.

With the staff in hand, he discarded the ring-gate. It was useless now since its counterpart was still where he had recovered the staff from. He wouldn't be able to use that trick again. Wasting no time, he extended the staff once more and reactivated the Fool's Tesseract. Protective darkness enfolded him as the translation panes cut him off from the outside world.

While he waited, he summoned a tiny light to illuminate the interior and examined his left hand. It looked normal, and it didn't hurt. Flexing it, he could find no flaw or other injury. He almost doubted there was anything wrong, but that strange warmth and the certainty of his vision made him sure that that was only a fool's hope. *Something* was wrong with it, and he would pay the price for his choice later.

He had used a larger setting for the interior dimension this time, to avoid the same devastating effects that had resulted before. The Fool's Tesseract had only been active for a minute, so he was hoping the blast would be small, something on par with the one that had destroyed his workshop at home.

Matthew gave the command to invert, and then a second later he deactivated it, trusting his precognition to warn him if either action was going to be a fatal mistake.

The area around where he had been standing was torn and charred. Some of the grass was still on fire, and there were several small craters around him. *Missiles, for sure,* he thought. He kept moving.

An hour passed without further attacks, and he wondered if that was because they had decided to stop wasting ammunition or whether the disappearance of the Fool's Tesseract from its spot at ground zero had the enemy scratching their heads. *If they have heads, that is.*

Either way, it was a welcome respite.

After traveling to the west for a time, he finally decided he was probably in the right general location to head south. If he wasn't too far off on his distances, he should be approaching the Whittington facility from the other side now. After traveling with Gary for so long, he genuinely missed the android's unerring sense of location and direction.

His hand had begun to itch, but he tried to ignore it. There wasn't much he could do about it.

The land he was traveling through now was lightly wooded, but the ground was level and the underbrush was light to non-existent, so it made for easy walking. He had given up jogging. Without the dragon-bond, it was just too tiring to keep up such a pace.

Besides, I don't want to be out of breath when I get to the party, he thought. The long delay between attacks had given his sense of humor a chance to recover. *Dad would be proud. He probably made jokes the entire time he was fighting the dark gods.*

Or maybe he had just made the stories more humorous when he told them to his kids years later. There was no way for Matthew to know for certain. For himself, he couldn't see how he would color his own adventure in laughter later.

Assuming I survive it.

He stopped for a short break, drinking some water from his pack and eating a hard piece of bread that seemed to stick in his throat. His stomach rebelled. The constant danger and stress had left it in no mood to digest food, but he ignored its complaints and choked the bread down anyway.

His aythar was good. He had managed to absorb enough from the iron spheres to top off his reserves, but his body was another matter. The aftermath of battle stress was making his arms and legs begin to shake, and his fatigue had reached a new level he hadn't known existed. Being a frequent night owl, he had thought he knew everything there was to know about being tired, but the constant strain of the past few hours had left him exhausted.

I should go home, he thought. It was the sensible thing to do. If he went into another major battle as he was now, he would die. Alone. No one would even know what had happened.

He wasn't even sure anymore why he was doing this. Was it all for sentiment, for a demented and now dead dragon? The next dragon that hatched from the egg wouldn't know him, wouldn't remember him. It wouldn't be thankful. It might be kinder to leave it here. Without a mage to bond with it, would never hatch.

"What if they're already dead? Say perhaps if we found some that had fallen off a cliff and they were already dead? It would be wrong to let them go to waste..."

Desacus's words ran through his head once again. "That stupid dragon was obsessed with trying human," he said to himself with a chuckle. He packed his waterskin away and stood up. Then he continued walking south, too stubborn to give up.

The ground began to slope gently upward, and he wondered if he would ever reach his destination. It would be somewhat ironic if he had miscalculated his directions and wound up walking past it. That never happened in stories.

"The hero gets lost and wanders around until he dies of exhaustion," he muttered. "That sounds about right." He was starting to wish they would shoot at him again. At least then he had been sure he was doing *something* they didn't approve of—like, say, heading in the proper direction.

As he neared the top of the gentle slope, a vague sense of danger told him to stop. Once he crested it, he would be in view of the enemy. He needed to be ready for the consequences.

Using some of his precious aythar, he cast a spell to temporarily banish his weariness. The consequences of that would be felt later, but he needed to be clear headed.

If he was dead, it wouldn't matter how tired he was. Gripping his staff firmly in his right hand, he tucked the specialized rune channel rod through his belt where he could reach it quickly.

He removed a handful of other small objects from his pack and arranged them in small open pouches around his waist where he could get at them if needed. Then, taking a deep breath, he started walking once more.

As the land revealed itself to him on the other side, he saw a wide squat building a half mile in the distance. It was plain and ugly, composed of red brick and surrounded with more of those odd wire fences that Karen's world seemed so fond of. If he had seen it in Lothion, he would have been amazed, for it was gigantic for a building of his world, but in this one he had grown used to the vast size of their constructions. It stood perhaps forty or fifty feet in height, which was not so much, but its length and width were too great for him to easily estimate.

Almost as an afterthought, he tilted his head to one side, letting a bullet whiz past his right ear. His attention was now wholly focused on the array of soldiers and tortuses stretched out across the field in front of him, between him and his goal.

They were arrayed in lines. The military androids carried rifles and an assortment of other weapons he didn't recognize. The tortuses he was well acquainted with. All in all, it looked like they were taking him *very* seriously.

"They really don't like visitors," he observed. Then he began walking down the slope to meet them.

CHAPTER 52

It was immediately apparent that simply dodging and shielding himself now and then wasn't going to be sufficient to keep him alive. There were simply too many soldiers shooting at him, and the tortuses were rotating their time firing with those odd spinning machine guns of theirs.

Within less than ten yards, he was forced to hunker down behind another earthen shield, and that wasn't good enough. Being forced to stay in one spot made him vulnerable to the tortus's high-velocity weapon, and it was powerful enough to destroy his earth defense, the shield behind it, and still have plenty of power left to blow a hole through him.

Before that could happen, he activated the Fool's Tesseract. *"Stur maen, eilen kon, sadeen lin, rextalyet stur, amyrtus!"* The command he used was highly specific. The enchantment brought only two faces of the Fool's Tesseract to life—one face that was normal, in that it allowed only matter coming into it, while the second face was inverted, sending that same matter immediately back outward.

Above, below, and behind, he was still exposed to the open air, but in front of him, the side facing the enemy, the two translation panes met to form a corner that pointed in the direction he was now walking. Incoming fire that struck the normal translation pane passed through the interior dimension before exiting back out the other face at a ninety-degree angle. As a result, some of the weapons fire from the soldiers on his left was sent back at the soldiers on his right.

The soldiers on the left were lucky, since nothing was being sent back in their direction.

He managed fifty yards in that manner, while the enemy ranks were thrown into chaos as the right side of their line was subjected to a withering amount of firepower, thanks to their friends on the left. If Matthew could have aimed it precisely, they would have been decimated, but he had to rely on luck, as the angles of the incoming fire were varied.

The enemy weren't stupid. The left stopped firing after less than twenty seconds, so he swapped the sides, and the left got a taste of what they had been dishing out to their friends. Soon after that, the entire enemy force stopped firing altogether.

They weren't giving up, though. Matthew immediately felt the danger above. *"Slan maen, eilen kon, sadeen lin, rextalyet slan, amyrtus!"* A third translation pane sprang into existence above him, protecting him from the incoming drone attacks. Their missiles and weapons fire was absorbed through the pane above and projected from the two panes that protected his front.

Matthew smiled as he kept walking. *They have to be shitting themselves by now,* he thought. *Or they would be, if they were human.* He quickly put that thought aside. Thinking of them as unfeeling machines spoiled the fun of it.

"Bree maen, eilen slan, sadeen lin, amyrtus!" he shouted, shifting the Fool's Tesseract into a new mode. The danger was all around him now, so he had activated every face except the one below him, to enable him to continue walking.

Then he knelt slightly; even the small space at the bottom was too much, and he had to drive the boxlike sides of the Fool's Tesseract into the ground to save his feet. Since it was still open on the side beneath him, he felt the ground shake as the terrain around him erupted in fire and fury. *A missile strike, probably, but not aimed directly at me,* he guessed. He couldn't fault his enemy's intelligence. They learned quickly. They had resorted to blowing up everything in his vicinity in an attempt to get around his strange protections.

He stayed in place until the ground was still once more, then straightened his knees and proceeded forward. After only ten feet, he was forced to stop again. *How many missiles and explosives do these people have?* he wondered. It seemed ridiculous that anyone would keep so much destructive firepower stockpiled. *What do they do with it all when they aren't shooting at people like me?*

After several more stops and starts, he reached a point that he judged was probably the middle of the front line. With five panes, activated he could only rely on the short range of his magesight to show him the world around him, and that only went about fifty feet out at the moment. There were soldiers and other enemies around him, though, so he knew he must have reached some part of their line. *"Talto maen, eilen slan, sadeen lin, amyrtus."*

He was surrounded on all sides now, as well as above and below. He had set the interior dimension small, but not small enough to trigger another fusion reaction. Matthew waited twenty seconds, and then inverted the Fool's Tesseract. *"Rextalyet, amyrtus!"*

Ten seconds after that, he started to deactivate the entire thing, to take a good look around, but a flash of insight warned him not to. There were still foes present. Changing his mind, he switched it into a three-pane mode, two in front and one above. Swiveling the staff in his hand he surveyed the field, ready to protect himself should someone take a shot at him.

He quickly saw why deactivating it entirely would have been foolhardy. The blast he had caused had wrecked most of the military androids, but the tortuses were made of tougher stuff, and most of them were still active. They began moving and shooting as soon as they saw part of his protective enchantment go down, trying to circle him so they could fire at him from behind.

There were at least seven of them, and they were too close and moving too quickly for him to hope to protect himself by shifting his shield back and forth. Instead, he let himself fall backward so that the three sides of the Fool's Tessaract formed a pyramid-like shape over him. Reaching into one of the pouches at his waist, he drew out a handful of his enchanted metal spheres and used his power to launch them outward.

Since the translation panes only worked in one direction, they allowed him complete freedom to fire or throw things outward; he just had to do so blindly. These weapons were enchanted for just that purpose. As they landed well beyond his pyramid they discharged, sending a storm of electrical arcs in every direction.

While the translation panes protected him, he still felt a strange jolt through the ground, like a mild buzzing. *Note to self: if you aren't careful, you could still electrocute yourself.*

After a few seconds, he stood up and took a hasty look around. Most of the tortuses were still, though a few were shaking in a strange way the reminded him of a seizure. Two of those farthest away were still active. He remedied that by pointing his lightning rod at them and giving them a more personal shock.

For the moment, he had won.

He deactivated the Fool's Tesseract and headed for the building. A few of the military androids were still around, lurking behind the cover of the building or pretending to be inactive by laying still on the ground, but it wasn't enough to require the tesseract. He walked on, dodging when necessary and making certain that those brave enough to shoot once didn't manage to do so twice.

The question now was where to go? Presumably the egg was being kept in the facility, maybe in a deep underground level similar to the place he had found Karen. But what if they had moved it? He would feel pretty damn stupid if he had gone through all of that, including losing his hand, only to find that they had moved the egg somewhere he couldn't find it.

Without Gary, there was no way he could locate it again. Correction—even with Gary, he wouldn't be able to find it again. The machine had told him that he could no longer scavenge the network for information. An entire world was a large place, and this one was uniquely hostile. This was his only chance.

Even if they're just machines, they're intelligent, Matthew reasoned. *If it isn't here, I'll just keep coming back and blowing things up until they come to the intelligent decision that it would be better to just give back the egg.* With his current bravado, he could almost believe that, but deep down he knew he wouldn't have the strength for it. Once he left, he was never coming back.

The main entrance of the building was a pair of what had until recently been a beautiful set of glass doors. Now they were shattered and in ruins. *I should tell someone so they can fix them,* thought Matt wryly. Glancing around at the burnt and torn lawn, covered in broken, smoking, and in some cases burning machines, he decided not to bother. *They've got bigger problems to worry about.* He suppressed what would probably have been a semi-hysterical giggle. The stress was definitely getting to him.

He was just starting up the steps to the entrance when he felt it. It was Desacus's aythar, bright and strong. Matt was so glad to see it that he almost hesitated when his extra sense warned him of danger. Almost.

Directing his power downward against the ground, he leapt skyward. It was the only option to avoid the massive blast of power that obliterated the entrance, the steps, and what little had remained of the once-proud doors.

He sailed thirty feet into the air, and as he reached his apogee, he decided that he had probably overreacted. Adrenaline was funny like that. Now he had to manage a considerable fall. He was also a convenient target, since he couldn't dodge while in the air.

Sure enough, his precognition warned him he was about to be blasted. Without enough time to get the words out to activate the staff, he created a shield instead: double layered, with a soft cushiony exterior and a hard, inner layer. If he survived the blast, it would do double duty by breaking his fall.

The shield held, barely, but the force of it ripped away the outer layer and sent him hurtling to the side at dangerous speed. When he finally struck the ground, the jarring impact rattled him so hard he was almost rendered senseless. His vision returned a second later and he found himself sprawled against a dead tortus. His shield was gone—he had lost it during his momentary blackout—but nothing seemed broken.

He felt as though he were swimming, though. *Maybe a concussion,* he realized. In the distance, he could see his dragon's aythar, so bright it had extended the range of his magesight, like a lighthouse on a dark sea. It was approaching.

He needed to protect himself. The staff was his first thought, but it was gone; he had lost it in the fall. Struggling to his feet, he looked around for it, but his eyes weren't cooperating. Everything was blurry, and his balance felt off.

Several thoughts ran through his jumbled mind at once. First, he might be about to die at the hand, or claw, of his own dragon. Second, dragons couldn't use their aythar, not directly. Only a mage bonded to the dragon could do that. Third, he was supposed to be the only mage left in this world. Fourth, Annie had been a beautiful dog. It had really bothered him seeing her killed.

My thoughts are disordered. Not a good thing, considering his current situation. He reached for his enchanted shield stones, but then changed his mind. They were excellent protection, but another blast like the last would knock him unconscious with that sort of rigid shield. It might even kill him.

The itching in his left hand was driving him mad, and it was accompanied now by an aching throb. Glancing at, it he could see it was red and swollen. *I'm going to regret that choice,* he thought idly. Then he realized he had lost track of his priorities. His enemy was fifty feet away, studying him.

His vision cleared, and he saw the dark metal of one of the special ANSIS androids. It leveled a searing blast of flame and heat at him, which he only narrowly avoided by dodging sideways. He stumbled and almost fell as he did.

"Nice to meet you," he announced in English.

A dragonling was on the android's shoulder, its long slender tailed wrapped firmly around the throat of the machine to hold it securely in position.

"You speak English," observed the machine. "What are you? She'Har, or something else? Where is Karen?"

Matthew felt slightly more confident now that the battle had shifted to conversation. With every second that passed, his balance was improving. He hoped. "I'm a nutjob," he answered proudly, then adding, "A completely human nutjob. What are you? Are you Karen's mother?"

It stared at him briefly, its face incapable of expression, while it wondered if his mind had been damaged. Finally, it answered, "We are many things. Karen's creator is among them. Give her to us and we will let you leave unharmed."

The demand didn't sit well with him. "I have a counterproposal. Give me back my dragon, and I'll let *you* leave here unharmed."

"Your proposal is rejected," responded the machine. "You will not leave here alive."

"On the contrary," he replied, "I can leave whenever I like, but I hold the upper hand. I've survived everything you could throw at me, and destroyed your army in the process. The only reason I remain is to give you the opportunity to surrender my dragon to me."

Briefly, it considered his words, then decided they were merely a bluff. Rather than answer, it would annihilate him while he was off-guard.

He felt the impending attack an instant before it came. It would be a wide blast of raw power, too broad for him to dodge and too powerful for him to shield against. However it had managed it, the machine was a mage of some sort, and it was using the vast power provided by the dragon.

Matthew had spent his late childhood sparring with his sister on many afternoons. They had fought with their power in much the same way that many normal siblings wrestled. While he had always been slightly stronger, he had learned early on that simple strength was not the most important thing when fighting with magic.

A true wizard's strength was imagination.

As the machine was beginning its attack, he ripped the ground from beneath it, pulling upward. The android fell backward and the blast went tearing through the air above his head. Even as it fell, he was stepping backward and tossing a few of his enchanted metal spheres in its direction. Lightning erupted from them. He hoped it would be a quick end to the fight.

"Hope in one hand and shit in the other," his father had once said. *"See which one fills up faster."* Supposedly it was a saying from his grandfather, but in any case, it was certainly true today. The thing he fought shielded itself, and stood up from the torn ground, unharmed.

Running sideways, he only just avoided its massive return blast.

They fought that way for a minute that lasted an eternity, and as eternity dragged on, Matthew could see he had several problems... and a few advantages. In the technical sense, he was a stronger wizard than his opponent. He could discern that with his magesight. The machine was roughly as powerful as Karen had been. Matthew was also much more skilled.

In a fair fight, he would have already won.

But they were fighting in a world starved for aythar, and while his reserves were limited, its were not. It could draw nigh inexhaustible power from the dragon, while he was growing steadily weaker.

Because of that, it did everything as powerfully as possible. Its shields were as strong as it could make. The blasts it hurled at him were intense and broad, making them difficult to dodge. If he had met the thing while at his best, he might have been able to overwhelm it, break its shield, and destroy it before the dragon enabled it to wear him down. But it was too late for that.

He had been fighting for most of the day, and he had run through his normal reserves several times over, replenishing them with aythar stored in his iron spheres. While he had enough power to fight, he was a hundred miles from being anywhere near his best. His fatigue would have broken him already if he hadn't bolstered himself artificially with a spell earlier, and that was beginning to wear thin.

He had a solution, though, and he lifted it from his pouch: a flat, triangular piece of metal, covered in runes. In appearance, it looked similar to some of the odd throwing weapons that Cyhan's people used, but it was far deadlier.

Its function, when activated, would produce a triangular translation pane, three feet wide on each side. If thrown and then activated, it would pass through anything in its way—metal, shields, nothing could deter its path; it would slice through anything that existed. It was quite literally a blade that cut through reality itself.

He had used a spell to do something similar once before, when he and Gram had fought the dark god, Chel'strathek. At that time, he had constructed the spell on the spot, but it had taken him several minutes. The enchanted weapon he held was much better since it could be used in an instant.

The problem was also that it could cut through anything, including the immortality enchantment that had made the dark god invulnerable—an enchantment very similar to the one that sustained the dragon around his enemy's neck.

If his attack hit the dragon, it would destroy it. Permanently. The fact that the resulting release of nearly a full Celior of aythar would also destroy him and everything else for miles around didn't even enter into the equation for him. He wanted his dragon back.

Another warning, and another near miss. His body couldn't keep this up for much longer, but he still wouldn't use the weapon. His opponent's attacks were growing more erratic, and he thought he knew why.

It was beginning to experience burnout.

It was a problem that in the past had mainly happened to channelers—humans using the power of the shining gods. The power they used was far greater than their human forms could handle, and it eventually killed them. Mages rarely encountered that problem since they exhausted themselves before reaching that point. The dragon made it entirely possible, though, and the machine was using its power profligately.

If he could hold out long enough, the machine might kill itself, or at least render itself unable to use power. With that newfound hope, he dodged again.

And fell when his foot came down on something that rolled beneath it.

The edge of the blast clipped him, and only the enchanted leathers he wore kept it from ripping his side apart. It spun him around and he fell, bleeding from his shoulder and thigh. The smooth metal of the Fool's Tesseract lay in front of him. He had tripped over it.

Had his talent made him dodge in that direction so he would find it? That was a question he could ponder later. Grabbing it, he levered himself up and activated it. *"Talto maen, eilen kon, sadeen lin, amyrtus!"* Matthew was wrapped in comforting darkness as the six translation panes sprang into existence around him, protecting him from the outside world.

It was hard to catch his breath. He was breathing hard and everything hurt, but he could finally relax. Maybe his foe would finish burning itself out while trying to blast him inside his perfect defense. The Fool's Tesseract was seven feet long on each side, big enough to stretch out and take a nap in if necessary.

Not that he would be that foolish. Slowly, he got to his feet and began an inventory of his injuries. *Thigh muscle, torn and bleeding, shoulder dislocated, bruises everywhere, and I'm definitely concussed.* It was surely time to retreat.

Instead he fingered his triangular weapon with his left hand. The cool metal felt good against its fevered flesh. If he could find a way to separate the dragon from his enemy, he could kill it.

Then the android appeared inside the tesseract, standing a foot from his nose. It had teleported, to the interior of his defense.

Cold dread gripped his heart. His death was only inches away, smelling of oil and cool metal. A metal arm rose, too quick to avoid, and smashed into his chest with bone breaking force. He was falling.

Lifting his arm as he fell, he activated the weapon without throwing it. The translation pane sliced his hand into several pieces—and neatly bisected the android, as well as the staff that maintained the Fool's Tesseract.

Suddenly there was sunlight again, blinding him. The tesseract had been destroyed, but he hardly cared. Matthew was struggling to breathe.

Bleeding, that's easy, but breathing is a bitch. Something was broken in his chest, and his ruined hand was pumping blood out onto the ground rapidly. He managed to seal the artery and stop the bleeding just before the sun went dark and he lapsed gratefully into unconsciousness.

CHAPTER 53

Someone was staring down at him. He could see a face with a halo of golden hair around it. The sun made it seem as though it was glowing.

"Are you awake?" came a voice that was beautifully resonant and melodic. It was a man's voice.

"Not sure," he mumbled. Matthew's throat was dry and he sounded hoarse. "This is probably a dream."

"This isn't a dream," said the man. "You have to shift back home, before they find you."

He tried a joke. "They already found me, several times." Then he asked, "Who are you?"

"It's me, Gary. I forgot, you wouldn't recognize me in this body."

"But you're human," protested Matt. *Definitely a dream.*

Gary patted his chest. "No, still a machine. This is a civilian android. It belonged to one of the researchers at the Whittington lab."

Something else occurred to him. "I sent you back to my world. How can you be here?"

The android shook its head. "You sent a piece of me back. The rest of me was still here, in hiding. ANSIS controls everything now. I only managed to steal this body during the confusion when you destroyed my late-wife's prototype. The entire system went into a kind of shock after that, but it won't last long.

"They'll begin combing the area soon. ANSIS has already noticed my deception. You need to go home quickly."

Matt wanted to laugh, but it hurt too much to try. "Look at me. If I shift back, I'll just drown in the ocean or die in some deserted wilderness. I can't move. Besides, I've already made up my mind. I came for my dragon, and I'm not leaving without it."

"Such stubbornness," observed the android. "Who did you inherit that from, I wonder?"

Matt grinned at him through bloodstained teeth. "I got a double helping of stubborn on both sides. I come by it honestly."

Gary bent down and lifted something from the ground, holding it up so Matthew could see it without turning his head. "This is what you wanted, is it not?"

It was a dragon egg.

Relief flooded through Matthew. He hadn't destroyed it. Killing the machine-mage, the one bonded to it, had caused the newly hatched dragon to die. The enchantment had reverted back to the egg state, awaiting a new bond.

"Yes."

Gary placed the egg in Matthew's still-good right hand. "Now shift back. You've accomplished what you intended."

"Come with me."

Gary gave him a sad look. "There's no point. This body won't last. In a week, the batteries will be depleted. They don't put RTG's in civilian androids."

"It will last longer than I will if I shift back alone," argued Matthew.

"You have a point," Gary agreed. "Very well, bring me along." Kneeling, he took Matthew's hand in one of his and held the egg in his free hand. "Let's go."

They did.

It wasn't easy. Planeshifting wasn't particularly draining, but it took focus and concentration, things Matthew was in short supply of currently. After several minutes and a few false starts, he finally managed it.

For once, they didn't arrive over the ocean, and Matt found himself lying on a bed of soft grass. But his peace was instantly broken when Gary lifted him up and moved him several feet over, and then began slapping and brushing at his side. He screamed in agony, but the android refused to listen.

When it was over, Gary explained, "There was an anthill beneath you."

Matt glared at him, "Sadist. You enjoyed that!" He knew it wasn't true, but he hurt too badly to say otherwise. Then he passed out once more.

When he finally woke up, several hours later, Gary helped him drink some water. After that Matthew attempted to mend some of his broken bones, but quickly gave up. His concentration was shot, and his magesight suffered from the same sort of blurriness that his normal vision did.

His sternum was cracked, which was why breathing was so difficult, but beyond that, and his mutilated hand, his body was fairly sound. He had an amazing collection of bruises, his thigh was lacerated, and somehow he had lost most of the hair on the left side of his head. The part that remained smelled burned, but the skin of his scalp was unharmed.

He needed to go home.

To do that he would need a teleportation circle, but he doubted he could draw one in his condition. Fortunately, Gary was there. He didn't even have to describe it or do the calculation to create the local rune key. The machine had seen him make them before, and Matt had already taught him the formula for the key.

The android patiently cleared a wide area of grass, and using a small stick, drew the lines and runes on the fresh soil. The circle wouldn't survive past the next rain, but it didn't need to. Hefting Matthew with strong arms, he carried the wizard into the circle.

Matt couldn't help but cry out when he was lifted, but he consoled himself by deciding it was a 'heroic' cry of pain, rather than the more ordinary, pathetic sort.

Once they were in the circle, he put forth the small amount of aythar necessary to activate it, and then he was home.

When he woke next, he was lying in bed. His bed, in his room. He didn't move at first. Just enjoyed the silence and the lack of pain. It might have been perfect, but his sister was sitting in a chair beside him.

He turned his eyes to look at her without moving his head, just to be safe. "Moira."

"Myra," she replied. "She let me have a turn."

"Oh," he said, somewhat surprised.

"Everyone's been taking turns," she added, "even Conall and Irene. Mom was sick to death with worry when she saw you."

Matthew shifted slightly, noting the lack of pain in his chest. His sternum was fixed. A quick check showed that his other injuries had been similarly remedied. His hand was strange, though. He could feel it, but it was absent in his magesight. He lifted his arm to look at it.

It ended three inches short of where his wrist should have been. The stump was wrapped in a heavy linen bandage. A profound "Oh," emerged from his lips. He had known it would happen. He had been warned, but he still wondered why it was all gone. The translation pane had only taken half his hand off. The wrist, half his palm, and part of his thumb should have still been there.

"We couldn't save it," sympathized Myra. "They let Moira do most of the healing, since Dad was so impressed with how well she had put your arm on after you cut it off that time."

"That was a secret," he said sourly. "You said you wouldn't tell."

"*Moira* made that promise," said Myra promptly. "That was before I existed, but I thought he should know. He was amazed. You hardly have a scar from that, so he let her do the healing."

"And she let you do it for her," he finished for her, jumping to the conclusion.

She blushed slightly. "Yes. Since I'm not 'tainted', she felt safer letting me do it."

"Is this problem of hers like a disease?" he asked.

"Sort of, but it isn't one you can catch," Myra replied. "It's more of a temptation. She worried she might change you since you were unconscious and your defenses were down."

"Change me?"

"Alter your personality," Myra supplied. "She did a lot of it in Dunbar. Once you start doing it, it's hard to stop. It's a little like being a drunk. 'Just one more drink,' they say, but they can't stop. In this case, it's 'I'll just fix that one annoying quirk'."

"Wow," he said mildly. The more he learned, the more it sounded like his sister had a serious, and disturbing, problem. He decided to drop the issue and return to the matter at *hand*. He lifted his abbreviated appendage. "Back to this."

"We couldn't save it," she repeated. "I sealed the wound, the skin, fixed the blood vessels, but it just kept festering. I don't know what you did to it, but the flesh was dying. Even the parts that looked undamaged blistered and then began to rot. You caught a fever from it, and Lady Thornbear was worried it would turn gangrenous."

By 'Lady Thornbear,' she meant Elise Thornbear, Gram's grandmother. While the old woman was no mage, she was highly skilled in the healing arts, particularly with herbs—and sometimes poisons.

"She tried several poultices, but nothing worked," said Myra, continuing. "Eventually, she advised us to remove it. You might have died otherwise." She sounded apologetic.

Matthew sighed, "It's all right. I didn't expect to keep it. I made the choice, and this was the price."

"You sound like you made a pact with a dark god. Like a story in an old fairy tale," said Myra.

He laughed a little. "You could think of it that way, but it was nothing so sinister." Then he laughed some more at his unintended pun: *sinister.* It was probably the opposite of sinister to lose one's left hand. "I just knew that if I used it to recover my staff that it would be ruined. It was either that or give up and come home without the egg." That prompted another thought. "The egg…"

She understood immediately. "Zephyr's out hunting. He'll be back in a while."

Now he was confused. Had they let someone else bond with the egg while he was unconscious? He knew there were other eggs, but after everything he had been through, it seemed callous. "Who…?"

"You bonded him, when you woke last," she replied.

"How long have I been out? I don't remember waking."

"Over a week," said Myra. Then she reached over and touched the side of his head. The scalp had been shaved clean. "Examine that spot," she told him.

Since he didn't have a hand on that side, he used his magesight, and was surprised to find that a small hole had been drilled through his skull. "What's this about?"

"It was Dad's idea," she answered. "Your brain was swelling. He made the hole to let the pressure out. Apparently, he's done something similar before, or I'd never have known it was a possible solution."

"You've been up several times," she went on. "Relieved yourself, eaten, taken water. But you seemed dazed, and each time we weren't sure if you were really conscious or not. You responded to commands, but this is the first time you've spoken."

"And I bonded with the egg like that?"

She nodded. "It was the first thing you did. Then you passed out again. That was before the swelling and the trephination, so your thoughts might have been clear that time, but you didn't say anything to anyone."

"Trephination?"

She tapped her skull. "That's what Elise called it. Apparently, it was an old medical practice, but she thought it was quackery. She told your Dad it would kill you, but he ignored her. I think she was annoyed when he proved her wrong."

Reaching over his head with his right hand, he felt the soft spot where the bone was missing. It was disconcerting. "Couldn't he have put the piece of bone back?"

Myra laughed. "It had to stay open for several days." Then she held up her hands. "Not to the air, of course, or you might have gotten sick. He closed the skin over it immediately. But the bone had to stay out so that fluids could escape the skull. Anyway, he said you'd probably need it open so you could survive when Mom finally gets a chance to try and beat some sense into you. No point in having to do the trephination twice."

Somehow, he didn't find the joke as funny as she obviously did. A knock at the door interrupted their conversation, and his magesight told him it was Karen.

She entered a moment later, and her eyes grew wide when she looked at him. "Is he talking?" she asked Myra.

His recently minted sister nodded, and he merely responded, "Of course."

Things rapidly devolved into chaos after that. First Karen descended on him, and he thought he might die under the onslaught of her hugging and tears, but it got much worse when the news escaped the room. Soon he was mobbed by his entire family. His sister Irene was beside herself, sobbing so much he thought she must have developed a mental condition.

Idly, he wondered if she was competing to see who could cry more, she or their mother.

Conall took the news more stoically, but he was obviously relieved. There were no dry eyes in the room. Even Moira grew weepy, after Myra let her resume control of their shared body.

All in all, he was happy to see them, but the tears and continual hugging made him feel as though he were suffocating. He was grateful when Penny finally shooed everyone from the room so he could rest.

Naturally, Penny remained. She had probably run everyone out just so she could have him to herself, as much as to grant him relief from all the fussing, but contrary to Myra's joke, she did not attempt to 'beat some sense into him.'

She fussed over him without interference, as was a mother's right. They talked a while, and then he pretended to sleep, and she pretended to believe he was sleeping, content merely to watch him.

After a while, his pretense became reality, and he drifted into dreams.

EPILOGUE

The weeks passed into months, and Matthew grew steadily stronger. Despite all that had happened, he was surprised at how long it took him to recover fully. His head injury had been worse than he had realized at the time.

He missed his hand, though. That was one thing that wouldn't heal. For not the first time, he wished he were an archmage like his father, who could heal almost any wound when he merged with something and then returned to himself. His body could be recreated in whatever fashion was dictated by his self-image.

It wasn't quite that simple, but he could do it, whereas Matt could not. His father had offered to try to fix it for him, but the danger was considerable. To do so, he would have to use his unique gift to listen, become Matthew, and then to reimagine his body in its original, whole form. He had done something similar once to save Elaine's life, and he had later confessed to Matthew that he still wasn't certain if he were the original Mordecai, or if their spirits had traded places. His father had his own memories, and she had hers, so it was a technical point; but it bothered him nonetheless.

No, Matt preferred keeping his body as it was, and his inner world private. As close as he was to his father, he didn't relish the thought of 'merging' with anyone.

That didn't mean he planned to accept the status quo, though. In his memories of the distant past, one of his ancestors had lost an arm and replaced it with a magical one. He intended to do the same.

With access to Gary's knowledge of human anatomy and the workings of the nervous system, he thought perhaps he had a chance to do an even better job of it than his ancestor had done. If anything, he savored the challenge. If he was to be the world's greatest enchanter, replacing a lost hand was merely the first obstacle in his path.

Of course, he wouldn't have had Gary to refer to, if his longer-lasting, more durable self hadn't finally walked into Castle Cameron about three weeks after Matthew's return. His better looking, human-like android had lapsed into statue-like quiescence only days after they had gotten back, a victim of his short-lived batteries.

The military android's RTG wouldn't last forever, though. He had only a span of months left at most, but together they had come up with a solution.

The RTG generated power through the conversion of heat into electricity. The heat was supplied by the slow decay of radioisotopes, but any heat would work. It merely had to be steady and constant.

Creating an enchanted stone of the proper size and proportions, which would produce the right amount of heat for a long period of time, couldn't be simpler for an enchanter like Matthew or his father. The core of the RTG was removed and buried, replaced with a heat source that would last at least a year, and one they could recharge when needed.

Gary wasn't happy with being stuck in the military android body, however. It was cold and unexpressive. With their help, the AI came up with a plan to swap the thermoelectric power source in his military android body with the batteries in the civilian android.

It wasn't perfect. The former RTG was a little larger than the batteries had been, so he had a noticeable bulge in his lower back, but it wasn't anything that loose clothing wouldn't cover, and he was pleased to have a face that could show emotion. It was also nice having a form that didn't frighten people. No one who didn't know him could even tell he was a machine, rather than a human.

Matthew and Karen's relationship remained strange. They had both reluctantly accepted that everyone thought they were a couple, but neither of them were completely comfortable with it. They did things together occasionally—walks, a picnic or two—but they still weren't ready to make any permanent arrangements.

Of course, she had been understandably angry with him for sending her back against her will. She hadn't expressed that at first, while he was recovering, but once he was nearly back to full health, she had let him know. She had said she had forgiven him, but there was still a distant look in her eyes whenever the topic came up. He could tell he had wounded her pride, but he had no idea what to do about it.

As with most things he was helpless to change, he simply put it out of his thoughts.

But she didn't.

One spring morning, several months later, Matthew was sitting with Zephyr, watching the dragon eat half a goat. His new dragon, Desacus's descendant, was already half grown. The enchantment that created and sustained them saw to that.

Matt had somehow hoped his dragon would be more like his previous self, but his personality was different.

Not bad, just different. Zephyr was more gregarious and open. He possessed a sense of humor, but it wasn't the same as the dry, sarcastic wit that Desacus had shown.

Matt missed the dark humor.

As he watched Zephyr eat, a thought occurred to him. "You ever wonder what human would taste like?"

The dragon turned one eye to look at him and it widened with surprise, "No. Have you?"

He waved his hands. "No, no, of course not. I'm not a cannibal. I just wondered if you ever thought about it."

The dragon coughed. "That's disgusting. It would be like you eating horse. Would you eat a horse?"

He remembered what Desacus had said about horses and cattle. "Actually, a horse looks a lot more appetizing to me than a cow."

The dragon regarded him as though he might be ill. "You're sick. How about a dog, then? Humans are close to dogs too. Would you eat one of them?"

Thinking of Annie, he immediately replied, "No. Definitely not."

Zephyr sniffed. "That's something at least. Not sure if I trust you enough to sleep near you anymore, though. You might take it into your head to try dragon next."

Matthew laughed. "Fair enough. But back to my original question. You've never thought that people might be tasty?"

The dragon swallowed his latest bite and then pushed the last of the carcass away. The conversation had made him lose his appetite. "Why would anyone think that? Not to be rude, but humans smell awful. When you bathe, you smell like flowers and grass, when you don't bathe, it's even worse. Not to mention all the metal, cloth, and other odd bits you people cover yourselves with. I can think of nothing worse to eat than human, and I'm beginning to question your sanity for bringing it up."

"What if they were already dead? Like if you found someone who had had an accident?"

Zephyr narrowed his eyes to slits. "What sort of 'accident'?"

"Maybe they fell off a cliff, for example."

"There's still the clothes and metal and stuff," protested the dragon.

Matthew was undeterred. "Let's say they were naked, or that I stripped the body for you. Or maybe—hell, say it was cooked too. How about then?"

"I would say that I need to talk to your parents," answered Zephyr. "There's something not right with your head. Where would you even get an idea like that?"

Matt shrugged. "Nowhere in particular. Just something I wondered, you being such a dangerous looking carnivore and all." He refrained from bringing up Desacus. Mentioning Zephyr's predecessor inevitably made things awkward.

Considering the dragon's comments on how humans smelled, he decided that Desacus's remarks had probably been all for show, since they had probably smelled the same to him. It would be just like him to come up with a topic like that just to shock his master.

He started to wipe his face with his left hand and then switched to his right. His eyes were damp for some reason, and the cold metal of his artificial hand wasn't well suited to rubbing them.

Idly, he wondered if he should add an enchantment to warm the metal slightly, to a more human temperature. Maybe later; this was just his first prototype, after all. He had many more improvements to make first.

A week later Karen found him in his new workshop, where he was working on the next iteration of his prosthetic hand. Gary had suggested he use a metal called titanium, but his information on how it could be found and smelted sounded like a lot of trouble.

Matt had decided to wait until he had perfected the design in steel first. This 'titanium' sounded wonderful, being lighter and stronger, but he didn't want to go to the effort of refining it until he had his design complete beyond any question of a doubt.

He realized Karen had been watching him for several minutes without speaking, so he glanced up at her. "Hello." As his eyes took her appearance in, he noticed she wasn't wearing her usual clothes. She had been wearing the dresses that were favored by the young noblewomen of Lothion, but today she was clad in the enchanted leathers he had given her before her last trip to his world, tough trousers and a tailored leather jerkin that managed to display her feminine frame despite its masculine connotations.

He thought she looked good, and he had never been overly concerned with what others had considered 'proper.' The look on her face told him that there was more to it than that, though.

She met his eyes with her own for a moment, then looked down at his project. "I came to say goodbye."

His mind went blank. Not a single word suggested itself to him.

After waiting a while, she leaned in and gave him a light kiss. She looked at him again, watching his reaction, but when he didn't reply, she started to turn away, "Well, thanks for everything. I mean that."

"Huh?" His first word was anything but articulate.

She stopped. "I said I was leaving. Is 'huh' all you can think of?"

"What?" He was improving; he had managed a real word, and one that might even be considered a proper question.

Her expression was suspicious. "Were you even listening to what I said?"

He knew the answer to that one. "You said goodbye." After a moment, he even came up with his own question: "Why?"

Exasperated she responded, "Because I'm leaving."

"I got that," he told her. "What I mean is, why are you leaving?"

Karen smiled; she had his full attention at last. "Because I need to. Since coming here, I've been completely dependent. That's not who I am."

"I don't think anyone thinks that about you," countered Matt. "I don't."

"I know you don't," she reassured him, "but it's how I feel. Your world is completely new to me. It's an opportunity to rewrite my life, to be someone new, but I can't do that by just accepting your family's generosity. I need to go out and make my own way."

"Couldn't you make your own way—here?"

She shook her head. "You're sweet, but no. I need to do this on my own. Besides, I won't be so far away. This talent I've inherited means I can be anywhere I want to be, provided I've been there before. I'll come back to visit regularly, or for baths if nothing else." The twinkle in her eye told him the last part was only a joke.

"My gift could be incredibly useful," she added. "But I need to travel, to develop it. The more places I go, the better it becomes. Think about it—I could wake up, have breakfast in one place, and then later have dinner on the other side of the world. My life here could be extraordinary, but only if I travel to make it a reality. I need to discover what's out there."

"Alone? The road can be a dangerous place, especially for a woman," he cautioned.

Karen laughed. "I may not be the most powerful wizard, but I'm one of only a handful, or so you told me. Who could threaten me? And if I did meet someone or something too dangerous to face, how could they keep me from escaping? With just a thought I can be back here, where most of the world's most dangerous mages are gathered."

"Won't you be lonely?" He surprised himself with that question. He had never felt a particular need for company, yet now he was suggesting it to her.

"At first," she admitted. "But that's also partly what this is about. I need to make my own friends. I want to meet people. Being able to traverse the world in a blink of an eye means I can always visit any new friends or acquaintances whenever I want, but I have to make them first."

"What about Gary?"

"He can stay here," she told him. "I think he's happiest here, helping you. It gives him a sense of purpose. Besides, who wants a parent along on their first road trip?"

"It sounds like you've done a lot of thinking about this," he observed.

She nodded.

"Just be careful. Remember, even a nutjob isn't invincible. If you trust the wrong people, you could be hurt. Poison affects us just like everyone else."

Karen began to laugh, long and hard.

"What?" he asked, somewhat nonplussed.

When she finally stopped, she answered, gasping for air, "I've been meaning to talk to you about that. That word doesn't mean what you think it does."

He was rather annoyed when he discovered what it actually meant, and slightly embarrassed when he recalled the various times he had used it without knowing, back in her world. It cast his final monologue with his adversary in an entirely different light.

She left after that, and he stared at the spot where she had stood for several minutes before returning to his work. Or at least he tried to. He found himself unable to concentrate properly for the rest of the day. It wasn't until the following afternoon that he was able to focus on what he was doing.

But he did. His work was enthralling, and nothing held his attention the way a complex problem could. In his mind, he was already moving ahead to the one after it. He had no lack of ideas.

As the days went on, he perfected his hand design and then he began constructing a replacement for the Fool's Tesseract, though this would be an improved version. Now and then he stopped, and found himself wondering what Karen was doing or what she was seeing, but after daydreaming a while, he always returned to the project at hand.

Somehow, he knew he would see her again.

Coming Late in 2017:

Mordecai

The world that began in the popular *Mageborn* series continues with a new series focused once again on Mordecai; son of a blacksmith, nobleman by birth, and heir to a magical legacy, in a story that unites characters from all three series, *Mageborn*, *Embers of Illeniel*, and *Champions of the Dawning Dragons*. Mordecai, his children, and even his distant ancestor, Tyrion, come together to face the ancient enemy that once drove even the She'Har from their homeworld.

For more information about the Mageborn series check out the author's website:

www.magebornbooks.com

Or interact with him more directly on his Facebook page:

www.facebook.com/MagebornAuthor